I0608729

The
MX Book
of
New
Sherlock
Holmes
Stories

Part XLVIII
Occupants of the
Canonical Realm
(1861-1889)

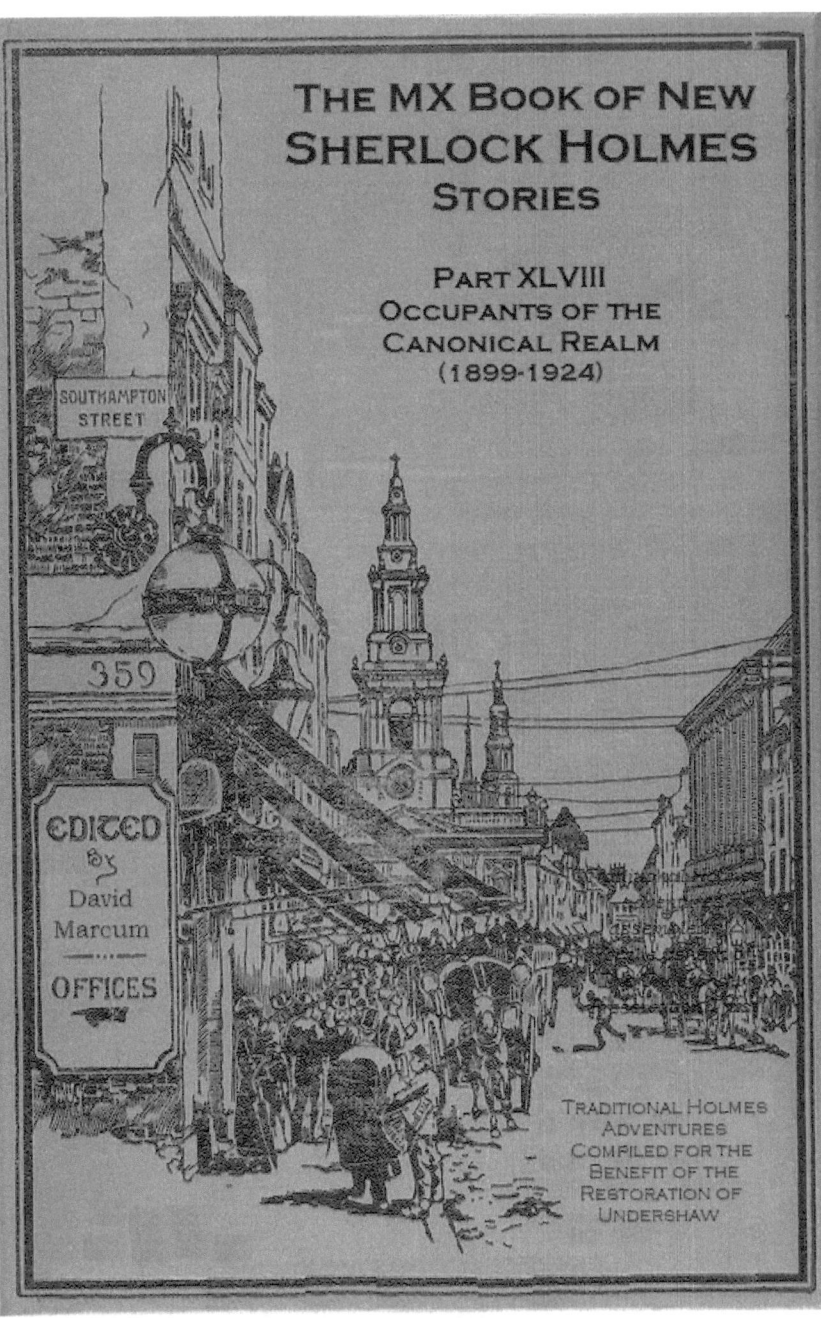

THE MX BOOK OF NEW SHERLOCK HOLMES STORIES

PART XLVIII
OCCUPANTS OF THE
CANONICAL REALM
(1899-1924)

SOUTHAMPTON STREET

359

EDITED
By
David
Marcum

OFFICES

TRADITIONAL HOLMES
ADVENTURES
COMPILED FOR THE
BENEFIT OF THE
RESTORATION OF
UNDERSHAW

First edition published in 2024
© Copyright 2024

The right of the individuals listed on the Copyright Information page to be identified as the authors of this work has been asserted by them in accordance with the Copyright, Designs, and Patents Act 1998.

All rights reserved. No reproduction, copy, or transmission of this publication may be made without express prior written permission. No paragraph of this publication may be reproduced, copied, or transmitted except with express prior written permission or in accordance with the provisions of the Copyright Act 1956 (as amended). Any person who commits any unauthorised act in relation to this publication may be liable to criminal prosecution and civil claims for damage.

All characters appearing in this work are fictitious or used fictitiously. Except for certain historical personages, any resemblance to real persons, living or dead, is purely coincidental. The opinions expressed herein are those of the authors and not of MX Publishing.

ISBN Hardback 978-1-80424-567-5
ISBN Paperback 978-1-80424-568-2
AUK ePub ISBN 978-1-80424-569-9
AUK PDF ISBN 978-1-80424-570-5

Published in the UK by
MX Publishing
335 Princess Park Manor, Royal Drive,
London, N11 3GX
www.mxpublishing.co.uk

David Marcum can be reached at:
thepapersofsherlockholmes@gmail.com

Cover design by Brian Belanger
www.belangerbooks.com and *www.redbubble.com/people/zhahadun*

Internal Illustrations by Sidney Paget

CONTENTS

Forewords

Adventures

(Continued on the next page . . .)

These additional adventures are contained in
Part XLVI: Occupants of the Canonical Realm
(1861-1889)

Part XLVII: Occupants of the Canonical Realm
(1890-1898)

(Continued on the next page . . .)

These additional Sherlock Holmes adventures
can be found in the previous volumes of
The MX Book of New Sherlock Holmes Stories

(Continued on the next page . . . .)

PART III: 1896-1929

PART IV – 2016 Annual

(Continued on the next page . . . .)

PART V – Christmas Adventures

(Continued on the next page . . . .)

PART VI – 2017 Annual

(Continued on the next page . . . .)

The Unwelcome Client – Keith Hann
The Tempest of Lyme – David Ruffle
The Problem of the Holy Oil – David Marcum
A Scandal in Serbia – Thomas A. Turley
The Curious Case of Mr. Marconi – Jan Edwards
Mr. Holmes and Dr. Watson Learn to Fly – C. Edward Davis
Die Weisse Frau – Tim Symonds
A Case of Mistaken Identity – Daniel D. Victor

PART VII – Eliminate the Impossible: 1880-1891
Foreword – Lee Child
Foreword – Rand B. Lee
Foreword – Michael Cox
Foreword – Roger Johnson
Foreword – Melissa Farnham
Foreword – David Marcum
No Ghosts Need Apply (A Poem) – Jacquelynn Morris
The Melancholy Methodist – Mark Mower
The Curious Case of the Sweated Horse – Jan Edwards
The Adventure of the Second William Wilson – Daniel D. Victor
The Adventure of the Marchindale Stiletto – James Lovegrove
The Case of the Cursed Clock – Gayle Lange Puhl
The Tranquility of the Morning – Mike Hogan
A Ghost from Christmas Past – Thomas A. Turley
The Blank Photograph – James Moffett
The Adventure of A Rat. – Adrian Middleton
The Adventure of Vanaprastha – Hugh Ashton
The Ghost of Lincoln – Geri Schear
The Manor House Ghost – S. Subramanian
The Case of the Unquiet Grave – John Hall
The Adventure of the Mortal Combat – Jayantika Ganguly
The Last Encore of Quentin Carol – S.F. Bennett
The Case of the Petty Curses – Steven Philip Jones
The Tuttman Gallery – Jim French
The Second Life of Jabez Salt – John Linwood Grant
The Mystery of the Scarab Earrings – Thomas Fortenberry
The Adventure of the Haunted Room – Mike Chinn
The Pharaoh's Curse – Robert V. Stapleton
The Vampire of the Lyceum – Charles Veley and Anna Elliott
The Adventure of the Mind's Eye – Shane Simmons

PART VIII – Eliminate the Impossible: 1892-1905
Foreword – Lee Child
Foreword – Rand B. Lee
Foreword – Michael Cox
Foreword – Roger Johnson
Foreword – Melissa Farnham

(Continued on the next page . . . .)

Part IX – 2018 Annual (1879-1895)

(Continued on the next page . . . .)

(Continued on the next page . . . .)

Part XII: Some Untold Cases (1894-1902)

PART XIII: 2019 Annual (1881-1890)

(Continued on the next page . . . .)

PART XIV: 2019 Annual (1891 -1897)

(Continued on the next page . . . .)

(Continued on the next page . . . .)

The Adventure of the Headless Lady – Tracy J. Revels
Angelus Domini Nuntiavit – Kevin P. Thornton
The Blue Lady of Dunraven – Andrew Bryant
The Adventure of the Ghoulish Grenadier – Josh Anderson and David Friend
The Curse of Barcombe Keep – Brenda Seabrooke
The Affair of the Regressive Man – David Marcum
The Adventure of the Giant's Wife – I.A. Watson
The Adventure of Miss Anna Truegrace – Arthur Hall
The Haunting of Bottomly's Grandmother – Tim Gambrell
The Adventure of the Intrusive Spirit – Shane Simmons
The Paddington Poltergeist – Bob Bishop
The Spectral Pterosaur – Mark Mower
The Weird of Caxton – Kelvin Jones
The Adventure of the Obsessive Ghost – Jayantika Ganguly

Part XVII – Whatever Remains . . . Must Be the Truth (1891-1898)
Foreword – Kareem Abdul-Jabbar
Foreword – Roger Johnson
Foreword – Steve Emecz
Foreword – David Marcum
The Violin Thief (*A Poem*) – Christopher James
The Spectre of Scarborough Castle – Charles Veley and Anna Elliott
The Case for Which the World is Not Yet Prepared – Steven Philip Jones
The Adventure of the Returning Spirit – Arthur Hall
The Adventure of the Bewitched Tenant – Michael Mallory
The Misadventures of the Bonnie Boy – Will Murray
The Adventure of the *Danse Macabre* – Paul D. Gilbert
The Strange Persecution of John Vincent Harden – S. Subramanian
The Dead Quiet Library – Roger Riccard
The Adventure of the Sugar Merchant – Stephen Herczeg
The Adventure of the Undertaker's Fetch – Tracy J. Revels
The Holloway Ghosts – Hugh Ashton
The Diogenes Club Poltergeist – Chris Chan
The Madness of Colonel Warburton – Bert Coules
The Return of the Noble Bachelor – Jane Rubino
The Reappearance of Mr. James Phillimore – David Marcum
The Miracle Worker – Geri Schear
The Hand of Mesmer – Dick Gillman

Part XVIII – Whatever Remains . . . Must Be the Truth (1899-1925)
Foreword – Kareem Abdul-Jabbar
Foreword – Roger Johnson
Foreword – Steve Emecz
Foreword – David Marcum
The Adventure of the Lighthouse on the Moor (*A Poem*) – Christopher James
The Witch of Ellenby – Thomas A. Burns, Jr.

(Continued on the next page . . . .)

Part XIX: 2020 Annual (1882-1890)

(Continued on the next page . . . .)

The Adventure of the Matched Set – Peter Coe Verbica
When the Prince First Dined at the Diogenes Club – Sean M. Wright
The Sweetenbury Safe Affair – Tim Gambrell

Part XX: 2020 Annual (1891-1897)

Foreword – John Lescroart
Foreword – Roger Johnson
Foreword – Lizzy Butler
Foreword – Steve Emecz
Foreword – David Marcum
The Sibling (*A Poem*) – Jacquelynn Morris
Blood and Gunpowder – Thomas A. Burns, Jr.
The Atelier of Death – Harry DeMaio
The Adventure of the Beauty Trap – Tracy Revels
A Case of Unfinished Business – Steven Philip Jones
The Case of the S.S. Bokhara – Mark Mower
The Adventure of the American Opera Singer – Deanna Baran
The Keadby Cross – David Marcum
The Adventure at Dead Man's Hole – Stephen Herczeg
The Elusive Mr. Chester – Arthur Hall
The Adventure of Old Black Duffel – Will Murray
The Blood-Spattered Bridge – Gayle Lange Puhl
The Tomorrow Man – S.F. Bennett
The Sweet Science of Bruising – Kevin P. Thornton
The Mystery of Sherlock Holmes – Christopher Todd
The Elusive Mr. Phillimore – Matthew J. Elliott
The Murders in the Maharajah's Railway Carriage – Charles Veley and Anna Elliott
The Ransomed Miracle – I.A. Watson
The Adventure of the Unkind Turn – Robert Perret
The Perplexing X'ing – Sonia Fetherston
The Case of the Short-Sighted Clown – Susan Knight

Part XXI: 2020 Annual (1898-1923)

Foreword – John Lescroart
Foreword – Roger Johnson
Foreword – Lizzy Butler
Foreword – Steve Emecz
Foreword – David Marcum
The Case of the Missing Rhyme (*A Poem*) – Joseph W. Svec III
The Problem of the St. Francis Parish Robbery – R.K. Radek
The Adventure of the Grand Vizier – Arthur Hall
The Mummy's Curse – DJ Tyrer
The Fractured Freemason of Fitzrovia – David L. Leal
The Bleeding Heart – Paula Hammond
The Secret Admirer – Jayantika Ganguly

(Continued on the next page . . . .)

Part XXII: Some More Untold Cases (1877-1887)

(Continued on the next page . . . .)

The Dundas Separation Case – Kevin P. Thornton
The Broken Glass – Denis O. Smith

Part XXIII: Some More Untold Cases (1888-1894)
Foreword – Otto Penzler
Foreword – Roger Johnson
Foreword – Steve Emecz
Foreword – Jacqueline Silver
Foreword – David Marcum
The Housekeeper (*A Poem*) – John Linwood Grant
The Uncanny Adventure of the Hammersmith Wonder – Will Murray
Mrs. Forrester's Domestic Complication– Tim Gambrell
The Adventure of the Abducted Bard – I.A. Watson
The Adventure of the Loring Riddle – Craig Janacek
To the Manor Bound – Jane Rubino
The Crimes of John Clay – Paul Hiscock
The Adventure of the Nonpareil Club – Hugh Ashton
The Adventure of the Singular Worm – Mike Chinn
The Adventure of the Forgotten Brolly – Shane Simmons
The Adventure of the Tired Captain – Dacre Stoker and Leverett Butts
The Rhayader Legacy – David Marcum
The Adventure of the Tired Captain – Matthew J. Elliott
The Secret of Colonel Warburton's Insanity – Paul D. Gilbert
The Adventure of Merridew of Abominable Memory – Tracy J. Revels
The Affair of the Hellingstone Rubies – Margaret Walsh
The Adventure of the Drewhampton Poisoner – Arthur Hall
The Incident of the Dual Intrusions – Barry Clay
The Case of the Un-Paralleled Adventures – Steven Philip Jones
The Affair of the Friesland – Jan van Koningsveld
The Forgetful Detective – Marcia Wilson
The Smith-Mortimer Succession – Tim Gambrell
The Repulsive Matter of the Bloodless Banker – Will Murray

Part XXIV: Some More Untold Cases (1895-1903)
Foreword – Otto Penzler
Foreword – Roger Johnson
Foreword – Steve Emecz
Foreword – Jacqueline Silver
Foreword – David Marcum
Sherlock Holmes and the Return of the Missing Rhyme (*A Poem*) – Joseph W. Svec III
The Comet Wine's Funeral – Marcia Wilson
The Case of the Accused Cook – Brenda Seabrooke
The Case of Vanderbilt and the Yeggman – Stephen Herczeg

(Continued on the next page . . . .)

Part XXV: 2021 Annual (1881-1888)

(Continued on the next page . . . .)

(Continued on the next page . . . .)

Part XXVIII: More Christmas Adventures (1869-1888)

(Continued on the next page . . . .)

Part XXIX: More Christmas Adventures (1889-1896)

Part XXX: More Christmas Adventures (1897-1928)

(Continued on the next page . . . .)

Part XXXI: 2022 Annual (1875-1887)

Part XXXII: 2022 Annual (1888-1895)

(Continued on the next page . . . .)

Part XXXIII: 2022 Annual (1896-1919)

(Continued on the next page . . . .)

(Continued on the next page . . . .)

Part XXXVI: "However Improbable . . . ." (1897-1919)

(Continued on the next page . . . .)

(Continued on the next page . . . .)

Part XXXIX: 2023 Annual (1897-1923)

Part XL: Further Untold Cases (1879-1886)

(Continued on the next page . . . .)

Part XLI: Further Untold Cases (1877-1892)

Part XLII: Further Untold Cases (1894-1922)

(Continued on the next page . . . .)

Part XLIII: 2024 Annual (1874-1888)

(Continued on the next page . . . .)

(Continued on the next page . . . .)

The following contributors appear in this volume:
The MX Book of New Sherlock Holmes Stories
Part XLVIII – Occupants of the Canonical Realm (1899-1924)

"Foreword" ©2024 by Dan Andriacco. All Rights Reserved. First publication, original to this collection. Printed by permission of the author.

"The Arc of Redemption" ©2024 by Gustavo Bondoni. All Rights Reserved. First publication, original to this collection. Printed by permission of the author.

"The Adventure of the Tall, Slim, Dark Woman" ©2024 by Craig Stephen Copland. All Rights Reserved. First publication, original to this collection. Printed by permission of the author.

"The Perfect Spy" ©2024 by Martin Daley. All Rights Reserved. First publication, original to this collection. Printed by permission of the author.

"An Ongoing Legacy for Sherlock Holmes" ©2024 by Steve Emecz. All Rights Reserved. First publication, original to this collection. Printed by permission of the author.

"The Adventure of the New Da Vinci" *and* "The Adventure of the Deadly Threat" ©2024 by Arthur Hall. All Rights Reserved. First publication, original to this collection. Printed by permission of the author.

"The Ghost of Mycroft Holmes" ©2024 by Paul Hiscock. All Rights Reserved. First publication, original to this collection. Printed by permission of the author.

"The Adventure of the Bishop's Gambit" ©2024 by Jeremy Branton Holstein. All Rights Reserved. First publication, original to this collection. Printed by permission of the author.

"Last Words for Watson" (*A Poem*) ©2024 by Christopher James. All Rights Reserved. First publication, original to this collection. Printed by permission of the author.

"'In the Old Rooms in Baker Street'" ©2024 by Roger Johnson. Originally presented to the Baker Street Irregulars Dinner, January 1994. All Rights Reserved. Printed by permission of the author.

"Editor's Foreword: More are Still in the Works" and "The Swapped Names of the Saviour" ©2024 by David Marcum. All Rights Reserved. First publication, original to this collection. Printed by permission of the author.

"The Case of the Purloined Pistols" ©2024 by Mark Mower. All Rights Reserved. First publication, original to this collection. Printed by permission of the author.

"The Return of Agatha Davis" ©2024 by Ember Pepper. All Rights Reserved. First publication, original to this collection. Printed by permission of the author.

"The Adventure of the Stolen Savant" ©2024 by Tracy Revels. All Rights Reserved. First publication, original to this collection. Printed by permission of the author.

"The Ebony Bastet" ©2024 by Roger Riccard. All Rights Reserved. First publication, original to this collection. Printed by permission of the author.

"The Adventure of the Surprises" ©2024 by Daniel A. Rowley. All Rights Reserved. First publication, original to this collection. Printed by permission of the author.

"The Case of the Circumspect Client" ©2024 by Daniel A. Rowley and Donald L. Baxter Jr. All Rights Reserved. First publication, original to this collection. Printed by permission of the author.

"The Intrigue of the Torn Treaty" ©2024 by Shane Simmons. All Rights Reserved. First publication, original to this collection. Printed by permission of the author.

"The Due Debentures" ©2024 by I.A. Watson. All Rights Reserved. Printed by permission of the author.

"A Word from Undershaw" ©2024 by Emma West. All Rights Reserved. First publication, original to this collection. Printed by permission of the author.

The following contributors appear in these companion volumes:
Part XLVI – Occupants of the Canonical Realm (1861-1889)
Part XLVII – Occupants of the Canonical Realm (1890-1898)

"The Case of the Many Marshal Mendlers" ©2024 by Ian Ableson. All Rights Reserved. First publication, original to this collection. Printed by permission of the author.

"The Wolf of Kensington" *and* "Such Profitable Treason" *and* "The Dockers' Tanner" ©2024 by Mike Adamson. All Rights Reserved. First publication, original to this collection. Printed by permission of the author.

"The Georgian Dragon" ©2024 by Tim Newton Anderson. All Rights Reserved. First publication, original to this collection. Printed by permission of the author.

"Misson (Some Sort of Sonnet)" (*A Poem*) ©2024 by "Anon.". All Rights Reserved. First publication, original to this collection. Printed by permission of the author.

"The Unpaid Bills" ©2024 by Chris Chan. All Rights Reserved. First publication, original to this collection. Printed by permission of the author.

"The Adventure of the Stradivarius" ©2024 by Steven Connelly. All Rights Reserved. First publication, original to this collection. Printed by permission of the author.

"Dinner at St. Lukes" *and* "The Disappearance of the Cutter *Alicia*" *and* "The Adventure of the Unfortunate Cardinal" ©2024 by Alan Dimes. All Rights Reserved. First publication, original to this collection. Printed by permission of the author.

"The Voice in the Night" ©2024 by Arthur Hall. All Rights Reserved. First publication, original to this collection. Printed by permission of the author.

"And UnChristian Act" *and* "The Violated Grave" ©2024 by Paula Hammond. All Rights Reserved. First publication, original to this collection. Printed by permission of the author.

"The Case of the Spitalfields Man" ©2024 by Stephen Herczeg. All Rights Reserved. First publication, original to this collection. Printed by permission of the author.

"The Case of the Benevolent Professor" ©2024 by Naching T. Kassa. All Rights Reserved. First publication, original to this collection. Printed by permission of the author.

"Inspector Gregson at Bay" ©2024 by Susan Knight. All Rights Reserved. First publication, original to this collection. Printed by permission of the author.

"The Adventure of the Willing Suspect" ©2024 by Gordon Linzner. All Rights Reserved. First publication, original to this collection. Printed by permission of the author.

"The Adventure of the Scottish Coffins" ©2024 by David MacGregor. All Rights Reserved. First publication, original to this collection. Printed by permission of the author.

"The Notting Hill Murderer" ©2024 by Michael Mallory. All Rights Reserved. First publication, original to this collection. Printed by permission of the author.

"The *X*-Marked Boxes" *and* "The Debt to Jabez Wilson" ©2024 by David Marcum. All Rights Reserved. First publication, original to this collection. Printed by permission of the author.

"The Question of the Rival Criminalist" *and* "The Return of the Rival Criminalist" *and* "The Weird Adventure of the Particular Phantom" ©2024 by Will Murray. All Rights Reserved. First publication, original to this collection. Printed by permission of the author.

"The Adventure of the Two Brothers" *and* "The Adventure of the Deadly Bird" *and* "The Adventure of the Illustrious Author" *and* "The Adventure of the Unexpected Corpse" ©2024 by Tracy Revels. All Rights Reserved. First publication, original to this collection. Printed by permission of the author.

"The Neopolitan Complexity" *and* "Death of a Sails Man" ©2024 by Roger Riccard. All Rights Reserved. First publication, original to this collection. Printed by permission of the author.

"The Romance of Reginald Musgrave" ©2024 by Jane Rubino. All Rights Reserved. First publication, original to this collection. Printed by permission of the author.

"The Boarding House Adventure" *and* "A Penny for the Guy" ©2024 by Brenda Seabrooke. All Rights Reserved. First publication, original to this collection. Printed by permission of the author.

"Sophy Kratides in Peril" ©2024 by P.C. Shumway. All Rights Reserved. First publication, original to this collection. Printed by permission of the author.

"The First Problem" *and* "In the Flesh" ©2024 by Elbert Henry Smith. All Rights Reserved. First publication, original to this collection. Printed by permission of the author.

"*Lady Dragonfly*" ©2024 by Robert V. Stapleton. All Rights Reserved. First publication, original to this collection. Printed by permission of the author.

"Sherlock Holmes" (*A Poem*) ©2024 by Joseph W. Svec III. All Rights Reserved. First publication, original to this collection. Printed by permission of the author.

"The Last False Step" ©2024 by Tom Turley. All Rights Reserved. First publication, original to this collection. Printed by permission of the author.

"The Neckinger Mills Mystery" ©2024 by DJ Tyner. All Rights Reserved. First publication, original to this collection. Printed by permission of the author.

"The Mystery of the Major's Music Box" ©2024 by Margaret Walsh. All Rights Reserved. Printed by permission of the author.

"The Widow's Pique" ©2024 by Victoria Weisfeld. All Rights Reserved. Originally published online October 2010. Revised 2024. Printed by permission of the author.

"Behind the Wells of Light" (Originally published online August 2009. Revised 2024, ©2024) *and* "The Lilac Flame" ©2024 by Marcia Wilson. All Rights Reserved. Printed by permission of the author.

The MX Book of New Sherlock Holmes Stories
Occupants of the Canonical Realm
Parts XLVI, XLVII, and XLVIII

are dedicated to

Kelvin Jones *and* David Stuart Davies

Both of these long-time Friends of the MX Anthologies
passed as these volumes were being prepared.
The world – Sherlockian and otherwise – will miss them both greatly.

R.I.P.

Editor's Foreword:
More are Still in the Works
by David Marcum

In his essay, "Who Shall Ever Forget?", * Ellery Queen related his first encounter with Sherlock Holmes. At age twelve – in 1917, since Ellery was born in 1905 – the young future Great Detective was in bed with his annual earache and, as a distraction, his grandmother brought him a copy of *The Adventures of Sherlock Holmes* The first story wasn't too inspiring for a lad of that age – "A Scandal in Bohemia", with an illustration labeled *"The gentleman in the pew handed it up to her . . ."* – but the other tales fired his imagination. He wrote that he finished the book that day, passed the night without any sleep while thinking of Holmes – *"All the Queen's horses and all the Queen's men couldn't put Ellery together again."* – and early the next morning, before the city had arisen, he bundled himself up, a wad of stained cotton protruding from his ear, and set forth to visit the public library, where he expected to find shelves upon shelves – entire rooms and wings – devoted to further adventures of Mr. Sherlock Holmes.

Alas, after waiting hours for the place to open, sitting huddled on the cold stone front steps, he discovered that such was not the case. In the entire library, he found just three previous volumes, *A Study in Scarlet*, *The Memoirs of Sherlock Holmes*, and *The Hound of the Baskervilles*. I was about that age, a couple of full generations later, when I discovered Sherlock Holmes, and I completely shared his disappointment – because even though there were a few more Holmes adventures available by then, there weren't shelves upon shelves and entire rooms and wings of them.

I was ten in 1975 when I first picked up an abridged copy of *The Adventures*, and then *The Return* – unknowingly skipping "The Final Problem" and reading "The Empty House" first, thus (*Spoiler alert!*) learning that Holmes didn't die at Reichenbach, and how he survived. (NOTE: *Always always always* read chronologically if possible.) I quickly devoured the rest of The Canon, acquiring the remaining books in the form of Berkeley paperbacks with excellent cover paintings by Guy Deel, and then I purchased the flawed Doubleday edition (with the wrong versions of "The Resident Patient" and "The Cardboard Box") – my first great Sherlockian purchase, setting me back a whole ten dollars! (My dad gave me a big months-ahead advance on my fifty-cent-per-week allowance, and then he even drove me to the bookstore that night after supper. I remember riding home with that big book perched carefully on my lap, almost afraid

1

to start reading it because it was so new and perfect. It was the first major monetary loan of my life, and very much worth it.)

As I was reading the Canonical sixty stories, I was unknowingly treading closer and closer to that Great Grimpen Mire where all new Sherlockians eventually find themselves: *I've read them all! Now what?*

Of course, I re-read the Canonical stories. And I was very grateful a few months later when my parents, ordering from a catalog of remaindered books that regularly arrived at our house, bought three Holmes-related volumes as a Christmas gift: *Holmes of the Movies* by David Stuart Davies, *The Sherlock Holmes Scrapbook* as edited by Peter Haining, and a true game-changer, *Sherlock Holmes of Baker Street* by William S. Baring-Gould.

I actually read Baring-Gould's brilliant biography before I'd finished all of the Canonical stories. I don't remember feeling that any of the narratives were spoiled by meeting them early that way. Instead, it presented Holmes from a different perspective that raised him in my mind to an even higher level. At that young age, I observed and understood that Holmes and Watson were historical figures existing in a fixed place in time. I saw them both young and old, and not presented and locked into some fixed middle age. I was exposed to the idea of *chronology*, wherein the adventures occurred at specific times, influencing and being influenced by what came before and after. And I saw that there was more to the *entire lives* of Holmes and Watson than the pitifully few sixty Canonical tales.

The Holmes Canon references approximately 140 *Untold Cases* besides the published adventures – from the famed Giant Rat of Sumatra to the oft-forgotten case where Holmes caught a coiner by the zinc and copper filings in the seam of his cuff. But even these Canonical hints of other cases weren't enough. Fortunately, I was primed and hungry for more post-Canonical adventures when I picked Nicholas Meyer's *The Seven-Per-Cent Solution* (1974) at a school Reading-is-Fundamental (RIF) event, and not long after, when I bought the next related volume, *The West End Horror* (1976). *The Seven-Per-Cent Solution* touched the flame to ignite the current modern Sherlockian Golden Age that we all enjoy now, and the fire has only burned hotter and hotter over the subsequent decades . . . but it wasn't an inferno at first.

The Seven-Per-Cent Solution showed that, for members of the starving public – Like me! – additional Watsonian manuscripts were out there in the world, waiting to be found and shared, beyond those too-few "official" titles that had crossed the First Literary Agent's desk. One simply had to put forth enough effort to excavate these adventures and publish them. They initially appeared in dribs and drabs – *Enter the Lion* (1979) by Sean Wright and Michael Hodel, for instance, and *Hellbirds* and

2

The Earthquake Machine by Nick Utechen and Austin Mitchelson – but at least they did appear. And I was lucky enough and diligent enough to find them, grabbing them as they were published because, even at that early age, I understood that I'd better get them and hold on to them when I could, because finding them later would be either expensive or time-consuming pesterments, or both.

The New Sherlockian Golden Age began in 1974 and has never ended, but it still took a few decades for Sherlockian adventure addicts like me to start to feel satisfied. If it was up to the traditional publishing dinosaurs to lumber into motion and recognize the need, we'd all still be waiting with great yearning disappointment. Thank heavens for MX Books, and later Belanger Books, which spun into motion from MX's initial efforts. With these two defining Sherlockian publishers now in place, so many more of Watson's discovered manuscripts can finally reach a desperately hungry public.

With the availability of so many more Holmes adventures, there is room to revisit all aspects of that world – including the other occupants of the Canonical realm. The World of Sherlock Holmes is wide and deep, and it has many Canonical individuals besides Our Heroes and the regular stalwarts like Mycrft and Mrs. Hudson, and Lestrade and Gregson. The theme of this set of MX anthologies was simple: To include a Canonical character – possibly in a large role, or sometimes just in passing. All of the contributing authors did a wonderful job, and now the game is afoot for the readers to spot some of those in some stories who are less well known.

When Ellery Queen went to the library as a boy in 1917, the entire Canon wasn't yet in existence. When I was about the same age as that, in the mid-1970's, the amount of available tales – Canonical and post-Canonical – was just about as slim. Now, thank Heavens, we finally have thousands of traditional Canonical adventures, set in the correct time period, and featuring the *True* Sherlock Holmes – not a modernized sociopathic murderer or continent-shifted tattoo-covered prostitute-paying drug addict, or a Van Helsing substitute or an anachronistic era-hopping Time Lord. I'm very proud that this latest set of MX anthologies brings us to almost 1,000 of these new True Holmes adventures – and as of this writing, more are still in the works. Stay tuned . . . .

* * * * *

"Of course, I could only stammer out my thanks."
– *The unhappy John Hector McFarlane,* "The Norwood Builder"

As always when one of these sets is finished, I want to first thank with all my heart my incredible wonderful wife of over thirty-six years,

3

Rebecca, and our amazing son and my friend, Dan. I love you both, and you are everything to me!

I can never express enough gratitude for all of the contributors who have donated their time and royalties to this ongoing project. I'm constantly amazed at the incredible stories that you send, and I'm so glad to have gotten to know so many of you through this process. It's an undeniable fact that Sherlock Holmes authors are the *best* people!

The contributors of these stories have donated their royalties for this project to support the Stepping Stones School for special needs children, located at Undershaw, one of Sir Arthur Conan Doyle's former homes. As of this writing, and as mentioned above, these MX anthologies have raised over $125,000 for the school, with no end in sight, and of even more importance, they have helped raise awareness about the school all over the world. These books are making a real difference to the school, and the participation of both contributors and purchasers is most appreciated.

I also want to particularly thank the following:

☐ *Dan Andriacco* – I first met Dan in 2011 at the third *From Gillette to Brett* conference, where he was in the Dealer's Room selling his books. I saw him again the next year at *A Gathering of Southern Sherlockians* in Chattanooga. From there, we began to correspond, and run into each other on occasion at various Sherlockian events – which attends a lot, and me quite a bit less.

Over the years, he's risen from success to success in the Sherlockian World. He's written a number of Holmes novels, and additionally the ever-growning McCabe and Cody series, which I dearly love. They are Golden Age-type mysteries, heavily influenced by Nero Wolfe and Archie Goodwin, and with all kinds of Sherlockian aspects. In addition to all the other rich deep characters in the books, the setting of Erin, Ohio is a character too. I look forward to each new volume. And after all this, Dan took over as the editor of *The Baker Street Journal*.

I've been trying to recruit him for years to contribute a story these books – and I'm still trying! – and with his foreword, I'm glad that he's now part of the MX Anthology family.

Thank you, Dan!

☐ *Roger Johnson* – I'm more grateful than I can say that I know Roger. His Sherlockian knowledge is exceptional, as is the work that he does to further the cause of The Master. But even more than that, both Roger and his wonderful wife, Jean Upton, are simply the finest and best kind of people, and I'm very lucky to know both of them – and I was lucky enough to see them in June 2024, during my fourth Holmes Pilgrimage to England and Scotland. I can't thank you enough, and I can't imagine these books without you.

☐ *Steve Emecz* – When I first emailed Steve from out of the blue back in late 2012 and early 2013, I was interested in MX re-publishing my previously published first book. Even then, as a guy who works to accumulate *all* traditional Sherlockian pastiches, I could see that MX (under Steve's leadership) was *the* fast-rising superstar of the Sherlockian publishing world.

The publication of that first book with MX was an amazing life-changing event for me, leading to writing and then editing more books, unexpected Holmes Pilgrimages to England, and these incredible anthologies. When I had the idea for these books in early 2015, I thought that it might, with any luck, be one small volume of perhaps a dozen stories. Since then they've grown and grown, and by way of them I've been able to make some incredible Sherlockian friends and play in the Holmesian Sandbox in ways that I'd never before dreamed possible.

All through it, Steve has been one of the most positive and supportive people I've ever known, letting me explore various Sherlockian projects and opening up my own personal possibilities in ways that otherwise would have never been possible. Thank you Steve for every opportunity!

☐ *Brian Belanger* – Brian is one of the nicest and most talented of people. His gifts are amazing, and his skills improve and grow from project to project. He's amazingly great to work with, and once again I thank him for another incredible contribution.

And finally, last but certainly *not* least, thanks to **Sir Arthur Conan Doyle**: Author, doctor, adventurer, and the Founder of the Sherlockian Feast. Honored, and present in spirit.

As I always note when putting together an anthology of Holmes stories, the effort has been a labor of love. These adventures are just more tiny threads woven into the ongoing Great Holmes Tapestry, continuing to grow and grow, for there can *never* be enough stories about the man whom Watson described as *"the best and wisest . . . whom I have ever known."*

David Marcum
September 25th, 2024
The 136th Anniversary of
the first day of
The Hound of the Baskervilles

Questions, comments, or story submissions
may be addressed to David Marcum at
thepapersofsherlockholmes@gmail.com

NOTE

* Ellery Queen's essay regarding his first meeting with Sherlock Holmes has appeared in at least three different versions. The best and most succinct is his foreword to the 1975 Ballantine edition of *The Adventures of Sherlock Holmes.* Versions also appear in *In the Queen's Parlor* (1969, as "Who Shall Ever Forget?") and also – much reduced – as "Who Shall Ever Forget?" in *The Golden Summer* (1953, by "Daniel Nathan").

Foreword
by Dan Andriacco

"*And so, reader, farewell to Sherlock Holmes!*" Arthur Conan Doyle wrote in the Preface to *The Case Book of Sherlock Holmes*. The exclamation point is telling. Conan Doyle was excited to be finished at last with that annoying consulting detective.

But the world was not.

The author's efforts to shed himself of his most famous creation are well known to all Sherlockians. He wanted to stop writing about Holmes after the sixth of the *Adventures,* and then after the twelfth, and then believed that he had finally done with deed with the ominously named "The Final Problem" at the end of what became *The Memoirs*. Many of us can recite most of the opening words of that story by heart: "*It is with heavy heart that I take up my pen to write these last words in which I ever record the singular gifts by which my friend Mr. Sherlock Holmes was distinguished.*"

The author was wrong, of course. One of my favorite cartoons related to Sherlock Holmes is by Jeff Decker (reprinted in the Summer 2023 *Baker Street Journal*) showing Conan Doyle at his desk, pipe in hand and a startled look on his face as a dripping Sherlock Holmes stands at the open-door yelling, "*Nice try, Doyle!*"

Two novels and thirty-two short stories would follow before the Canon was complete at sixty stories. One of the later tales, my favorite, is called "His Last Bow." But it wasn't.

Why is that man so hard to get rid of? Even the death of the canonical author couldn't stop the flow of new adventures of Sherlock Holmes. (I have been guilty of a few myself.) The reason is elementary economics: Supply meets demand. As long as there are legions of us around the world who want to go back again and again to Baker Street – which is likely to be forever – new stories will be produced.

It is not entirely about Holmes, however. The world of The Canon is also peopled with dozens of other characters worth spending more time with as well. And you will find many of these occupants of the Canonical realm within the pages of these volumes – Parts XLVI, XLVII, and XVLIII of *The MX Book of New Sherlock Holmes Stories*. Some surprises await!

Dan Andriacco
Editor – *The Baker Street Journal*
July 2024

"In the Old Rooms
in Baker Street"
by Roger Johnson

The Festival of Britain in 1951 was intended as "a tonic to the nation" in the austere years after the Second World War, and every local authority was expected to make its own contribution to the festival. The Borough of St. Marylebone chose to mount a Sherlock Holmes Exhibition, with a re-creation of Holmes and Watson's sitting room as its centrepiece, and the Abbey National Building Society offered space in its headquarters, located in what had been, until 1930, Upper Baker Street. Abbey House, completed in 1932, occupied a site that had briefly included the only house that ever legitimately bore the address *221 Baker Street*, and for nearly twenty years a member of the staff had acted as Sherlock Holmes's secretary, to answer the many letters that arrived addressed to Mr. Holmes or Dr. Watson. *

The exhibition was a great success, attracting more than fifty-thousand visitors before it closed, and during that five-month period the little group of volunteers and professionals who created it had founded *The Sherlock Holmes Society of London*. Eventually the various exhibits that had been loaned were returned to their owners, and many of those that remained, including the sitting room, were bought by Whitbread, the brewers, and installed in a handsome old public house called the *Northumberland Arms*, in Northumberland Street, near Charing Cross Station. In December 1957, it was formally opened as the *Sherlock Holmes*. The sitting room is approximately one-third of its original size, but all the important landmarks are present. Diners in the restaurant can view it through the plate glass window that replaces the fourth wall of the room. There are also viewing windows in the door and corridor alongside the room and in the patio area.

In early 1992, my wife Jean Upton was having lunch at the pub and noticed that the sitting room looked very shabby. The managers told her that they had only recently taken over, and were faced with several problems, including water damage from a washing machine that had overflowed in the room above the sitting room. Jean offered to help with cleaning and restoring the items in the sitting room, and as she clearly knew a good deal about Sherlock Holmes, her offer was gratefully accepted.

That was the start of our direct involvement. We discovered that some items had been damaged, and some had disappeared, so we have done our best to repair, restore, and replace. It took nearly a year to find an affordable pair of brown leather boxing gloves to replace the missing originals, but other items have proved less elusive — suitable oil lamps, a handsome mantel clock in working order, a tea service that looks very much like the one Jeremy Brett and his two Watsons used in the Granada Television series . . . The deerstalker and cape now hanging behind the door were given by the director of a television programme for which I was interviewed at the pub.

Among the many things we have added are the *Legend of the Hound of the Baskervilles* — the manuscript read aloud by Dr. Mortimer to Holmes and Watson, the plans of the Bruce-Partington submarine, Watson's commission as an army surgeon, various letters and other documents. These are items that we have made ourselves. Many years ago I bought a swordstick as a theatre prop. It now has a place in the sitting room at the pub, because it is identical to the stick carried by Jude Law in *Sherlock Holmes* and *Sherlock Holmes: A Game of Shadows*.

We do our best to make sure that the room looks as if it really exists in the late 1890's. We cannot disguise the smoke alarm on the ceiling, but we were able to provide a pinboard, with appropriate documents attached, to hide a modern electric socket on the wall beside the chemistry table.

During our three decades as curators of the sitting room, the *Sherlock Holmes* has undergone two changes of ownership, several changes of management, and at least two extensive refurbishments. It is an honour for us to maintain the long relationship between *The Sherlock Holmes Society of London* and the *Sherlock Holmes* pub. Just to be able to enter the sitting -room is exciting. To be trusted with ensuring that it always looks authentic is a great privilege and a great pleasure.

The side door of the pub opens on to Craven Passage. Look to your left at the building opposite and you'll see three formidable wooden doors, above which are attractive oriental arches and decorative blue-and-white tiles. This is all that remains of the Turkish Baths where we find Holmes and Watson at the beginning of "The Illustrious Client".

Now, bear with me, please. You may remember that Neville St. Clair – alias Hugh Boone, the Man with the Twisted Lip – lived at a house called The Cedars, near Lee in Kent. Remarkably, The Cedars is a real house: It stands on Belmont Hill in Blackheath, very close to the neighbouring town of Lee, and until his death in 1878 it was the home of one John Penn, whose widow was apparently still living there in 1907.

9

John Penn was an English marine engineer whose innovations in engine and propeller systems led to his company becoming the major supplier to the Royal Navy as it made the transition from sail to steam power. By the time of his death, Penn's firm had built engines for 735 ships, ranging from river ferries to battleships. He was elected a Fellow of the Royal Society in 1859, and the following year he was a founder-member of the Royal Institution of Naval Architects.

Back in Northumberland Street, next door to the *Sherlock Holmes* pub, we find – Guess what! – the Royal Institution of Naval Architects.

As Mycroft Holmes remarked at his first meeting with Dr. Watson, *"I hear of Sherlock everywhere . . . ."*

Roger Johnson, BSI, ASH
Editor: *The Sherlock Holmes Journal*
August 2024

NOTE

*   That rôle ceased in 2005, when the building society sold Abbey House and departed from Baker Street.

An Ongoing Legacy
for Sherlock Holmes
by Steve Emecz

Undershaw
Circa 1900

As we head into the autumn of 2024, we're delighted to have some more volumes of *The MX Book of New Sherlock Holmes Stories*, which continues to support the wonderful school at Undershaw. It's one of several projects we work with that you can read about on our website:

https://mxpublishing.com/pages/about-us

We continue to release dozens of new titles every year, and are entering our seventh year providing cases for the mystery subscription series *Dear Holmes*, which has now had over 50,000 aspiring detectives take part.

We look forward to another busy season with a variety of books from authors old and new.

Steve Emecz
August 2024

The Doyle Room at Undershaw
Partially funded through royalties from
The MX Book of New Sherlock Holmes Stories

A Word from Undershaw
by Emma West

Undershaw
September 9, 2016
Grand Opening of the Stepping Stones School
(Now *Undershaw*)
(Photograph courtesy of Roger Johnson)

It is always a pleasure to share the latest news from Undershaw, especially on such a momentous occasion. This year, we are not only celebrating the 20th anniversary of our school's founding, but also the 8th year of being housed in the historic and inspiring building of Undershaw, the former home of Sir Arthur Conan Doyle. Moving into this incredible space in 2016 marked the beginning of a new chapter for our school, and in 2021, we renamed the school to honour its legacy, recognising its deep connection to one of literature's most beloved creators, the mind behind Sherlock Holmes.

The journey we've taken as a school has been filled with milestones, and we have been fortunate to be supported by many, but none more so than MX Publishing. The interest, encouragement, and partnership we have received from MX Publishing has helped shape our community into what it is today. Just as Sir Arthur Conan Doyle enriched the world with his stories, MX Publishing has enriched our journey, and we are deeply grateful for their friendship and support.

As we reflect on our growth, we also celebrate being shortlisted for the prestigious "Outstanding Impact" award by the National Association of Special Schools. Out of more than four-hundred schools, being in the top three finalists is a testament to the dedication of our staff and the incredible impact of the Undershaw Diploma. Designed to develop the skills young people need to succeed in life, this diploma reflects our mission to tackle the challenging statistic that only 4.8% of adults with learning needs are in full-time employment. Through our accredited program, we are equipping students with the essential skills to ensure their futures are filled with opportunity and that they can be socially and economically engaged.

In addition to these achievements, we were honoured to receive the Gold-standard Anti-Bullying Charter Mark from Surrey County Council, a recognition that speaks volumes about the culture we nurture at Undershaw. The assessment team were impressed by the ethos of our school and the positive experiences shared by students, staff, and parents alike. We take pride in creating a school environment where every student feels valued and safe, as one student beautifully expressed: "Undershaw is like a second home."

We look ahead with excitement to what the future holds. As we continue to grow, we remain committed to the legacy of Sir Arthur Conan Doyle, using the skills of creativity, resilience, and curiosity that he embodied. And as we celebrate our twenty years of transformation and success, we extend our deepest thanks to MX Publishing for their unwavering support and their role in helping us thrive.

Undershaw is more than a school. It's a community, a home, and a place where young people are empowered to become the best versions of themselves. We are proud of all we have achieved so far and excited for the road ahead.

Until next time . . . .

Emma West
Headteacher
September 2024

"Undershaw," Hindhead, Conan Doyle's House.

Editor's *Caveats*

When these anthologies first began back in 2015, I noted that the authors were from all over the world – and thus, there would be British spelling and American spelling. As I explained then, I didn't want to take the responsibility of changing American spelling to British and vice-versa. I would undoubtedly miss something, leading to inconsistencies, or I'd change something incorrectly.

Some readers are bothered by this, made nervous and irate when encountering American spelling as written by Watson, and in stories set in England. However, here in America, the versions of The Canon that we read have long-ago has their spelling Americanized, so it isn't quite as shocking for us.

Additionally, I offer my apologies up front for any typographical errors that have slipped through. As a print-on-demand publisher, MX does not have squadrons of editors as some readers believe. The business consists of three part-time people who also have busy lives elsewhere – Steve Emecz, Sharon Emecz, and Timi Emecz – so the editing effort largely falls on the contributors. Some readers and consumers out there in the world are unhappy with this – apparently forgetting about all of those self-produced Holmes stories and volumes from decades ago (typed and Xeroxed) with awkward self-published formatting and loads of errors that are now prized as very expensive collector's items.

I'm personally mortified when errors slip through – ironically, there will probably be errors in these *caveats* – and I apologize now, but without a regiment of professional full-time editors looking over my shoulder, this is as good as it gets. Real life is more important than writing and editing – even in such a good cause as promoting the True and Traditional Canonical Holmes – and only so much time can be spent preparing these books before they're released into the wild. I hope that you can look past any errors, small or huge, and simply enjoy these stories, and appreciate the efforts of everyone involved, and the sincere desire to add to The Great Holmes Tapestry.

And in spite of any errors here, there are more Sherlock Holmes stories in the world than there were before, and that's a good thing.

David Marcum
Editor

Sherlock Holmes (1854-1957) was born in Yorkshire, England, on 6 January, 1854. In the mid-1870's, he moved to 24 Montague Street, London, where he established himself as the world's first Consulting Detective. After meeting Dr. John H. Watson in early 1881, he and Watson moved to rooms at 221b Baker Street, where his reputation as the world's greatest detective grew for several decades. He was presumed to have died battling noted criminal Professor James Moriarty on 4 May, 1891, but he returned to London on 5 April, 1894, resuming his consulting practice in Baker Street. Retiring to the Sussex coast near Beachy Head in October 1903, he continued to be associated in various private and government investigations while giving the impression of being a reclusive apiarist. He was very involved in the events encompassing World War I, and to a lesser degree those of World War II. He passed away peacefully upon the cliffs above his Sussex home on his 103rd birthday, 6 January, 1957.

Dr. John Hamish Watson (1852-1929) was born in Stranraer, Scotland on 7 August, 1852. In 1878, he took his Doctor of Medicine Degree from the University of London, and later joined the army as a surgeon. Wounded at the Battle of Maiwand in Afghanistan (27 July, 1880), he returned to London late that same year. On New Year's Day, 1881, he was introduced to Sherlock Holmes in the chemical laboratory at Barts. Agreeing to share rooms with Holmes in Baker Street, Watson became invaluable to Holmes's consulting detective practice. Watson was married and widowed three times, and from the late 1880's onward, in addition to his participation in Holmes's investigations and his medical practice, he chronicled Holmes's adventures, with the assistance of his literary agent, Sir Arthur Conan Doyle, in a series of popular narratives, most of which were first published in *The Strand* magazine. Watson's later years were spent preparing a vast number of his notes of Holmes's cases for future publication. Following a final important investigation with Holmes, Watson contracted pneumonia and passed away on 24 July, 1929.

Photos of Sherlock Holmes and Dr. John H. Watson courtesy of Roger Johnson

The
MX Book
of
New
Sherlock
Holmes
Stories

Part XLVIII
Occupants of the
Canonical Realm
(1861-1889)

Last Words for Watson
by Christopher James

This is your time to walk the Earth.
To live life brightly, for all its worth.
Claim the moon and pocket the stars.
What once were theirs, now are ours.
Lose your shoes, go open-toed,
Call on a friend and take to the road.
Walk the hills, float down the rivers,
Do things that sometimes give you the shivers.
Laugh at yourself, make someone smile,
Go out of your way; the extra mile.
Dare to say yes, the time is ripe,
Then treat yourself to an extra pipe.
Take days off and take it easy,
Or paddle a bathtub down the Zambezi.
Don't let a minute go to waste
Try grass sledging on a double bass.
Say no to the dull, same old weeks,
Blow an old trumpet 'til it hurts your cheeks.
On rainy Mondays, wear Sunday best,
Take a train to Budapest.
Wear your bowler with checkered socks
Post a five-pound note through a letterbox.
Dash into the sea, leapfrog the surf
O lucky Inheritor of the Earth.
You are the now, the spark, the light,
The bright of day before the night.

The Adventure of the Bishop's Gambit
by Jeremy Branton Holstein

The Raven and the Bishop strolled down beside the sea.
The day was lovely for a walk, the waters calm and free.
They stumbled 'cross a gull, gasping for its final breath.
"Consider," said the Raven, "how the living fear their death."

My name is Watson – Doctor John H. Watson – and it was my honor to share the adventures of Sherlock Holmes.

It was in the fall of the year 1899, as I have cause to remember, that Holmes and I became involved in the case that I have come to think of as "The Bishop's Gambit". It had been a busy year for Holmes, with his investigating, amongst others, the cases of Charles Augustus Milverton, which I have recorded elsewhere, and the Giant Rat of Sumatra, for which the world is still not prepared. Although Holmes's return from his supposed death and the very real death of my beloved wife Mary had occurred more than half-a-decade prior, both felt to me as if they had happened only the day before. It is true that the past never truly dies.

The London fog had been especially thick for days now, confining Holmes and myself within the walls of 221b. I believe that Mrs. Hudson was secretly pleased at this, as she showered excessive food and drink upon us at every opportunity. I reveled in it. Rarely had I eaten so well – but Holmes, as always, chafed at the inactivity. He had an infuriating habit of turning his deductive powers toward me whenever the London criminal class failed to provide fodder for his busy mind. Even as I scrawled down notes upon a recent case, I could sense Holmes staring at me, and steeled myself for what was to come.

"I say, Watson," said Holmes. "I do believe you've put on a quarter-stone since we began this cursed imprisonment."

"Hardly an imprisonment," I said. "And I doubt a few days indoors could have such an impact."

"Mrs. Hudson's cooking begs to differ," said Holmes, and then sneezed explosively.

"Are you coming down with something?" I asked.

"Just a mild cold," said Holmes. "I'll be better in a day or two. In the meantime, it keeps me from smelling Mrs. Hudson's dreadful curdled kipper."

"Perhaps you need a distraction. I see that the circus is in town, and they offer many unusual acts: Fortune tellers, elephants, and even a trainer of exotic birds!"

"One cannot enjoy what one cannot see. Perhaps once this fog dissipates . . . ."

Holmes's thought was not to be completed, as the sound of the bell below signaled the arrival of a visitor.

"At last!" said Holmes. "If fortune favors us, it will be a client."

"You should be resting – " I attempted.

"Rest be damned!" said Holmes, listening to the heavy tread upon our steps. "No, not a client, but perhaps someone better. It is Gregson."

The door opened, and in stepped a man I had known now for almost twenty years: Inspector Tobias Gregson of Scotland Yard, rival to Inspector Lestrade and one of Sherlock Holmes's most frequent visitors. He carried with him a package and an envelope, both of which he promptly handed over to Holmes even as he spoke.

"I've a puzzle, Mister Holmes," he said, "and I know how you enjoy such things."

Holmes examined the package and the envelope. "Your case might be puzzling, Gregson, but what you have presented me with is rather commonplace."

"Oh!" said Gregson. "I do apologize. It's the envelope I wish you to consider. The package was upon your doorstep. I thought I'd bring it up with me."

"Commendable," said Holmes, putting the package aside. "What do you have for me, Gregson?"

"A murder," said Gregson. "Or, at least, I think it was . . . ."

"There is some doubt?"

"Aye," said Gregson. "Did you not hear of Bishop Marley's death?"

"I have," said Holmes. "A heart attack, or so the papers say."

"That might be true," said Gregson, "but we withheld certain details from the papers."

"You intrigue me, Gregson," said Holmes. "Pray, continue."

"I think before I do you should look inside the envelope."

Holmes picked up the envelope, held its fiber up to the light. He then tried to smell the paper, but his cold prevented this, and he finally opened it in frustration. From within he withdrew a small sliver of paper, which he unfolded and read. He frowned and handed it to me. I took it, noting the tell-tale red stains upon the paper stock, and read the baffling message.

32

"*R x B*" said the note in careful block lettering.

"That note was found in the pocket of the deceased Bishop," said Gregson.

"And the blood?" asked Holmes.

"The Bishop's as well," said Gregson. "You see, Mr. Holmes, that while it's true the Bishop's heart gave out, it wasn't the primary cause of death. He was attacked, you see."

"Attacked!" said Holmes. "By who?"

"It's more a *what* than a *who*," said Gregson. "According to a witness, he was swarmed and pecked to death by a flock of *ravens*."

"Hmm," said Holmes. "I see what you mean. The note now takes on a rather sinister meaning.

"It does indeed," said Gregson. "When I realized what it said, I knew you would be intrigued."

"Forgive me," I said, "but I fail to see what is meant by the three characters."

"Are you not familiar with chess notation, Watson?" asked Holmes.

"I am," I said.

"And what is another name for a raven?" he added.

"A crow," I said. "Or a rook." I blanched as the meaning struck me full on. "Rook takes Bishop. My God."

"Precisely," said Holmes. "Murder, then, but carried out in a most unique method. Yes, this case does appeal to me quite a bit. How has your own investigation progressed?"

"Not well," said Gregson. "Bishop Marley had been at the diocese for nigh on twenty years, and was well regarded by the parishioners and staff."

"And the other clergy? What do they say?"

"That's just it, Mister Holmes," said Gregson. "They are being evasive, declaring the Bishop's death as an Act of God."

"Surely they would wish to help apprehend the Bishop's murderer," I said.

"A fair point," said Holmes. "Which means, in all likelihood, that they are protecting an even greater secret than murder. Very well, Gregson. I shall visit the Bishop's church and see if my reputation can open doors barred to the official force. I'll keep you updated on our investigation."

"Which means you'll contact me once you've figured the whole bloody thing out," said Gregson. "I know your ways, Mister Holmes. Good day."

Gregson departed, and Holmes collapsed into his armchair with a sigh of satisfaction. "What do you make of it?"

"Murder by raven seems rather outlandish to me," I said.

"Yes, and that's the beauty of the thing," said Holmes. "There may be nothing new under the sun, but every so often the sun still manages to surprise us with a new variation. I suggest we make haste to the Bishop's church at once. Are you game to accompany me?"

"I am," I said. "But you sure you should be out and about with your cold?"

"Nonsense," said Holmes. "I crave activity, not bedrest. Get your coat."

I was retrieving my overcoat from the rack when my eyes strayed over the package that Gregson had brought in with the envelope. "Who is the package for?" I asked.

Holmes stopped in mid-stride. "Bless you, Watson, but in the excitement of a new case I had all but forgotten." He picked it up and turned it about in his hands, studying the parcel. "Common enough paper," he said, "similar to that you might find in any butcher's shop. No name, but the address is clearly meant for us: *221b Baker Street*. No postmark, though, so it must have been hand delivered."

""What do you suppose it is?" I asked.

"There is but one way to find out," said Holmes. He picked up a letter opener, and carefully cut open the paper.

I smelled it before I even knew what was happening, a scent I shall never forget from my time in Maiwand.

"Explosive!" I tried to say, but before I could there was a wave of heat, and I knew nothing more.

"It is only natural," said the Bishop kindly to the bird.
"Death is the last mystery of life, our God's final word."
"I do not know many things," said the Raven, his eyes a deep dull black,
"But I know this gull is on a journey
from which there is no turning back."

My return to consciousness was agony. My eyes opened to such a harsh light that I cried out and immediately shut them.

"Saints be praised!" said a familiar voice.

"Mrs. Hudson?" I said, my voice dry and cracked.

"Don't you go exerting yourself, Doctor," she said. "Drink this."

I felt a glass pressed to my lips, and drank down cool water. In all my years, I don't believe I have ever tasted anything so sweet. I opened my eyes again, and this time the light was but a minor sting.

I was in a white room, lying in a low bed. Mrs. Hudson sat by my bedside, concern etched upon her maternal features.

The memory of the explosion rushed back in. "Holmes – !" I said, struggling to rise, but Mrs. Hudson stopped me.

"Never you mind about Mister Holmes," said Mrs. Hudson. "You need to take care of yourself." With the seeming strength of a giant, she pushed me back onto my bed.

"But where is he?" I protested. "Is Holmes all right?"

"He's alive, thank God," she said. "Given the number of attempts upon his life over the years, it would be ironic if it were a bomb that finally caught up to him, but his injuries are worse than yours. They say he took the brunt of the blast."

"I must see him," I said.

"And you shall," she said, "just as soon as you're able."

"I am ready now," I said.

"Are you sure, Doctor?" she said. "You've been unconscious the better part of a day. The hospital wants to keep you for at least another night."

"I'm not sure at all," I said, "but Holmes needs me."

Mrs. Hudson regarded me, and then nodded her assent. She helped me stand and led me down a corridor to another room.

Lying in the hospital bed, eyes closed and face covered in bandages, was Holmes. Seated by his side, both portly hands perched upon the end of an umbrella, was his brother, Mycroft. Neither looked up as I entered.

"They say he shall recover, Doctor," said Mycroft. "Never fear."

"How badly was he hurt?" I asked.

"I do not believe in luck," said Mycroft, "but if I did, I would say my brother was extraordinarily blessed. He is concussed, of course, and is experiencing *pulmonary barotrauma*. He also has some minor burns on his hands, although he was able to shield himself from the worst by using his coat. The two of you were en route somewhere? A church, perhaps?"

"Why, yes," I said, astonished. "How on earth did you know that?"

"Calm yourself, Doctor," said Mycroft. "It is not a deduction this time. Sherlock told me."

"Yes, Doctor," said Holmes, his voice muffled by bandages. "You cannot get rid of me that easily."

"Holmes!" I said. "I'm so relieved you're all right."

"Hardly that," Holmes replied. "However, I fear I shall be here several days at least . . ."

"Of course," I said. "You must rest and recover."

". . . which is why it is imperative that you travel to the Bishop Marley's church immediately,"

"Me!" I cried. "But my name doesn't carry the weight of Sherlock Holmes."

35

"You do yourself a disservice," said Holmes. "Thanks to your stories, your name – for better or worse – is now almost as famous as my own."

"My brother does not exaggerate," said Mycroft. "Even within the halls of the Ministry we have all heard of Doctor Watson, the companion of – forgive me, Brother – the so-called 'Great Detective'."

I rarely blush, but I might have at that moment.

"Are you strong enough, Watson?" asked Holmes.

I would have answered differently only moments before, but now I felt reborn – full of energy and, yes, I admit, pride.

"You can count on me," I said.

"I knew that I could," said Holmes.

"What am I to look for?"

"Evidence, patterns. Strange occurrences around the parish, and – Dare we hope? – more transcribed chess moves."

"But what of you?" I said. "Are you safe here? There has already been one attempt upon your life. And what about the bomb? Perhaps Scotland Yard . . . ?"

"I shall remain by his side, Doctor," interrupted Mycroft, "and I have ordered extra protection for my brother's room at all hours. The Holmes line shall endure."

"You see, Watson?" said Holmes. "I am quite safe. Talk to Scotland Yard about the bomb, if you must, but your focus should be on the incident at the church. Now go. Report back as soon as you are able."

The Bishop said a prayer while the Raven waited,
and once the priest was done, the Raven's hunger was promptly sated.
"Delicious," said the Raven, his meal now complete.
"I rarely make it to the beach, so this gull is quite a treat."

Despite Holmes's instruction that I focus upon the church, I still made Scotland Yard my first destination on that foggy day. There I was met by Inspector Gregson, who was relieved to see me upright and alert. Pushing aside his concerns as politely as I could, I inquired about the bombing at Baker Street.

"Not a clue, Doctor," said Gregson with obvious chagrin.

"But surely there must be something?" I asked. "The powder used, the type of paper . . . ."

"There wasn't much left of either," said Gregson, "but the few scraps of paper we've been able to recover show it to be fairly ordinary, the kind used in any butcher's shop across London."

"And the powder?"

"Gunpowder, as far as we can tell," said Gregson. "You know as well as I just how easy that is to obtain."

This was true. Pistols and cartridges were widely available, from gunsmith's, hardware stores, or even by post.

"Have you inquired around Baker Street? Perhaps someone saw the package being delivered . . . ?"

"In this bloody fog?" laughed Gregson. "Honestly, Doctor, you must have taken quite a blow to your head to ask me that. We inquired, of course, but no one saw a blasted thing. They could hardly see their hands in front of their noses, let alone someone delivering an ordinary parcel."

My optimism for a fresh lead withered with every word from Gregson. The good inspector noticed my sad expression.

"Oh, cheer up, Doctor," he said. "The fog is finally starting to dissipate, and we at the Yard never give up that easily. We shall continue to investigate, and we'll find the blaggard who tried to kill you and Mister Holmes, never fear."

I thanked Gregson and decided that Holmes had, as always, been correct. It was best to put the bomb mystery aside for the time being, and focus instead upon the Bishop's murder.

They walked further on, footprints trailing in the sand;
A claw beside a shoe showed the path of this odd band.
"This prayer you uttered," said the Raven. "It sounded very old."
"You consume the dead," said the Bishop,
"I give comfort to their souls."

The cathedral of Bishop Marley's parish loomed in the foggy sky, its spires silhouetted against the hazy gloom. I was met at the front door by a sandy-haired young man whose collar marked him as a priest.

"You must be Doctor Watson," he said.

"I am," I said, "but I'm afraid you have me at a disadvantage, Father."

"Oh!" he said. "Where are my manners? My name is Forrester, although I must point out that I am not yet a priest, and thus have not yet earned the title of Father."

"You are a Seminarian," I said.

"Yes," he said, "though if all goes well I should complete my studies by next year. Now, I understand from Inspector Gregson that you are looking into the death of Bishop Marley?"

"I am."

"The church doesn't wish me to talk with you," said Forrester, "but with so much tragedy within our congregation recently, I want to help you as best I can. Please, follow me."

I walkded behind the young man inside the chapel, down its aisles, and into a small and sparse side room. A simple bed and side-table strewn with stacks of books dominated the dingy chamber, with a single chair its only luxury. On the wall, hung side by side with a cross, was a set of gardening tools.

"These are my humble chambers while I complete my studies. It isn't much, but I have come to think of it as home."

Forrester sat himself down on his bed, and bade me to take the chair.

"Now then, Doctor," said Forrester, "tell me how I can assist you."

"Tell me the circumstances of Bishop Marley's death," I said.

"It isn't a memory upon which I wish to dwell," said Forrester. "Bishop Marley was a man of ritual, and would take his nightly prayers alone each night in the cathedral's courtyard. I was in my own bed, reading, when I heard a most unholy commotion, the sound of a multitude of wings outside my window, their tumult so loud that they almost overwhelmed the Bishop's horrible screams. I ran to the courtyard and saw the most incredible sight: A flock of ravens all piled one on top of each other, all pecking away at something hidden by their combined mass. I charged at the birds, and they took flight, revealing the mortally wounded figure of the Bishop. I cradled him in my arms, but the attack had been too savage for him to survive."

I shuddered at the grotesque image but soldiered on. "Do you have any theories as to what caused this attack?"

"I do," said Forrester. "Bishop Marley's death was clearly an act of the Devil. There can be no other explanation."

"Even the Devil needs human hands to accomplish his work," I offered.

"We all have a piece of the Devil in us, Doctor," said Forrester.

Privately, I thought there could be numerous other explanations, but chose a more tactful approach. "Can you show me this courtyard where the Bishop died?"

"Of course," he said. "This way."

He led me through one of the chapel's side doors and out to an enclosed clearing along the eastern side. A solitary cobblestone path led to a bench under a withering tree, and I saw immediately the dark stain upon the stones marking where the savage attack had occurred. I knelt down and ran my hand over the cold surface. Even as I did so, I heard the call of a bird, and looked up to see a solitary raven, watching me from above.

"Where is your room, Mister Forrester?"

The young man pointed to a small glass overlooking the courtyard. "That is my window."

"You must have been here almost immediately."

Forrester nodded. "I was. Others joined me soon after, but by then he was gone."

"Did the Bishop say anything before he died?"

"He did, but it was only a whisper. 'Forgive me,' he said."

"How very strange," I said. "Why should he ask for forgiveness?"

The young man shrugged. "Who can say?" he said. "We all seek forgiveness for our sins, no matter how small they may seem to others."

"You mentioned other tragedies," I said.

"Oh, but those were accidents," he said. "I really don't think they're relevant to your investigation."

"Sherlock Holmes often says that no detail is too small."

Forrester sighed and held up his hands in surrender. "Very well," he said. "Three months ago, we lost our Emeritus, Bishop Roberts, to a sudden heart attack. Then, just as we had laid him to rest, we lost our Auxiliary, Bishop Mortimer, to an accident involving a carriage."

"Three tragedies in three months!" I said. "That is a burden of sorrow no congregation should bear."

"It has been difficult," said the young man, "but we endure, content that we are serving God's plan. I wish you good fortune in your investigation, Doctor."

I bade Forrester goodbye and took my leave.

As I wandered down the pathway away from the church, I pondered the case. What would Holmes's next move be? I could go back to the hospital and consult with him, but I wished to try to make some sort of progress on my own, to prove that I had absorbed some of Holmes's methods over the years. The other tragedies Forrester mentioned – the three deaths so close together, all Bishops – seemed too much a coincidence to be trusted. Perhaps this was the way forward?

My carriage rattled away toward my destination, and I fell into a light slumber. Little did I realize as I slept how connected the three deaths actually were, or how those same deaths were interwoven with my own past.

"Their flesh is my domain," said the Raven. "I leave their souls to you."
"You are very gracious," said the Bishop. "To yourself be true."
"I believe in nature," said the Raven. "I believe in ancient truths."
"That is why we are friends," said the Bishop. "For, you see, I do too."

Bishop Mortimer's home wasn't far from the cathedral where he had once served, and his widow, a graying woman of middle age, seemed grateful for the opportunity to talk about his memory.

"He was such a kind man," she said. "So good to all his flock, especially the children."

"I'm so sorry for your loss," I said.

"That's what everyone says," she responded, "but it doesn't bring him back or solve the mystery of his death."

"Mystery?" I asked. "I was told he died in a carriage accident."

"That's what the police said," she grumbled, "but I think there's more to it than just mere chance."

"What makes you think so?"

"Letters, Doctor. For a month before he was killed, he'd been receiving these strange letters with nonsense inside. George thought it were just a joke, but I suspected otherwise."

"Do you still have the letters?"

"Only the last. George burned the others. Here it is." She handed me an ordinary envelope. I studied it, and noted its lack of post-mark. Hand delivered, then, just as the bomb had been. I opened the envelope and removed a small card. Printed upon it, in careful block letters were the letters "*P x B*".

"May I keep this?" I asked. "It may be important."

"Don't see why not," said the widow. "A portent of tragedy, it was. But if it helps you catch whoever did this to my poor George, then take it with my blessing."

I thanked the widow and bade her goodbye. My heart was beating rapidly, as I had found what seemed a vital connection. Without context those letters might not mean anything, but combined with the card that Holmes had examined back in Baker Street, its message seemed clear: *Pawn takes Bishop*. The identity of the Bishop was clear enough, but who, I wondered, was the pawn?

I attempted to visit Bishop Roberts' flat, but too much time had passed and his rooms had been cleared out, his possessions disposed of. Had I been able, I was sure I would have found another chess move mixed in amongst his personal papers. Alas, I was never to know.

Birds killing a man in the fashion that Forrester described was clearly unnatural. Perhaps they had been trained in some way by a malicious actor? I needed to seek out an individual whose trade was taming the untamed, and after some deep thought, and a consultation with the most recent edition of *The Standard*, I knew just where to look.

They left the ocean sand, and wandered the cobbled streets.
The sun was high above, yet the townsfolk were asleep.
"Lazy people," said the Raven, a growl within his gut.
"They do not know how to work for the meals that they sup.'

"Lord George Sanger's Royal Circus, Beloved by the Queen Herself!" proclaimed the banner strung over the entrance. Despite this audacious slogan, I found the fairgrounds beyond to be anything but royal – a distended field overrun by a veritable army of tents and trailers, creating a miniature labyrinth through which I wandered. The advertisement for this circus had run in the morning paper for several days now, including a lengthy list of the amusements they offered. I was seeking one amusement in particular.

Upon inquiry, I was soon directed to the tent for Whistler the bird trainer. With no door to knock upon, I instead drew back the canvas flap and stepped within.

Inside stood a tall and exceedingly thin man surrounded by numerous bird cages. Currently, though, he was ignoring his birds and was instead intently studying a chess board. He calmly moved one of the chess pieces to a new square, playing a game alone against an unseen opponent.

"Be sure to secure the tent-flap, whoever you are," he said, without turning to face me. "I don't want any of my darlings to escape into the London air."

"I beg your pardon for entering unannounced," I said, closing the flap behind me. "My name is John Watson."

The man, who I presumed to be Whistler, finally looked up from his game to regard me, crooking one of his lengthy eyebrows in suspicion. "Not merely John, is it?" he said. "I presume I have the honor of addressing none other than *Doctor* Watson?"

"That is my title, yes. And you must be Whistler, the bird trainer."

"Surely you can deduce as much?" said the man. "You are, after all, familiar with Sherlock Holmes's methods."

"Mr. Whistler," I said with as much gravitas as I could muster, "I am here on official business.

"A case, perhaps?" said Whistler, He carefully moved a pawn on the board, capturing one of the pieces and moving it aside. "Unless I am very much mistaken, this has to do with the death of the Bishop? A Bishop murdered by a group of ravens?"

"Why, yes," I said. "But, sir, that fact hasn't been made public. How did you hear of it?"

"The newspapers aren't the only sources of information," said Whistler. "We here in the circus are often privy to rumors and scuttlebutt not known to the general public. In the wake of such an unusual death, I was warned that someone might come and inquire."

"And has anyone?"

"No," said Whistler. "Honestly, it's been a bit disappointing. I tell you that there are no bird trainers in this world with more skill than myself, and only a few who can even approach my level, and yet you are the first investigator to grace my tent. Such a pity. But, please. You are here to ask questions. Ask away."

"Is it possible to train a flock of ravens to kill a man?" I asked.

"Quite possible," said Whistler. "Ravens are very intelligent birds – perhaps one of the most intelligent of the species."

"And have you, sir," I asked, "ever trained a raven?"

"No," said Whistler. "Sadly that same intelligence makes ravens terribly stubborn. I much prefer simpler birds. Pigeons, for example. Or canaries." He made an odd whistling chirp with his lips and held his hand out at an unusual angle. In response a small, yellow bird flew down from one of the tent's eaves and perched itself on the side of his hand. Whistler rewarded the bird with a seed which the bird promptly devoured. "You see?" said Whistler, smiling proudly. "Much more cooperative."

"I don't suppose that you know anyone who has trained a raven?"

"Well, yes," he said. "In fact, I do. Years ago a child came to me, wishing to be trained in the art of working with birds. He was quite good with all of my feathered flock, but had an almost supernatural affinity for the ravens. He seemed to speak their language, and they responded to him with affection and loyalty."

"What was his name?" I asked. "Where might I find him?"

"I have no idea," said Whistler. "He left my tutelage quite some time ago, one of many who try the carnival life only to discover its hardships. As for his name – Well, we here in the circus often trade under aliases, lest an unfortunate past be uncovered. This particular boy introduced himself as Timothy, nothing more."

Whistler must have seen my crestfallen expression, for he smiled and clapped me upon the shoulder.

"Oh, cheer up, Doctor! Seek out the ravens themselves and there you may find Timothy."

"And where would you suggest I look?"

"Ravens are everywhere throughout the city of London, but there are two places where they are known to congregate. The first is The Tower of London. The second is Hyde Park."

Despite feeling as if I had learned next to nothing, I still thanked Whistler for his assistance and made my departure from his tent.

As I strode toward the circus entrance, I thought I heard another step behind me, echoing my own. Turning about I saw no one.

I shook my head. Paranoia is only natural after facing your own mortality. Still, it never hurt to keep one's guard up.

42

With that in mind I summoned a cab, and proceeded on to The Tower.

"Is that jealousy I hear?" said the Bishop to the rook.
"Do you wish to play human games, and read a human book?"
"Not I," said the Raven. "I want forever to be free."
"Free to walk the streets," said the Bishop, "and wander by the sea."

The fog had mostly lifted by the time my cab approached the Thames. The Tower of London stood proud on the north bank of the river, silhouetted in the slowly dying light of day. Its solid stones had been a source of English identity for hundreds of years, despite its terrible and bloody past. Approaching by the roadway along the river, one couldn't help but feel the weight of history contained within.

As I drew nearer, I could see a small crowd of people waiting for admittance at the Byward Tower. A few Beefeaters were chatting and giving guidance to the visitors (after a small payment was exchanged, of course). Paying my cabbie, I disembarked and approached the oldest, hoping he would prove the most knowledgeable.

"May I help you, sir?" the Beefeater inquired, resplendent in attire steeped in English tradition.

"Yes, I have what might seem an odd question."

"Go right ahead, sir," he said. "It is my job to answer inquiries."

"Are the legends true?" I asked. "Do you have ravens here?"

The Beefeater laughed. "Not so odd a question, sir. For the price of admission, I shall gladly show you."

I handed over my coin, and followed the Beefeater. He guided me to one of the many towers within, and pointed above. There, perched on the stonework, were dozens of the black birds, all eyeing us below, their dark eyes filled with unknowable emotion.

"There, sir," said the Beefeater, "with more to be found about the grounds. They say that the ravens must never leave The Tower, lest England herself should fall."

"They are quite striking," I said.

"That's one word for it, sir," said the Beefeater. "Creepy is more the word I'd use."

"I have another odd question to ask," I said. "Has anyone ever tried to train them?"

The Beefeater stroked his beard in thought. "Now that is an odd question, sir," he said. "And now that you mention it, there was one bloke who came through here a few years back offering to work with our ravens."

"Was his name Timothy?" I asked.

"Can't say that I remember, sir," said the Beefeater. "We turned him away, but he kept coming back. Finally I said that if he wanted to work with ravens, he might try those in Hyde Park. There are more there than here, or so I've heard. Indeed, I . . . ." He broke off, and then, before I even knew what was happening, he'd pushed me to the ground as a chunk of masonry smashed into the cobbles where I had just been standing.

"That was close, sir," said the Beefeater, helping me up. "Are you all right?"

"Yes, thanks to your quick action," I said. "What the devil happened?"

"A stone fell from one of the towers," he said. "Happens now and again. Nothing to worry about – provided you aren't standing below."

I looked to the towers above, and the throng of ravens which surrounded them. A sense of threat emanated back.

I thanked the Beefeater and set out for Hyde Park, determined to use the last few hours of daylight to my advantage.

A carriage rattled toward them, drawn by two white mares.
The Raven flew into the Bishop's arms, startled by the pair.
"Maniacs!" said the bird. "They think they own the street!'
"I could have died had they knocked me from my feet!"

I'd hoped that a long constitutional through Hyde Park might be just what I needed to clear the remaining pain from my bones and ponder the case, but alas, it all proved only more baffling. Who was this mysterious raven trainer, and how could I find him? I had no choice but to stay the course and hope that fate and chance would provide me with answers.

I entered the park and made my way through the meadows toward the Reformer's Tree. Walking the myriad paths of Hyde Park is a meditative experience, especially if fortune favors one with isolation. Luck was with me that day, and I saw few other souls until I approached the tree.

The title of "Reformer's Tree" is, sadly, a misnomer. They say that once a mighty oak stood at the site, but it had burned down decades ago and now retained the title for sentiment alone. Since then, it had become a focal point for radical voices, one of which now carried to my ear.

A man stood there upon a literal soap box, surrounded by a small crowd who exuded a potent disinterest. This didn't dissuade the speaker, who only spoke louder in an effort to spur them to action. "Our Uitlander brothers," said the speaker, holding that day's paper aloft. "They are being mistreated and exploited by the Boer government! We must fight to liberate them from tyranny!" The current tensions between England and the Transvaal Republic did indeed seem to be headed toward some kind of

44

conflict, and I prayed that our politicians could avoid bloodshed. I had seen enough war to last my lifetime.

I passed beyond the Reformer's Tree, headed toward the Serpentine, when I noticed a flock of black birds gathered in a field near the foot path. Moving closer, I confirmed what I had already suspected: They were ravens, and what was more, they were gathered around a child.

She was a small girl, well-clothed with a child's pouch slung over her shoulder. She was seated cross legged upon the ground and making odd gestures with her hands, gestures which fascinated the ravens circled about her, all watching with dark, black eyes. She picked up a stick and threw it beyond the assembled fowl. Cued by another gesture from the girl, one of the ravens hopped over and retrieved the stick, plucking it from the ground as if it were a worm, and, with a quick flap of its wings, it returned the stick to the girl's open hand. She rewarded the bird with a nut from her pouch which it gobbled greedily

I was astonished. I had seen this trick performed by mongrels before, but never by birds.

"That is quite remarkable," I said. The girl started, so focused had she been upon her ravens that she hadn't noticed my approach until I spoke. She eyed me with suspicion, but still managed a polite nod.

I knelt down to the girl's level and smiled my most charming smile. "Tell me," I said, "where on earth did you learn to do that?"

"I learned it," said the girl. "I figured it out."

"By yourself?" I asked.

She shook her head.

"Someone taught you, then. Who was that? I would like to meet this teacher."

"He said not to tell anyone," the girl said. She was wary of me, pulling back. I had to try something desperate to keep her engaged.

"But I'm not just anyone," I said. "My name is Doctor John Watson. Perhaps you have heard of me."

As much as I disliked using my notoriety as an author, it had the desired effect. Her eyes widened, and for the first time since I'd laid eyes on her she smiled.

"You're Doctor Watson?" she said. "Papa's read me some of your stories from *The Strand*."

"I'm flattered," I said.

"They were sort of scary, your stories," she said, "but I still liked them. I especially like your friend, that Herlock Scholmes. Is he with you?"

"Sherlock Holmes," I corrected, "and I'm sorry to say he isn't."
Privately I wondered if anyone would ever be happy to see just me without
mentioning my famous friend.

"That's too bad," she said. "I think he'd like my bird tricks."

"I am sure he would," I said. "Can you show me another?"

Wordlessly she untied the ribbon from the back of her hair, and held
it aloft, gesturing with two of her fingers. A pair of ravens from the circle
around her perked up immediately. She tossed the ribbon into the sky, and
the two ravens took flight, snatching it out of mid-air by the ends before it
hit the ground. There they hovered while the girl stood and retrieved the
cloth from the pair, retying it into her hair with practiced ease. Finally she
produced from her bag a handful of seeds that she cast upon the ground,
where they were set upon by the entire flock in a frenzy of naked hunger.
I clapped, and the girl bowed as her birds continued to feast.

"That was astounding," I said. "Can I learn to do that?"

"I'm not sure," said the girl. "He only teaches certain people."

"I should like to try," I said.

"All right," said the girl. "But only if you promise that next time you
come here you'll bring Mr. Scholmes."

"Holmes," I corrected. "But, yes. I promise."

She reached into her bag, and produced a card which she handed to
me. I looked at the name printed upon the card, and the pieces of the puzzle
fell into place. It was a name very familiar to me indeed.

"Calm yourself, my foolish friend," the Bishop kindly said.
"That trap did not harm a feather 'pon your coward's head."
He put the bird gently down upon the rocky street.
"It will take more than a mere carriage for us death to meet."

The windows of Baker Street were dark, an unusual sight. Most
nights, the lights within would blaze under the gentle hand of our landlady,
Mrs. Hudson, who would keep the lamps filled and lit even when her
tenants weren't at home. As I approached 221b, I was surprised to find no
constable guarding the door. Normally, in the hours after a tragedy,
Scotland Yard would station a bobby outside to keep away naysayers, but
tonight, with Mrs. Hudson watching over Holmes at the hospital, there was
no one to observe my return. I let myself in with my key, climbing the
familiar steps to the first floor, and on up to my bedroom on the second.

Opening the door, I headed straight to retrieve my service revolver.
There was a confrontation approaching, one for which it would be best if
I were armed. Then I went back downstairs one floor to the sitting room.
Unfortunately, someone had gotten there first.

"That's far enough, Doctor," said a voice from the darkness.

I turned to see a shadow seated in the chair by our cold fireplace. I heard the unmistakable sound of a revolver's hammer being cocked.

"Hello, Mister Forrester," I said.

With the strike of a match, a candle was lit and I saw the placid face of the Seminarian glaring at me from out of the dark, my own revolver clutched in his hand.

"Good," he said. "I'm glad that you know. I don't want any secrets between us here in this final hour."

"Then you intend to kill me, as you did the Bishops?" I said. "As you attempted with Sherlock Holmes?"

He stared at me with an unreadable expression, until his lips moved, slithering like a serpent into a cold smile.

"Sherlock Holmes?" he said with a laugh. "Oh, no, Doctor. The bomb wasn't meant for Mr. Holmes, but for you!"

I started in surprise. "For me?" I whispered. "But why?"

"Because you let her die," said Forrester. From inside a pocket, he produced a slip of paper which he placed upon the side table. Even in the dim light I could see the inscribed chess move on its surface.

"*P x K.*"

I puzzled at his cryptic comment, until the answer clicked in my mind. "Mary," I said.

Forrester nodded.

"That's unfair,"I said. "I would have done anything to save my wife." Forrester said nothing, merely fidgeting with the revolver's trigger in a way I found most unsettling. I knew I had to play for time. "You know, Forrester," I began, "Mary often talked of the children she governed before our marriage – in particular of a boy named Timothy. You, I presume."

"She was good to me," said Forrester. "She protected me."

"I'm sure she did. She was one of the most loving souls I've ever met . . ." I began, but a shot from my own revolver cut my words short. The bullet hadn't hit me, but it was close enough that I could feel its passing before it hit the wall behind me.

"A lie," said Forrester. "You all lie."

"I assure you – "

Another shot, this one passing so close to my cheek that I jumped back.

"You took her from me," said Forrester, rising from the chair, the revolver clutched in a death grip within his hand. He advanced a step toward me, and then another, his eyes possessed of a strange mania. "She assured me that you were a good man, that you would protect and provide for her, but once you were in her heart there was no more room for us. For *me!*"

"Sir, I – " I began.

Another shot, so close that I could feel the hot sting of blood as it grazed my cheek. Outside I could hear bobby whistles, the constables at last aware of my danger, summoned forth from the night by the sound of gunshots.

"She forgot me, Doctor," he said with suspicious calm. "Who would protect me once she was gone?" His rage bubbled over, his cheeks and eyes turning the color of raw anger. "Who?" he screamed. "Answer me that!"

I had faced death many times, but never before had it seemed so close, so personified. I knew what I had to do.

Before Forrester could react, I sprang at the man.

He fired again, his shot going wild and shattering one of Holmes's test tubes. I hit him squarely in the chest, tackling him to the ground. His gun went sprawling from his grip, but he still possessed the strength of a madman, and even as I attempted to pin him down his hands clasped around my throat.

"You should have died with the bomb, Doctor!" he cried. "It would have been easier that way."

I clutched at his hands, struggling to get purchase even as spots began to swim before my eyes. Somewhere in the distance I could hear Mary, calling for me.

Then the door to our sitting room flew open, and Gregson and two constables burst into the room. One of them grabbed at Forrester, attempting to wrest him away from my throat, but the madman's grip was strong, his mania fully unleashed. I thought for sure my time had finally come when a gunshot issued forth and Timothy Forrester collapsed, his devil's strength gone in an instant. I gasped for breath, strong hands seeking to help me up from where I lay, but darkness called and I knew no more.

I dreamed of Mary.

The day was fading, the hours long
as they approached the Bishop's church.
The shadow of the cross loomed down upon them
from atop its lofty perch.
The Bishop crossed himself, but then lurched forward with a start.
"Raven, oh friend Raven, dear, I think it is my heart."

"Well, Watson, you've certainly outdone yourself this time."

48

I opened my eyes to the same hospital room in which I had awakened only a day before. Or had it been more than a day? I looked to my bedside to see Holmes smiling down at me. His bandages were gone, but he was still garbed in a hospital robe and clasped a cane in his angular hands. Despite this, his eyes radiated his familiar energy, and I knew he was well on the road to recovery.

"Holmes!" I said, my voice overwhelmed immediately by a hacking cough.

"Calm yourself, my friend," said Holmes. "Not many survive two attacks upon their life within so many hours. You should count yourself fortunate."

"How long . . . ?" I said, my voice a rasp.

"Two days," said Holmes. "Really, Watson. I should be very cross with you if I weren't so relieved. You were supposed to report back to me, not confront the perpetrator alone."

The memory came back in a flash. "Forrester!" I croaked. "Is he – ?"

"He is no threat," said Holmes. "Gregson's shot was true."

"I didn't know he was there," I whispered, finding the less I pushed my voice the less pain.

"Come now, Watson. Surely you must have suspected something was amiss when you found no constable at the front door?"

"I did notice," I whispered, "but I assumed he had been called away."

"He had," said Holmes. "Forrester had staged a fire a few streets over, and reported it to the officer. Then he slipped into Baker Street as neat as you please. But perhaps it would be best if you now told me all that transpired since we last spoke. Here is some tea. Take your time, refresh yourself and tell me of your adventures."

Slowly, haltingly, I told Holmes all that had occurred since I had bade him farewell from this same hospital. He listened, his eyes closed, and when I finished my tale he sat in silence for some time, pondering.

"This case continues to be unique," he said at last, "made all the more by the connection to your past."

"He wanted to kill me for not protecting Mary," I whispered.

"Yes, but that doesn't explain why he wished the same fate for the Bishops, nor why he chose such outlandish methods to achieve his ends. This would be a three-pipe problem, if not for my cursed doctor prohibiting tobacco. Still, let me ponder the matter. You should enjoy a well-deserved rest until you are better."

The Raven looked on as the Bishop fell down to the ground,
and from his blood-stained beak came a most peculiar sound.
As the Bishop writhed, the bird began to peck his face,

his beak drawing blood that flowed at an increasing pace.

Four days later, we were both back in Baker Street.

Mrs. Hudson had cleaned up our rooms as best she could. The table damaged by the bomb had been replaced, the soot scrubbed away, and fresh plaster covered up the new bullet holes Forrester had made during our struggle. Strangely, she had chosen to preserve the letters "*V*" and "*R*" which Holmes himself had shot into our wall during a particularly savage spate of boredom. I never asked her motives for preserving this memento of Holmes's peculiar habits, but the two letters had been on our wall now for nigh on a decade.

Holmes was seated by the fire smoking his pipe, while I was opposite reading the morning newspaper. The headlines that particular morning told of the escalation of tensions within the Empire, as the Boers had apparently laid siege to some of our colonies, yet I found myself distracted by other matters. I was healing, my voice almost back to its normal baritone, but still felt weary from my body's exertions and trauma. My war wound ached, as it often did at this time of year. I looked over the top of my paper at my companion and marveled at his strange and remarkable constitution. Seeing the man's energy now, I would never have guessed that he had been in the hospital only days before.

Holmes sensed my gaze. "What troubles you, Watson?" he asked. "Is it the Forrester affair?"

"It is," I said. "I don't mean to sound ungrateful, but it has been four days since we've had any developments in the case."

"Things progress, my friend," said Holmes. "Indeed, I suspect we shall have all the answers we require before the day is through."

"You've made inquiries?" I said.

"Of course," he said. "In fact, I shall be headed out shortly myself."

"But Holmes," I said, "the doctors ordered you to rest."

"And I have," said Holmes. "Indeed, I haven't left Baker Street since we returned. As you know, I have other methods of investigation still open to me, but I think that those have run their course." He paused and looked at me with an expression that veered dangerously close to affection. "I must warn you, I begin to suspect that what I find may be upsetting to you. Are you sure you wish to know?"

"It is more than a wish," I said. "It is a necessity. I suspect I will not sleep soundly again until I know the truth."

"Very well," said Holmes. He grabbed his hat and coat and made for the door. "You may have a visitor before long," he said enigmatically, and then departed before I could respond.

50

Some time later, the bell below rang, and soon I could hear someone ascending the stairs. The door opened, and in shuffled a young man I recognized as the current lieutenant of the Baker Street Irregulars.

"Afternoon, Mister Doctor, sir," said the child. "Mr. Holmes in?"

"No, Billy, he's out, I'm afraid," I said. "Do you have news? I can relay it."

"We do, sir," said Billy. "Took a bit too, but we found her."

"Found who?"

"That child," said Billy. "That girl you met in the park. You'll find her here." He reached into his shabby coat and withdrew a slip of paper, which he handed to me. Printed clumsily on the paper, and mis-spelled besides, was a London address.

"You have done good work, Billy," I said. "Here are your wages, compliments of Mr. Holmes." I handed Billy a bag of coins, which Billy accepted with naked hunger. "Share these with the other Irregulars."

"I will, sir." He bowed, with a grace that belied his awkward appearance, and vanished from our rooms.

It was night before Holmes returned, entering the sitting room without a word, and I could see from his expression that he was troubled. He sat down in his chair and regarded me.

"These are very dark waters, Watson," he said.

"What have you discovered?" I asked.

"I was able to secret myself into Timothy Forrester's rooms at the church and, after a quick search, discovered these." He produced from inside his coat a tin box, a set of pruning shears, and a battered notebook bound in faded blue leather. "The book and tin box were hidden behind a stone behind his bed," said Holmes. "The shears were left behind by Scotland Yard when Gregson searched the place."

I picked up the tin box and sniffed at it.

"Gunpowder," I said. "No doubt the same which produced the bomb which was hand delivered to our rooms." I picked up the blue book, opened it, and started at the title page. "Why," I said, "this is Timothy Forrester's journal!"

"Quite so," said Holmes, "and the tale that it tells is a tragedy. Within those pages lies an unspeakable crime that led to the death of the three Bishops, and the subsequent attempt upon your life. I'm afraid, Watson, that you will not like the story that these pages tell. There is poetry to his madness, but it is poetry that may only add to your pain."

"Holmes, you speak in riddles," I said. "Normally I am content to let your obfuscations play out to the end, but just now I am in far too much pain. Please. Tell me what you have learned."

"Very well," said Holmes. "You already know that Mary was a governess for the Forrester family when you first met."

"Yes," I said. "And Timothy was one of her charges."

"Indeed," said Holmes. "Along with two others: Daniel, the oldest, and Samantha, who was but an infant when Mary left the Forrester's employ."

"I know all this," I said with growing impatience.

"Of course," said Holmes, "but did you know that you met Samantha not five days ago?"

I froze in astonishment.

"Yes," said Holmes. "The girl from Hyde Park. You could say that affinity for ravens runs in the family."

"Are you suggesting," I sputtered, "that little girl with the ribbons in her hair is somehow involved in this nefarious affair? Was she the one who trained the ravens?"

Holmes held up his hand. "Calm yourself, Doctor. I am suggesting nothing of the sort. Indeed, I suspect that Samantha is completely ignorant of her brother's activities, as one of his stated goals was to protect her."

"Yes," I said, "but protect her from what?"

"From the church," said Holmes, "or, more specifically, from its Bishops."

"I don't understand," I said.

"It is all there in Timothy's diary," said Holmes. "How the three Bishops from Forrester's church all paid Timothy attentions most unnatural when he was but a child. How your Mary tried to shield him from these attentions, and even succeeded until she left the household for marriage. Alas, the subsequent governess wasn't as attentive as Mary to her charge's needs, and Timothy soon fell prey to the Bishop's unholy affections. The experience left him both traumatized and bitter, and he plotted against those he blamed, partly for revenge, but also to prevent his sister from suffering a similar fate."

"That's monstrous," I whispered. "Mary never said anything about this to me."

"Mary protected those she loved," said Holmes. "That included you, Watson, as she knew such knowledge would upset you."

"But why would Timothy use such outlandish methods of murder?" I said. "Why inscribed chess moves, bombs, and ravens?"

"I told you that there was poetry to Timothy's madness," said Holmes, "and indeed his inspiration for his reign of terror comes from exactly that. Open the diary to the final page, Doctor."

I did as Holmes requested, and discovered a tattered piece of paper pasted inside. Inscribed upon the page was a poem.

"'*The Bishop and the Raven*'" I read aloud.

"We all draw inspiration from what we read, Watson. Alas, we cannot ask Timothy himself, but we can make some suppositions from his diary. Given the age of the of paper, I would say that Timothy discovered that poem when he was very young, and saw within its words a path towards vengeance."

"Rooks and Bishops," I said. "Bishops and Rooks. The game of chess."

"Indeed," said Holmes. "A game young Timothy learned during his time at the circus, and excelled at. But we shall return to Whistler in a moment. The imagery of the poem took hold within the young man's mind, and a plan was formed. It was around this time that the Forresters died."

"They died?" I said, shocked. "Mary never said anything to me."

"I am uncertain if your wife even knew," said Holmes. "An accident at sea. Subsequently Timothy and his siblings were put into the charge of a wealthy relative. Timothy never felt affection for his new family, and soon ran away, anxious to put his long plan into action.

"He had heard of the Canary Trainer, the man named Whistler, and sought him out with the intention of learning how to train birds, particularly ravens. He proved to be rather talented at this skill, and soon could inspire these birds to feats almost supernatural. Once Whistler had taught him everything he needed to know, he left the circus and began the next portion of his plan, his training at the church as a Seminarian. The Bishops who had once wounded him as a child now welcomed him as a man, never suspecting Forrester's vendetta against them. Once his place within the church was established, he began to implement his plan. First he disposed of Bishop Roberts, utilizing a poison to simulate a heart attack. Given Roberts' advanced age, nothing was suspected.".

"And yet no chess move was discovered for Roberts."

"Bless you, Watson. As the death wasn't considered suspicious, the police didn't know to look for anything out of place. I would venture that you were correct and that particular piece of paper is forever lost. Next was Bishop Mortimer, run down in the street by an out-of-control carriage."

"I have the chess move sent to Mortimer in my possession." I produced the piece of paper I had received from Mortimer's widow and handed it to Holmes. He examined it and placed it upon the side table.

"Same make of paper as the one given to us by Gregson, along with the same careful lettering in black India ink. Not conclusively by the same hand, but given the circumstances, we can be fairly certain that Mr. Forrester was the author."

"'*Pawn takes Bishop*'. I suppose that Timothy represents the pawn in this game."'

"I am certain that he fancied himself that way, yes," said Holmes. "Content now that his machinations hadn't been discovered, Forrester decided to dispose of Bishop Marley in his most brazen method yet. He waited for the Bishop to walk down the garden path, and then attacked him."

"You mean ordered his ravens to attack," I said.

"No, Watson," said Holmes. "I mean he attacked him using the pruning shears to simulate an assault by ravens. I was suspicious from the first that even the most well-trained bird could commit so bloodthirsty a crime, and my discovery of the shears in Forrester's room confirmed my hypothesis."

I lifted up the shears and examined their blades. He had done his best to wash away the blood, but the reddish tinge upon the blades was unmistakable.

"But his training," I said. "The time with Whistler . . . ."

"Oh, I have no doubt he intended for the ravens to kill the Bishop, but, when faced with the reality that they wouldn't, he took the murder into his own hands. We only have his testimony for what occurred, after all. The other parishioners only saw ravens, not the attack itself."

"My God," I said.

"No, Watson," said Holmes. "Forrester may have been wrong about many things, but he was right about one: God had nothing to do with this."

"And then Forrester turned his attentions to us," I said.

"Not us, Watson," said Holmes. "*You*. In Forrester's mind, you had taken Mary away from him, removing the protection she offered. Your death would have represented his final revenge. It is all there in the diary, if you wish to peruse."

I looked at the diary in my hands, but then laid it down.

"I'm not sure I can read this," I said. "It seems unthinkable to me that my happiness with Mary could have caused so much pain to this young man."

"You know my views on both women and marriage, Watson," said Holmes, "but even I could tell that you brought great joy to Mary Watson in the final years of her life. You shouldn't blame yourself for that."

"Thank you," I said, but in my heart I knew that I would be wrestling with my own demons and doubts for some time to come.

"And now, dear fellow, grab your hat," said Holmes, rising from his chair. "There is still one loose end that we must tie up, and I think it would be best if we did it together."

"What is that, Holmes?"

54

"Do you have the piece of paper that Billy brought you?" said Holmes. "That is the home where we will find Samantha Forrester. It is important that she knows of her brother's fate, and that we be the ones to tell her."

With a grim sense of duty I retrieved my hat, and together we set out into the streets of London to deliver one of the most difficult messages of my life to an innocent soul.

"Why do you wound me, Raven friend?" said the Bishop as he cowered.
"I need help, not hurt, from you here in my final hour."
The bird smirked, and pecked out the Bishop's eye.
"To myself be true," said the bird, and flew away as the Bishop died.

The Arc of Redemption
by Gustavo Bondoni

The blood drained from my face as Mrs. Hudson led the man into our sitting room at 221b Baker Street. Though his features appeared slightly darker, as if cooked by the sun, and despite not having seen him in over a decade, I recognized the man immediately. His was a countenance I would not soon forget.

I reacted immediately. Lacking my revolver – I was unaccustomed to carry my trusty Webley with me in domestic circumstances – I was determined to reach my hefty walking cane before the fiend in our midst could carry out whatever nefarious vengeance he had in mind.

Holmes's hand on my shoulder halted my progress. "I don't think there is any need for that. I suspect John Clay comes to us as a supplicant, as opposed to an old enemy."

The man stood peacefully before us in a light-grey suit whose cut had been out of fashion for years and which, furthermore, sat loosely on his frame. He nodded to Holmes. "They told me you were hard but fair," he said. Then, with a slight smile he continued. "I have firsthand experience of your being hard, so I thought I might as well see if they were right about the fairness."

"Please sit," Holmes said, motioning towards the chair left over from the interview we'd concluded just minutes earlier. "You have been waiting since noon?"

"I asked your landlady to send for me when your last potential client departed. I was disinclined to be an annoyance."

It being past four, and a cool autumn day, I found myself warming to the man. Holmes studied him silently for a moment. "For that I thank you, but I suppose this is quite consistent with your newfound views, so I might as well thank the Separate System."

John Clay, a hardened criminal that Holmes and I had apprehended in the very act of attempting to rob the Coburg branch of the City and Suburban Bank, nodded. "I'm not certain that every man put into our prisons emerges reformed," he said, "but I found that the hard labor brought clarity of mind. Within two years, I realized I would emerge while still, if not in my prime, at least young enough to make a real go at it, and by the fifth I had a plan to become a solid citizen, one that, perhaps, wouldn't make me wealthy, but would at least reconcile me to my family."

"And that plan has been undone," I prompted.

"I don't understand it," he said. "My family gave me their word that they did nothing to disturb the money."

Holmes waited for some beats, then finally answered. "Perhaps it would be best if you started at the beginning." He raised his voice and called for Mrs. Hudson to bring our guest a small repast left over from our luncheon.

The man nodded and bit into a pastry. "Thank you. I haven't eaten since early morning."

"I deduced as much," Holmes replied. "Now, tell me how you managed to become the secretary to the Gaolor of Winchester Prison."

The man allowed a smile to form at the ends of his lips. "Though I have had cause to regret those powers of deduction you are rightly famous for, I admit to curiosity as to how you managed to glean that information."

"It's more observation than deduction," Holmes said. "In the first place, the last time we crossed paths, you had a skin color more suitable to a city gentleman of nocturnal habits than that of a man accustomed to spending time outdoors. In the Metropolis, prison labor tends to be of the treadmill type, not an activity calculated to give one the complexion of an outdoorsman.

"Inasmuch as you were once a gentleman, the likelihood of being sent to a prison far afield of the Capital was small, and Winchester is tolerably nearby. Hence my deduction of where you spent the time.

"As for my asseveration that you were the gaoler's secretary, it's quite clear that the shirt you are wearing isn't new, and that the cuffs are stained with ink. It is also the only piece of your attire that fits correctly. Your suit, on the contrary, was clearly recovered from the effects you left behind when you were imprisoned. Hence, it is now slightly large on your frame. This leads me to conclude that the shirt is something you wore until your release. The single person who would be exposed to ink in the prison is the gaoler's secretary, and that is the origin of my conclusion."

The man nodded. "I have often wondered, while awaiting my return to liberty, whether my capture might have been in some way avoidable." He held up a hand. "Please don't think I would have preferred not to be captured: I now understand that having been caught was my salvation. But I must admit to having gone over every particular of the caper that led to my apprehension, and wonder if I could have arranged things in a way to outsmart you." He sighed. "With this recent piece of deduction, I understand that such an enterprise would have been impossible, and my last doubts are laid to rest. For this, even were you not able to solve my principal problem, I have cause to be grateful."

He took a sip of the tea Mrs. Hudson had supplied him with and began his tale. "As you know, I was sentenced to ten years of labor, a judgement not as lenient as I then felt I deserved for a crime I only intended to commit. Nevertheless, the judge, swayed by witnesses who came forward to speak of other things in which I'd been involved, gave me a decade and said that I should count my blessings that he wasn't swayed to give more by my career criminality. He also expounded at length about how I should be grateful that transportation was no longer an option."

As the man paused to sip his tea with evident relish, I took the opportunity to observe Holmes. Far from the impatience I expected at this lengthy *apologia* of this man's criminality, he seemed genuinely interested. Perhaps I should have expected that: The criminal mind fascinated him.

"During the first months of my penance," Clay continued, "I admit that I was a prisoner like any other. Sullen, enraged, and quite simply overcome with the unfairness of my lot. I was the plaything of the guards' clubs and the despair of the parson they brought in on the Sabbath to attempt to mend our ways."

"From what I see before me," I said, "the parson was successful."

"The change in me didn't start by an opening of my ears to the Word of God," the former prisoner replied, "but with an opening of my eyes to the men around me. I looked and saw creatures that, had I seen them on the street, I would have been certain of their criminality. A less-inspiring group of sniveling, cringing degenerates you would have been hard pressed to find." He shook his head. "At first, I'm ashamed to admit, I felt infinitely superior to my companions in misfortune, but then I found myself hearing the echoes of my words in theirs. On my first day, when a man said a magistrate had been unfair, I simply thought that he couldn't claim injustice unless he was in my place.

"Gradually, though, I came to realize that all sang the same song as I did, and many were in gaol for much the same reasons as I, and that made me wonder whether I – seen from the outside – might be just as unworthy as those men surrounding me." He sipped his tea. "The idea, on the face of it, appeared ridiculous to me. After all, was I not a gentleman of good breeding? But as the months went by, I realized it wasn't breeding that brought these wretches together, but the meanness of our actions. In that, I was no better – if also no worse – than the men around me. Having managed that realization, I was free to see myself as I really was . . . and to improve."

"And the gaoler took note," Holmes said.

"The parson first. I told him that I had a certain amount of money – not ill-gotten, but from the time when my family gave me an allowance, before they disowned me – set aside to put up a shop front and establish a bookseller's concern. When the gaoler found out I enjoyed books – and after I had been a model prisoner for more than a year – he allowed me to serve as his secretary, and I was released at the earliest possible moment allowed for in my sentence."

Holmes nodded. "And when you emerged, you found the unassailable hiding place of your coin to have been violated, and the coin gone."

Clay nodded glumly. "It must have been a singular act of misfortune that led to its discovery. But the hiding place is in the country, so I assume an honest person likely encountered it. If you can track that person, I'm certain he can be convinced to return it."

Holmes took a long puff of his pipe. "And where is this place located?"

"Wanstead," the man replied.

Holmes said nothing, merely puffed some more, the great mind already involved in gymnastics I could only follow once he explained them to me at a later date.

The day dawned bright and crisp. The coach we'd hired was prompt and, somewhat to my surprise, so was John Clay. At some point in the night, I'd become convinced that the man would make us wait, that his protestations of having turned a new leaf were empty shells meant to convince Holmes to assist him. I was quite certain that, once he had no further use for us, the miscreant would return to his former ways.

I had said as much to Holmes, and he simply shook his head and replied that, even if that were true, this case promised much in the way of interest, and made arrangements to have the coach waiting.

My duties had never before taken me to Wanstead, so I was pleasantly surprised to discover that it was a mere four miles north of the metropolis proper, and set in a wooded area.

"That there's the orphanage," John Clay said. "If we stop here, I can find the way."

He pointed to a walled compound inside which could be discerned an edification in the style of the early part of the last century, resplendent in exposed brick, and which had a plaque on the gate that read *Royal Wanstead Children's Foundation*. Upon seeing the name, I immediately recognized the institution as a traditional beneficent society with a good reputation. I was acquainted with doctors who gave their time to the place out of charity, and I made a note to see if I could be of assistance.

Clay took us to the northeastern corner of the walled space and led us directly into the woods from there, following a path that seemed even less pronounced than a game trail. We walked among the brambles for some while, and I thanked the autumn for having defoliated the vicinity to a certain degree, before we arrived at a small clearing beside a bubbling brook. Our guide located a rock on the brook and counted three paces inward before showing us a hole in the loam. "This was covered with dirt and leaves when I was arrested – I would always conceal my capital whenever there was a risky job afoot. When I got out, I found the hole and nothing more, except this." He held up a pin that looked like something a schoolboy would affix to a tie, rusted around the edges where the enamel didn't cover the metal. "That is how I know I wasn't mistaken about the location. This is mine, and it was in the hole. I pulled it out just last week."

Holmes studied the pin, then knelt beside the excavation. "This looks like it was dug out some years ago. Look at the way the sides of the top have eroded. I assume the new digging at the bottom is yours, in the attempt to recover your property? By the look of it I would say it was three days past."

"That was me, yes." He looked up, his eyes imploring. "Can you help me?"

"Let us retire to the public house," Holmes said. "I have some questions."

Once seated comfortably near the fire, John Clay refused to drink until Holmes assured him that his pint would come at our cost. Then Holmes spoke.

"I'm certain you have suspicions about who might have removed the money. I would advise you to inform us who knew you had funds in hiding, and also the amount in question."

John Clay hesitated. "There were eight-hundred pounds in the hole," he said.

"You had eight-hundred pounds and you still thought it necessary to rob a bank vault via an underground tunnel?" I asked. That amount represented a reasonable year's income for many men. A comfortable life.

"I know it may be difficult to understand for people such as yourselves, but the prospect of living with eight-hundred pounds wasn't satisfactory when there were twenty-thousand – and also stocks and bonds to an equal sum – within easy reach. In my present, more-enlightened state, I wouldn't succumb to that particular temptation, but this was before." He looked from Holmes to me. "You must understand that I was brought up a gentleman, accustomed to an allowance that would permit me to enjoy myself without a care. My own excesses led to my family to disown me – and any appeal to them now would be sterile as all family wealth has been willed to a cousin who despised me from birth – and left me with a dwindling capital which, as you saw, I have also now lost."

"Why would you bury it in a hole?" I asked.

"At the time, I had a marked distrust of the safety of banks. I'm certain you can imagine the reason for my prejudice." He smiled.

"Who else knew of this?" Holmes asked. "I assume you told the parson in the prison."

He nodded. "I did. And his duty likely compelled him to inform the gaoler. But I never told them where the money was located."

"Quite apart from that," I said, "a parson and a high official in His Majesty's prison administration don't seem the kind to dig up a man's wealth."

"Is there anyone else who might have suspected you weren't simply living off the wages paid to you by Mr. Wilson? Your accomplice, Archie?"

"Poor Archie. He was a career criminal, and though he might have been involved in fewer unsavory things than I was, they proved more on him. He won't be seeing the streets for another five years yet."

"It is quite fortunate for you that your tracks were well covered," I interjected. "A couple of the things you were reputed to have done would have implied a long fall at the end of a short rope."

"Perhaps there is a plan for my life, still," John Clay said.

Holmes cleared his throat. "And other criminals from your past life? What of them?"

Clay shrugged and pushed his pint along the wood of the table. "I assume some must have suspected. Certainly, they seemed to often go out of their way to touch me for a spot of coin, as if attempting to see how deep my pockets were." He looked up. "Do you think one of them could have done it? If they followed me . . . I would think it was Dirty Bill or Maria the Dancer who might have done this to me. Maybe the Whispering Man."

"We can look into it," Holmes replied.

He cocked his head. "I'm not certain that would be wise," he said. "I know you're a formidable opponent, Mr. Holmes, but Bill's killed four men that I know of with his bare hands. And while the Whispering Man and Maria aren't deadly themselves, they can snap their fingers," he demonstrated with a loud cracking that made the people at the next table look our way in annoyance, "and call up several men who make Bill appear an altar boy."

"I am well aware of that, but there is little risk in making enquiries," Holmes said. "And if any of these individuals suddenly found themselves in possession of additional funds, it's quite certain that someone will have noted the change in their habits." He shook his head. "Sadly, I fear that it's most unlikely that you will recover the money in any of those cases."

"I fear you may be right." Clay stood to go. "I'm sorry to have been a burden on your time."

"It has been a most invigorating morning," Holmes said. "And please don't worry on our account – we would be most happy to share our coach back to the city."

"I don't want to impose further . . ." Clay began, but Holmes waved away his objections.

"No imposition at all. It is the same to us whether the seat returns empty or occupied. Furthermore, Watson and I have ample opportunity to exchange views. It will be refreshing to have a third member of the party to break up our usual discussions."

Though I got the impression that he would have preferred to remain in the neighborhood of Wanstead, the man allowed himself to be persuaded, and on the return trip, Holmes said that, if he were willing, he knew of a position for an assistant or secretary that he could fill, beginning the following day. It was, sadly, only a temporary spot, as it was in a brewery whose secretary had had his foot broken by a wagon, but it would help tide the man over during the first few days.

John Clay accepted gratefully.

My duties kept me from Baker Street that afternoon and well into the evening, but I returned before Holmes retired for the night. As I drank a small glass of sherry and he smoked his pipe, I asked the question that had been praying on my mind the whole day.

"Do you think it's wise to send John Clay into a position of responsibility on your recommendation?" I asked.

"In what way could it be unwise?" Holmes asked, with that superior half-smile he displayed when he knew perfectly well what I was insinuating, but wanted to force me to say it anyway. When confronted, he claimed the process of discussing things helped him to think about them from different vantage points. As I wasn't in possession of mental faculties approaching his, I refrained from arguing the point.

I merely sighed and said, "A secretarial position is a role of trust. I merely thought it might be better to let the man prove himself before allowing him to attain such positions."

"And I agree with you absolutely. That's why Mr. Yardley's brewery is such a perfect position for him. There is nothing he can carry off, unless prison life has strengthened him to the point where he can lift a hogshead without assistance, and there is little chance he can organize sufficient men to make a night-time raid in the time he will be there. Also, I have warned Mr. Yardley to check his numbers quite thoroughly."

"But what is the point of employing a secretary if his employer will have to go through and revisit the records? It is a duplication of . . . ." I let my voice trail off. "Of course. Yardley owes you goodwill for your help with the case of the watered spirits. You want to know exactly where John Clay is for some reason."

Holmes beamed. "Very good, Watson!" he said. "I wish to keep him out of the way until Sunday, when he will not be working. It is Tuesday, and that gives us four days to see if we can solve his case. While I am thus employed, Mr. Clay will find that the hours at the brewery are quite long. He should arrive at his lodgings quite tired out from the day's activities."

"And us? Will we be tracking these people he told us about? This Dirty Bill and Maria the Dancer and the other one?"

"The Whispering Man. Yes. It would be irresponsible of us not to investigate the possibility that one of them might still be in possession of Mr. Clay's fortune."

I drank my sherry, my earlier irritation erased by the fact that I'd actually managed to guess one of Holmes's ploys. "But do you think there will be anything left to recover? From what I know of Clay's life, his criminal acquaintances are unlikely to have retained the money. They are more likely to have dilapidated it on the wildest and most immediate extravagances to which the sum stretched."

"Yes," Holmes replied. "That is likely. Still, it's an avenue we must pursue, if only for the sake of elimination." Then, knowing my curiosity was far from sated, he went on. "I conclude that Mr. Clay thought we'd be able to garner clues from the site of the burial, but unfortunately, not even I can make many deductions from a hole in the ground last disturbed years ago. However, I think we could profit from a judicious study of the area without Mr. Clay present. His involvement in the subject is too close, and I prefer a more cool-headed approach."

On the following morning, the sense of the game being afoot was quite alive in the air. Messengers came and went, the Irregulars – and a few of the former Irregulars grown to man's estate and therefore able to penetrate redoubts closed to urchins – reported on an hourly basis, and a picture of our three prime suspects gradually came into focus.

Dirty Bill, whose reputation as a hard man had been well-deserved, was the first of the suspects to be discarded. He'd been knifed by a sailor in the Isle of Dogs, agonizing for twelve days, cursing both his attacker and his doctors, until he succumbed to the wounds. The incident occurred almost at the same time as John Clay was put in prison. Thereafter, his gang had scattered and any money – if there was any to be found – had long since disappeared.

Maria the Dancer appeared to be a more complicated proposition. A decade before, she had already been the mistress of a house of ill repute, and the intervening years had seen her premises move several times, creeping gradually west from her original location in Limehouse to her current abode in Verulam Street. Likewise, her clientele, had evolved from sailors and men who made their living on the street to gentlemen attracted by proximity to the theater district.

Unfortunately, her rise seemed more consistent with the abilities of a rapacious but capable businesswoman than with someone encountering an unexpected windfall. After some discussion, we set her aside. In my case, it was with reluctance that I accepted that she probably wasn't the culprit. Had she been, she would likely have been the only one able to return the funds.

On the other hand, the Whispering Man was unlikely to have more than the clothes on his back. In the days when Clay had been a free man, the Whispering Man operated a group of urchins that patrolled Canary Wharf and, aside from begging for alms, they specialized in stealing small things and then bolting for cover. He, himself, had supervised their activities while pretending to be a blind beggar stooped under an overhang on the street.

Ironically, this mummery had caught up with the Whispering Man, and true blindness affected him to the point where he was reduced to subsisting on the alms in reality. I marveled at the generosity of the human spirit. The fact that the very neighbors he'd once robbed gave enough to keep him from starvation once he fell into misfortune was a marvel.

But once again, the suspect was unprofitable. If that man had ever had eight-hundred pounds, he certainly didn't have them now.

"Well, we've done our duty when it comes to Clay's suspects," Holmes said, rubbing his hands together against the evening chill. "It now falls to us to generate new avenues of investigation. Retire early tonight, my friend, for tomorrow, we have an early appointment."

We left on another hired coach quite early the following morning, the sound of hooves on wet cobblestones echoing against the buildings along the street. A thick fog had rolled in, making the going slow, the coachman tentative.

Once more, however, we rode only a short way, and once again our journey brought us to Wanstead before an hour had passed.

Descending from the coach, I had the sense that the place had been transformed by the mist. A solid blankness marked the wall of the orphanage. Dimly seen structures loomed like distant mountains. A darkness encroached on the road from all sides.

A moment passed before I realized that it concealed the forest beyond the lane, and the massive structures were the walls of the orphanage. Had

I been a less-modern man, the creeping shadows would have brought visions of monsters and gods.

Even in our more enlightened age, I breathed easier once the man who opened the gates of the orphanage led us across large, fog-covered grounds to seat ourselves in a well-lit room with a warm fire and a young girl with a tea-tray. I sat gratefully, despite descending from the coach mere minutes before.

"Miss Perkins will be with you shortly," the doorman said. He must have been a gardener, at least to judge by his attire of heavy boots and a thick jacket. He certainly didn't look as if he belonged inside the house, but rather a creature more comfortable in the primeval gloom outside.

The house itself was well-built and solid, and the room in which we were seated had darkened wood on the furniture and a well-worn rug beside the fire, but there were no signs of the opulence one naturally assumed for an edifice like this one in a rural setting. The furniture was more solid than delicate, the carpet more functional than ornate, and even the walls were devoid of ornamentation except for a single hunting picture in one corner. Clearly, any funds sent to the Royal Wanstead School were used for things other than decoration.

The tea, on the other hand, was excellent.

"Good morning, gentlemen," a lady's voice said. "I thank you for your punctuality. You would be surprised how many people underestimate either the interval it takes to come up from London or the importance of my own time. We have more than a hundred children here, as you likely you know, and I must keep one eye on everything that happens."

Miss Perkins was a woman in her sixties, thin to the point of emaciation, with greying hair tied almost carelessly back in a single pigtail. She peered at us from behind round glasses, and she wore a blue dress that, like the house itself, spoke more to ruggedness than to frills.

"And I thank you for agreeing to meet with us on such short notice," Holmes replied after we'd introduced ourselves.

"You mentioned that time could be of the essence," she replied.

"In one way, it is absolutely critical that we resolve this matter in the most expedient manner possible," Holmes said. "Unfortunately, in another sense, the time to act would have been a decade ago."

The mistress of the orphanage peered at Holmes, then said, "You appear to be a serious man, Mr. Holmes," she said. "I would appreciate it if you would refrain from speaking in riddles."

"Of course, and I apologize," Holmes replied. I admit that I found myself having to suppress my smile at hearing the great detective chastened like a schoolboy. "On Monday, Dr. Watson and I were approached by a man . . . ."

He proceeded to tell the woman about the case of John Clay, our earlier visit to the neighborhood, and the missing treasure from the hole in the ground. The woman listened impassively, nodding every few moments to show she was following along, but never interrupting until Holmes finished speaking.

"And what is the reason you saw fit to bring this to me?" she asked.

"In the first place, I am aware that the woods behind the School, though not enclosed by the wall, are part of the grounds, and as such, I felt you should be informed in case any of Mr. Clay's former connections come looking for the treasure. My colleague, Dr. Watson, will be able to show your groundskeeper the location of the hiding place. For my own part, I was interested in knowing if any members of your staff during the year in question might suddenly have come into money and departed. In a case of that sort, I would be interested in the person's address and to interview him. I believe that, as a public charity, your records are open to inspection by any member of the public?"

Now Miss Perkins seemed uncertain. "It has never come up before, but I suppose you are correct. I have no reason to doubt you." She gave him a hard gaze. "I would like you to know, however, that I take a very dim view of anyone snooping into the affairs of my staff. This is an orphanage, not a public ministry, and some of the people in my employ were hired in much the same way as my wards are selected – because there is nowhere else for them to go. I would be sorely disappointed if you attempted to use this case as a way to dig into their pasts regarding unconnected matters."

"Nothing could be farther from my thoughts," Holmes replied. "In fact, I would welcome your presence as I search the archives in order that you may ascertain that I'm only looking over the time period we discussed. Any activity of anyone prior to entering your employ need not be touched upon."

Somewhat mollified, Miss Perkins arranged for the gardener to be located, and I found myself leading that worthy to the site of the hole, wondering how it was that Holmes was ensconced in the relatively warm building while I was out trampling through foggy cold woods with a man who, for all I knew, might have been a killer that the mistress of the orphanage had taken under her charitable wing. The shovel he carried around with him could have made the perfect weapon. A blow to dispose of me and an hour of hard labor to dig the concealing hole – no one would have known to where I disappeared . . . particularly if Miss Perkins had the good sense to poison Holmes as well.

Despite my misgivings, however, the gardener limited himself to grunting when I showed him the hole and leading me back to the grounds in sullen silence.

Once there, we found Holmes waiting, his demeanor much brighter than my own, for which I grumbled at him. We were halfway back to Baker Street before my mood lifted. "I sincerely hope your own morning was more fruitfully spent than mine," I said.

"I cannot know. We seem to have a habit of leaving Wanstead with a list of names to investigate," he replied. "We'll know more when I've had a chance to think, and the Irregulars have had a chance to ask questions."

As a longtime student of Holmes's expression, I was convinced he had either found something in his perusal of the orphanage records or the trip had ignited a different fuse, which, even as we traveled, was burning down to the inevitable conclusion. Despite the time that had passed, I began to think that John Clay might be recovering his money after all.

My doubts about whether he would ever deserve that, however, would remain.

Since Holmes was convinced that John Clay would do something to disrupt our investigations on the first day of freedom from his employment, we worked with a sense of urgency. Holmes, typically enough, refrained from sharing his suspicions regarding what form that interference might take, but he appeared energized by the strict time limit he'd set for us.

Checking the list of former employees of the orphanage involved not only writing letters – and waiting for the reply by return post – but also traipsing hither and yon all across London.

One former Wanstead School secretary had become a successful banker. A maid had married a publican and now served pints until time was called. Both of those lived a short walk from Baker Street.

The man who appeared to interest Holmes the most, however, was a butcher in Lambeth who had been a cook's assistant at the orphanage as a young man, and who'd married one of the maids. Looking around at the man's place of business, the corner of a rundown house a minute's walk from the Thames, I found it hard to imagine that the man would have had eight-hundred pounds all together at any point in his life.

Still, that didn't seem to affect him. He greeted us with the bonhomie of a man who truly enjoyed his station in life. Holmes and I walked into the room he occupied, a place quite saturated with the smell of fresh meat, and found him wearing a blood-stained apron. Despite his age – he didn't seem to be much over thirty – he was bald and quite unimposing.

His wife sat in a corner reading *The Illustrated Police News*, and my sympathies immediately opened to her, as that particular instrument of dreadful information was quite close to my heart. The sympathy deepened as she looked up at us, since her features were as beautiful as her husband's were nondescript. It seemed an unusual match, but one that surely brought much joy to the husband, as the fresh face and open expression would have made any man's burdens easier to bear. Like her husband, she was likely less than thirty.

A young boy darted inside, had a quick conference with the mother, and was quickly shooed out. "These men seem to be important visitors," she told him, and the urchin rushed out again, pausing only to doff his cap at us, a gesture I found oddly civilized for an boy who looked no older than nine or ten years of age.

"Not important in the least, my good woman," Holmes said. "But it's true we've come to talk and not to purchase any meat."

"That's no matter," the man said as he brought his cleaver onto a stubborn cut. "Few enough people from across the bridge stop to talk here. It will make for a nice change."

"Do you enjoy the neighborhood?" Holmes asked.

"Oh yes, very much," the butcher replied. "Been here these three years. Originally had my business up Wanstead way, but the custom could be slow at times. When Ginny heard that this place could be rented, she reckoned a smart butcher might do well here." He smiled fondly. "She was right. Londoners don't know good meat except when they taste it, so a country boy who appreciates what he's selling will always do well for himself, won't he?"

"I see you have," Holmes said. "I'm actually here to discuss the time you spent in Wanstead."

The man beamed. "That's where I met Ginny. I was a cook's boy at the orphanage, though I was a little too old to really be a boy. Still, the cook was the one who gave the good word that helped me become a butcher's assistant, so I can't really complain, can I?"

Holmes looked around and shook his head. "You do seem to be a man moving up in the world. And in a way, that's related to what I wanted to talk to you about. In your time at the orphanage, maybe ten years ago, did you hear about any of the other employees suddenly coming into money?"

The butcher shook his head. "Can't honestly say I did," he replied. He turned to his wife. "Ginny?"

She laughed. "It certainly wasn't us." Then she thought a moment before continuing. "I'm sure none of the employees came into any money. But I hear old Remus is a rich man now."

"But he wasn't really one of us, was he?" the butcher said. "He was always an educated man."

"Well," Holmes said, handing the man a card, "if you think of anyone, could you write to me here?"

"I will," the butcher replied.

We left just as the boy rushed back. He was small but stoutly built, strong but not fat, the kind of child who would have been the terror of the neighboring youngsters. He didn't resemble either parent except for the shape of his mother's mouth. Of course, it was quite possible he would have had his father's hair . . . but that worthy had none of it left for comparison purposes.

"That seemed to me to be a singularly honest woman. Scrupulously so, in fact," Holmes said thoughtfully. "We have one final stop to see before I am satisfied that we have exhausted all possible alternatives."

"Ah, yes, the retired former nurse," I said. "I expect she must be over seventy, as she left the orphanage well past sixty."

"Yes," Holmes replied. "Perhaps we should stop to buy her something. A bunch of flowers might ease the abruptness of our appearance, I think."

I doubted an old woman living alone would need much in the way of flowers to allow someone inside. In my limited experience, pensioners of any sex were quite content to speak to any visitors for extended lengths of time. Still, I allowed Holmes's opinion on the matter to rule our actions, perhaps by force of habit, or perhaps because I felt that this case was taking a particularly unusual turn, especially as we appeared to be acting in the interests of a client without keeping that worthy informed of our intentions. If I'd read the situation correctly, we appeared to be acting to keep John Clay from acting on his own behalf.

That state of affairs made me wonder, once again, if perhaps the man's reformation was an act. Were that the case, I had the utmost faith in Holmes to identify the signs from some action of the man's, and to keep Clay from managing whatever nefarious purpose had brought him to us.

A mere five minutes after leaving the butcher, still not across the bridge, Holmes arrested our progress. "This shop should do nicely," he said.

I could claim many skills among my accomplishments, from the medical arts to marksmanship. I couldn't claim to be an expert horticulturist.

Nevertheless, even my meager skills in that particular field allowed me to discern that the flower shop in question wasn't a shining example of the type. The window was grimy, the selection poor, and the counter covered in what appeared to be dirt from a delivery of potted houseplants.

However, I was willing to overlook those characteristics in order to avoid going out of our way to locate another shop in the vicinity. Lambeth wasn't a place I'd scouted for florists.

Inside, the initial impression was somewhat mitigated. The shop was warm and smelled of fresh loam, and a faint but not unpleasant perfume. A young woman smiled from the counter and greeted me with a curtsy, and I was suddenly overcome with the sense that I'd seen her face somewhere quite recently.

But even though I studied the pale features, thin hair tied back in a bun and pleasantly rotund physique, I couldn't quite place her. She looked, however, to be of that age between eighteen and twenty in which young girls began to take on the harder planes and more severe beauty of adult women.

"What's that you'll be wanting then?" she asked.

Holmes selected a small tie of flowers already looking dry and made conversation with the girl. "I hadn't noticed this shop the last time I came here," he said.

"You wouldn't have, would you?" the girl replied. "Not if you only come by every once in a while. I sold on the street until just last April. But I thought to myself that summer is too hot to be pulling that cart everywhere, and that I was starting to get too old for it, and me with my bad ankle. I was always afraid to pay rent, but the people roundabouts have been good. They buy from the shops that are near them, and help when they can."

"And have you been here for a long time?"

"Long enough. Came to Lambeth when I was a girl of twelve."

"Well," Holmes said, taking the flowers, "I hope you continue to prosper."

We emerged into the chilly air and continued on to the old woman, who lived with her sister a mile from the florist. She didn't seem particularly concerned with the flowers but, true to my expectations, she did keep us entertained with tales of the orphans – though no intelligence regarding anyone digging up treasure – until the late hours of the afternoon.

When we retired, I was considerably annoyed with Sherlock Holmes. I was certain he had a solution to all of this, and I was equally certain that the lost afternoon listening to the ramblings of an eccentric elderly woman had little to do with the eventual *denouement*.

Unfortunately, I was quite ensnared. To have asked him for the answer would have meant exposing myself to his expressed conviction that I would be able to deduce things for myself, were I just to apply myself to the problem. Worse still, to allow my frustration to lead me to abandon

70

the quest would have meant leaving my curiosity unfulfilled. This I was under no circumstances willing to do.

Sunday dawned dreary, raining just hard enough to dampen spirits and make the footing on cobbled streets treacherous, but not quite sufficiently to soak through clothing. I would have preferred to remain indoors on such a day, but Holmes had risen early.

"We're off to intercept our man," he said.

I followed in his wake. We'd long since had the Irregulars ascertain where John Clay had established his lodgings, and made haste there.

It wasn't quite an inn, instead being one of those places where one could rent a mattress in a common room. And while Clay might be there temporarily – a man with his abilities would soon move up to other quarters – his companions might be there for life, ever fearful of the day they wouldn't be able to bring together the coin for a mattress and be consigned to a place on a rope and a night on their feet.

Clay emerged holding a walking stick, and wearing stout boots. His suit and shirt, on the other hand, were the same as he'd worn to the interview at Baker Street. He wore no cloak.

"It is a bad day to be walking four miles without a coat," Holmes said to him as he emerged.

John Clay looked surprised to see us there, but not alarmed. He cocked his head at Holmes. "Have you come to tell me that your enquiries bore fruit?" he asked. "I am in a bit of a hurry. As you've surmised, I have a long walk ahead of me."

"A walk I can save you from embarking upon," Holmes replied. "What you seek isn't four miles north, but in actual fact it lays just south of the Thames."

"I'm less concerned about my money today than . . . other things. I calculate that I can earn my way out of these premises in another week at the brewer's. And with his recommendation, I can find another position when his man gets well."

"It is those other things that I'm here to tell you about. And in the telling, I will also endeavor to show you the disposition of your eight-hundred pounds. Most of all, however," Holmes added, "I believe you will learn more about yourself than of the other things you want to know."

John Clay said nothing, and I hope Holmes didn't catch my own incredulous expression.

At Holmes's insistence, we waited until eight-thirty in the morning at a small establishment that was open on the Sunday, and then caught a hansom across the river. To my surprise, Holmes led us to the butcher's

71

shop, closed and shuttered for the day. We arrived a few minutes before the man opened the door and led his family from the place.

"That's Ginny Morgan," John Clay said.

"She is Virginia Fulton now. The man's name is Fulton, and he is a good man," Holmes said.

The butcher and his family were dressed in their Sunday best. The tiny domestic procession clearly headed to the nearest church for the nine o'clock service.

John Clay's face showed no expression. "When were they married?" he asked.

"A month after you were sentenced."

"Ah. She didn't wait then."

Holmes shook his head. "She couldn't, as I think you knew. It's just fortunate that she found a good man. A man who understood that one mistake didn't make her any less valuable. A man who made a home for her. A family man."

Jon Clay nodded. "Did she keep the money?"

"Do you think Virginia would be capable of stealing?" Holmes asked.

"Never," John Clay replied. "She was always the most honest thing, confessing to the smallest transgressions that no one else would ever notice. She wouldn't even willingly tell a lie." He grimaced. "How I despised her for it then. I spent the first part of my prison term thinking she was the most perfect imbecile I'd ever encountered . . . until I came to realize that she would be happy whatever her lot in life, while I was a wretch." He watched them walk off, and I realized that they must have had an amorous connection in the times before we captured him. Strangely, he didn't follow her with his eyes, but seemed to be distracted by the gamboling, from one side of the street to the other, of the couple's child.

Then he gave Holmes the last look I'd have expected from a man who'd been forced to watch his former sweetheart married to another man: A look of hope. "Then the money . . . ."

Holmes nodded. "Come."

Eschewing hansoms, Holmes led us across streets we'd walked the day before. I found myself once again at the door of the flower shop. The young woman was just opening for the day.

John Clay gasped. "So beautiful," he said. "I never imagined."

I frowned and tensed. The flower girl couldn't have been more than ten years old when he was condemned. Holmes, however, didn't seem to make the connection. He stood impassively.

"Is she well-treated by the owner of the shop?" he asked.

Now, Holmes smiled. "I suppose that depends on her mood," he replied.

John Clay looked up, confused. "Whose mood would that be?"

"Her own," Holmes said. "For she is the proprietress."

Clay stood, unspeaking, for several moments. "Ginny did this. This is where my money went."

"That was my conclusion, yes."

"That woman is an angel."

Holmes turned to survey him. "What will you do?"

"I think I will just watch her."

"You won't talk to her?"

"Not yet," Clay said. "Not until I can meet her in a suit of clothes that fits me. Not until I can be of help to her, and never have to ask her for assistance."

Holmes nodded. "I would have been disappointed to hear otherwise," he replied. We shook hands and took our leave.

"The flower girl was his daughter," I said once we'd established ourselves before the fire. I had no rounds to make. My patients appeared to have decided that they would, despite the climate, be in rude health on that day, which, truth be told, was a considerable relief. "And he and the butcher's wife had been in difficulties as a result of her inappropriate liaison with Clay."

"Very good, Watson," he said nodding. "And of course, you understood how it was that I deduced these facts."

"No," I admitted. "I deduced them from John Clay's reaction."

He picked up his pipe. "The first clue I had came not last Monday, but when I learned that John Clay had been disowned by his family." He paused to light it and puffed. "He'd been working at cross-purposes with the law long before his kin took any action on that front, so I felt it safe to assume they weren't overly concerned about his criminal activities. There is typically one thing, however, that brings the head of the house into a rage, and that is when a scion disgraces the family name in genealogical questions. By disowning the son, one severs ties with the unwanted offspring."

"The flower-girl."

Holmes nodded. "Her mother was deemed inappropriate, and when she died, the family thought it best that the girl be abandoned to her fate. John Clay felt otherwise and took her to the orphanage as a foundling. He must have confessed to it . . . and his father was furious.

"Even during his criminal heyday, Clay became a frequent visitor to Wanstead. It might have been the first sign of his underlying goodness, because he was there to ensure that his daughter did as well as could be expected. At some point, he brought Virginia Morgan into his orbit. He must have told her about the money. And she did as he expected her to: She gave it to his daughter to help her along her way." Holmes shook his head. "The strength of that woman amazes me. You saw them . . . They could have found unnumbered uses for eight-hundred pounds. A weaker woman would have justified it to herself by saying that she would be ensuring the future of John Clay's son, even as she abandoned the daughter. Instead, she solved both problems by finding a man with an understanding disposition and a heart as kind as her own. A remarkable woman."

"But we could have let Clay find all of this out on his own," I said. "We've been quite inconvenienced by all of this."

Holmes nodded. "I concluded that, by searching myself, I could keep certain truths from emerging before their time. And perhaps certain other truths from emerging at all."

I thought about everything I'd learned, and how the parts that I'd only half-seen, as through a thick fog, now fit together like the stones on a castle battlement. "And do you think the right truths will come to light at the right time?"

Holmes held my gaze, puffed on his pipe, two short pulls, and looked away. "That will depend entirely on John Clay." He paused. "I have trusted him with the truth. What he does with it will show how far along the road to redemption he has come. I like to think he can be trusted with the burden."

I said nothing, simply marveling at Holmes's calm confidence that he had done the logical thing.

The Case of the
Circumspect Client
by Dan Rowley and Don Baxter

*"I have not had occasion to mention Shinwell Johnson in these memoirs
. . . During the first years of the century he became a valuable assistant."*
– Dr. John H. Watson
"The Adventure of the Illustrious Client"

"What, may I ask, are you doing here?"

"I'm waiting for Mister Holmes."

I had come down from my room to sit by the fire to ward off the chill of the early morning, and I eyed with suspicion the man lounging in my habitual place in the sitting room that Sherlock Holmes and I shared. He was large and rather porcine, with coarse, red-faced features. I detected symptoms of scurvy, while he appraised me with his glittering black eyes, which betrayed an intelligence belied by his exterior manifestation

Before I could proceed, the door to Holmes's bedroom opened. "Ah, Watson, I see you have met Johnson."

"We have not been properly introduced," I replied, somewhat stiffly.

"Then allow me to do the honours. This is Shinwell Johnson, also known as 'Porky'. He was a recent resident of Parkhurst and asked to come see me. Johnson, this is my colleague, Doctor Watson. Now, what is it you wanted to see me about?"

"Well, Mister Holmes, two 'visits' to Parkhurst are enough for me. I have decided to mend my ways and seek legitimate employment. I thought, seeing as how you facilitated my latest visit, you might be willing to employ me in some capacity."

"I do not have regular employees, Johnson, so I cannot offer you anything steady. But are you sincere about abandoning your former life of crime?"

"Indeed I am. I had plenty of time to think about it, as you might suspect. I still have all my former contacts and could pretend to be my old self, but actually work for you."

"Yes, I imagine two terms of incarceration would enhance your reputation in certain quarters. But you realize, do you not, that only certain types of cases would be appropriate for your involvement."

"How do you mean?"

"You could never be involved with me in anything that might eventually be in the courts. Otherwise, your confederates would realize your duplicity, and your usefulness would be at an end."

The corpulent man grinned at Holmes. "That's fine with me. I'm happy to let you determine when to involve me. I can get into any night-club, doss house, gambling den, and similar places in the city. And if you're worried about my ability to fool people, my acting ability was on display in some of my earlier, umm, jobs."

"I'm aware of that talent on your part. I make it a practice to study the crimes and criminals of our city, and had my eye on you for some time before making your acquaintance. Allow me to make a proposal to you, which, if you are sincere in your repentance, might well be mutually satisfactory: Maintain your contacts in the criminal underworld, acting as if nothing has changed. If a matter of the type I outlined comes to my attention that could benefit from your involvement, I'll contact you for a trial of your abilities and our compatibility in working together. Assuming that resolves itself in a satisfactory manner, you can become my agent in similar matters. What say you, Johnson?"

"Sounds fair by me, Mister Holmes. Let's give it a go."

"Fine. How may I contact you?"

Johnson mentioned a disreputable public house down by the river, and Holmes nodded. The two shook hands, Johnson gave me a leering look, and he departed.

"Holmes, do you really intend to associate that ruffian in your work? He hardly seems the type to be amenable to your methods, let alone the standard of gentlemanly conduct to which you adhere."

"Watson, there are times when a workman needs a particular type of tool for a particular job. I believe Johnson could be useful – provided he has truly reformed. That is why I want to test him in the proper way."

"I'm not familiar with the case to which he alluded. You have never mentioned it."

"It was some time before I left on my journey abroad. As I mentioned, I had become aware of Johnson's various activities, which proved to me he was a dangerous man. He specialized in extortion and robbery, and had some experience in disposing of stolen goods. After his first term in prison, he seemed to me to become even more violent than before. He assembled different people for each separate misadventure and varied his mode of operating, so didn't have a steady group or gang or create identifiable patterns, and was thus more difficult for the police to apprehend. He was always large, but I had heard that he had begun to put on more weight.

"One night there was a burglary in Mayfair, where the owner came home and surprised the culprits. They severely beat him, but he did recall that one of the men was large and rather fat. Inspector Lestrade had the sense to call me in immediately. I was able to determine from the shoe impressions in the thick carpet, which could only have been made by a heavy man, and some soil in those impressions that I identified as coming from a known haunt of Johnson by the docks, that he was likely the leader. Lestrade quickly found Johnson in his lair with some of the stolen goods. Apparently Johnson inquired how they had found him so quickly, to which Lestrade replied he had me to thank for that."

"Very interesting. You must tell me more details at some point, as it might warrant a write up." Holmes gave me a wry look, picked up the newspaper, and became absorbed in it.

Several weeks passed, and February 1901 was promising to continue the cold spell we had been experiencing. We were in our sitting room, and I was staring out the window, when Holmes startled me. "No, I don't believe dreams could assist me in my work. Facts and logical reasoning are what really matter."

I looked at him, I suppose with some surprise, although I should have been accustomed to this trait of his. "Please elucidate how you knew what I was thinking."

"It's quite simple: You were reading that medical journal on your lap for the past half-hour. You continually stopped and looked at me out of the corner of your eyes. When I came out of my room. I overheard you asking Mrs. Hudson if she dreams at night while she was laying out our breakfast. I took a cursory look at the journal last night before retiring, and noticed that it contains a *précis* of the latest book by that Viennese chap who so fascinates you."

"Yes, Sigmund Freud. His latest work discusses the hidden meaning of dreams. I hope it will be translated into English soon."

"Quite so. You were obviously reading the summary and kept looking at me, wondering how I would react. When you finished it, you stared out the window, as you often do when pondering something. The conclusion was obvious that you were contemplating whether I would use this dream theory in any of my investigations. I will not go so far as to say it has no merit, but for now I'll continue to study human nature through solid facts."

I sighed, but before I could say anything, we heard a knock at the front door and the murmur of Mrs. Hudson and some man talking.

"Ah, Watson, perhaps a client. Please go down and bring him up."

I obliged my friend and went down the stairs. In the front hallway, I found a man in his mid-forties, rather slim with greying and receding reddish hair, a *pince-nez*, and a somewhat thin, reedy voice. Mrs. Hudson introduced him as Sir Percy Reeves. He explained that he had a rather delicate matter he wished to discuss with Sherlock Holmes. I bade him to remove his overcoat and hat and follow me upstairs. After introductions, I moved the basket chair over by where Holmes and I were sitting.

"Well, Sir Percy, what is it you wanted to talk about? You can say anything in front of Watson, as he is the soul of discretion and my invaluable colleague."

"Yes, er, umm . . . I don't know where quite to begin."

"Start at the beginning and leave nothing out, however trivial you may believe it to be."

"Fine. I have a townhouse here in London, over in Belgravia. It was my father's, Sir James, and I inherited it when he passed away."

"Does anyone else live there with you?"

"I am unmarried – or, as my sister would say, married to my work at the Foreign Office. My mother, Lady Margaret, lives mostly at our country place, but she likes to come to London for the social events when Parliament is in session, at which times she stays with me."

"I see. Proceed." Holmes leaned back in his chair and shut his eyes. Sir Percy seemed a bit disconcerted, but I motioned for him to proceed, as I knew this merely meant Holmes was concentrating his powerful mind on every word his potential client uttered.

"*Ahem*. I have a collection of antique items in my study, some inherited from both my paternal and maternal grandparents, some that I have acquired myself. Last night, several of them were stolen. Of course, I would like to recover all of them, but there is one item in particular that I must have back.

"I cannot determine how the thief got into the house. We actually have a fairly full house now, as several relatives are staying with us to visit my mother. They were all there last night, and a cousin and my nephew also came for dinner. My study is at the back of the house, and the kitchen is across the hall, so either my relatives or the servants would have seen a stranger, if the thief came in before midnight. At that time, my cousin and nephew left, and I locked the front door. At the same time, our butler locked the back entrance and checked all the windows on the ground floor, as is his habit. He and the maids who live there have been with us for years, and I would swear to their reliability."

Holmes sat up. "Did you enter the study before retiring?"

"I went straight up to bed. When I came down this morning, I needed to retrieve some papers from the study. That is when I discovered the theft."

"This seems like a matter better handled by the police, if I may say so."

"No, please, Mister Holmes, I don't want to involve the police."

"Why not?"

"I would rather not say, sir. Please help me."

I could see by the glimmer in his eyes that this was beginning to interest Holmes, probably because of Sir Percy's reticence. "What was stolen?"

"Rather small items. Old writing implements. A letter signed by Disraeli. Some buttons from military uniforms, and cuff links supposedly worn by Palmerston. A jeweled casket. There may be a few other things, but I didn't do a complete inventory, as I wanted to hasten here to meet you."

"You mentioned one item you wanted to retrieve. Which is that?"

"The casket. It's approximately sixteen-inches-by-ten-inches, and ten-inches deep. It's encrusted with diamonds and rubies. It came down through my mother's side of the family."

"And why that item?"

"Erm, sentimental value, I suppose."

"What other relatives are staying at the house?"

"My sister, Agatha Pinchlin, and my aunts Ethel, Lydia, and Ruth."

"And the cousin and nephew who came to dinner?"

"My nephew, Montague Pinchlin, Agatha's son, and my cousin, Samuel Breverton, my Aunt Ethel's son. Montagu is hoping to obtain a position in the Foreign Office, and Samuel currently is living a life of leisure."

"Are the three aunts all sisters of your mother?"

"Ethel and Lydia are my mother's sisters, and Ruth is married to my Uncle Charles Deane, my mother's brother."

"What of the husbands of these women?"

"Aunt Ethel's husband, William Breverton, has passed away. Fergus MacDonald, Lydia's husband, has a business up in Edinburgh. In fact, he – my Uncle Charles – and Agatha's husband William, are all partners in that business. They are there now."

"I see. Well, Sir Percy, I'll provisionally take this case. I say 'provisionally', because I must satisfy myself that it's suitable for my methods. I would like to come to your house and meet the ladies – this afternoon if that would be convenient."

"*Ahem*, I suppose so. But I must insist that no one knows the purpose of your visit. I'll tell them you are interested in looking at my rare book collection. My mother normally serves tea at about four o'clock. Would that be satisfactory? I could be there as well. Please don't let on why you are there, but I leave it to you how to accomplish with them what you want."

"Fine. Watson will accompany me. Please write your address on that piece of paper over there." He abruptly got up and left the room. Our startled client wrote down the address, shook my hand, and left.

A few moments later, Holmes reentered the room. He had in his hand a copy of *Burke's Peerage* that he kept in his room. "Well, what do you make of our new client?"

"A bit odd. Seemed very nervous. He doesn't seem the sentimental type, so I suspect there's more to this jeweled casket than he is telling us."

"Good. And there is the matter of not wanting to involve the police or allowing any of his relatives to know why we are there. You see, your observations will tell you more than any dream."

"I have no time to debate that now, as I have some patients to see. I'll return by three o'clock. I don't see how we'll accomplish anything if you cannot question anyone in your normal manner or otherwise follow your normal methods. But I'm confident you will determine some way to accomplish what you need, despite the client's rather peculiar restrictions." By that time, he was intently studying the book he had brought in with him and said nothing, so I left.

When I returned, more books were scattered on the floor, including several on military history that I keep in my room. Holmes was deep in conversation with the loutish Johnson.

"So, Johnson, do you comprehend the assignment?"

"Of course, Mister Holmes, I hope to have an answer for you by tomorrow morning. I'll stay out all night if necessary."

"Good. We'll see you in the morning."

As Johnson left, he once again gave me a leering look and clumped off down the stairs.

"Watson, I know you don't care for Johnson, as it's manifest on your face. But beneath that exterior is a rather fine mind, which we hopefully can put to use."

"Whatever you have given him to do, let us pray he doesn't betray your confidence in him by warning his former confederates."

"That indeed is how we shall test him. Come, let us depart for Sir Percy's residence."

We arrived shortly at a stately Georgian town house. The brick was white-washed, and large windows on the first three floors looked out over a park. When we rang the doorbell, Sir Percy himself opened the door."

"*Ahem*, er . . . I thought I should be here to let you to confirm I have told my relatives about your interest in my book collection. Come this way, as the ladies are assembled in the drawing room." He led us to a large mahogany door to the left of the entrance. The room was sumptuously furnished with floral wallpaper, sofas and chairs covered with green Chinese silk, mahogany side tables, and a comforting fire in the grate.

Sir Percy made the introductions. Lady Margaret, his mother, was a plump woman in her early sixties, with white hair, alert blue eyes, and rosy cheeks. Her two sisters, while not as plump, bore a strong family resemblance. Ethel Breverton was in her late fifties and, unlike her sister, had a full head of luxurious auburn hair. I imagined she had been quite the beauty in her youth. The other sister, Lydia MacDonald, was somewhat plain looking. In her early fifties, she likely had spent her youth in the shadow of her two older sisters. Lady Margaret's sister-in-law, Ruth Deane, was about the same age as Ethel. She had a pixie-like quality and seemed always to have a smile on her face, which I couldn't quite determine was from amusement or detachment. Rounding out the company was a far younger woman (I would venture in her mid thirties) who looked remarkably like a female version of our client – In fact, it was his sister, Agatha Pinchlin.

After the introductions, Lady Margaret smiled at my friend. "I am sure, Mister Holmes, that you and Percy want to get straight away to his study and those tiresome books. I have read several of the stories about you, and am sure you would be bored sitting here as we discuss our various ailments, which seems to have become our favorite topic of conversation lately."

"Thank you kindly, Madame. We shall do so. But might I be so bold as to suggest Watson remain here with you. He is quite a good doctor, and may have some suggestions to make."

The ladies all murmured their approval, and I was soon left alone with them. I quickly realized that Holmes's intent was actually that I gather information for him. He always has believed I have a special expertise when it comes to the fairer sex. But in this case, I believed my medical knowledge would be more useful, as it's my experience that people tend to confide in a doctor rather quickly.

Holmes and Sir Percy left and, as the ladies and I settled in, I smiled at Lady Margaret. "I find it hard to believe, my Lady, that some one with such a robust appearance as yours could be suffering from any ailment."

"Well, you are quite charming but wrong, Doctor. I have the beginnings of arthritis in my joints, especially my hands. I am slowly becoming unable to write."

"Mother," interrupted Agatha Pinchlin compared to me, you are the picture of health. You see, Doctor, I have very severe headaches at times, so severe that I must lie down in a darkened room."

Her Aunt Lydia spoke up. "My dear, I do believe the weather in Edinburgh doesn't agree with you. Perhaps you and William should consider moving away to a better climate."

Lady Margaret looked her sister. "I am sure William will not leave until the business matters with the firm are straightened out, Lydia. In fact, I suspect that has more to do with her headaches than the weather."

Ruth Hill spoke up. "Margaret, could Agatha's symptoms be similar to Montagu's, erm, *condition*?"

"Certainly not. He never had headaches and has been healthy for years. Doctor, what about *my* condition."

"I assume you have only consulted your local physician. I would suggest you seek a specialist here in London, as there have been real advances in the last decade distinguishing arthritis, rheumatism, gout, and so forth. If you wish, I could recommend someone."

That seemed to open a floodgate, as the good ladies bombarded me for the next hour or so with various complaints. I was on the brink of desperation, hoping for Holmes's return, when he and Sir Percy rejoined us.

"Ah, Ladies, I see you have made good use of Watson while Sir Percy and I were examining his marvelous collection. If I may tear him away, we are going to return to our flat. And Sir Percy: We will see you later this evening, as discussed."

The good ladies fussed over us for a few minutes, promising me to continue reading our adventures. Holmes had a half-smile on his lips as he heard this, but thankfully he refrained from his usual complaints about the accuracy of my accounts.

We finally extracted ourselves and found a hansom outside. I turned to my friend. "What was that about seeing Sir Percy later this evening?"

"His nephew, Montagu, had expressed disappointment not to be there this afternoon to meet me. Apparently he is another reader of your melodramas. In any event, I wanted to meet him. When I learned he and the cousin Samuel were accompanying Sir Percy to the theatre, I suggested they stop by Baker Street first. Sir Percy agreed, but said something odd.

"He said, 'Well, I at least will know Samuel isn't dragging off Montagu during that time.' It suggests Samuel may have some bad habits that Sir Percy wishes to shield Montagu from. Given that he is 'at leisure', it may be that he is gambling. In Sir Percy's circles, that is often what 'at leisure' signifies. If he has experienced a recent string of losses, that could explain why he is living with Montagu. Now, what did you learn from the ladies?"

I recounted all that had been said, then asked, "And I assume you didn't spend all that time in the study?"

Holmes chuckled. "You do know my methods. When we stepped out, I asked Sir Percy if I could inspect the rooms of the house, especially the bedrooms. At first he hesitated, until I reminded him that I would be quick and no one would be the wiser. Although not my usual comprehensive search, I was able to ascertain that no doors or windows showed evidence of tampering, and none of the bedrooms of the ladies contained the stolen items. Given the size of the items, especially the box, that narrowed my work to things like bureaus, wardrobes, writing desks, and so forth. I also decided it was unlikely a thief would hide something in one of the public areas, as discovery might be too easy. I found none of the stolen items."

"So you believe the thief was someone not staying in the house?"

"Not necessarily. The thief could have passed the items to a confederate before we arrived. I ascertained the front and back doors are normally open during the day, so someone could have slipped out for a few minutes to pass the items along to another person outside. Or, of course, Sir Percy could have done so on his way to see us."

"Surely you don't suspect him. He came to see you. "

"He wouldn't be the first person to assume he could fool Sherlock Holmes. For now, I am maintaining an open mind. Ah, here we are. I'm going to do a bit more research before our guests arrive. Would you be so kind as to ask Mrs. Hudson to refresh the drink decanters and hold our evening meal until they depart."

I went in to talk to Mrs. Hudson, who, worried I might become hungry, insisted I sit with her and have some of her wonderful biscuits with homemade jam and tea. Not wanting to disappoint her, I of course complied. I told her to send Sir Percy and his two relatives up to the sitting room when they arrived.

A few hours later, I was sitting by the fire reading the newspaper while Holmes was pasting items in one of the indices in which he keeps regarding crimes and other items of interest, when the doorbell rang. I heard Mrs. Hudson tell the visitor he was expected and to go upstairs. I went to the door as Sir Percy and his two companions reached the top of the staircase. He introduced first his nephew, Montagu Pinchlin, Agatha's son. He was a thin, earnest looking young man in his mid-twenties, clean-shaven, with sandy hair and facial features similar to his Uncle's. We next learned that the other companion was Samuel Breverton, Ethel's son, and thus Sir Percy's cousin. He was about thirty and, unlike Montagu, was rather tall and stout, with receding black hair, pointed nose and chin, with an affected look of boredom as he peered through a monocle at Holmes and me. Although all three of our visitors were clad in evening clothes, I noticed that those of Sir Percy and Montagu were rather traditional, while

Samuel sported attire trimmed in satin with a ruffled shirt, gold studs and cuff links, and a bright scarlet bow tie.

Holmes indicated that they should take seats and offered refreshments. Montagu and his uncle had sherry, while Samuel took a healthy draught of whisky. When we were all settled, Holmes gave a slight bow. "Sir, Percy, I'm grateful you could stop by before your evening out. The doctor and I have been discussing nothing but your delightful collection since we returned."

"Thank you kindly, Mister Holmes. I mentioned your visit to Montagu and Samuel earlier and suggested we stop by this evening. Montagu has read several of Doctor Watson's tales and was eager to meet you."

"Yes, Mister Holmes, when Uncle told us of your visit, I implored him to introduce us. My work at the Foreign Office so far has been rather routine, so it's quite enjoyable to obtain a vicarious sense of adventure through you."

Holmes again refrained from mentioning his disagreement with my style and instead turned to Samuel. "And do you also indulge in Watson's tales?"

Samuel sniffed and drawled, "I should say not, old chap. Not my cup of tea, if I may say so. I prefer to generate my sense of adventure in other ways – such as at the gaming tables."

"I see. We met your delightful relatives this afternoon as well. I understand you were at dinner last night."

Montagu smiled. "Yes, we both were there – although Samuel kept wandering off, and Aunt Ethel had to ask me to go look for him and bring him back. He often does that."

Another sniff. "One can only withstand Mater and her siblings for so long before one must walk about to clear one's brain cells of the incessant chatter of medical details."

Sir Percy coughed. "Now, now, Cousin. They mean well. I'm sorry I don't have your collection of sketches and prints so that you might amuse yourself when you visit."

Holmes sat up. "You are a collector. I would love to see your collection some time, as Watson and I dabble from time to time."

I trust I didn't allow the astonishment I felt show on my face, as Holmes always says I'm too honest to dissemble. But Samuel showed the first signs of actually being interested in Holmes. "Oh, quite, old chap. I have assembled some unique items with my winnings, including a drawing by Blake and a study by Rossetti. If you would like, you could drop by our place, as Montagu has been kind enough to put me up whilst I search for more-suitable accommodations."

I suspected that perhaps Samuel's "winnings" had been rather low lately, which, as Holmes had deduced, was the real reason he was living with Montagu. Holmes smiled and asked, "Might we stop by tomorrow? I believe Watson and I will be free."

"Certainly, old chap, if Montagu doesn't mind. But not before noon, as I shall be asleep until then."

"I'll be at work," added Montagu, "but of course, Mister Holmes, you and the Doctor are welcome to stop by." He provided us with an address in the West End and then looked over at his Uncle. "I say, Uncle Percy – should we be on our way?"

Sir Percy agreed. We all shook hands and our visitors departed. I turned to Holmes. "I assume that you actually wanted to go there to perform a similar search."

"Of course. And I observed that you took note of Samuel's reference to his enjoying the gaming tables, which as we discussed must be the bad habit to which Sir Percy referred. Ah, here is Mrs. Hudson with our meal. Let us enjoy it and not discuss this further tonight. I wish to have a pipe or two after we eat to consider our next course of action."

After an excellent repast of broiled sirloin, boiled potatoes, snap peas, and trifle for dessert, accompanied by a delicious claret, we moved by the fire. I had a cigar and Holmes lit his favorite pipe, after filling it with shag from the Persian slipper hanging on the mantel. I read for a bit and then retired. I didn't bother to say good night, as Holmes was deep in thought while the room turned blue from his smoking.

The next morning, I had to arise early, as I needed to go to a hospital to see a patient. I had a quick breakfast of coffee and toasted crumpets with Mrs. Hudson's homemade marmalade, and left before Holmes was up. When I returned, Mrs. Hudson informed me that my friend had departed and hadn't indicated when he would be back, but had instructed her that I was to wait for him.

At about two o'clock, Holmes entered our sitting room. "Watson, capital that you're here. Shall we go over to Master Pinchlin's apartment to view the art collection?"

I knew better than to inquire where he had been, so I donned my overcoat, scarf, and hat, ready to brave the chilling wind. We quickly found a passing cab and Holmes gave the address to the driver. Once in, he was sunk deep in thought, but upon our arrival, he came alive. "Good. Follow my lead as always."

The apartment was on the top floor of a rather modest red-brick building, with a bay window on each floor and no particular ornamentation. It appeared quite respectable and suitable for a rising young man at the Foreign Office. I mused that Samuel likely wished to escape its confines as soon as possible. We climbed the stairs to the top landing, where Holmes gave the bell pull a tug. A moment later, Samuel, who only seemed partially awake, came and let us in. The apartment had a central hall running to the back of the building. There were three doors on each side, and all were closed. Samuel led us to the first door on the left, which led into a simply furnished room with hardwood floors, several area carpets, some leather chairs, and a sofa that looked a bit worse for wear. The walls were lined with shelves on three sides, and the window at the front of the house let in some feeble light from the overcast sky. Next to the window was a battered trolly holding several decanters and glasses and a humidor. The sofa had a low table in front of us, and Samuel indicated we should sit there.

"Here you go, chaps. Care for a drop? No? Well, I don't mind if I do. Let me fetch the first batch of prints from that box over there." He went to the trolly and fussed with a glass a few minutes, then proceeded to one of the shelves and brought over a veneered box, which turned out to have a number of prints and etchings, interlayered with velvet to protect them. He removed the top picture, lovingly handled it, then smiled at it. "This is one of my real prizes. Found it in Florence, you know. Small shop off the Piazza Republica. Ever been? You must see it. In any event, the dealer, a rather shady character if I may say so, attempted to claim its provenance was Fifteenth Century, but I believe it's more likely Eighteenth."

He went on in that way through the rest of the box for the following hour. He was about to bring down another box when Holmes politely cleared his throat. "I fear I have an appointment and must take my leave. But please continue with Doctor Watson, so that he may share it with me later this evening. Thank you so much for this. It has been a highlight of the year for me, as I'm sure it's for my friend here."

"Thanks. Glad to keep at it with our medical savant."

"No need to see me out. Watson, I envy you. Take your time, and I'll see you back at Baker Street."

With that, he left, closing the door behind him. I endured several more hours of Breverton's inane drawling banter and finally extracted myself and returned to our abode. Holmes was sitting by the fire contentedly puffing on his pipe. "Enjoy yourself?"

"I realized you wanted me to divert him, so I did, but I must say, I think I would rather prefer one of our more strenuous adventures than go through that again."

"All for a good cause. A good cause indeed. Now, what do you make of the state of this matter at this juncture?"

"Well, it would appear that the theft was committed the night of the dinner party. Your inspection of the house showed that no one broke in after the doors were locked, so I would think one of the dinner guests must be the thief, unless a servant committed the crime. "

"Excellent. I see that after all these years you are beginning to observe and deduce, not just see what is in front of you. For now, let us take Sir Percy at his word that it wasn't one of the servants. What do you deduce about opportunity."

"As to the two young men not staying at the house, Montagu stated that Samuel kept 'wandering off', and his Aunt had to ask him to go and bring Samuel back. So they both have time unaccounted for. The ladies staying there, not to mention Sir Percy, undoubtedly were all at one time or another alone by themselves. Although we are hampered by our client's insistence that we be discreet, I suspect rigorous questioning would reveal nothing more."

"You likely are correct. And motive?"

"Financial need seems the most probable to me. Although the other items seem rather mundane and difficult to sell, the jewels on the box could be pried out and sold separately. The other items may have been taken to mislead."

"Quite so."

"When we look at financial need, it's clear that the firm in Edinburgh has suffered financial losses. That means the wives of the three partners could have a financial interest in obtaining the jewels, which would point to Agatha Pinchlin, Lydia MacDonald, or Ruth Deane."

"Next would be Samuel Breverton, who clearly has a gambling habit, given his remark about how he prefers his adventure. Those pictures of his aren't inexpensive. Likewise his attire. And I sense he would prefer more fashionable quarters than he presently inhabits. As a widow, his mother, Ethel, may not have ready access to funds, which could be encumbered or in trust — again, we cannot question her. But, of course, a mother often will do anything to save a son in distress."

"A fine summary. What of Lady Margaret, Sir Percy, and young Pinchlin?"

"Montagu might feel a need to help his father out of the Edinburgh mess, but he would be more likely to ask his uncle or grandmother for assistance, rather than steal. Seems too-weak a motive. Likewise, Lady Margaret might wish to avoid a family scandal, either because of Edinburgh or Samuel's gambling, but she would have a dower from her deceased husband or, like Montagu, ask her son for money. And as for Lord Percy, I respect what you said earlier about being foolish enough to consult you, but I just don't see him as the culprit."

Before Holmes could respond, there was a knock at the door. "Ah, that will be Sir Percy himself. I sent him a telegram earlier and told Mrs. Hudson to be expecting him. And here he is now."

The door opened, and our client, looking haggard and nervous, entered, removed his overcoat, and sat by the fire. He declined anything to drink, so Holmes began.

"Sir Percy, I'm happy to report I have something for you." His sense of the dramatic led him to turn his back to us, walk over his chemical table, and abruptly turn around. In his hand was a gleaming coffin as described by Sir Percy, with the jewels glittering in the firelight.

Our client gasped. "But how on earth did you find it?"

"I'll explain everything in due course. I had the assistance of an associate of mine – "

"What! I assumed you would tell no one!"

"You have no need to concern yourself. Disclosure of his involvement would render him useless to me, not to mention dangerous to him. Our pact is that I'll only utilize him cases of this nature. Perhaps it would be clearer if I commenced with my train of thought.

"As Watson has correctly deduced, no one broke into your residence the night of the theft. That means someone in the house that evening must have been the thief. Taking you at your word that your servants are trustworthy, along with my assessment of your intelligence, which means you would not be so reckless to request my assistance if you were the culprit, that means a member of your family must have been the thief."

"That – that – that is *preposterous*!"

"Allow me to continue without interruption. We determined that all the family members in the house that evening at one time or another must have been alone, and thus had the opportunity to slip down the hall into your study. That left us with the question of who had reason to steal the items. Based on Watson's conversations with your mother, aunts, and sister, we learned that the Edinburgh business of your uncles and brother-in-law is in financial difficulty. That could indicate a possible motive for your Aunts Ethel or Ruth, or your sister Agatha to purloin the coffin. I also inferred from your comments and his behavior that your cousin Samuel likely has sizable gambling debts and is constrained to live with your nephew. That could be a motive for Samuel or his mother, Ethel. Pardon me for saying so, but your mother might want to avoid a scandal, as might your nephew Montagu, although I felt that rather unlikely.

"My next line of thought was whether any of the stolen items could have alleviated any of this financial distress. It was clear to me, based on what you said at our first meeting, that the item of real value was that coffin. Could it provide such relief, either intact, or with the jewels detached? I made a discreet inquiry yesterday of a banker for whom I resolved a matter of some forged stock certificates and learned that the debts of the Edinburgh venture are rather enormous. I also suspected that Samuel's gambling debts are rather substantial – which my associate was able to confirm last night. Thus, I began to doubt that the coffin could have helped any of your relatives materially enough to warrant the desperate recourse to theft. While you were anxious to obtain the return of the coffin, it didn't seem that financial value was the primary reason, which suggests that the coffin and its jewels have something other than monetary value to you.

"But what if the thief was unaware of the intrinsic value to you and had a lesser financial pressure than the ones we discovered? That led me to the thought that there might be another motive, one that would explain why the thief didn't come to you for a smaller sum, but instead stole the casket, with the other items being taken as a blind. I realized that the simplest answer might be that the thief is a victim of blackmail. I therefore instructed my associate to make two inquiries last night of his underworld acquaintances. First, he spoke to a number of dealers in stolen goods and finally obtained a description of someone offering to sell some jewels. Second, he also asked about anyone attempting to implement a blackmail scheme. He finally located the culprit and, based on his somewhat fearsome reputation, persuaded the would-be miscreant to drop the scheme and sell the materials to him, ostensibly so that he himself could implement the dastardly plan.

"This morning, my associate gave me the description of the would-be seller and handed over the intended blackmail materials. I then knew who the thief was. We paid a visit to Samuel this afternoon, and, while Watson distracted him, I retrieved the casket you have there."

Sir Percy groaned and held his head in his hands. "I cannot believe Samuel would do such a thing. I don't approve of his way of life, but to stoop to this – "

"You are mistaken, Sir Percy. It was your nephew, Montagu. Watson heard a remark while spending time with your mother about Montagu's weakness. The blackmail papers refer to his stay in Bedlam ten years ago for treatment of a breakdown. I assume he was concerned this would ruin his career at the Foreign Office, and he likely was ashamed to come to you and admit his predicament. It might also tarnish your reputation with your superiors, as it's likely you have vouched for him, or perhaps they would begin to worry that you suffer from a similar malady. People continue to have unacceptable prejudices concerning whether such mental issues 'run in the family', as I believe they so crudely put it. But the matter now is safely put to rest, and you may be assured that my associate, Watson, and I will never reveal it."

"Mister Holmes, I don't know how to thank you. I'll see Montagu this evening and assure him that his torment is over."

"Ah, but we haven't yet gotten to the real reason why I took your case. Why was the casket so important to *you*, and why did you want to be so secretive about the efforts to recover it?

"You mentioned when we first met that the casket had descended through your mother's side of the family. I consulted *Burke's* after your departure and learned that one of your ancestors, Norbert Deane, served in the Army during the Napoleonic Wars. Looking into the matter in one of Watson's tomes on military history, I ascertained this Deane was an aide to Major General Robert Ross. Am I on the correct path, Sir Percy?"

"Yes," was the barely audible response.

"As I'm sure you know, Ross commanded all the British troops on the eastern coast of the United States in 1814 during the American War of 1812, although most people in this country aren't familiar with that conflict, as it's overshadowed by the struggle against Napoleon. Ross, along with Rear Admiral George Cockburn, led the troops that captured and burned the capital of the United States in August 1814. Your ancestor was with them when they entered the President's House during that operation, was he not?"

"Yes."

"And the casket was taken from the President's House before it was set ablaze, and Norbert Deane returned to England with it. Presumably few family members realize that this casket is actually war booty."

"Yes. It passed down through the males, and only we knew. My grandfather gave it to me and swore me to secrecy."

"And there isn't only that oath. As an official of the Foreign Office, you are well aware of the current efforts of our country to improve relations with the United States. It would be highly embarrassing for you and the country to learn the coffin has been in your family's possession all this time. That is why you were so guarded about the investigation, but also why you were desperate to obtain the coffin's return.

"And," he concluded, "there is also the matter of the paper inside the hidden compartment."

Sir Percy jerked upright, his eyes and mouth wide open. "You know that as well? Mister Holmes, whatever shall I do? I cannot stand this burden any longer! Since the theft, I have lain awake at night agonizing over this situation. I wish I had never come into possession of the cursed thing. I don't feel it proper to destroy it, given its historical significance.

90

And yet, I cannot turn it over to my superiors without explaining how I came to have it. Please – do you have any suggestions?"

"You no doubt know of my brother, Mycroft. If you agree, I'll turn the casket and the paper over to him. Perhaps the Government can return the casket to the United States as a gesture of goodwill, thereby strengthening the ties of the two nations. As to the paper, we can leave it to Mycroft to decide its fate."

"Yes, yes. I'll leave it to you and your brother. This is a great weight off my conscience. I'll go now and similarly relieve Montagu. I am forever in your debt, Mister Holmes." With more profuse expressions of gratitude, Sir Percy departed.

"That was," I stated, "as usual, an amazing recital. But the paper: How could it be more astonishing than the origin of the casket?"

"History, as it often does, supplies the answer. General Ross wasn't in North America during the early stages of the American War of 1812. He was wounded in France in early 1814 fighting Napoleon. He then came back to England to recover. Thus, he was in direct contact with Lord Liverpool's Government when Napoleon was sent in exile to Elba and the decision was made to reinforce the Army fighting in North America. Ross was sent to Maryland shortly before the attack on Washington.

"Most accounts, including the one you possess, state that the British troops burned Washington simply because they were enraged by the American burning of York in Canada in 1813. In fact, the paper hidden in the casket is a copy of the direct orders of the Cabinet in London that Ross should spare no effort to burn Washington to the ground."

"That is extraordinary. Whatever goodwill might be garnered by return of the casket would be obliterated, and then some, by the disclosure of such an order."

"Undoubtedly. I'm confident Mycroft will agree with me that it should never see the light of day in our lifetime."

The Adventure of the
New Da Vinci
by Arthur Hall

I recall that the evening had turned very wet when I again encountered Mr. Grant Munro.

I'd left Charing Cross Station, struggling with my umbrella, when I caught sight of a hansom delivering a fare. Intent on reaching it before it could be taken I hurried along the pavement, only to be beaten by a younger and more nimble fellow who leapt aboard while I was still yards away.

With a sigh I turned to look for another conveyance, but at that moment a figure who was vaguely familiar to me emerged from a nearby shop. He apparently recognised me, for he paused in mid-stride and stared uncertainly in my direction. As I watched, his face lit up and he approached.

"Doctor Watson? It is you, is it not, sir?"

"Mr. Grant Munro!" I replied. He was a little older and heavier, but my memory had not betrayed me. He was indeed the man who Holmes had assisted in the circumstances I later described in my account entitled "The Yellow Face".

He nodded enthusiastically. "How are you, sir? How is Mr. Holmes? Only a few days ago, Effie and I were reminiscing about you both."

"We are both in good health. Yourself and your wife?"

"We are also doing well. The hop business is flourishing too."

"Excellent."

I saw him glance at my suitcase as I moved my umbrella towards him to extend its shelter. "You have returned from a journey?"

"A friend from my army years invited me for a few days." I turned to the shop he had visited, and saw that its window featured a display of paintings. "But I was unaware of your interest in art."

He laughed. "No such thing. David Crowe is a former customer. Also, I was curious as to the portrait you see there."

My eyes followed the direction he indicated. The picture showed a woman wearing the apparel of a past age, with shining dark hair and of considerable beauty. Her eyes held an expression that could not be ignored. I have very little knowledge of the subject, but the resemblance to the celebrated *Mona Lisa* was unmistakable.

"Is it a Da Vinci?" I asked him.

"That was what I enquired of Mr. Crowe. He explained that there is now a school producing paintings in Da Vinci's style, but never claiming their work to be his – although some unscrupulous dealers have attempted to pass them of as such."

I looked again. "She is certainly a handsome woman."

"Whether real or contrived, I have no way of knowing. I imagine the object of such work is to make it possible for interested parties who would otherwise have no hope of owning work of this sort – to purchase something reminiscent of classical art." He consulted his pocket-watch. "I regret that I must now keep an appointment, but why not visit Mr. Crowe to see what he has to say? You appear to like the portrait, and I can assure you that he is a most agreeable fellow."

We exchanged more words about how pleasant it had been to renew our acquaintance, and I promised to give his regards to Holmes. He left me then, quickly disappearing into the thickening crowd.

After a minute or two spent admiring the portrait further, I folded down my umbrella and entered the shop.

The short, middle-aged man behind the counter put down the sketch he was examining and welcomed me.

"I saw that you are acquainted with Mr. Munro." With a gesture, he explained that he had been watching from the window.

"Our paths have crossed before, some years ago."

"I also have had dealings with him before now. Satisfactory transactions, I am pleased to say. Now sir, what is it that I can show you?"

I allowed my eyes to sweep over portraits and seascapes and a faithful representation of Loch Lomond before my attention was brought back to the magnetic gaze of the woman who had fascinated Mr. Munro.

"It was this portrait that attracted both Mr. Munro and myself. I noticed that its style was similar to that of the great Leonardo, and he informed me that you had indicated it to be the work of a school dedicated to his achievements."

"That is so. They have appeared recently, and are in no way to be thought of as imitations of the great master's work. The style is consistent, or intended to be. This example came into my possession only yesterday, and I confess to paying less for it than I expected. Therefore, if you're interested, I could let you have it quite reasonably."

I imagined for a moment how it would appear in our sitting room at Baker Street, and what Holmes's response was likely to be. Then I reflected that my regular investments in horse-racing had returned favourably on two recent occasions, and made my decision.

"What sum would you consider appropriate?" I asked Mr. Crowe.

He suggested an amount that was rather too high for my purse, but after some minutes of good-natured haggling, we arrived at a mutually acceptable figure. Ten minutes later I had written the cheque and boarded a hansom, carrying the picture wrapped in brown paper and string.

Shortly after we were reunited, Holmes sat in his armchair, viewing the picture thoughtfully.

"I see the resemblance to Da Vinci's style, but I'm uncertain as to whether I can be comfortable with the portrait as part of my permanent surroundings." He blew out a final cloud of fragrant smoke before putting his old briar away. "It might be better as an adornment in your own room, where you can admire it at your leisure."

We hadn't long finished breakfast. When I'd returned to Baker Street the previous day, it was to find my friend absent. He reappeared not more than half-an-hour later, reaching the top of the stairs as our landlady served my meal. I saw at once that his weary expression indicated that he hadn't slept, and he gave no explanation other than to remark that Jason Norris would do no more harm in this world. He requested a pot of strong coffee, which he consumed as we spoke.

"But Holmes," I said in objection to his dismissal of the painting, "surely you will become accustomed to – "

He held up a hand to silence me, and the doorbell rang again. Moments later Mrs. Hudson entered after knocking, preceding a young woman of about twenty-six years.

"Miss Agnes Groom," our good landlady announced, "to see Doctor Watson."

I confess to being surprised for I expected no visitor, nor had I any outstanding cases of clients who would seek me out. Further, the young lady's name was unfamiliar to me.

Nevertheless, Holmes and I rose as one and welcomed her. My friend was in the habit of retreating to his own room on the rare occasions when callers sought my advice rather than his, but now he politely requested that we tolerate his presence at the far end of the room, where he would peruse the several morning editions that had been delivered. We both agreed and he retrieved the papers, walking the length of the room with the open *Standard* held before him.

"Now, Miss Groom," I began when all three of us were seated and settled, "how can I be of assistance? Are you a new patient?"

As I spoke, I noticed the way her long auburn hair was piled beneath her bonnet, and her provocative movements as she took up a position facing me. The morning light shone brightly on the subtle blue of her costume, which was exquisitely styled.

"Oh, I am sorry to have given the wrong impression, Doctor." She appeared mildly embarrassed. "I'm not here on a medical matter, but something quite different."

"What is the purpose of your visit then?" I asked with some curiosity. I fancied, rather than saw, that Holmes's attention had been aroused.

She gave me an uncertain glance, as if wondering if her action had been presumptuous. "Please allow me to explain. I am the daughter of Mr. Micah Groom, who owns the Groom Galleries near Regent Street. My father sent me to Charing Cross yesterday afternoon to purchase a portrait from Mr. David Crowe, who owns an establishment selling fine art. Unfortunately," I noticed her cheeks begin to redden, "I chanced to meet an old friend, a young man who I . . . knew several years ago. He insisted that I have tea with him and, not wishing to appear rude, I did. Consequently, when I arrived late at Mr. Crowe's shop the picture had been sold. I enquired of him the name of the purchaser and he was reluctant to disclose it at first, but when I mentioned my father's name, he relented."

"But the portrait isn't a Da Vinci," I told her, "merely an imitation of his style. It cannot be valuable. Mr. Crowe was good enough to point this out before I made the purchase."

"My father is aware of that, but he has a very rich and influential client who has been a regular customer for some years. This man has made a collection of the works of this new school. I suspect he considers them to be an amusing novelty, and wishes to continue the series. I am authorised to offer twice the price you paid, if the transaction takes place today. Tell me, sir, is that acceptable to you?"

I was rather taken aback at this, and unaware that Holmes had risen and approached until he spoke from beside Miss Groom.

"It is regrettable that you were unable to secure the portrait, Miss Groom, but the fact is that I took an intense liking to it. Consequently, Doctor Watson bought it for me as a gift, and I couldn't think of replying to such a kind gesture in this way. I'm sure that more such works will come into Mr. Crowe's possession soon, and your father's client will then be able to further his collection."

I glanced in the direction where I had left the picture, and saw that it was no longer there. Holmes, for some reason, had removed it.

To my surprise, a flash of anger momentarily altered the girl's expression, although Holmes's impassive look suggested that he expected it.

"I'm certain that my father wouldn't object to three times the sum you paid," she said with a hint of irritation in her voice.

For a moment all was silent, except for the faint newsboy's cry that reached us from Baker Street.

"I am sorry," my friend assured her then, "but that is my final word on the matter."

"But – "

"I'm sorry," Holmes repeated.

"In that case, gentlemen, I will bid you good morning."

She rose abruptly and strutted from the room, and we heard the door slam behind her moments later. Holmes had already moved to the window.

"As I suspected, a carriage awaited her."

"Holmes! I exclaimed. "What did you mean by that? You appear indifferent to the picture, and then claim it as your own. I confess to being baffled."

"Come, Watson!" He laughed shortly as we took our seats on either side of the fireplace. "Surely you weren't deceived. As soon as I saw that woman, I knew she was here for an undisclosed purpose. I mentioned earlier that I've ensured that Jason Norris will meet the hangman, and there are no other enquiries immediately on hand. What connection then can this woman have with us, other than something very recent? Your new Da Vinci sprang instantly to mind."

"Miss Groom didn't take well your refusal to oblige her. What is it about her that you see as deceitful?"

"I know her of old, by reputation. She disappeared from the London underworld a year or two ago. You will have noticed that her accent is now that of the Midlands, but I recognised her at once. Her appearance is much changed and improved, suggesting that she has done better for herself in whatever enterprise she is now involved, but she is still Martha Vincent, confidence trickster and pickpocket. In addition, I'm quite certain that the newspapers have stated that Micah Groom is unmarried and childless. The man is in love with art."

"I am quite astonished. You have no doubt of this?"

"Watson, if these rooms had been unattended, she would have thought nothing of stealing the picture."

"But why? We have established that it is of little value."

"Have we? Clearly, it has some worth to someone. If you are free, I suggest we visit Charing Cross to see Mr. Crowe. He may be able to tell us more of the painting's origin."

I saw the day stretching out tediously before me, and I accepted.

"Capital!" Holmes acknowledged, as I retrieved our hats and coats.

I can recall speaking to my friend but once, as our hansom neared Charing Cross.

"Are you sure that something is amiss here? Could it not be that someone sees eventual value in the work of this new school?"

He shook his head slowly. "Your account of this sudden rise in imitations that aren't imitations of Da Vinci's work didn't sit well with me when you produced the painting. With the introduction of Martha Vincent into the drama, there is certain to be a criminal element involved. She is a woman who will undertake any task, regardless of its legality, for anyone who will pay her sufficiently."

Shortly afterwards, we stood before the shop I had visited the day before. I was about to inform my friend that a notice indicating that the establishment was closed featured prominently in the window, but he had already grasped the door-handle and turned it.

Surprisingly, the door opened soundlessly.

We glanced at each other with curious expressions, then entered the shop before closing the door behind us. Standing still, we looked around us at the undisturbed portraits and landscapes tastefully displayed. A coach, travelling quickly, passed along the street, leaving the heavy silence that had been before. Twice, Holmes shouted to alert Mr. Crowe of our presence, but this brought no response.

"Can the fellow have left yesterday and forgotten to lock the door?" I wondered aloud.

"I doubt that. Some of this work is sure to be valuable." His eyes roamed around the room again.

"Perhaps he has stepped out for a moment."

Holmes's expression became flint-like. "Come this way."

He led me behind the counter, along the short enclosure that ended with a doorway from which hung a beaded curtain. He brushed it aside and we passed into the room beyond.

Here there was less light, but our eyes accustomed themselves quickly. Not surprisingly, we were in a storehouse, with racks of paintings and sculptures set out in rows. Holmes moved quickly, inspecting the corridors between them one by one before coming to sudden halt somewhere to the left.

"Watson!"

I hurried to join him and understood at once the alarm in his voice.

Mr. Crowe sat in a chair, the meagre light glinting on his unseeing eyes. There were no manacles or ropes restraining his wrists, but patches of raw flesh suggested that they had recently been tightly compressed. Several pools of congealed blood gleamed dully on the stone floor, and I swear that I have rarely seen such an expression of agony and terror that I beheld frozen on his face.

Despite my experiences at Maiwand, and those encountered since while assisting my friend with his investigations, the effect on me was profound. My surroundings whirled around me, the sensation threatening to disturb my balance, while nausea added its unpleasant presence also.

Holmes, apparently unaffected, walked slowly around the corpse while maintaining a short distance. He peered at it from several angles, but at no time did he allow himself to touch.

"I take it that these are the remains of the man from whom you bought the portrait?"

I steeled myself to look again and nodded. "What has been done to him?"

"He has been brutally tortured. I've seen the like before, but I'll spare you the gruesome details. It tells us, though, of the lengths these people will go to, and what they are capable of."

"You believe this to be connected with my picture?"

"What else am I to conclude? Miss Vincent understated the situation considerably when she informed us of Mr. Crowe's reluctance to divulge the name of the purchaser. It wasn't the mention of Mr. Micah Groom that loosened his tongue." He shot a sudden glance in my direction. "Are you quite well?"

I swallowed and took a grip on myself with difficulty.

"Thank you. What are we to do now? It isn't lost on me that there may be further attempts to secure the portrait, which could be dangerous for us, and Mrs. Hudson."

He took my arm and guided us out of that place of horror.

"First a telegram to Scotland Yard. Lestrade must be made aware of this, and may be able to assist us. Second, we will immediately return to Baker Street and attempt to discover why this painting holds such importance and, possibly, for whom."

On leaving the premises, Holmes locked the door with the key that had been left inside. Before procuring a hansom, we walked the short distance to the telegraph office near Charing Cross Station, from where he dispatched a message to Inspector Lestrade, also informing him of our likely visit later.

By the time of our return to our lodgings I felt better, and had, with some effort, largely dismissed the distressing image of Mr. Crowe's demise from my mind. Hence, I was able to do justice to our luncheon, which our landlady served immediately in the shape of a delicious chicken pie.

"A rather objectionable gentleman came to see you earlier, Mr. Holmes," she informed him as she placed the steaming plates before us.

"Did he leave a card, or any indication of his identity, or reason for requiring a consultation?"

"No, sir. In fact, he implied that he knew of your absence, since he said you were aware that he would call for a picture you had sold to him. I couldn't believe that you had given him permission to enter your rooms to collect it."

"Nor should you, for I did not."

She nodded. "I told him that I had received no such instruction, and that he would have to call again after you returned, and he became very insistent. In fact, sir, I believe that he would have forced an entrance, had I not shut the door without further ado."

"Did he leave then?" I interjected.

"To my relief, Doctor, he did."

"And there have been no similar callers or events since?" Holmes enquired.

"None, sir."

"Capital. Thank you, Mrs. Hudson. You acted correctly."

A faint smile crossed her face as she withdrew.

"They seem increasingly desperate to gain possession of the picture," I observed.

"Indeed. As soon as our meal is concluded, I'll see what can be made of it. By then, Lestrade will undoubtedly wish to see us regarding the unfortunate Mr. Crowe."

No sooner had Mrs. Hudson cleared away the remains of our meal than my friend stood in the centre of our sitting room, holding the picture up to the light. He turned it this way and that, scrutinizing it from every angle and peering at the beautifully painted face at length.

"Have you discovered anything?" I asked to break the silence.

He lowered it thoughtfully. "The style is certainly reminiscent of that of Leonardo, in as much as I'm familiar with it, and you have said that no attempt has been made to claim it as a newly-discovered example of his work. This would be easily disproved in any case, since the paint itself bears little sign of age. I saw nothing to indicate hidden value, but then I asked myself why such new canvas would be stretched on an obviously much older frame. This type was in common use during the last century, and is different to those of today because its back is angled at the point where it meets the canvas and restrains it." He put down the portrait and took a small landscape from its place on the wall. "You see, Watson?"

I examined the back of both paintings, as he had directed. Certainly that of the frame of the landscape was flat, whereas the portrait was contained within a bevelled rim.

"Surely it is a matter of style or fashion," I suggested. "It has no bearing on any other feature of either painting."

He replaced the landscape and again picked up the portrait. "Perhaps, and yet what secrets may it conceal?"

I watched as he produced a small mirror and pressed it against the back of the portrait, so that the inner surface of angled edge was reflected. He moved the glass slowly along in silence, his expression curious.

"Halloa! What have we here?" He exclaimed suddenly. "Strange symbols indeed. Watson, be so good as to bring your notebook and a pencil, and we will do our best to transcribe them."

I held the picture while he copied the reflected mixture of letters, numbers, and characters that were totally unfamiliar to me.

"That is like no language that I've ever seen," I said as he completed his task.

"No, not a language, but a code of some sort, and a complicated one." He consulted his pocket-watch. "But I see that the afternoon is passing quickly, and we have yet to see Friend Lestrade. Watson, I think it best if we take this picture to Scotland Yard, where it will be safe and can be forwarded to those who can more readily identify this message. Retrieve the wrappings, if Mrs. Hudson hasn't yet disposed of them, and we can be on our way."

We left Baker Street with the portrait suitably disguised. Holmes refused the first two cabs that presented themselves, as was his way when he suspected that danger was near, and we arrived at our destination without incident.

"I had just returned from a case near the Brixton Road when I received your message," Inspector Lestrade told us when we were seated in his office and had refused his offer of tea. "I took two constables to Charing Cross. I tell you, Mr. Holmes, I have rarely seen a body treated like that, and I shan't mind if I never do again."

"It was the work of someone desperate to learn of the whereabouts of the buyer of this painting," Holmes indicated the wrapped package, and related his discoveries. "It requires someone more skilled than I to decipher what is contained there. I suspect its meaning to be of the first importance."

"Art," the little detective mused. "This seems to be the week for that."

"How so?" Holmes queried.

The inspector picked up a printed sheet from a pile on his desk. "We have a report of a gang operating in the Midlands, selling old and famous works to rich collectors. They are probably the results of burglaries elsewhere in the country, but there are some who will accept them with no questions asked. We suspect they're now at work in the capital, also."

Holmes nodded slowly. "I wish you well in your efforts to apprehend them, Inspector, and of course in identifying and arresting the murderers of Mr. Crowe." He placed the picture on the desk and received a puzzled look. "In view of the events I have related to you, will you be good enough to see that this, together with my attached note, reaches a quarter where it can be fully decoded? I would suggest the higher echelons of Whitehall, rather than your own people, since this affair has every indication of crime at a highly-organised level."

"Very well, Mr. Holmes," the official detective hesitated, possibly to overcome the resentment of Holmes's implication that the divisions of Scotland Yard might be unequal to the task. "I'll determine the most appropriate destination before dispatching it under guard."

"Excellent. Then, if all goes well, our combined efforts will bring an end to this affair."

I recognised this last remark as an intention to soothe Lestrade's pride which was apparently successful, for his smile was friendly as we rose to leave.

"I'm certain that they will. Good afternoon, gentlemen."

We boarded a cab near the building's entrance.

"Holmes, I fail to see that the gang mentioned by the inspector is the same as whoever is pursuing the portrait. After all, it is a copy, whereas they are stealing and selling genuine works of art."

He turned from his observation of the passing scene as the hansom halted to allow a barrel-laden dray to cross its path.

"Lestrade mentioned that the gang operates from the Midlands, did he not?"

"That is what I understood him to say."

"And you will recall my observation that Martha Vincent's accent had changed, since she ceased to live in London."

"To that of the Midland counties – Of course! The two cases are connected, or are one and the same."

"Precisely," he said as we entered Baker Street.

I poured brandy for both of us as we settled into our armchairs. A glance at my watch revealed that there was still an hour before dinner.

"Before we retire later, I would suggest we each pack a bag with whatever we may need for one, possibly two, nights. We leave early in the morning." He sipped his drink slowly, his thin form upright in his chair.

"For the Midlands, of course," I ventured.

"For Birmingham," he specified.

"How have you arrived at that?"

He gave a slight shrug. "I have not, at least not by deduction. It is our destination because the only man I know in the area who was once concerned with dishonest art transactions now runs an honest business there. However, do not yet consider our departure to be certain. I'm expecting to hear from Mycroft, and that could change everything."

He seemed distracted during our meal of steak-and-kidney pudding, and refused dessert as he often did. He called for another pot of strong coffee and drank it in silence, and I saw that he was alert for the chime of the doorbell.

Inspector Lestrade must have acted quickly, for the expected telegram arrived not long after nine o'clock. Holmes had been explaining his line of reasoning that solved a recent counterfeiting case for the Bank of England when his sharp ears caught the sound of a bicycle coming to rest near our front door. Minutes later Mrs. Hudson delivered a yellow envelope into his hand.

"As I anticipated." He resumed his seat after handing the telegram to me. Its message was short and precise.

Come tomorrow. Eight o'clock. Imperative.

Mycroft

"It seems as if our departure will be later, after all," I remarked.

"There is more in this as I feared, if it arouses my brother's interest so."

Holmes had already left by breakfast-time the following morning. The coffee pot, the only sign that he had sat at the table, was cold.

I had emptied the toast rack when I heard our front door close loudly, and then his quick tread upon the stairs. He burst into the room and threw his hat and coat onto a chair, waving away my suggestion that he allow me to order food for him, and calling for another pot of coffee as he sat opposite.

He had drunk several cups and I had finished eating before he spoke again.

"There is more to this business, Watson."

"You were correct then, in surmising that your brother knew of it previously?"

He nodded. "He had heard vague rumours. His people recognised the characters on the picture frame at once, but are still working on the message."

"What is the meaning of them, then?"

"They are details of a new type of field gun, a weapon of unprecedented accuracy, being constructed secretly. Mycroft wouldn't tell me where, but he is well aware that the place must contain at least one foreign agent, or someone betraying the information to an enemy power."

I pushed away my plate. "Our adversary is Imperial Germany."

"Precisely. I had already suspected as much. Before now, I have mentioned that war is becoming increasingly likely. The fact that Martha Vincent is working on their behalf doesn't surprise me, since I've long held that she would work for the Devil if he paid her sufficiently."

"It appears that the Kaiser's agents have lost none of their ruthlessness, given their treatment of Mr. Crowe. It suggests that it is vital for them to obtain the picture."

"As they have demonstrated. Doubtless their arrangement to direct their line of supply through his shop was without his knowledge. He probably never knew why he was undergoing torture for the sake of a picture of apparently little value."

"At least that is safe from them now." The doorbell rang and we both listened, but it proved to be a delivery for Mrs. Hudson.

"If your appetite is satisfied," Holmes said to me then, "I think we should depart. According to my *Bradshaw*, the morning train to Birmingham leaves within the hour."

Our next actions, the taking up of our overnight bags, the journey in the hansom, and our installation in a first-class smoker, are recorded indistinctly in my memory. I can recall also Holmes's wariness as we boarded the cab, his interest apparently captured by a loafer who loitered near our lodgings.

"Our journey will take about seventy minutes," he said as we smoked cigarettes after settling ourselves in our seats. "It would be as well, I think, to review certain points of this affair as we travel."

With the beginning of our discussion, I noticed a certain uncertainty about him, in as much as the constant flow of passengers along the corridor seemed to interrupt his train of thought. The conversation was unexpectedly cut short however, for after about twenty minutes, the door of our compartment was flung open and a man almost as tall as Holmes and bearing some strong resemblance to him, entered.

"Sir, this is a private compartment," I informed him at once.

He looked as us with a blank expression, then tottered for a moment before falling heavily onto the seat next to me.

Holmes was on his feet at once, standing over him.

"He appears to be unconscious. Watson, see what you can do for him."

We laid the man flat on his back and I peeled back an eyelid before listening to his breathing.

Abruptly his eyes opened and he sat upright, clearly embarrassed.

"Gentlemen, my sincere apologies. I hardly know what I'm about."

"Are you ill?" I asked him.

He smiled faintly. "Not ill, sir, but unable to sleep. My wife, my

Annie, passed on not three weeks ago, and I swear to you that I have managed barely a wink since. It must be that exhaustion overcame me for a moment so that I sought a place to lie down, not realising that you were here."

Holmes, I could see, was suspicious. Nevertheless, we expressed our condolences.

Our new acquaintance acknowledged and regarded us nervously. "I am Nicholas Earley," he said.

"I'm a doctor," said I, and introduced us both. "I have a few items from my medical bag with me. I feel sure that I can find something to help you."

With my friend looking on, I retrieved a small bottle from my overnight bag. It contained a strong sleeping draught that I have resorted to only on rare occasions, but it had nevertheless become part of my travel impedimenta. Mr. Earley's face was full of strain and his body trembled, so that I had no doubt of the genuineness of his predicament.

As he drank a small amount, Holmes consulted his pocket-watch.

"I'll pull down the blinds to shut out most of the light. We should be able to allow him at least an hour, while we continue our discussion in the refreshment car."

"Gentlemen, my gratitude is immeasurable," the tired man said in a slurred voice. He was already asleep as we left.

"What do you make of that, Holmes?' I asked my friend a few moments later as we sat, watching the passing scene.

"At first, I was suspicious, then I saw that the man was genuinely in distress. Hopefully, we have been of some assistance."

As we ate, I noticed that he was especially watchful of the other passengers.

"Holmes, do you believe that we have been followed here?"

He impaled a piece of roast chicken on his fork. "I'm quite certain of it. Before we left Baker Street, we were under observation by at least two men loitering in the vicinity. Since then, I've watched our fellow-travellers carefully, and one of them has gone to great pains to conceal his interest in us."

"Is he here, with us in the dining-coach?"

"No. As you saw, the train has stopped twice since we began our meal, so he may have alighted. You will have realised that the passengers are fewer by many than before."

The remainder of our time there was spent mostly in silence, though I confess to experiencing some unease that our adversary could be so close. We returned to our compartment after almost an hour to find it empty.

We saw nothing more of Mr. Earley for the remainder of the journey, nor was he among the passengers who disembarked with us at New Street Station. I imagined that he must have left the train, but Holmes made no comment as to this other than to say that the man following us, if indeed he was, must be doing so by description only and had probably never set eyes on us previously.

Holmes, I could tell, was constantly watchful for pursuit. As we left the station, he led us on a haphazard route through nearby backstreets to emerge not far from our starting point, looking somewhat relieved as we booked into one of a number of small boarding houses for two nights.

"I do not anticipate that a longer stay will be necessary," he told me. Then, when we had placed our scant luggage in our rooms, "Watson, has the journey tired you?"

"Not especially."

"Excellent. I see from the notice-board that dinner here is served rather later than we are accustomed to, so I propose we make our first enquiry this afternoon.

I nodded. "Very well. Where do we begin?"

"Unless I'm much mistaken, our destination is within walking distance. An art shop, a similar establishment to that of the late Mr. Crowe, is situated in Corporation Street, which leads directly from New Street. It is run by one Archie Vine, who I once helped to convict for his part in a scandalous attempt to steal a Rembrandt from the British Museum in exchange for a substantial sum from an unscrupulous private collector."

"But would such a man be prepared to assist us, since you were instrumental in sending him to prison?"

"Oh, yes," Holmes smiled faintly, "Mr. Vine is not a man who bears grudges. In fact, he is a most cheerful fellow, without a shred of malice. When it became apparent that this case was concerned with *objets d'art,* I thought of him instantly, especially when a connection with the Midlands was established. However, when murder became a feature, I dismissed him as a possibility. But the world of art is a specialized one, and Archie Vine can be depended upon to keep his ear to the ground."

Not long after, we found ourselves walking steadily past the variety of shops in Corporation Street. Once there, the place began to appear familiar to me, for Holmes and I were here while concerned with the events which I have documented elsewhere as "The Stockbroker's Clerk". It seemed that little had changed, with hansoms and private carriages crowding the street continually.

Mr. Vine's shop was unmistakable, its window display consisting of a set of impressive seascapes by an artist who I confess was unknown to me.

The man behind the counter in the rather loud check suit looked up from the catalogue he was reading and became initially very still. A moment later a wide smile spread across his face and he held out his hands before him, embracing the air.

"Why, Mr. Sherlock Holmes! And this must be the man who translates your activities so well into print – Doctor Watson! I would never have thought to see you here."

"Good afternoon, Mr. Vine," Holmes replied.

"Look around," he went on proudly. "Do you see all those pictures, portraits, landscapes, seascapes, displayed across the walls? What a business I've created using my knowledge of art, with money coming in regularly and without need to worry about the law. I swear I've never been better off, and it's all thanks to you, Mr. Holmes, for showing me the error of my former ways! I suppose I should thank you for it, since I could have drawn a much longer sentence had you not explained the case properly in court."

"You weren't the worst of those involved."

"No, sir, I don't suppose I was. Crooked museum guards, and rich men who'd risk the life and limb of others, just so their collection would look good and greater than that of the next fellow. All I wanted was to make a few pounds to get by." He ceased to speak suddenly, adopting a different expression. "I didn't know you were interested in art though, Mr. Holmes." He paused again, taking on a furtive look. "Or is it something from my past, something from the grapevine, that I can help you with?"

"I'm looking into an incident connected with art, and with murder."

His expression changed. "Murder, you say? That's certainly not beneficial to business – unless of course it's to do with one concerned in the past with a well-known piece. Is that the case?"

Holmes shook his head. "Regretfully, it is not. A dealer was killed in the capital, it is thought because he sold a portrait that was intended for someone else. The painting is not valuable, but part of a series from an emerging school that specializes in reproducing the styles of the famous. I should emphasize that this isn't an instance of attempting to sell such a work as if it were an original, but something else entirely."

Mr. Vine hesitated for barely a moment, glancing around the empty shop as if he were afraid of being overheard.

"Are you referring to those Da Vinci copies that have been circulating lately?" he asked with narrowed eyes.

"I am."

"They are but a novelty, and not to be taken seriously – at least that is how the art world considers them."

"Nevertheless," said Holmes, "they are connected to my investigation, and possibly to the security of our country."

106

Mr. Vine fell silent as someone peered into the shop window, his expression now downcast. I thought I detected a trace of fear in his voice when he next spoke.

"There are bad rumours, very bad rumours, going about regarding the people who distribute these works. A representative of the Da Vinci Society, a sort of club devoted to his works, recently visited the warehouse where they're kept to make enquiries. He was found a couple of days later near the railway track, about a mile from the local station. It looked as if he'd been hit by a train, but the police can't understand how it could have come about. There have been other incidents, too."

"This 'warehouse' you mentioned. Presumably, the portraits are stored there as they become available?"

Mr. Vine shrugged. "No one knows any more than I have told you. It is said that all who work there keep very much to themselves."

Holmes nodded, his expression thoughtful.

"Do you know where this place is?" I asked.

Mr. Vine looked at me uncertainly, then glanced at Holmes.

"I will write down the address," he answered, reaching for a pencil.

Dinner that evening was edible, though not remarkable. I believe that Holmes also missed Mrs. Hudson's fare, although he usually appeared indifferent to food.

"Where is this place – *Hockley*?" I asked as I finished a rather tasteless dessert. I had ensured that we were seated well out of earshot at a table in the corner of the dining room.

"Not too far from here. A short cab ride, according to the map. The light has almost gone now, and I suggest that we change to darker clothing before leaving."

"You're certain that a better course of action wouldn't be to wait until tomorrow – When we are rested, perhaps?"

"We have no way of knowing how far advanced the enemy's plans are, and therefore the extent of the danger to us. No, I want this affair ended, so unless you feel unable to accompany me, we'll see to it tonight."

"How are we to proceed?"

"We'll know that when we arrive. Evidence or information will enable Mycroft to act. We will secure what we can."

Our driver gave us a peculiar look when Holmes told him of our destination. We were quick to realise why when the hansom left us in deserted poorly-lit streets. Hockley, we soon discovered, was a district where goldsmiths, jewellers, sculptors, artists, and warehouses containing various imported cargoes were much in evidence during working hours, but it became a silent wasteland at night.

107

Holmes led us along soot-blackened streets that betrayed the presence of small industry, occasionally reading his map or an indistinct street sign to determine our path. We came upon a square with a four-faced clock atop a tower in its centre, containing a post office and local branches of well-known banks. He held up the map and lit his dark lantern with a vesta.

"This place is like a maze," he whispered, although there was no one to overhear. "That street opposite seems to be composed of factory buildings and, if Mr. Vine's information is to be relied upon, we will find the warehouse we seek there."

We walked slowly and quietly along that dull thoroughfare, our shadows cast by moonlight as we passed between dark and silent structures. None of the small factories were signposted or otherwise identified, but some of the warehouses bore numbers. My friend paused at one of these, then moved on to the next.

"Is this the place?" I asked in a low voice.

He leaned forward and held up his dark lantern until he could make out a number scrawled in chalk upon a crumbling wall.

"It appears so. I see that there is a gate between this and the next building, probably leading to a rear entrance. It would be as well to gain entry that way, so as to conceal ourselves from the street. Complications could arise if we were disturbed by a local constable on his beat."

"Holmes, we are committing burglary."

"Not for the first time. We have discovered before now that extreme circumstances require extreme measures to set things straight."

He then closed the shutter of his dark lantern and confronted the gate. I've seen him employ such methods in the past, but I was nevertheless surprised when he suddenly leapt into the air and grasped the cross-piece above it. In an instant he had raised himself until he could hook a leg over, and then the other. I heard him drop to the ground on the other side. The noise of bolts being drawn back was muted, as he performed the actions slowly.

The gate opened and he beckoned me into a passage barely visible in the meagre light. He closed it after us and we crept slowly along the side of the building to the corner. Here in the moonlight was revealed a tangle of metal and many empty crates on what must once have been a lawn. Weeds and thistles had grown to knee-height, evident also among the rows of flagstones adjoining the rear wall. I could just make out Holmes's shadowy figure, placing a finger to his lips to ensure silence.

We were now faced with a stout door, wide and unyielding. He stood very still for a few moments with his face near the lock. Apparently satisfied with his observation, he produced his pick-lock and gained our entry in a surprisingly short time. As we entered into blackness, I felt the reassuring weight of my service revolver in my pocket, and told myself that we would quickly discover the evidence we sought before emerging from this Tartarus unscathed.

I felt Holmes's hand on my arm and we both remained still. After some moments had passed all became clearer, and I realised that some illumination was admitted through the skylights above. Our eyes having adjusted, we moved into the centre of the revealed space before us.

Our surroundings were much as I had imagined. As far as I could see, the walls were hung with landscapes and portraits, most of them unfamiliar to me. I recognised a reproduction of Leonardo's *Head of a Woman* and a copy of the mural *The Last Supper* before Holmes whispered to me softly.

"It seems they do copy the originals, as well as their style. This has been operating for some time, I think. If we can determine that the same symbols are present on some of these examples and take some with us, that should suffice."

The silence was absolute as we began our examination. I was about to lift a picture, as Holmes had done, from the wall when the lamps above, hidden until now by the gloom and somehow lit by a remote source, sputtered and exploded into light. A heavy internal wooden door slid open causing a loud impact. Three men, each armed with revolvers, descended the few steps.

I saw at once that the man in the centre of the trio was the leader. He was dressed smartly in attire of the Continental style, and had the bearing of a nobleman, while his companions had the appearance of street roughs.

He looked first at Holmes, then at me. In the increased light, the full expanse of the warehouse was now visible.

"Good evening, gentlemen," he began in a voice with no more than a trace of accent. "I'm not surprised to see you, since I knew that your investigation would soon lead you here." He paused, staring at me, and then at Holmes. "What does astonish me however, is that Doctor Watson isn't alone. I had received information that Mr. Holmes had been accounted for, since his unconscious body was thrown from the London train earlier today. Who then, was that unfortunate fellow?"

Thrown from the train? I thought, wondering who he meant. Then, it suddenly occurred to me: Poor Mr. Earley, who had looked so much like Holmes, and whom we had left in our compartment to catch up on his sleep. It was he who had been killed, simply for being in the wrong place at the wrong time, and because he looked like someone else.

"It matters little," continued the man, "since he will now take no part in the coming conflict."

"I thought I saw your hand in this," Holmes answered. "Watson, be aware that you have made the acquaintance of the head of the Kaiser's network of spies in England – *Count von Swemberger*."

"You flatter me," von Swemberger said. "It would be more accurate to say that I control our activities in this *region* of England. You know, gentlemen, our network was operating very smoothly, and our agents in various places were most efficient in their obtaining and transmitting useful information. Germany is using it to improve our own engines of war and for the destruction of all who resist us. Then one of our supply lines was discovered, so that we were forced to depend temporarily upon that shopkeeper in Charing Cross to act as an unconscious conduit. It was intended that the picture you are so interested in would be bought by our contact before it could be sold elsewhere, but you, Doctor Watson – " He gave me a humourless smile. " – purchased it before he could arrive. The shopkeeper was most reluctant to divulge to me your name and address, but I was able to persuade him in a short while. Naturally he couldn't be allowed to speak afterwards of our interest in the matter."

"Murderer!" I retorted. "What harm could Mr. Crowe or Mr. Earley have caused you. They were innocent civilians."

"Were those their names? It is certain than many others will share their fate before my country completes its fight to victory, but that is the way of things."

"And what will you accomplish now?" Holmes enquired of him. "Your plot has been discovered. If you continue, your entire network will fail."

"We have alternatives, of course. But first we must clear up the remnants left by our unfortunate failure here." He pointed with his free hand into the depths that had been invisible to us in the darkness. "Doctor Watson, be so good as to open the crate standing near the statue of Mars." He gave a mirthless laugh again. "The God of War. Appropriate, wouldn't you say?"

Conscious that the weapons of the Count and his silent companions were pointed at me, I did as he ordered. The crate was of sturdy construction and the lid was heavy. I lifted it back and peered within. The sight that was revealed appalled me.

"She failed, and we had no further use for her. Besides, she turned against her own people for money, so how long would it be before someone else offered her more to work against us?" He glanced at the man standing nearest to him. "I was glad to see that you were thorough, Otto."

"What is in there, Watson?" Holmes asked.

"The body of Martha Vincent," I answered. "Brutally strangled."

"With the addition of you gentlemen," von Swemberger continued, "the crate will shortly be disposed of in a river. I believe the nearest are the Severn or the Avon. Thus, all will be removed from the scene without trace. We will then set about some alterations to our network, and all will be well."

"Hardly," Holmes disputed. "Scotland Yard and others know more of you and your activities than you seem to be aware."

"Then why have they not acted before now? No, Mr. Holmes, you cannot delay the inevitable like that." He gestured to his companions. "Otto, Hermann: Dispose of them."

I took cover behind the crate as Otto levelled his weapon. His quick footsteps drew nearer and it occurred to me that he was expecting me to be unarmed. It surprised me that Count von Swemberger hadn't had us searched for weapons, but I remembered several occasions when Holmes had mentioned how often it is that the most confident of adversaries forget the obvious or the elementary.

A shot rang out, its echoes fading slowly. I prayed that it hadn't found its mark if my friend was the target. Otto didn't appear suddenly around the corner of the crate as I expected, but approached warily. His revolver was aimed at my heart and he muttered something in German an instant before I brought my hand from its concealment behind my back and fired my service revolver. Blood spurted from his chest and he toppled towards me with his features frozen in astonishment. I ensured that his weapon was out of his reach, an old precaution, and altered my position so that I could see across the room.

My worst fear – that I would see Holmes's body lying there – proved groundless. I peered around the crate and immediately drew back as a bullet struck it, inches away from my head. By changing my angle of view, I saw von Swemberger edging his way along the wall between a group of statues in classical pose. I was unable to fire because to do so would have partially exposed me, and I was aware that the shot of a moment ago came from a different direction. Silence had fallen, except for a sound like an animal scuttling from somewhere among the grouped paintings and sculptures around me. I strained my ears and moved within the limitations of my protection, but there was no sign or sound of Holmes.

Again, I tried to see further. This time no firing resulted, but von Swemberger had disappeared. I listened once more, but all sound had ceased.

A tense silence had settled on the warehouse, made sinister by the effect of the flickering gaslight. I waited, conscious of the accelerated beating of my heart.

Then another shot, from much nearer, echoed like cannon fire, and something tore at the sleeve of my coat. Someone fired twice more and the body of Hermann crashed down, almost on top of me. I realised then how close I had come to death – he had approached silently, or almost so, from behind. Once more, I reflected, I owed my life to Sherlock Holmes.

Still, we had Count von Swemberger to deal with, and I knew not where he had hidden himself. I considered calling to my friend but instantly saw the foolishness of it, since that would reveal my position to our enemy also.

Minutes passed, with no occurrence.

Eventually I rose cautiously, praying that my impatience wouldn't cause my end. Slowly I peered in every direction, but saw no one. It came to me that this must be the way it is for a hunted animal, waiting for a sight of the hunter or a chance of escape. Then I asked myself: *Was I the hunter, or the prey?*

Moments later I crouched, as I had been taught to do during my army days when under fire, as two quick reports were followed by a cry of pain.

That it had been Holmes's voice, I had no doubt. A terrible crash shook the warehouse, and I fought down an instant of panic.

I crept into an aisle bordered by statues that dwarfed the others, and wondered how much information must be concealed within them. They appeared to be fashioned from white marble, and were doubtless of great weight. No sound reached my ears as I pressed slowly forward, determined to avenge Holmes if, God forbid, that proved to be necessary. Every minute or so I stopped, my eyes searching for von Swemberger and dreading what might soon confront me.

Another aisle led away at an angle and I considered where it was likely to take me. I had taken four paces when the silence was broken.

"Not that way, Watson. Continue on your previous path."

Relief all but engulfed me, but I ignored it in my desperation to find my way.

I came upon Holmes near the end of the aisle of statues, with blood dripping from his hand and the broken remains of an overturned figure of Neptune before him.

Beneath the statue, and impaled upon the trident that Neptune held, lay Count von Swemberger.

"Are you all right?" I stammered.

He glanced at his hand and wrapped a handkerchief around it. "It's nothing. The Count shot my revolver from my hand. He was a marksman of considerable skill. My only recourse then was to sever the ropes holding the statue aloft – in preparation for shipping I assume – at the moment he passed beneath. Fortunately, my judgement was sound."

"Let me examine your hand," I offered with concern.

He shook his head. "That will not be immediately necessary, I think. It can be attended to later. As for now, it would be better to leave this place to seek out a constable who can then summon help. I must confess, I will

112

be glad to return to Baker Street on the early train – providing we can answer satisfactorily the many questions to which we will inevitably be subjected."

The Return of Agatha Davis
by Ember Pepper

In my long association with Sherlock Holmes, we had encountered murderers, robbers, scoundrels, and frauds both in England and on an international scale. However, one personage who crossed our threshold left him more unsettled than I had ever seen him. Until now, I had kept this particular tale off the page, sensitive to Holmes's feelings and averse to causing him embarrassment. However, twenty years hence, I know Holmes looks back on the affair with a sort of resigned amusement that only time can foster.

It was May of 1901, and Holmes was at his writing desk distracting himself from his current monograph by falling deeply engrossed in the morning edition of *The Gloucester Journal*, one of dozens of newspapers he had delivered every day. He emerged only to begin a virulent, albeit justified, tirade against the police and their handling of the murder of another unfortunate woman in Whitechapel. "Have you seen this drivel, Watson? This poor girl was brutally murdered in the most horrific manner, and the police are bungling everything."

He twisted in his chair and tossed the journal on the morass of newsprint covering the middle of the sitting room floor. I leaned over the arm of my comfortable armchair and swiped the paper up to see what had so soured my friend's mood.

Murder in a Whitechapel Lodging House

Within a stone's throw of the house in which Mary Kelly was murdered and mutilated in November 1888, when police and public alike were staggered by the extraordinary series of atrocities known as "The Ripper Murders", a tragedy of a somewhat similar character occurred in the early hours of Sunday morning.

The story went on to desgive the strangulation of Mary Ann Davis, a poor widow. I sighed, a feeling of resignation washing over me. "Do you think it's him?" I asked quietly.

Holmes didn't answer at first, staring resolutely down at the blank paper of his yet-to-be-started monograph on matching specific blood spatter patterns with types of violence, his gaze turned inwards.

114

Finally, he gave a small shake of his head. "No, it isn't *him*. He is dead."

He said no more, applying himself to his task with a concentration that seemed specifically designed to discourage conversation.

"Will you look into the case?"

"My services have not been requested."

"That's never stopped you before."

"There's a more interesting story on page two."

I glanced at it. A man had been found hanging from the iron fence of the London Hospital.

"Why leave a body in such a public manner?" Holmes asked. "It may have some meaning that I think is curious."

"How is this any more unique than the murder of Mary Ann Davis?"

"Because it means there is a third party at play – whoever the message was for. Besides, as I said, the police have not tried to consult me about the woman's death."

Surprisingly, it seemed he did not wish to be consulted, but before I could wonder too much at this, we heard the step of our landlady ascending the stairs, followed by a quieter click of heels.

Mrs. Hudson peeked her head around the door. "Mr. Holmes, I know you asked not to be bothered, but there is a young lady here that seems desperate to see you, if you could spare a moment."

Holmes sighed, tapping his pencil against his paper before throwing it down irritably. "I'm getting nowhere with this. Let the lady in, Mrs. Hudson. A distraction may be a fine thing right now."

He stood and bent down to gather the mess of papers into a pile to clear a path for our guest. I stood as a woman of about thirty years of age stepped into the room, nodding her thanks to Mrs. Hudson as she closed the door behind her. She was a pretty girl, with a very unique shade of dark brown hair and elfish features. She smiled politely at me, revealing a very pleasing dimple in her right cheek.

She gave me a small, awkward curtsy, as if someone had told her it was a customary thing to do, and waited to be given permission to sit. In my long acquaintance with Holmes, I had learned something about deduction, and recognized immediately by the faded patches of her skirt near her knees and the faint remnants of coal dust along the edges of a few of her fingernails that she was likely a housemaid.

Holmes turned, his hand already raised to welcome our guest into our usual client's chair when he saw her and drew up short. His face paled with what I could now easily recognize as mortification, his stance suddenly tense.

I looked between the two, confused. It seemed my friend knew this woman, but she made no indication that she had ever met him before. She frowned a bit at his behavior, glancing at me.

Braving through the discomfort of the moment, she smiled. "Your landlady told me that you didn't want visitors, so I'm sorry to interrupt, but it's very important that I speak to you. I need your help, Mr. Holmes."

Holmes still said nothing. My gaze shifted back and forth between them in a way that I'm sure would appear comical from an outside view. I imagined a gigantic puppet master twisting my little wooden head to-and-fro for a delighted audience.

The awkward *tableau* was becoming unbearable. I had finally decided that I would be polite and urge her to sit when Holmes seemed to shake himself free of whatever horror had gripped him. "You need my help?" he echoed. The response struck me as quite dumb, particularly for Holmes, and I gaped a bit at him in shock as he finally gathered his wits.

He cleared his throat. "Of course, forgive me. My mind was elsewhere. Please sit."

Once settled, Holmes stayed silent for a painfully long moment, and I decided to begin the interview, if only to save us from this torture.

"I'm Doctor Watson," I said kindly. "This, as you evidently know, is Mr. Holmes. Can you describe your problem for us?"

She nodded, appearing relieved to have some concrete directions. "Yes, it's a pleasure to meet both of you. My name is Agatha Davis. I was born in Whitechapel but, because my Mum had a problem with drink, I went to live with my uncle, my Mum's brother-in-law, whose home was a bit more stable. He died, though, when I was twelve, and I went back to my Mum who, by that time, had eased off the drink and was doing better. Like many young girls, I quickly went into service as a maid. I served in one household for about thirteen years before the couple passed, and then I went to work for a man. You may have heard of him – it was in the papers about two years ago – Mr. Milverton? He was shot in his home, but his murderer was never found." She glanced between us in question.

I nodded idiotically, my face flushing a bit even though I had nothing of which to be guilty. I snuck a glance at Holmes and saw he was blushing as well, trying valiantly to look as if he didn't notice my stare.

"Yes," I confirmed, my voice a bit scratchy, "I think I read something of it." At my own words, I felt an inescapable burst of irrational laughter crawling up my throat that I just barely repressed.

Thank the Heavens that the girl didn't seem to notice. She continued on. "It wasn't a personal loss. He was a horrible man, but it did mean I no longer had a position there. After that, I went to work for a young man in

Harley Street – you know, where all the doctors live. I still work for him. His name is Dr. Chambers."

I gave her a curious frown. Not quite able to stop myself, I asked innocently, "Pardon the inquiry, but you never married?"

Holmes made a noise in his throat that I took as a warning, but I pretended I didn't hear it.

She smiled prettily. "Oh, no. I had a few suitors, but none of them went as far as marriage. It's all right. In any case, I live with Dr. Chambers and visit my mother at the end of the week. I have more than most, I suppose. This brings me to my current problem." A sadness crossed over her face. "I said that I visit my mother, but I should have spoken in the past tense. You see, her name was Mary Ann Davis, and she was murdered yesterday." As I recalled the name from the news story, she swallowed back a well of tears. "I went home to her little room in Dorset Street, and found her on the floor. The police think she was strangled, but they don't want to help, because people die all the time in Whitechapel."

"So you wish us to investigate?" I asked.

"Yes, but, I beg your pardon, I'm not finished, Doctor. After her death, as I was walking along the street to Dr. Chambers' home, two men sprang from the darkness between the trees and tried to carry me off! I fought hard and bit one of them on his hand. When he let me go, I kicked wildly and managed to scream while running down the lane. Dr. Chambers heard and opened the door to let me in. He went out to find the men, but they were already gone. He told me not to leave the house again until we knew it was safe, but I had to come see you."

"That must have been very frightening for you," I commented, feeling increasingly out of my depth as Holmes had still not said a word.

I turned my gaze to him pointedly.

He cleared his throat and stood up abruptly. "I cannot look into this personally."

Her face fell. The pathetic look of absolute dismay seemed to have some effect on the detective. His teeth clenched and then he gave an inch, "I will contact the police in charge and see what I can find out for you. That is the best I can do at this moment, Agg – Miss Davis."

She perked up at that. "Here, I have a note with my current address on it. Please tell me if you have any information." She pulled a torn piece of writing paper from the cuff of her sleeve and held it out. The action forced Holmes to lean over to take it, coming close to her. At the proximity, she frowned and gave him a probing look. "Have we met before?"

He shook his head firmly. "No. No, not at all. I understand this matter is of great importance to you. I'll do what I can." It was an obvious dismissal, so she stood and thanked us profusely, if a bit confusedly, taking Holmes's hand without asking and pressing it between hers warmly. The detective endured the action with unease, and she swirled from the room.

An oppressive silence settled over us in her wake.

I let out a chuckle. "Well, she is delightful."

"Watson – " he warned.

"Holmes, I do think she recognized your smell!"

His face grew even redder, and he turned his back, fiddling with the papers on his desk. "She did not," he countered. "That's impossible."

"Mmm. I presume you don't mean to confess to her, so I'll try my very best to keep myself under control – "

"I'm not taking her case."

"What? She needs your help. You *owe* her that much."

"I owe her nothing," he snapped, but he stared down at the address she had given him for some time before folding it and putting it into his pocket.

"I don't agree with this. It seems in poor character to refuse her."

"Your objections are noted."

This argument seemed a dead end. I was disappointed in my friend, but I strove to be understanding of how uncomfortable the situation was for him.

"I'm frankly shocked she didn't recognize you," I said instead.

"My disguises are professional, as you know. Coupled with dim lighting, they are impenetrable."

"Yes, but . . ." I trailed off.

"But what?" he challenged.

I cleared my throat. "It's just that you courted her to the point of engagement."

"And?"

I fluttered my hands in affected disinterest. "Nothing. Never mind."

He pressed his fingers to the bridge of his nose. "Good God, I thought she was here to confront me! I never imagined I'd see her again."

"You assumed she'd disappear into the great mire of poor people, never to be of concern to you again?"

A look of startled hurt painted his face. I'm not sure why I said it. I knew Holmes never looked down or disregarded anyone due to their status in society. He was simply not that sort of man. But his nonchalance about his own cold-hearted ploy with the woman had always chafed at me. It was unlike him, driven by his obsession with ridding the world of Milverton.

He glared at me and then, in a flurry of sudden energy, he twisted on his coat and swept up his walking stick. "Come, Watson. Don't let me brave Whitechapel alone."

I stood to follow. "So you will take her case?"

"Indeed not. I want to find out who was left hanging from that fence a few days ago."

Holmes's stubbornness here was inexplicable to me. He was adamant, in my opinion, to choose the mystery that seemed the least remarkable. I understood his reticence in the matter of the delightful Agatha, abandoned fiancée, but the revolting murder of her mother seemed most vicious and worrisome.

I followed, keeping my opinions to myself for now.

The police in Whitechapel were notorious for various reasons. Not the least, the failure to catch the Ripper. Before that, they had garnered a reputation for being overworked and, therefore, a bit lax in their investigative policies. Holmes had had trouble with them before, irritated by the disdain with which they treated the very community they were meant to protect. Now we met with an Inspector Lockhart who, while not overtly contemptuous, seemed annoyed that we were bothering him.

"Forgive me," he said as we shook hands, "but we are understandably busy, as always. I can't imagine what could draw you here. Your skills are renowned, so I can't see why you'd lower yourself to apply them to the mundane crimes of the East End."

"On the contrary, sir, I spend a great deal of time here," Holmes answered. "The lovely denizens of Whitechapel have so few to advocate for them. I do what I can."

If the inspector noticed the subtle censure, he didn't show it. He only said, "Well, what can I help you with?"

"Three days ago, you discovered a man hanging from the fence of the hospital on Whitechapel Road. This seems a strangely public display, and it piqued my interest. Are you holding the body?"

"I'm afraid you're too late for that, Mr. Holmes. We buried him yesterday."

"Who was he?"

"No way to identify him. No one came forward."

"It seems you could have given it more time."

"We needed the mortuary space."

Holmes visibly reigned himself in. "Are you in possession of any of his effects? Or did you burn them?"

Inspector Lockhart bristled. "I'm not pleased with your implication, sir! We do what we can here. Just because it's been thirteen years and the

Ripper has taken a break, doesn't mean he isn't still out there. In any case, the unidentified man's possessions, as well as the rope he was hanging from, should still be at the Shoreditch Mortuary in one of the boxes, if the coroner hasn't disposed of them yet."

Holmes nodded and, without bidding him a good day, spun on his heel to leave.

The day was pleasant, so we walked the short distance to the mortuary, a small rectangular building next to St. Leonard's Church. Holmes stood staring at the door for a moment before entering. We were met by Henry Wilton, a man just beyond the threshold of eighty who had been the undertaker during the inquest of Mary Kelly and who had, reportedly, paid for her burial. There was a body on the table, covered by a sheet that had seen better days. Holmes studiously ignored it. There were two other bodies on rickety tables cramped together, both covered by sheets that had seen better days. Holmes studiously ignored them as well.

Holmes shook the man's hand. "Wilton," he nodded respectfully. I had never met the man, but it seemed obvious Holmes had had some dealings with him and viewed him with upmost regard.

Henry Wilton seemed equally deferential. "Detective," he said warmly, "I am pleased to see you, though I know you must be here on business. No one enters the mortuary for recreational purposes."

"Certainly not," Holmes murmured. "I hope you can help us. Inspector Lockhart says you handled the body of the unidentified man found at the London Hospital?"

"Oh, yes. Strange affair. I protested how quickly they discarded the corpse. I know those who pass my doorway aren't lords, but we could at least see if they have family. In any case, if you wanted to examine him, he's in the earth now, Mr. Holmes."

"Yes, so I was told. Do you have his effects?"

"You're lucky. I haven't disposed of them yet." He moved to a crowded corner of the room and shifted through some boxes, some tin and some old repurposed bandboxes. "Here you are." He put a faded floral hat box on the small wash table and opened it.

"There is little here," he explained. "He had nothing on him but his clothes and this pocketknife. The rope is the one found around his neck."

Holmes examined the knife. "This is a sailor's knot knife."

"That's what I thought as well," Wilton agreed, "but the police didn't seem too interested."

"This rope is very telling," Holmes said, peering closely at the knot on the noose. "It's a Portuguese bowline. Sailors use this to make a boatswain's chair. Clearly the victim and the murderers are sailors of some sort. I doubt the official Navy. This knife isn't a Navy issue, but it is very well used."

He handed me the rope, a habit he had formed after years of allowing me to tag along. I doubted I could provide any helpful insights, but I dutifully turned it over in my hands.

"It is wire rope," I pointed out. "Often used on ships."

"That seals it," Holmes said, returning the items to the box.

"It doesn't seem very helpful, if you don't mind me saying," Wilton offered. "How do you find one sailor in a town with a port as busy as London's?"

"I've done it before," Holmes said simply. "Thank you."

Though he seemed eager to quit the morgue, he faltered, staring at the two sheet covered bodies.

"Is one of these women named Davis?" he asked reluctantly.

"The one to the left," Wilton answering, stepping to the table with a questioning look.

Holmes sighed and nodded, and the old man pulled back the dirty sheet.

Like most strangulation victims, the woman's face was swollen and mottled. Beyond the colour of her hair, I could not make out any features of her face. Time had not hardened me to the sight. Holmes and I both flinched in sympathy. She was stripped, but clearly hadn't yet been washed. Holmes, as usual, was pleased.

"Perfect," Holmes said, as if talking to himself.

He started with the ligature at her neck, using his magnifying glass to peer closely at the marks. "This was done by a rope," he murmured. He sucked in a surprised breath and straightened. "Wire rope, to be more specific."

He stood and looked back at the box of deceased man's effects, a small frown creasing his wide brow.

"Wait a moment," I said. "What are you suggesting?"

"I suggest nothing. This is a fact."

He retrieved the rope from the box without asking permission and spent some time with his magnifying glass at the woman's neck, comparing the wound to the material. Wilton and I waited patiently.

"This is not the same rope, obviously, but the same type was clearly used to kill both our mystery man and Agatha's mother," he said at last, straightening. His tone was flat, purposefully emotionless.

"Does it mean that this murder and our unknown sailor are connected?"

He clucked his tongue thoughtfully but didn't answer, scurrying down and examining the rest of the body.

121

"There is evidence here of some torture," he declared. "I suspect she didn't give them something they wanted, and they killed her in anger."

"What signs of torture?" I asked, horrified.

"Her fingers were broken, and there are bruises on her sternum and around her shoulders. Hullo, what is this?"

He was looking closely are her bare wrist. I stepped close to peep over his shoulder. "See here?" he said. "These scratches." A series of vertical, haphazard scratches, red and angry, marred her wrists and hands.

"More torture?" I asked.

Holmes looked unconvinced. He continued downwards until he reached her legs, making another exclamation of discovery. "They are here too, limited to a very specific horizontal band around her lower leg." He leaned back, resting his arm on his knee and thinking. "Watson, correct me if I am wrong, but this area of the leg is roughly where a woman's socks would end but before the cuff of her pantaloons? Protected only by a layer of stocking?"

"Yes, I'd guess that could be true."

"Well, I've found all I can here." He covered the body once more with the sheet.

The first tendrils of sunset were reaching across the sky when we exited. We had put some distance between us and the mortuary before Holmes stopped on the kerb at the crossing of Church Street and spent some time tapping his knuckles against his chin, his expression far off, deep in thought. I waited patiently until he came back to himself with a large, frankly dramatic sigh, and signaled for a passing cab.

"Get in, Watson," he ordered as the driver slowed next to us.

"Where are we going?"

"I said get in," he repeated crossly. He turned to the driver. "Take us to 34 Harley Street."

When he turned back, he shook his head at my smirk. "Not a word, Doctor. Not a word."

Harley Street was familiar to me. Though I had lived in Paddington when I was in practice, the sight of the rooms – likely filled with happily married medical men much like myself, once upon a time – caused a slight pang of grief as I was reminded of the small flat I had shared with Mary before her tragic death and my return to Baker Street. I wondered who resided in our old rooms, living their everyday lives within the walls of our comfortable home where we had eaten together, read together, slept together.

Holmes drew me from my thoughts with a soft tap against my knee. "Are you all right?" he asked gently.

I nodded. "Merely reminiscing."

He hummed sympathetically.

"You know how it is to look back on those meaningful moments with the woman you love," I continued.

He gave me a surprised, suspicious look before he realized I was teasing him. He sighed. "It isn't amusing."

I shrugged. "I suppose it isn't, but that doesn't mean I can't find some humour in your embarrassment."

"Ah, the mark of true friendship."

I laughed. "Actually, yes."

No. 34 Harley Street was a modest-sized, two-story house that spoke of admirable success but not extreme wealth. The three steps leading to the doorway were recently white-washed, and the flower boxes in the windows were carefully tended to.

The door was answered by a pleasant butler who seemed not at all surprised by our request to see Agatha. We were let into an airy sitting room and asked to wait. I suppose I shouldn't have been astonished when it wasn't Agatha who entered the room a few minutes later but, rather, a handsome man of about forty years.

He closed the door and immediately approached Holmes, holding out his hand. "Dr. Chambers, sir. I presume you're Mr. Holmes. The illustrations in *The Strand* are hardly accurate, but I judge from the lack of a mustache that you are the detective." He shook my friend's hand before shaking mine. "And you are the doctor and biographer. An absolute pleasure to meet both you, gentlemen. You're one of the few men whose renown, I believe, is actually earned."

Holmes took this praise with modest appreciation. As he had gotten older, he had become more inured to the praise that was often heaped upon him, both sincere and insincere.

"I wondered if you would meet us," my friend remarked. "Agatha's description of you was one of a man admirably protective."

A flicker of a frown crossed the doctor's face at Holmes's use of the maid's first name, but his expression cleared when Holmes explained that Miss Davis had asked us to look into her mother's death and her subsequent attempted kidnapping.

"I can confirm her telling of events," said the man, "I heard her screaming last night, and when I opened the door, she was running up the street. I thought I saw two men behind her, but by the time she was safely inside, they were gone. I went out to look around, but they must have realized that this area isn't one wherein thugs can simply carry off a struggling woman without notice."

"It seems too coincidental that this attack on her came so close on the heels of her mother's murder. I'd like to look into it, if I can speak to her and get her mother's address."

"Of course. I feel much relieved that she has more able-bodied men on her side to keep her safe. I'll ask Paxton to fetch her." As he went to the door to call for the butler, I cast Holmes an amused glance. It was clear this man's affection for Miss Davis went much deeper than merely a protective employer.

Agatha rushed into the room in a flurry of emotion. She went straight away to Holmes, grasping at his hands and thanking him profusely for deigning to help her. Holmes took her attentions with aplomb but looked immensely relieved when Dr. Chambers gently removed her.

"I can't express how happy I am that you are going to help me find out what happened to my Mum!" she exclaimed, her eyes wet.

Holmes, a safe distance away, nodded. "All I require, Miss, is the address of your mother's flat."

"Oh!" she exclaimed, "I'll take you there! Allow me to put on my shawl." She hurried from the room before Holmes could protest.

"You have no objection to her accompanying us?" Holmes asked Chambers. I suspected he was hopeful the man would object and deter her, but the doctor nodded.

"I see no problem. I don't worry for her safety in the company of two men such as yourself. I trust you will not allow her to be snatched away."

"All right then," Holmes muttered, resigned.

We fetched a four-wheeler, and my friend said nothing as the girl sat next to him on the bench chair, oblivious to his discomfort.

I took pity on him and asked her questions about her mother. This prompted a steady stream of speech that spoke of her grief, but also her ease with words. I remembered Holmes making an off-hand jest about his long talks with the maid while masquerading as that rakish plumber and understood what he meant. I found it endearing, however. She was a sweet woman and her voice was pleasing. I couldn't imagine that Holmes had really been that put out by her company.

Her mother had lived in a makeshift flat off a dim and dreary alley in Dorset Street. A few police still remained loitering about, and we were stopped at the doorway by a man who introduced himself, quite rudely, as Inspector Matheson. When we explained our business, he scoffed.

"Not much to see but the messy room of an old dead crone. One of many around here. She must have gotten on the bad side of her latest bully."

"Sir," I admonished, horrified by such speech in front of a woman, and the victim's daughter, no less.

Agatha, though pale-faced at her mother being spoken of in this way, seemed unsurprised by the inspector's attitude.

"We only wish to look around," Holmes ground out. "Surely, if as you say it is a commonplace murder, then no harm can come from our examination."

The man shrugged. "I have no objection, but the landlady is coming to clean out all the bric-a-brac and rubbish, so you best hurry."

Holmes didn't waste time continuing the conversation. He pushed past the man and into the small flat, eager to start his examination as quickly as possible.

The room was square, barely the size of our sitting room with a layer of old mattresses in the corner, blanketed carefully in a way that spoke of a woman trying to make the best of her situation. The rest of the room was occupied by a water basin, a stove, and a few bookshelves with old books that appeared to be fished from the trash.

Agatha noticed my observation. "My Mum wasn't a good reader, but she enjoyed it. She made sure my uncle gave me a good education in reading and writing. She said it was the pathway to a better life." Her eyes were wet, but she laughed at a sudden memory. "She gave one doctor a tongue lashing when he told her that reading led a woman to being unable to have children – an idea that Dr. Chambers, thankfully, strongly disagrees with." She gave me a questioning look.

"It is a ridiculous notion," I confirmed. She nodded. I felt strangely pleased as if I had just passed some sort of test.

She glanced around her mother's rooms and swallowed thickly. "Pardon me, sirs, but I think I'll step outside. Please call me if you think I can be of some help."

Holmes and I nodded sympathetically, and it was only after the crooked door had closed behind her that Holmes sprang into action, darting to-and-fro seemingly at random to different corners in the small room. At one point, he stood for some time as if in deep thought, staring at the small wallet portrait of Agatha that had seemingly fluttered to the floor near the water basin, before he dropped with his magnifying glass and, with most intense concentration, examined every scratch and mark on the old unvarnished wood. His face showed that his quest was not a successful one.

I leaned down over the picture that had captured his attention before, peering at the faded, smiling face of a much younger Agatha and wondered at the unfairness of such a sweet girl being born into such disadvantaged circumstances.

I saw nothing else in that sepia visage that could have been of note to the crime, so I stood and looked around. It was clear that the tiny flat had been rummaged through. The woman's books and clothes were scattered around. I guessed the search was both quick and fruitless.

"They were looking for something."

Holmes grunted. "Yes, likely whatever it is they were interrogating her about." He took the two steps that centered him in the room and pocketed his magnifying glass. "There were two of them. Both sailors. One has a slight limp and shoes that are somewhat too large for him. They used rope to secure her and spent some time roughing her up before strangling her which, I suspect, was due to a fit of anger and not part of a premeditated plan. They saw the picture of Agatha and made some connection. How they discovered her name or whereabouts, I'm not sure. I can hardly believe her mother would endanger her. If she was so hell-bent in staying silent that she was willing to die, I'm sure she would not have divulged details of her daughter that would put her in harm's way."

Agatha stepped back in. "The inspector is coming down the alley, sir," she warned us with a waver in her voice.

Holmes sprung to his feet and continued his harried examination of the room, clearly adverse to bandying words with another doltish member of the official police force. It was helpful that the space was so small. He paused at the fireplace, digging around in the ashes and pulling out a charred remnant of paper. He held it up to the light, but no words could be seen.

"Do you think the killers burned this?"

"Difficult to know." He glanced around until he found a small pocket-sized book and carefully slipped the brittle paper into the pages and placed it into his pocket for safekeeping.

"Are you able to see what is written on there?" Agatha asked.

"There may be some way to expose the writing," Holmes said, "but it isn't guaranteed."

The inspector and the landlady entered then and brusquely rushed us out of the room. Holmes went with no protestation only because he had found everything he could discover.

Once back in Dorset Street, Agatha took desperate hold of Holmes's arm. "What did you see, Mr. Holmes? Do you know why someone would do such a thing to Mum? There could be no reason to hurt her. As you saw, she had nothing. She meant nothing to anyone except to me."

Holmes gently disentangled himself. "I know nothing for sure. Allow me to work on this note. For now, we'll escort you back to your home to make sure you're safe under the benevolent watch of Dr. Chambers."

If the sniffling housemaid noticed the slight humour behind Holmes's use of the word *benevolent*, she didn't make any outward show of it. I handed her my handkerchief as Holmes flagged down a passing cab, and we bustled in.

Agatha fell into a sad reverie, staring out of the cab's window. It was clear that brief glimpse of her mother's room had affected her deeply. Once the strained air in the carriage became overpowering, I felt it my duty to distract her from her thoughts.

I directed my question to the detective, "Once a paper is burned, Holmes, I was under the impression it was impossible to recover what it contained."

"Difficult, but not impossible," he answered. "There has been success with an alcohol and glycerin solution, diluted with water. When you place the charred item into the solution, as it immerses, decipherment can be made to varying degrees."

Agatha sniffed and used the edge of my pocket square to wipe at her eyes. "Do you think my Mum burned the paper, or her killers?"

"Likely your mother, in order to hide whatever it is the intruders were after."

"What could have been so important that she would die for it?"

Holmes's face softened with something startlingly close to affection. "You?" he suggested softly.

She looked very stunned by his words. "You believe my Mum died to protect me?"

"It seems an obvious fact. Forgive me for my bluntness, but as you yourself already said, your mother didn't have anything that seemed of any worth – except you. And there was an attempt to kidnap you very soon after her death."

"She never spoke of anything."

"It may have been a recent development. When did you last see your mother?"

"Last Saturday, when I went home to visit."

We arrived at the front of Chambers' door in peaceful Harley Street. Holmes disembarked the cab and offered his hand to the girl to help her down.

"Did your mother have any meaningful or extensive connection to sailors?" he asked as he knocked on Chambers' door.

Agatha frowned. "No, I don't think so. Of course, Whitechapel is an odd place, and people often find themselves in strange company. To be truthful. I only really have memories of her after my uncle died and I went back to live with her, but by that time, she kept mostly to herself. She wasn't one to socialize with anyone besides me."

"And why was that?"

"Because I'm a joy to be around," she replied smartly, a charming cleverness escaping even through her sniffles and tears.

Holmes hadn't been expecting the remark. He laughed, one of his rare bright laughs, that pleasant smile stretching across his face and serving to make him look as young as when I first met him.

Agatha visibly started, glancing at him quickly and then glancing again, a sudden look of recognition unfolding on her open face. I understood immediately what had just transpired, and a part of me wondered why it had taken so long. I felt myself tense, though I wasn't yet sure to whose defense I was preparing to come.

Holmes understood the moment as well. His stance became guarded, as readying himself for a blow.

We held our breath.

It didn't come.

Agatha stared for a long while, a sad look of disappointment marring her pretty face, and then the door opened, the warm light of the small foyer falling over her as Paxton allowed her entry.

She stepped in with a quiet goodbye.

Holmes was understandably subdued as we rode back to Baker Street. I didn't know what to say. My amusement at the entire debacle had faded now that I had seen that look of pitiful betrayal on the innocent girl's face.

As we neared our flat, I opened my mouth to offer some reassuring counsel, but Holmes shot me such a withering glare of forewarning that the words died on my tongue.

We ascended the stairs in tense silence. Upon entering our comfortably messy flat, Holmes hung up his coat and went straight away to his chemical desk, rummaging around the bottles and vials.

"Will you fetch me a half-gallon of water, Watson?"

When I brought the pitcher back upstairs, Holmes had filled a small tray with alcohol and glycerin. He took the water from me without thanks and poured some into the mixture. He didn't seem to be amenable to my company, so I took a seat and waited as he let the small piece of paper sink into the tray.

He hummed under his breath and used a spare piece of paper from his desk to write down the letters that appeared. He took his time with it, and was still writing long after the paper had sunk to the bottom and began to turn to mush.

I couldn't tell if the tightness of his shoulders was due to some failure of the test or the situation with our client, though I guessed it was the latter by the amount of writing he was absorbed in.

"You can't be too surprised," I ventured carefully.

He scoffed, still bent at his task. "I'm not surprised. This is precisely why I wanted to turn her away."

"Perhaps this will work out in the end. It will offer you an opportunity to explain. Apologize."

"I'm sure that will make everything all right," he sneered.

"It could at least reassure her that Escott's disappearance was due to no fault on her part."

"I'm no expert at women, but I don't think that will dull the sting."

Considering how quickly he had secured her hand in betrothal, I had my doubts that his knowledge of women was really as lacking as he professed. "She seems a forgiving sort – "

"I used her."

I was shocked at the admission. "For a noble cause," I offered.

"Again, the sting, Watson."

I sighed. "A frank talk with her may be inevitable – unless you intend to abandon this case."

"I will do nothing of the sort. In fact – " He passed the scrap of paper to me where he had been attempting to make sense of the few letters his experiment managed to reveal. " – I believe I have the first sentence of this letter – the best I could manage."

The sentence he uncovered was a simple but significant *Agatha dear, I have in my posses –*. The following letters were lost forever, but it didn't take a world-renowned intellect to know what it said.

"A shame we can't read the rest to know what she had in her possession that she was willing to die for. Or if it was found."

Holmes shook his head, "It wasn't found. If they had what they wanted, why would they risk taking Agatha in the middle of a well-to-do street? And we still don't have answers as to how this murder may be linked to the sailor left hanging in a very purposeful public display."

He disappeared into his room and emerged about an hour later dressed as a rough sailor, telling me not to wait up for his return.

The evening was young, and I felt suddenly adrift. I could smell the lamb shanks I had spied cooking when I went down to the kitchen to collect the water. The clock ticked by a few minutes as I sat and wondered how to spend my time, an increasingly common occurrence for me. In moments like these, I considered the wisdom of perhaps opening my own practice once again.

But that was hardly something I could do immediately. I shook myself. My publisher wanted my final draft of the Baskerville adventure, and I remembered that I had lent the notes to Holmes to get his comments. I poked around his desk, looking for my papers. I opened the top drawer and instead came upon copious documents he had written on beekeeping, of all things. I stood staring sort of dumbly at them for a long while. It wasn't that I was unaware of Holmes's interest. Indeed, he had spoken many times of his thoughts on the matter of apiology, but I didn't know he had made so much formal inquiry into it or written so very much.

I felt a pang of grief hit me. I had long suspected that Holmes was considering retirement. He wasn't old – in January he had turned forty-seven years of age and was still healthy and physically strong, but these last ten years or so had carried with them a sort of deep melancholy that was different than his youthful tendency to brood. His mind was as sharp as ever, and his love for his work hadn't waned, but it seemed his desire to be flush with the world had diminished. More and more, he sought out solitude and quiet, and I feared soon he might do so in a manner more permanent. And where would that leave me?

I set the bundle down carefully and found my own notes that I had been looking for. Holmes had written quick, helpful comments in the margins in that unique shorthand he used that I could now read like a second language.

I pushed all other thoughts from my mind and settled comfortably in my armchair to read through his edits on our harrowing adventure in Dartmoor.

Holmes didn't return until late the next morning. He was rubbing tiredly at his eyes and disappeared into his room without a word. I heard his wardrobe opening and closing.

He emerged clean and dressed in his favorite dressing gown. His eyes were still lined with exhaustion. I kindly pushed a plate of eggs and rashers in his direction. "Long night?" I ventured.

He poured a cup of tea from the cooling pot and downed it without complaint. "If you ever visit The Drunken Mermaid pub, I advise you to steer clear of their housemade gin. Vile stuff."

"You spent the entire night at the pub?"

"Part of it in a room behind the bar, as I didn't trust myself to walk." He ate a few bites of his eggs and then moved them away with a grimace.

He turned his attention once again to the tea. "I stationed myself there," said he, "to see if I could find any information about our dead man. It's a popular stop for sailors who have recently gotten into port. It took some time, and an unfortunate amount of gin, before I stumbled upon anything of interest."

"Care to share?"

He stood and filled his after-breakfast pipe. "The day before our sailor was found dead, a commercial fishing ship, *The Seafarer*, docked in port, cutting their expedition short because they lost their captain at sea. A group

130

of garrulous and quite-drunk men told me that one of the ship's men frequents the pub – a Mark Ingels. They then tried to ply me with absinthe, which I declined in favor of my healthy liver. I managed, I hope, to write out a note to this Ingels before the proprietor allowed me to sleep off my inebriation in the back room. If my note was legible, I expect a visit from the man sometime this afternoon." He shook his head ruefully. "I'm getting old. A little over-indulgence in spirits wouldn't have sent me under the table when I was thirty."

"Why would they try to ply you with absinthe?"

He shrugged. "They found it amusing. I wasn't familiar with the establishment, and thus didn't realize what a weathered crowd usually gathered there. Even in my rough attire, I evidently stood out." He grimaced. "They called me 'pretty boy' and bought me the first few rounds of gin to see how well I fared. I handled it admirably, if I do say so myself, but around the sixth glass, even I couldn't pretend to be unaffected."

I laughed. "I hardly think you could be described as a 'boy' anymore."

He glared. Indeed, Holmes had aged well, with only the beginnings of a frustratingly becoming grey appearing in his black hair and the whiskers on his face, which he hadn't yet shaved after his long night – but he was clearly no youth.

He cocked his head in the direction of the stairs. "If I'm not mistaken, there is our man now."

The door opened and the page showed in a small ribston-pippin of a man with a jovial smile and a twinkle in his eye that spoke of a good-natured disposition.

"'Ello there," he greeted us, "Old Onion Breath at The Mermaid said you were looking for me."

"I beg your pardon?" I stuttered.

Holmes just laughed, bidding the man to sit. "He means the pub owner, Watson. An affectionate – and apt – nickname."

"From what I could make of your note, you wish to speak to me of our last voyage." He held the note out, and Holmes took it. At the sight of his own unsteady handwriting, he grimaced.

"Yes. You're Mark Ingels, correct?"

"Yes, sir. A fisherman on *The Seafarer*. Our last trip had proved unusual, so I'm not too surprised it has become the topic of interest."

"Can you describe what about this trip was eventful?"

"Actually, in some ways it was very uneventful – we hardly caught anything. We were barely out at sea two days before the captain fell ill. His breathing was all wet, and then on the third day he died. That's why we returned so early and empty-handed."

131

"What was your captain's name?"

"Pattins."

"And what became of his body?"

"He was taken to the morgue and then buried. I was there with his wife."

Holmes frowned in disappointment.

The man recognized the expression. "I beg your pardon, sir, but are you looking for someone?"

"Did you hear of the man who was hung at the London Hospital?"

"Aye, I heard tale of it, but I don't know much about it. And I certainly had nothing to do with it."

"He was a sailor."

"Was he?" the man murmured curiously. "Do you have reason to think he was on my boat?"

"Has anyone gone missing?"

He waved his hand helplessly. "Most of us don't keep in company with each other while on land. We see enough of each other on that cramped ship. Though . . . ." He trailed off thoughtfully.

"Yes?" Holmes prompted with an edge of impatience.

"Jack Harper was acting sort of odd when we docked."

"Who is he?"

"First Mate. He was very close to Pattins. I think they'd been working together for about ten years now. In fact, he spent the day with him in his cabin when he fell ill."

"And this struck you as suspicious?"

"Not at all, but once we reached land, Jack was acting real skittish. He ran off – didn't even show up when Pattins was buried. Me and him get on just fine – better than fine, in fact – but he avoided me when he would normally spend some time with me at the pubs or watching the girls – " He broke off, eyes widening upon remembering that he wasn't speaking to fellow sailors. "What I mean is – "

"It's all right," Holmes waved away, eager to get on with it. "Continue."

"As I said, he scurried right off. I caught a glimpse of him later that night when I was at The Raven and Rat. He was going into Mrs. Miller's Inn across the street. I waved, but he darted into the building as if he didn't want to be seen."

"What does Jack Harper look like?"

"Sandy hair. Short at about five-and-half-feet tall. A stocky man. Do you think he was the man who was killed?"

"He fits the description," Holmes answered bluntly.

Ingels swore. "Why wouldn't he tell me what he had gotten into?"

132

"Did he appear to be in possession of a box, or any item that he didn't have when he boarded the ship?"

"No, just his ditty bag."

Holmes stared into the cold fireplace for a while before nodding. "You said Mrs. Miller's Inn on Red Lion Street?"

"Yes, sir."

Holmes stood and thanked the man. "I'm endeavoring to discover what happened to your friend. I'll send you word at The Mermaid when I have information. Do you expect to be in London for long?"

"I have no plans, as of yet, though my empty pockets will eventually compel me to find a position on board another boat."

"Well, then, let's hope I'm quick about it."

Once he was gone, Holmes tossed off his dressing gown. "I think a trip to Harper's rooms are in order. Would you care to join me?"

As we rode again to Whitechapel, I broached the topic of Agatha once more. "You know, once we discover the truth of this mystery, you will have to face the girl again."

Surprisingly, he didn't appear annoyed by my statement. He sighed. "I'm aware, Watson. In fact, it occurs to me that our housemaid is very intelligent, and has likely drawn the connection between her erstwhile fiancée's disappearance and the death of her former employer. The connection she may draw, however, may put us in a rough spot if she presumes we had some hand in his death."

"It would be unfortunate if she made a trip to Scotland Yard to turn us in," I said.

"I'm sure that would please Lestrade, but I've avoided a gaol cell – for the most part – thus far, and I have no intention of ending my illustrious career by being collared by the nitwits of the Metropolitan Police Force."

"You mustn't try to defend yourself when you speak to her," I advised, "Let her talk, and listen."

"I know how to converse with people."

"Not when you are so clearly in the wrong."

He grunted at that and took to watching the scenery move by as we descended into the spider-web streets of the East End.

Mrs. Miller's Inn was a depressing two-story rectangle building bracketed by a pawnshop on the left and a small alley leading to the back yard. Holmes didn't immediately approach the entrance, but instead gestured to the alley.

"I wish to see if there is any evidence of illegal entrance," he told me as we squeezed through the broken iron fence that led to the barren strip of dried grass that constituted the back yard. Center-right of the building was a sturdy but leafless tree with spindly branches that looked as if it would have been luxurious with proper tending-to. Its grey arms spread out across the first-story windows of the inn. Holmes pointed upwards.

"See that window? Its glass is broken."

One of the windows near the middle did have a broken windowpane. Holmes went to stand beneath it, staring at the pathway of the tree.

"It looks as if someone climbed here and broke the glass to unlock the window," he suggested. He touched the tree bark and then hefted himself up by one low hanging branch to test his theory. It held his weight, but he hissed and dropped back down, looking at his palm.

"Rough," he commented, showing me the scratches on his palm. "Look familiar?"

They looked identical to the marks we had seen on Agatha's mother. "Do you think she broke the window-pane?"

"Either she broke it, or simply used the fact that someone else broke it in order to enter. Come, let us see if Mrs. Miller will allow us to peruse her former tenant's room."

Mrs. Miller was cooperative once Holmes handed over a few shillings. She told us that Harper had vanished a few days ago, but he had paid a week in advance and his things were still there. She left us to find the place ourselves, and we ascended the dark, creaking staircase to a hallway lined with yellowing wallpaper.

Like most inns of this sort, Harper's room was a square space with a cot. A basin with questionable water stood on an uneven little table in one corner. The grimy covers and sheets were in disarray, as if someone had ripped them from the bed. The only item of Harper's present was his sailor's cloth bag crumpled on the ground, its contents poured from them. His extra clothes, sewing kit, a few books, and assorted toiletries were strewn around the room.

"Someone was looking for something," I commented.

"Astute observation. But did they find it? I think not, since they strung him up."

"But how would that help?"

"By sending a message to whoever *was* in possession of the valuables they were after."

"Evidently Miss Agatha's mother didn't get the message."

Holmes shook his head, sitting thoughtfully on the bed. "I think she did. I believe that is why they were unable to find the item – or items – on her. She must have hidden her treasure once she knew it was at risk."

"There was no place to hide it in her little flat. Perhaps Agatha knows of some of her mother's common haunts, places where she could put items away temporarily."

Holmes shook his head again. "I think the answer is much simpler. From the scratches on her hands and legs, we can presume she came here, entering through the window. Perhaps following the path of our killers."

"But why would she follow them? Do you think she was investigating them in some way?"

"No, I believe she came here for a much more ingenious reason. Where is the perfect place to hide something that you know others have been looking for?"

I had to think a second before it became obvious. "You believe she returned here and hid the item because she knew they wouldn't return to a place they had already searched?"

"Clever, hmm?"

He stood and lifted the flat mattress. Finding nothing, he began to shake out the bedding. I looked in Harper's discarded bag and then picked up one of the well-worn books: *Moby Dick.*

I ruffled through the novel and then felt my mouth fall open in shock. I stared mutely down at the papers that had been stuffed in the pages of the book.

"Holmes," I started, "I believe I found what we're looking for." I looked up as he took the two strides that brought him next to me. "Bearer bonds," I explained, removing them and letting the book drop to the ground. "Nearly one-thousand pounds worth of bearer bonds."

Holmes snatched some of them from me in excitement. "That'll do it," he murmured gleefully. "I wonder if Harper stole these from his dead captain."

"There's a letter here," I pointed out, showing him the small note handwritten on a cheap piece of paper. We read it together:

Dear Alice,

> *I cannot tell you how happy I was to see you last. The few days we spent together reminded me of when we were young and so ignorantly in love. I have always loved you, even after all these years. I understand why you did not tell me of Agatha. It stung to know you had kept my daughter from me, but when you explained you were only trying to avoid making me feel obligated, I knew you were a kind-hearted woman. Too kind, though. I would not have felt trapped. I would have done whatever I could to know her, care for her. I missed so much of her life, but from what you told me, she is a lovely, smart girl. And she knows how to read and write! My love, I cannot thank you enough for that blessing.*

135

I have the means to repay you for all you have struggled alone. My captain and friend fell very ill very suddenly on our last voyage. I stayed with him until his final breath. He was a simple man, at home at the sea, with no remaining family. As it became clear he was not long for this world, he told me a great secret. His grandfather, before he died, had passed onto him wealth in the form of bonds worth £980. Pattins – that was my friend's name – had no use for it. His home was The Seafarer, *his happiness the sea. He kept the notes in his safe, unsure what to do with them and possessing no kin to which to pass them. As he lay dying, he had me unlock this safe and told me to take them – that I had served him well and been like a son to him.*

I cannot tell you what a shock it was to have such wealth in my grasp. I instantly thought of Agatha, of you, and how I could save both of you from a life of dreadful servitude to others.

The day's journey back to land after his death were harrowing. I had to keep the bonds on me and knew that I could find myself in the depths of the sea if the other men discovered what I possessed. Two of them, Watkins and Quill, seemed suspicious. I hardly know how they could have learned of the bonds – perhaps the scoundrels were listening in somehow – but in any case, I sensed they were watching me. I am trying to stay out of sight, but I fear they may be on my heels.

I'm giving you the bonds. Please pass them to Agatha – I know she is safe with that fancy doctor of hers. Once I feel I am not being shadowed any longer, I will come to you. I wish to meet my daughter and be a part of her life. I wish to be a part of yours as well, but I will leave that decision up to you.

Be on guard.

All my love,
Jack

"I hardly think the man would have guessed all this would lead to his death, as well as the death of the mother of his child," Holmes said sadly. "The gross injustices people will commit for a little bit of money will never cease to dismay me."

"You realize," I pointed out, "that two people have died for these, and now we have them in our hands?"

136

Holmes plucked the letter from my grasp, folding it in with the bearer bonds and tucking the bundle into his pocket.

"I'm aware of that perilous fact," he said with entirely too much liveliness in his voice. "So I think it in our best interest to remove ourselves to Harley Street as soon as possible. I can send one of my Irregulars to Scotland Yard with the name of our two men, as well as directions to find Mark Ingels so he may provide a description. You have your revolver with you?"

"No, I do not," I answered testily. "I don't carry a firearm everywhere."

He *tsk*'ed. "No worries, I have my trusted walking stick and its secret blade, but I don't think we will be molested. The men have no reason to have eyes on this room now that they've killed Harper."

Holmes was correct, and we managed our journey with no dastardly interference. I had no doubt the house on Harley Street was being watched, our ruthless murderers on the lookout for any opportunity to grab the girl again. I shuddered to think of Agatha in the hands of men who weren't above torturing a woman. The quicker she cashed these bonds and secured the funds as hers, the quicker she would be out of harm's way.

Paxton once again let us in what that solemnity that seemed out of place on his relatively youthful face. We waited in the sitting room until Chambers entered and greeted us. An extremely fluffy calico cat followed him in, curling up on the divan like a queen.

"I'm so pleased to see you," he said, shaking our hands vigorously. "I hope you have news. I canceled all my patients today so as not to leave Agatha alone. Paxton is a hardy fellow, but two men are better than one, and I wouldn't have been able to concentrate on my work separated and unsure of what was happening."

I held back a smile, wondering if he knew how obvious his feelings were.

"We have plunged to the heart of the matter," Holmes reassured. "I can answer all her questions and furnish Miss Davis a pleasant surprise, if she will see me."

I understood the implication, but Chambers merely nodded and made haste to fetch her. I was thankful she had clearly kept her revelations about Holmes to herself, another mark of her fine character.

When the doctor returned with her, Agatha entered with much more reserve than usual. She clasped her hands and nodded stiffly, avoiding direct eye contact with either of us.

"Sirs," was all she said in greeting.

Holmes seemed unsure how to proceed for a moment. Glancing at Chambers, he chose to ignore the elephant in the room and barreled through with the mystery at hand.

"Miss Davis," he started, voice patently matter-of-fact, "I'm happy to tell you that we have discovered the motive for your mother's murder." He gave her a succinct overview of Harper's account, leaving out the letter or any reference to Agatha's mother.

"You see," he finished, "his captain had passed on a sort of inheritance, but the nature of the bearer bonds, being so similar to cash, put him in a perilous position. It is why he was killed and hung so publicly. You heard of this in the paper?"

She frowned. "I did, but I'm not sure why this story would interest me, frankly. Did you come here to brag of another case you solved instead of my mother's?"

Holmes visibly recoiled at the venom in her words. "No," he assured softly, "The two events are connected. Forgive my lack of brevity. Perhaps Jack Harper can explain better than I can." He removed the letter and with a careful air of respect passed it to her.

We all waited as she read, watching her face transform from confusion to shock. Long after I knew she was finished reading, she stared down at the words with a distant look in her eye.

At last, she raised her head and peered intently at Holmes. "So my Mum did die for me? She was so desperate that I receive this gift that she refused to tell them where it was?"

Holmes nodded. "Your father too. He didn't know you, but as you can see, that did not dull his love for you. I know, if given a choice, you would trade these pieces of paper for your parents, but the knowledge that you were that cared for I hope provides some solace."

I handed her the bonds. Chambers looked over her shoulder, clearly interested in making sure they were authentic.

"I will get these transferred to an account at The Bank of England under her name," he assured us. "I'll make sure the money is secured so no one may access the funds but Agatha."

With unquestioning trust, Agatha handed the bonds to him. "And the men that killed my Mum?" she asked.

"We know their names," Holmes explained, "and a shipmate of your father's can provide their descriptions. I will notify Scotland Yard immediately. We will secure the ports to be sure they cannot slip away on another ship." He paused as if unsure what else to say. Abruptly, he concluded, "You're a woman of some means now, Agatha. I sincerely wish you the best in your life."

He nodded at her, then at Chambers, turning to leave. I made to follow, but he stopped suddenly and turned, looking resigned. "Dr. Chambers, I know it may seem a bit improper, but would you allow me to speak to Miss Davis alone for a moment?"

The doctor looked surprised but nodded, evidently loathe to deny Holmes his request after the service he had provided. "You can step into the dining room here," he pointed to an adjoining room.

Holmes glanced at Agatha for permission. I thought she would refuse, but she went willingly into the next room. Holmes closed the door, leaving the doctor and me standing in confused silence.

"Do you know what that's about?" he asked me bluntly after some time had passed.

"I suspect I do," I admitted, "but it isn't my place to say anything."

"I see."

"Speaking of not my place," I began hesitantly, "I hope you'll forgive my forwardness, but Agatha's station in life has just made a turn for the better. Perhaps her circumstances may change in another area as well?" I suggested.

He reddened. "I am that obvious? Well, no need to urge me, Dr. Watson. I have been considering it for some time. I'm not the boldest or most confident of men when it comes to things of that sort."

"I think you may be confident. I do have some experience in this, and I believe she reciprocates your feelings."

He looked relieved, but merely nodded.

The door to the dining room opened and our two companions emerged. The air wasn't antagonistic, though Holmes was a bit flush. He jerked his chin down in a quick goodbye to our host, beckoning me to follow.

"Thank you, Mr. Holmes. You as well, Dr. Watson," Agatha said softly to our backs. I hesitate to say it was forgiveness I heard in her voice, but something close to it. I turned and bid her goodbye, pleased at the look of gentleness on her face.

As we regained the kerb, I asked Holmes what he had said to her.

"What needed to be said, Watson," he replied curtly, "and that's all you'll ever know. Now come along. I have a sudden need for my pipe and some peace and quiet."

The Adventure of the
Stolen Savant
by Tracy J. Revels

"Watson? Watson, wake up!"

A rough grasp on my shoulder and a firm shake expelled me from the delights of dreamland. I rolled over with a scowl and found Holmes looming above me, his long face made spectral by the yellow light of a candle.

"Good Lord, what – ?" I managed to glance at the watch that rested upon my nightstand. "It's barely five a.m.!"

"And yet it has already been a lengthy day for our friend in the official forces," Holmes said briskly. "We are needed, and there is not a moment to lose. A child's life is at stake. Into your clothes in five minutes, or you shall be left behind."

It was not so much an invitation as an order, and my friend's tone alarmed me. Without hesitation, I flung off the covers and dressed, meeting Holmes at the door, where a carriage driven by a constable waited.

"You were wise to add the scarf," Holmes said. "A cold wind is blowing. Watson. You recall Inspector Bradstreet?"

I offered my hand to the stalwart officer who shared the vehicle with us. He was a large and dignified man, who I remembered from a number of Holmes's cases. I was shocked to see that his hair and beard were nearly white, an uncomfortable reminder of the passage of time since he had watched Holmes wash the beggar Hugh Boone's face or travelled with us to Eryford in the matter of the engineer who barely escaped a gruesome death inside a hydraulic press. Bradstreet was a regular visitor at Baker Street, along with his colleagues Lestrade and Gregson.

"I am grateful for your assistance," Bradstreet said. "I regret evicting gentlemen from nice snug beds on such a morning, especially when my knees tell me we should have rain or snow by midday – it's a damned thing, getting old." He nodded towards Holmes. "You'll want the whole story, I know, and I think I should just have time to give it to you before we reach Brompton. Have you ever heard of 'The Girl Savant'?"

"Yes, but it was some years ago," Holmes said, while I confessed ignorance of the title or personage who bore it. Bradstreet leaned back, swaying with the rough movements. Our driver had clearly been given instructions not to spare his horse.

"She first appeared on the stage at the tender age of six," Bradstreet said. "Her name is Phoebe Clarke, and she is the daughter of Professor Adolphus Clarke, late of Camford University."

"The professor's area of specialty?" Holmes asked.

"Hanged if I know. Does it matter?"

"All things might matter," Holmes said, "but pray continue."

"I believe it was one of the sciences – astronomy or physics. Clarke was, like most professors, distinguished by his mind rather than his pocketbook. In fact, it was not until his daughter began achieving notoriety that he was able to retire from his classroom and elevate his family to a comfortable home in Brompton, in the very shadow of the great cemetery. The girl had an astonishing ability to perform calculations instantaneously. One might shout out a half-dozen ten-digit numbers, then demand they be added together and divided by nine, and in a twinkling, she would call back the answer, while a skilled accountant would need a minute or more to work the figure out on his paper. She was inevitably correct. Thus, her billing as the 'Girl Savant', and what began as an amusing parlor trick for her family became a career, leading to a command performance at Windsor when the child was nine. She is thirteen now, and her repertoire includes solving complex equations, including baffling calculus problems, on a chalkboard.

"Naturally, some suspected trickery – but none was proven. The child has been examined by dozens of physicians and alienists, all of whom have pronounced her the most incredible natural mathematician of the century. It is she, gentlemen, who has been abducted."

Holmes pulled out his cigarette case. Bradstreet accepted the offer with a grateful sigh. I could tell he was terribly fatigued.

"The message came to the police at three this morning. By good fortune, I reached the scene with two constables a half-hour later. I found the house in an uproar: The governess sick and distraught, still half-drugged. The mother screeching and pleading with God for mercy, and the father grim and white-faced, saying the ransom was beyond his means. The cook and the butler claimed to know nothing. There was an open window at the rear of the house, a set of man's footprints in the mud of the backyard, and the little girl gone missing. Oh – and this most remarkable letter was left behind."

The inspector pulled out a folded sheet of stationery and opened a small lantern on the seat. Holmes first lifted the paper to his nose, then glanced at the scribbled words.

"Written by a woman who wishes to disguise her hand. Surely you caught the whiff of perfume upon the paper?"

141

Bradstreet nodded. "Yes, but it could have easily been contaminated with perfume by virtue of being shuffled by Mrs. Clarke while she was reading it. I am more intrigued by the words than the odor."

"As am I," Holmes agreed. "Watson, will you read it?"

I scowled. I might as well have been decoding a cipher, but at last I was able to read the following aloud:

Dear Professor Clarke,

We are the minions of Aka Manah, Lord of the Dark Places, and followers of The Way of Death. Heed what we say if you wish to see your precious child again! We have her securely bound in the Underworld, and The Clock of Destruction is ticking.

You will take £5,422, all in new notes, and place the money in a blue bag. It must be blue, not black or grey, or we will know you do not keep faith with us. You must not alert the police, or we will know you do not keep faith with us. Bring the bag to the tomb of the Egyptian queens at noon and leave it as an offering. Return home and wait. When we are satisfied, we shall release the girl – but not before. Disobey us and we shall behead her, or burn her at the stake, or fling her from the cliffs at Dover. The manner of her death is commanded by Aka Manah, if you displease us.

Professor, you are reckoned a smart man – Now you must prove it!

"My word!" I gasped. "This is horrific!"

"It's nonsense," Holmes snapped.

"Madness," Bradstreet agreed. "Clearly the work of a lunatic . . . or two, or three, for it speaks of '*we*'."

Holmes took the paper back. "Yet it is oddly specific. And what a strange ransom."

"The man cannot raise it in a day's time," Bradstreet said.

Holmes waved his hand in annoyance. "I direct you to the figure! What abductor asks for five-thousand-four-hundred-and-twenty-two pounds? Surely even a madman can round his digits. There must be some significance to this number." Holmes folded the paper neatly and, with Bradstreet's permission, slipped it into the pocket of his coat. "Tell me how they claim the crime occurred."

"The child and her governess share a single bedroom. The governess, a Miss Harper, sleeps on a cot by the window. The pair retired at nine. The

142

parents' bedroom is in the opposite wing of the house, and they doused their lights at their usual hour of ten. The butler and housekeeper – Charles and Edith Wilson by name – worked at their chores until midnight, then went to their rooms which are just above the parents' chamber, on the second floor. There was nothing but peace and repose until just before three, when the governess began to scream and came staggering down the hallway in a half-swoon, saying Miss Phoebe had been taken. Indeed, the girl's bed was empty, and this note was found upon the staircase. Everyone flew about the house, searching, but Wilson had the presence of mind to notice that a kitchen window had been forced open. The ground in the yard was muddied from rain in the early evening, and it easily captured the impression of boot marks – I have already sent out for plaster."

"Only one set?" Holmes asked.

"Yes."

"Leading away from the house?"

"Yes."

"And none arriving?"

Bradstreet appeared suddenly flushed. His face turned rosy. "I did not see any. But perhaps the villain came from another direction, where he left no trace."

"Were any other windows found open?"

"No . . . and Wilson swears that the kitchen door, like all the others, was still bolted from inside. I confess that struck me as odd. Why not simply unlatch the door to exit, rather than scrambling through an open window with unconscious or perhaps struggling girl? Maybe there was a confederate, and he passed her along to him."

"Not an impossible conundrum to resolve," Holmes agreed. "But why did the family dog not bark? It's difficult for me to imagine a large home without a guardian canine."

If Bradstreet heard the sudden bite of sarcasm in my friend's tone, he was cool enough not to acknowledge it.

"I had meant to ask. I saw a chain and a collar on the ground but no animal. I thought perhaps the thief had stolen the dog as well."

Holmes barely suppressed a sigh. "What did the governess have to say?"

"Her testimony is that at around one in the morning, she awoke to find a man standing over her. He was – wait, let me be precise – " Bradstreet pulled out a little notebook and flipped several pages:

A tall man, with broad shoulders, dressed all in black. He had a mask all around his head and his nose, with his bright eyes peering through. He looked like an executioner from an old

143

*painting. His big hand was suddenly over my mouth, and he
bent down and popped the cork from a little bottle he held. He
pressed his face to my ear and whispered to me in French. He
had long side whiskers, and they scratched my cheek when he
spoke:* "Buvez ou la fillette va mourir!"

"'*Drink this or the little girl dies,*'" Holmes murmured. Bradstreet
nodded and continued:

*I had no choice. I swallowed down a nasty draught, and in
seconds the world began to fade. I tried to whisper for him not
to harm her, but my lips were numb. When I woke up, an hour
later, the bed was empty, and I began to scream.*

I shook my head in dismay. Inspector Bradstreet slipped his notebook
back into his pocket.

"That is all she could tell. I asked if any strangers or mysterious
figures had been seen about the home, but none were noticed. I inquired if
the household had a routine, one that a criminal might come to know. It
seems the professor travels a bit, giving lectures and taking Miss Phoebe
out to perform, but these excursions are less frequent, as a thirteen-year-
old phenomenon is much less remarkable than a six-year-old. Mrs. Clarke
is an invalid, and largely confined to a rolling chair, so she rarely ventures
out. The housekeeper and butler do the marketing. Miss Harper said that
she and her charge take an afternoon walk in pleasant weather, but the hour
and location vary according to their whims. I wonder . . . ."

Bradstreet's face turned grim. "She mentioned they stroll in the
cemetery and on the village heath. There are so many tramps and
vagabonds these days, sleeping rough among the tombs. Perhaps one of
those rascals laid eyes upon the girl."

"And conveniently penned such a remarkable ransom note?" Holmes
asked. "And spoke fluent French? It seems more likely that Professor
Clarke has some enemy."

"He could not think of any in particular, though I suppose like any
teacher he must have a legion of students who have vowed vengeance
upon him."

"What about the mother?" I asked. "Could this be some horrible plot
to hurt her?"

Bradstreet lowered his chin. His voice was barely above a whisper.

"I wondered the same thing. I was able to get the butler aside for a
few moments, and he revealed that these waters may be even deeper and
darker than they appear upon the surface."

144

Holmes had been staring out in the carriage window in an almost distracted manner. Now he turned, one brow elevated.

"How so?"

"Mrs. Amelia Clarke is the professor's second wife. His first spouse, the mother of his son Chester, committed suicide by leaping from a bridge when Chester was just seven years old. The youth has always believed his mother was driven to her death by his father's meanness. Clarke scandalously married his current wife less than a year after his first spouse died, and their daughter was born just five months after the wedding. Chester despises his stepmother, though the butler claims Chester has never been openly unkind to his half-sister. The youth has spent most of his life in boarding schools, and is currently completing his studies at Camford."

"He is not living in the home?"

Bradstreet shifted uncomfortably. "He visited two days ago. According to Wilson, there was an undignified squabble between father and son, and Chester departed with his personal effects, vowing never to set foot in the house again. But Wilson also told me, in a nervous rush, that he thought he glimpsed Chester in a local market yesterday afternoon, conversing with a rough-looking man." The inspector shook his head. "I feel as if I have slipped into a nest of vipers, Mr. Holmes, and I fear that if I err, the child may be killed. I hope you shall have better luck than I did, in the wee hours, in separating lies from truth and rescuing Miss Phoebe."

A short time later, we arrived at the Clarke home. As my friend had surmised, it was a large and pretentious dwelling, set comfortably back from Old Brompton Road, shaded by pleasant oaks and elms, and surrounded by a seven-foot-high wrought-iron fence.

"Another mystery," Bradstreet confessed, as we turned onto a gravel path. "Wilson swore the gate was locked when he ran out looking for the child. While it would not be impossible for an active man to scale the fence, he might think twice when considering those spikes. Nor could he easily slip between the posts. I'm beginning to think a ghost out of the cemetery next door stole the girl away."

Holmes did not dignify the statement with a response. Our carriage halted before the front door, and I considered the massive structure. It was built to resemble a Tudor mansion, but was clearly of modern construction and convenience. A constable stood at the doorway.

"Lloyd, I presume there has been no change since I left?" Bradstreet asked his man. "No further messages from abductors?"

"No, sir. However . . . we did our best to keep them all inside, as you said, but . . . Well, sir, Professor Clarke insisted on traipsing about the house, calling out for his daughter, as if he expected to find her hiding in the walls. Mrs. Clarke got to wailing and then . . . ."

"Out with it!" Bradstreet rumbled.

"The young gent, Mr. Chester, came running in, about ten minutes ago. He and his father went into the study. They have been shouting at each other nonstop and – "

The sharp retort of a pistol interrupted the officer's report. We instinctively jerked in response, but then the stalwart Bradstreet put his head down and charged like a bull. We were fortunate he had become familiar with the home's plan, for it was quite the labyrinth of hallways, odd niches, and sudden turns. We smelled gunpowder just as we reached the first-floor landing. The doorway to the study was open, and a young man stood in the hallway.

"You will not kill me as easily as you did my mother!" he shouted.

"And I shall not be extorted!" a thin voice screeched. "What have you done with your sister?"

Chester Clarke whirled at our approach, throwing up his hands. Bradstreet caught the youngster by his collar and dragged him back inside the study. Holmes quickly snatched the pistol away from the professor's trembling hand, sparing us from possible injury.

"This is disgraceful!" Bradstreet snorted, as I closed the door. "An innocent child is in danger, and you two bicker and brandish weapons? I will thank you to answer my questions honestly, or I will haul you in for disturbing the peace!"

The professor, a thin, sallow-faced man with a small fringe of white, wispy hair about his head, whimpered and collapsed into the chair behind his desk. He pointed a skeletal finger at us as his son dropped into the window seat and carelessly lit a cigarette.

"Who are these men?" he croaked at Bradstreet.

"They are the consultants of whom I spoke."

"My name is Sherlock Holmes," my friend said, "and this is my associate, Dr. John Watson. We have some experience in similar matters, and our discretion may be relied upon. The inspector has given us the gist of the matter. I fear our questions may make you uncomfortable, Professor Clarke, but without them, there is no hope for the return of your daughter."

"There's hardly the need for such drama," the younger man snorted. "Phoebe is probably locked in the attic or bound beneath the boards in a shed. The abduction is Father's doing! I would stake my life upon it."

The elder Clarke waved a clenched fist at his son. "How dare you! It is *you* who is the thief – who has stolen even our family dog and my best boots, and now you have taken you sister, to try to cheat me of my money!"

146

Holmes held out both hands for silence, then nodded to Chester. "Why do you accuse your father of this crime?"

"Because he is a desperate man who is running out of time to settle his debts. Phoebe's performances have dried up. Her novelty has worn thin. Without the money from her shows, my esteemed father will find himself in a deeper pit than he was before, when he stole my inheritance and spent it on that tramp he married."

"The money was not your mother's to bequeath."

"It was her legacy to me!" Chester cried as he rose from his seat. He was a handsome youth, with dark brown hair, long side-whiskers, and almost golden eyes, which now blazed with fratricidal fury. "My mother had funds she inherited from her maiden aunt. Before she died – driven to self-destruction by Father's cruelty and unfaithfulness – she wrote a letter to me, saying goodbye and bequeathing me her legacy. Father hid the note and never gave me what Mother wished me to have."

"You were a child!" the professor sneered. "Those words would only have caused you greater grief. And as for an inheritance: Your mother never made a will, so the law was on my side. I think I have done well-enough for you."

Chester shook his head and stepped forward, but Bradstreet's hand upon his arm prevented further violence.

"I found the note two days ago, while cleaning out some old drawers," the young man said. "I confronted Father with it. I freely admit that we quarreled, and I took everything I valued from this house, with the intention of never setting foot in it again, when I saw how profoundly I had been cheated."

"Did your items of value include the dog?" Holmes asked. The young man started.

"Why yes, I took old Melbourne – I raised him from a pup, and Father had nearly starved the poor beast while I was at school."

"You took my best boots, too!" Clarke shouted.

Chester shook his head. "I don't know what you're talking about. I had no interest in your footwear, only in my faithful hound. Melbourne is why I have't yet left London – the house where I board in Camford will not allow a pet, and I had to look up an old chum to see if I might let the rascal live with him, until I can find another lodging. I spent some time catching up with my friend, and it was he who spotted the constables lurking at the gate this morning and alerted me that something was amiss. Now I come in to find my stepsister kidnapped, and in such an improbable manner. Mark my words, Mr. Holmes, you have no need to look any further than right before you to find the fiend who took her."

"You are an ungrateful wretch!" the youth's father snapped.

Chester Clarke turned to Bradstreet. "Am I under arrest, Officer?"

I saw Holmes give the slightest shake of his head. Bradstreet coughed.

"No, but we will need more of an accounting of your whereabouts last night. And you must remain in London until this matter is resolved."

"Fair enough. You may ask my friend, Tobias Grey, where I was all evening, for I have not left his company since I met him in the market yesterday morning. If his word is not good enough, then you make speak to the publican of The Hat and Horse Inn. We stayed there until just after two this morning, socializing with some of the locals." He pulled a notebook from his coat and scribbled down his friend's address. "Please find Phoebe," he said, his words directed to my friend. "She is a good girl. I bear her no ill will, despite her disgraceful origin." He started for the door, then whirled at the threshold. "One more thing: Father recited the contents of the note – how it referenced demons. Look at Father's bookshelf. You will find his light reading most illuminating to your case!"

With that, the young man made his exit. I noted how the professor had slipped further and further down into his seat, growing grey about his mouth.

"I fear . . . I must be ill," he muttered, and staggered from the room on quivering legs. Bradstreet indicated he would follow. Meanwhile, Holmes walked over to the bookshelf behind the desk, running his nervous fingers along the spines of antique volumes. Following his example, I made a quick study of the room, noting the many framed commendations and testimonials to Clarke's daughter's talents. In pride of place was a signed letter from the Queen, calling Miss Phoebe "*a wonderously bright child*".

"What are you finding?" I asked Holmes.

"A keen interest in the occult," my friend said. "These are works on mythology and pagan practices. Here is the *Malleus Maleficarum* – the *Hammer of Witches*, in an early English edition. Our professor is quite the collector." He pulled down another book and flipped through the pages. "We assumed our kidnappers had simply plucked nonsensical letters from the air. But here I see that Aka Manah is a devil in the Zoroastrian tradition – a fiend of evil thinking who prevents mortals from fulfilling their moral duties. A charming fellow, no doubt."

"A most obscure reference."

"Indeed." Holmes reshelved the book and looked about the desk. He plucked up a silver-framed photograph. "Our victim, we may presume."

The girl was not an attractive child. Her hair hung in lank braids, and her eyes were overly large and protruding. She stared directly at the camera with a kind of defiance that her meek posture, with folded hands and slumped shoulders, belied.

"Forgive me," the professor said as he re-entered the library, still daubing at his lips with a handkerchief. "Dealing with Chester is never pleasant and this . . . My God, I do believe he is somehow responsible, and is trying to see that I am blamed. My reputation will be in tatters."

"Professor Clarke, did he speak truthfully about the state of your finances?" Holmes asked. The elderly man fell into his chair, slumping down as if battered by a fearsome opponent. Holmes walked around the desk and settled where he could face Clarke. My friend's gaze was firm, with little hint of sympathy. "If you truly wish us to find your daughter before some evil befalls her, you must not prevaricate."

Clarke hissed out air, and my doctor's ears heard an unhealthy wheeze. I looked closer at his color, the way his hands shook. The professor was clearly in poor health, and perhaps not long for this world.

"Chester speaks truthfully. I have never had much wisdom with money, and when Phoebe became famous, I over-extended us. This house bears a heavy mortgage, and my wife's medical care has been expensive. I should never have abandoned my chair at the university, for now they will not have me back. They claim I have become a 'carnival man' because of how I promoted Phoebe's natural gifts."

"Is your child's life insured?" Holmes asked. What small dollop of color remained in the professor's face leached away.

"Yes, of course. There was so much travel, especially when she was small, I felt it necessary. My life is insured as well."

Holmes nodded. "What of Chester's claim: That you deprived him of his maternal inheritance?"

"Foolishness! Yes, Margaret wrote that note, and I was a fool for not destroying it! I suppose I kept it because I feared, at the time, that Chester might someday blame himself for his mother's rash act. It was the only way to prove otherwise."

"And her legacy? Did it amount to five-thousand-four-hundred-and-twenty-two pounds?"

The professor flinched as if jabbed with a stiletto. "Exactly."

Holmes instructed Clarke to remain in his study while we walked about the house and grounds and spoke with the servants. The maid and butler had little to tell us, though Holmes put an astonishing question to Wilson just as we rose to leave the room.

"Has your master always had a strong interest in the occult?"

"Sir? You mean – "

"Witches, demons, supernatural events?"

149

The butler shook his head. "Ah, I see you have looked upon that shelf in his room. No, sir, the professor is a man of science. But his father was a vicar who was fascinated by the persecutions of King James I, and had many volumes on that subject."

"Ah. I noticed they were shelved rather high. I had to stretch to pull a book from its perch."

"That was my doing," Mrs. Wilson chirped. "I caught Miss Phoebe reading one of them and thought it unhealthy for a girl – all those dark and morbid stories. I did not think her imagination needed to be excited by such!"

Holmes thank the pair and together we followed Bradstreet to the nursery, where Miss Harper, the governess, had been asked to remain. We opened the door to a most remarkable scene, for the room might as well have been the cell of a monk. It lacked lacy curtains, or a fancy bedstead, or even a polished armoire, and instead of delightful pictures, the walls were hung with chalkboards, upon which equations were worked. There were no dolls or picture books, no toys of any kind. The single vanity bore only a comb and brush, and both the governesses and her charge's clothing hung on hooks. Two poorly covered cots completed the room's decorations. A prisoner in Dartmoor might have found his chamber more charming.

Miss Harper rose as we entered. She was pale and thin, with her dark hair pulled into a tight knot at the back of her head. Her only ornament was a *pince-nez* that hung from a silver chain at the waist of her dress. She lifted it, peering at us with the expression of the hopelessly myopic.

"Miss Harper," Holmes said, "I am sorry for the terrible fright you have endured, and I will put only a few questions to you."

"I will answer a thousand, sir, if they will return my bright one to me."

"How long have you had charge of the girl?"

"Since she was five. Her parents noted her precocious ways very early, and felt she should have a teacher rather than a nurse."

"I see. You inspired her capacity with numbers?"

The young woman shook her head. "No, sir, that was all her natural gift. I fear I struggle even with simple algebra. My job has been to advance her in reading, writing, and an appreciation of literature, as well as to tutor her in modern languages. Miss Phoebe, I am proud to say, is quite fluent in French, Spanish, and Italian, as well as English."

"The child's abductor spoke French to you – I presume quite crudely."

"Oh no, sir. His accent was perfect, like a gentleman's."

Holmes walked over to the chalkboard, his keen gaze running across the figures. He jabbed a finger in mid-equation.

"I see an error here. Perhaps the child is losing her gifts."

Miss Harper hurried to his side, donning her glasses and peering at the digits on the board. She shook her head briskly.

"No – no, forgive me for saying it, Mr. Holmes, but you are mistaken! The problem has been solved correctly."

"But the five here – "

"Do calculate again."

Holmes smiled slyly. "I . . . Indeed! My apologies to your charge." He turned and lifted an eyebrow. "But this is advanced calculus, a conundrum that would give even its inventor Sir Isaac Newton a headache. You said you are limited in mathematical faculties."

The lady blushed from her chin to her forehead. "Miss Phoebe has been instructing me. She is a gifted teacher. I confess it embarrasses me to take lessons from one so young, but it brings her great pleasure. So little does these days, I would be cruel to deny it to her."

"And what is the nature of her unhappiness?"

The lady removed her spectacles. She twisted them violently in her hands. I feared they would snap.

"You will likely be discharged," Holmes prodded, "and blamed for losing the child. Your only hope lies in total honesty, Miss Harper."

A single tear slipped down the young woman's cheek. "I fear . . . Phoebe's parents do not love her. Professor Clarke has been cold and sharp with her ever since the requests for her to perform began to taper off, and Mrs. Clarke rarely emerges from her sickroom. It was clear that Phoebe's labors supported the family, and even financed Master Chester's education at university. Miss Phoebe is quiet and reserved. She rarely speaks unless rattling off numbers. I know her better than her parents do, and I know she takes everyone's welfare to heart. I hear her when she cries at night. You will never meet a more gifted, yet sadder, child."

Holmes thanked the governess, assuring her the girl would be found safely. Miss Harper nodded, but as we exited, she curled back upon her cot, and began to weep copiously.

Inspector Bradstreet waited outside the door. He unfolded his arms and inclined his head.

"Well?"

"An intriguing interview," Holmes replied. "It has given me the idea that – Good Lord!"

The exclamation was inspired by a specter, a thin wraith clad only in a long white gown, who was racing down the hallway. We realized in an instant that it was Mrs. Clarke, who we had been told was insensible in her room, heavily sedated. She lunged at us, her hair loose and wild, her mouth an oval pit that emitted hideous moans. She would have toppled, but Bradstreet stepped forward and caught her in his arms.

"Madame, please – you must rest."

"He has the money!" the woman's cry was a banshee wail that echoed in the stately house. "Adolphus has it – It is mine – my dowry! He swears he has never touched it, that it was laid aside for Phoebe, when she wed! Make him pay! Oh, my dear girl! Sirs – make him pay the ransom. Do not allow him to sacrifice my child!"

"Watson, your expertise is needed," Holmes said. The lady had suddenly gone limp in the inspector's grasp. Bradstreet carried her back to her room. Her screams had brought the governess and housekeeper running to the scene and, with their aid, I was able to make Mrs. Clarke comfortable. I administered another mild sedative before leaving the overwrought lady to her employees' care. Afterward, I found Holmes, Bradstreet, and the professor back in the study.

"Ah," Holmes said. "And how is Mrs. Clarke?"

"Resting, for the moment. She was most insistent that the ransom be raised, without delay."

Professor Clarke dropped his head. "It is impossible. There is no money."

"Because you spent it?" Holmes asked.

"On necessary things," Clarke snapped. "Things that a woman would not understand!"

"I presume you keep an account book?" Holmes said, and the miserable man gestured to a red-leather volume on his desk. Holmes nodded to the inspector.

"Bradstreet, I think the best course of action is for us to divide our labors. If you will escort the professor to his bank, perhaps your presence will encourage the officials to advance him a loan. Without some sign of good faith, it will be impossible to retrieve his daughter."

"And what will you do, Mr. Holmes?"

My friend smiled.

"I believe Watson and I shall take a walk amid the tombstones."

Bradstreet and Clarke departed via the front door, while Holmes and I exited through the kitchen. Holmes paused for a moment to study the open window, inspecting the sill with his lens. As the butler had sworn, the door to the yard was still tightly fastened, and in fact was quite stubborn to unlatch. We moved into the yard, where a series of footprints were clearly visible in the muddy ground.

"Most singular, are they not?" Holmes asked.

I considered the tracks before me. They appeared to have been made by a man's square-toed boot, but they were admittedly irregular, and often at odd angles.

"He did not have an even stride," I observed. "But that might be explained if he was bearing an unconscious or bound child flung across his shoulders."

"You scintillate today, Watson."

It was not the tone of a compliment. I lifted an eyebrow, but Holmes did not elaborate on why he was mocking me.

"Is there anything else I should note?" I asked.

"Only the time. It's just now eleven in the morning. I wonder which of my cases holds the record for being resolved most expediently? This one will certainly stand among the finalists in that category."

"But you have not found the girl!"

"I have not produced her. I found her much earlier." he said, tapping his forehead. "*Here.*"

"If you know where she is, then go to her!" I fished into my coat pocket and drew out my army revolver. "We shall deal with these monsters as they deserve!"

"Your firearm will not be necessary, old friend. Come, let us complete our mission before the snow falls. Inspector Bradstreet's knee is a sure predictor."

Indeed, the clouds were dark and heavy, hanging in a threatening manner above our heads. Holmes led me across the street and into the vast Brompton Cemetery. The white marble tombs seemed even more spectral with such a gloomy sky above us, and visitors were few. Holmes hummed softly to himself, pausing only long enough to inquire of an aged sexton where a certain notable tomb was located. As we approached it, we passed a group of young ladies, clearly foreign tourists with oversized wraps and massive hats. They were chattering happily in Italian.

"Ah, now this is a singular bit of luck," Holmes said. "Wait here for a moment."

I did as he commanded, watching as he approached the little flock of ladies. Holmes tipped his hat, gave a courtly bow, and spoke to the women in their own language. After a moment's consultation, the youngest of the party – a strikingly lovely girl, with black hair and mischievous eyes – returned on Holmes's arm.

"Doctor Watson, may I have the pleasure of presenting Signorina Alessa Bernardi, from Milan? She will assist us in bringing this strange incident to a satisfactory conclusion."

I greeted the lady with my limited Italian, which only served to make her giggle. We walked another one-hundred paces, with her fellows trailing a safe distance behind, before Holmes stopped at a massive, Egyptian-style mausoleum. He motioned Signorina Bernardi forward, and she lifted her voice in a sharp cry.

"*Cara Phoebe, vieni fuori!*"

For an instant, nothing happened. The lady was about to repeat her call when, much to my surprise, the door of the mausoleum creaked open. Our linguist gave a cry and ran back to her friends. Together they made a frightened dash down the cemetery's main avenue, towards the exit. A small head peered through the gap in the mausoleum's portal, and would just as quickly have vanished, had not my friend possessed the reflexes of a cat. He caught the girl by one of her dark braids and pulled her forward, into the wane afternoon light.

"Miss Phoebe Clarke, I presume? Yes, I would know you by your boots."

I looked down. The child was clad in a simple black frock, and wrapped in a checkered blanket, but on her feet were oversized men's boots, which flopped about and made it difficult for her to struggle in Holmes's grasp.

"We are not here to harm you," Holmes said. "But you have given your family a terrible fright and placed your governess in great danger of being arrested for a crime. Surely you do not wish Miss Harper to pay the penalty for your tantrum?"

The girl twisted. Her voice was soft, but oddly deep.

"There is no need to be dramatic!"

Holmes chuckled. "Fine words, coming from a little lady who so expertly staged her own abduction. There is a tea shop just beyond the gate. Let us go there, where it's more comfortable, and we shall hear your side of this most-amazing story."

A short while later, we were seated in comfortable chairs in the warm and cozy establishment. It was clear to me that despite her blanket and heavy frock, the child had suffered from the chill and needed food. She sat with her head hung down, sullen and refusing to speak. I confess that had she been my own daughter, the urge to administer a slap or some other stern form of correction might have been irresistible. But Holmes possessed a special magic with children, and once a steaming cup of tea and a sugar-dusted cake were presented to her, the girl began to respond to his inquiries.

"Yes, I had been thinking of pulling the caper for months, and when I heard Chester quarrel with Papa, I knew a way I could do it and make it seem, to a very clever person, as if someone in my family was staging the crime. But it was impossible unless Miss Harper helped."

"Indeed – someone needed to 'witness' the abduction. If you had simply disappeared in the night, they would have suspected you of running away. The note was also a decidedly cunning touch." Holmes removed the paper from his coat and laid it upon the table. "You wrote it yourself – I recognized the family stationery and your handwriting from the blackboard in your room."

The girl nodded. "I tried to get Miss Harper to do it, but she refused. That would have been better, I think."

Holmes smiled. "The invocation of the demon, also known as *Manah*, was nothing short of genius. It certainly led your stepbrother to be convinced your father had abducted you for the notoriety and sympathy it would generate. And having Miss Harper give a description of her assailant that was uncomfortably close to Chester's physical appearance was also very provocative." Holmes observed the girl closely as she sipped her tea. "Obviously, you overheard the amount of your stepbrother's inheritance during your eavesdropping, and decided to use that sum for your ransom, throwing even more suspicion, on Chester."

The girl scowled. "No, you are *wrong*! Maybe you aren't as smart as your friend's stories claim! I found the letter from Chester's mother tucked in a drawer and read it. I had no difficulty remembering the figure she mentioned."

"How did you persuade your governess to go along with your scheme?" I asked. It disturbed me to think of that pale, nervous young woman being a willing accomplice. Miss Phoebe bit into her cake and offered a sugar-covered smile.

"She loves me, but she is timid. I told her there would be no harm in it. I would only give the family a scare until dinnertime, when I would race home and claim I had escaped from the clutches of villains. She hesitated, so I warned that if she would not help me, I would tell Papa about her young man who visits with her when we walk in the cemetery."

My jaw dropped. Holmes leaned back, folding his arms.

"Had you not made the '*tomb of the Egyptian queens*' the place to deposit the ransom, I would have had greater difficult in locating you and luring you out. The reference could only mean the mausoleum of Hannah Courtoy and her daughters, which is covered in scarabs, hieroglyphics, and other strange symbols, and is familiar to you from your many walks in the cemetery. Miss Harper's revelation that you are fluent in Italian suggested the strategy of having a female voice call to you in that language."

The girl looked up, her eyes narrowing. "Indeed, it was foolish of me to respond. A capital error on my part. Nor should I have been as dramatic in my letter's composition, but I knew it would send Papa into a frenzy."

"And you never once considered the feelings of your poor invalid mother?" I charged, with some passion, for I found the girl outrageous and lacking all normal sentimentality. She turned and favored me with a cool stare.

"You must be like all the other doctors she has deceived. Mother is not ill. She malingers and feigns sickness because it's the only way Father will show her any attention."

My jaw dropped with astonishment. Holmes inclined his head.

"The lady's movements in the hallway certainly belied her invalid status. Perhaps the reason no physician has found a cure for her ailments is because she lacks any."

"What will you do with me?" Miss Phoebe asked. I heard a weariness in her tone that almost drew my sympathies. The child had clearly never known a loving home, or even a true taste of innocent childhood. Holmes signaled for her to finish her cake.

"I will stay until you have made a complete confession and an apology. Beyond the terrible strain on your family was the wasting of police resources, for which your father may be held accountable. As for a punishment . . . ." Holmes hesitated. At that moment, I was once again aware of the kind heart that beat beneath the cool façade, and the compassion Holmes felt for young persons who were driven to wicked deeds by the failure of their elders.

"I will suggest you be sent away to a boarding school. My brother Mycroft will see to your tuition, so that your father may focus on resuming his career and improving his finances. You, in turn, will know a fresher and more wholesome environment as you come in a young lady's estate."

The girl's nose crinkled. "School? I doubt the instructors will have anything novel to teach me. And other girls are *boring*."

"Be that as it may," Holmes chuckled, taking her hand with surprising gentleness and leading her from the shop, "it is exceptionally dangerous to allow mathematicians to develop criminal tendencies. I have hopes, Miss Phoebe Clarke, that your scheming nature will be softened, and you will not follow in the footsteps of your infamous predecessor, who rests at the bottom of the Reichenbach Falls."

The Adventure of the Deadly Threat
by Arthur Hall

During my years of collaboration with my friend, the consulting detective Mr. Sherlock Holmes, I witnessed great variety among those who sought his services. There were the rich and the poor, the tall and the short, the elegant and those hopelessly lacking in decorum. Some of these possessed the presence of mind to state their difficulties in a calm and straightforward manner, while others were gripped by panic or overwhelmed by the urgency of their situation. When these last are considered, Mr. Lucas Burns springs inevitably to mind.

I thought it unfortunate, on such a beautiful May morning, that my friend should so adamantly decline my suggestion of a walk in St. James's Park. For several days, he had suffered one of the black moods that came upon him from time to time, and I feared that he might seek to alleviate it by means of the cocaine bottle of which, until now, I had thought him to be cured.

"Holmes, what troubles you?" I asked him.

"That should not be difficult for even you to deduce. I have had no worthy clients for almost two weeks. The resulting boredom is corrosive to my disposition."

"But you have been in this situation before!" I protested. "You are well aware that it never persists for long. In any case, the short outing that I proposed would lighten your spirits, as they have before."

"Pah! Flowers and trees! What I need is *work*!"

A knock at the door of our sitting room arrested our attention, and I bade the caller enter. Hope flitted across Holmes's hawk-like features momentarily as our landlady came in.

"Begging your pardon, gentlemen," she began, "but can I take it that you will be in for luncheon today? The butcher's boy has delivered some prime venison steaks."

I made to tell her that I would look forward to the meal, but Holmes forestalled me.

"We will be here today and everyday it seems, Mrs. Hudson. You may serve your steaks, but I cannot guarantee to partake."

She and I exchanged knowing looks. We had both seen him like this many times before, and felt concern in our different ways.

I believe she was about to speak again, when the momentary silence was interrupted by the chime of the doorbell.

Again, my friend's expression brightened, though for longer.

"Excuse me, gentlemen," Mrs. Hudson said then. "I will see who this is."

The man who accompanied her when she rejoined us was not familiar to me, but Holmes recognised him at once.

"Mr. Applegate!" he exclaimed, in a somewhat brighter tone. "I had not expected to see you again, certainly not so soon. Pray enlighten me as to what has brought you here. Surely you cannot be experiencing further difficulties.

Our visitor, a hearty giant of a man with a short beard and a tan that had begun to fade, shook my friend's hand vigorously. Holmes then introduced us.

"You will not know Mr. Applegate, Watson," he explained. "He once presented me with a case that I have myself recorded and may one day confide to you – 'The Counterfeit Marquis'. Shall I call for tea, Mr. Applegate?"

"I regret that I have no time, Mr. Holmes." He consulted his pocket-watch quickly. "You see, I have a train to catch soon, the result of a doubtful affair that is brewing in Parliament. I am here only to ascertain whether you will take the case of an acquaintance of mine. Mr. Lucas Burns has an extraordinary story to relate, and it is quite telling on his nerves. When he told me of the circumstances, I thought of you at once."

"My thanks to you, sir." Holmes replied. "It so happens that all my current enquiries have recently reached completion. When may I expect to hear from your friend?"

"I do not know him well," our visitor corrected. "I have had short conversations with him at my club on occasion, but that is all. He seemed in such distress, however, that I felt bound to help if I could. When I leave the train at Bristol, I will dispatch a telegram confirming your acceptance."

I recall little more of Applegate's visit, since he was anxious to be on his way. My memory is quite clear nevertheless, concerning the telegram that arrived for Holmes later. It said simply that Lucas Burns would call on us at nine the following morning, and that it was hoped that the time would be convenient.

Holmes was in better spirits, with the prospect of a new case before him. We enjoyed a late morning walk after all, and at luncheon he ate a fair proportion of his venison. The remainder of the day passed quickly for me, for I had allowed medical matters requiring my attention to accumulate. Holmes occupied himself with a chemical experiment, the results of which appeared to please him, while the unholy stench that it produced had the opposite effect upon me. We drank brandy during an hour or two of pleasant conversation after dinner, and retired shortly after.

My friend, I could see, was anxious for breakfast to be over. His food hardly touched, he quickly consumed the greater part of a pot of coffee, then called for another. I finished my meal and Mrs. Hudson cleared the table, ensuring that there was nothing else that we needed before leaving us.

At precisely nine o'clock, the doorbell rang.

Our landlady returned with a tall young man, clean-shaven except for a thin moustache and wearing a morning suit of good quality.

"Mr. Lucas Burns to see Mr. Holmes," she announced before withdrawing.

"My friend Mr. Applegate indicated that you would be prepared to see me, Mr. Holmes," our visitor began. "I hope I am causing you no inconvenience."

Holmes, now much lighter of demeanour, regarded out visitor with a steady gaze before greeting him with much enthusiasm.

"Not at all. Pray come in, sir. It is slightly chilly out despite the bright sunshine, don't you think? I believe you will find the basket chair comfortable. But first allow me to introduce my friend and colleague, Doctor John Watson, who, I do assure you, is the soul of discretion."

Burns and I acknowledged each other, and we were seated. It was apparent to me that he was in a state of considerable distress, but if Holmes had seen this, he had made no mention.

"I see that you work in a clerical occupation, probably a bank, but you must have come here today from your home, since it is still quite early."

Our client's mouth dropped open in surprise, as had many before him on hearing my friend's observations.

"This is true, but how on Earth did you know, sir?"

"It was a simple observation. Your hands show no sign of manual work, as they are far too smooth. But the tip of the forefinger of your right hand has a reddening, from repeatedly being rubbed against something of a rougher texture. I concluded that it was probably caused by counting banknotes."

"You are absolutely correct, Mr. Holmes."

"I further deduce that you are here to seek my help against a problem that is having a most detrimental effect upon you. You are trembling noticeably, and your eyes cannot settle, but continually move from one

159

side to the other as if expecting an attack from any quarter. Also, you are unhealthily pale."

Burns appeared positively shocked at the ease at which Holmes was able to reach these conclusions and I swear that he would have fainted, had not my friend gestured to me.

"Watson, if you will be so kind – our client is evidently in a very weak condition. A brandy, I think, will have a restorative effect."

I poured from the decanter and our client drank gratefully. As the harsh spirit began to warm him, he closed his eyes for a moment and leaned back in his chair.

"Thank you, gentlemen, for your consideration. For the last three days, I have been worried so that I feared I would lose my mind."

I saw that a spark of interest had appeared in Holmes's eyes.

"When you are ready then, tell us what has happened to you. You have my word that we will assist you in every way that we can. Pray be precise as to details."

Burns placed his empty glass on a side-table and inhaled deeply, I thought to further calm himself. He spoke hesitantly at first, but more confidently as his tale progressed.

"Three days ago, the morning began for me as a normal Sunday. My wife, Ellen, and I rose a little later than usual and breakfasted unhurriedly. We had not long finished our meal when a telegram arrived. I accepted it feeling rather puzzled, because I rarely receive telegrams – still less on a Sunday morning. Opening it did little to enlighten me, since it was from Mr. Elias Wilton, the manager of the Hampstead branch of the National Agricultural Bank, where I am employed as Head Cashier. It ordered me to meet him at once at an address in Highgate for an urgent but unspecified reason. I thought that this was highly irregular, but remembered that the bank had recently received a shipment of South African gold ingots, and considered that the summons might have some connection with that. It turned out that I was correct, but not in the way that I had envisaged."

"Did the bearer of the message appear to you as a genuine Post Office telegram boy," Holmes asked, removing his chin from his steepled fingers, "or was there anything that struck you as unusual about him?"

"No, he was quite ordinary."

"Pray continue, then."

"The telegram said to meet Mr. Wilton at No. 5 Goose Street, Highgate, and that the matter was sufficiently urgent as to require the attention of both he and I immediately. I explained to my wife that she would have to attend church alone, because a situation of some importance had arisen. This was unprecedented and caused me no little surprise, but I promptly put on my morning suit and took a hansom to the address. I arrived at a short street of rather dark old houses a little way past the cemetery, dismissed the cab, and knocked upon the door of No. 5 several times without answer. I ensured that I had come to the correct address and knocked once more before attempting entry. The door swung open at my touch, and I stepped into a dismal hall calling Mr. Wilton's name. I passed into the inner room before me and scarcely had time to realise that it was almost completely dark before the door was slammed shut behind me and a key was turned."

"Most curious," I commented.

"Did you hear the retreat of whoever locked you in?" Holmes enquired.

"I heard nothing except the closing of the outer door. After remaining still for a couple of minutes, in order to allow my sight to adjust to the lack of light, I was able to discern that the room was adorned with dark curtains all around. I stood in silence, wondering what I should do."

"There was no sign of Mr. Wilton?" I asked.

"None, not then or at any time. After several minutes had passed, I heard a voice speaking to me, but it was quite unlike his. It instructed me to take two gold ingots from the recent shipment, and secretly convey them to my home. Soon after I would receive directions as to their disposal."

"And what was to occur, should you fail to comply?"

"That was the worst of it, Mr. Holmes. The voice threatened that my Ellen would be killed horribly or taken from me, should I not obey within a week."

"The work of some scoundrel," said I.

"It is easy to understand, then, why you come to us in such an excited state," my friend acknowledged. "But there must have been more to this man's demands. Pray try to remember. Even the smallest detail is often most significant."

"He went on to assure me that he was not a greedy man," Burns recalled after a moment, "and therefore there would be no further demands for the remaining gold. I told him angrily that if this was some sort of joke I failed to be amused by it, whereupon he said that he spoke in deadly seriousness. He said that I would be convinced by a demonstration – that when I returned home, I would find my wife absent, but by then I could contain myself no longer. When he fell silent, I approached the curtains at the place from where the voice seemed to be emanating, and tore them away."

"Did you see your tormentor?" Holmes asked him.

Our visitor shook his head. "There was no one there, and clearly he had anticipated my action, for a screen of metal bars confronted me.

Beyond them was a single chair, and a half-open door leading to the street outside."

Holmes nodded slowly. "Then, of course, you hastily returned to your home and discovered that your wife had not attended church as you expected?"

Alarm passed over our visitor's features, as he recalled the memory. "When I arrived, the house was empty. There was no indication of where she might have gone. I tried to convince myself that she was late returning from church – perhaps the service had been longer than usual – but my mind kept returning to the words of the unknown voice. I began to imagine what terrible fates could have befallen her, what lengths my nameless enemy would take to convince me of his determination to secure my obedience. Finally, I could endure the suspense no longer. I ran into the street and reached its end in a confused state, mercifully relieved as I espied her turning a corner and approaching me."

"Did she then explain?"

Burns ran a hand over his brow, it was a confused and hopeless gesture. "She seemed surprised at my bewilderment, since she had received a message from me on the way to church. A small boy – a ragamuffin, she said – approached to say that I had sent him to tell her wait with him near the lych gate for my arrival. But after a while he glanced at the church clock, then thrust an envelope into her hand, indicating that she should give it to me. He then ran off without another word."

Holmes nodded. "Did your wife give it to you unopened?"

"Indeed, she did." He reached into his coat. "I have the enclosure here."

My friend took the sheet from him. "Rather stiff paper. Not intended for writing, I think. The edges reveal that it was torn in haste from something larger. The message, however, is more or less what one would expect."

He passed the paper to me. The text was short:

You see how easy it is, Mr. Burns. You have one week.

"Have you the envelope, also?" Holmes asked our client.

"No," he appeared mildly embarrassed. "I destroyed it. I did not think."

"Was it addressed to you?"

"It was blank. Off that I am quite certain."

Holmes looked faintly annoyed, but made no comment. A few moments of silence passed, except for the voices of passers-by that reached us from Baker Street.

162

A thought came to me. I was about to speak when Holmes forestalled me.

"What Watson has deduced, I believe, is my conclusion also: You may have realised, Mr. Burns, that the most likely person to be responsible for this is a colleague of yours."

"Impossible!" He sat up stiffly in the chair. "That cannot be. The bank employs only the most honest and respectable people. No, I cannot accept that, sir."

"But consider," Holmes explained patiently, "the knowledge that this man has at his disposal. He is aware of the name of your branch manager, as well as your own, the fact that you are married and live in Hampstead, and the church that you and your wife attend is also known to him. Then there is his familiarity with the fact that the bank has and is retaining South African gold ingots, which is an additional indication. Who else but a person in a similar position to yourself would know these things?"

Burns was clearly dumbfounded. "I cannot believe it," he shook his head hopelessly. "Can there be no other explanation?"

"Certainly there is," Holmes leaned forward in his chair. "For instance, that of a colleague divulging these facts to an outside party while making no use of them himself. But for now, let us concern ourselves with those who are most obviously suspect. Kindly list for us all that are employed at your bank, and their addresses if you know them."

He glanced at me quickly and I picked up my notebook at once.

"There are but three of us working as regular staff, as ours is a small branch," our visitor began. "I have already mentioned our manager, Mr. Elias Wilton, and that I myself serve as chief cashier. There is also Mr. Timothy Ferrows, our clerk. An elderly lady attends when required, to act as secretary to Mr. Wilton. She is Miss Agnes Hardiman." At Holmes's direction, I took down their home addresses.

"Very well." Holmes rose to his feet. "First, it would be prudent to examine the place in Highgate, I think. Watson, be a good fellow and retrieve our hats and coats."

The journey to No. 5 Goose Street wasn't a long one, and little was said until we arrived. The houses were, as our client had described, dark and rather dismal. Holmes didn't knock on the door but pushed it, and it swung open as it had for Burns.

My friend pointed to another door, set in a wall to the side as we entered.

"That, no doubt, is the closet where your tormentor concealed himself as you arrived, Mr. Burns. You will recall how quickly the door was

163

locked behind you when you had entered the room we see before us. How did you manage to leave, incidentally?"

"The door was no longer locked then. It opened easily."

Holmes paused to examine the lock, and I saw that it had been recently oiled. It probably could have been released silently at any time.

The room was as our client had described it. Black curtains, smelling of mould and damp, hung from every wall, save the one directly before us. There the curtains were strewn across the floor, presumably where he had furiously thrown them. The revealed space was an expanse of cracked plaster, with the single chair still in place and the door ajar, admitting minimal light.

"Our friend, or someone, has returned to the scene," Holmes remarked as he examined several sets of holes in both walls. The metal bars had been removed.

He then passed through the open door and reappeared, having verified that this was the escape to the street. He looked at the chair for barely a moment before turning his attention to the curtains.

"I suspect that these were here long before our adversary discovered this derelict place and decided to use this room," he said. "Apart from the fact that someone with long grey hair hung them or recently closed them, I can learn nothing."

Burns had been looking around with a mixture of disgust and awe, and seemed relieved to leave that place. As we made our way out, Holmes spent a few minutes examining the closet in the hall, but came away shaking his head.

"Did you consult the official force before approaching me?" he enquired of our client as we sought a cab.

"It was my first thought, naturally. The inspector at Scotland Yard insisted that these occurrences were no more than a joke, and suggested that I look among my friends."

Holmes, slightly perturbed at being second choice, I thought, asked, "Do you recall the name of the inspector?"

"I believe I heard a constable address him as 'Mr. Athelney Jones'."

"That explains much. Now sir, I recommend that you resume your employment as usual, and on no account mention any of this to anyone there. Should you hear from this man again, you must not fail to notify me at once."

We boarded our separate cabs and parted, after my friend had assured Burns that he would be hearing from us soon.

"Do you think the Irregulars could find the boy that accosted Mrs. Burns?" I enquired of Holmes as a hansom conveyed us back to Baker Street.

"Doubtless, it wouldn't be a difficult task for them. I have used that band of street Arabs many times, as you know, but this time I think their services will prove unnecessary. Burns' enemy will have told the boy little, beyond that he was required to stay with the lady until a specified time – you will recall how he gave her the envelope and left her immediately after consulting the church clock – which was to ensure that his house was empty when he returned. This of course, was intended as a demonstration of his power to manipulate. His control lies with the fact that his victim has no inclination as to where the threat originates."

"How, then, are we to proceed?"

"Whoever is behind this will become frustrated when he sees that our client is taking no action to comply with his demands. Burns will let us know if a further meeting is called for on or before the deadline of one week, and we will be there also."

"Might this man take further, possibly more serious, action against Mrs. Burns during this time, as an incentive to her husband not to delay the theft?"

"Perhaps. That's the reason why I think Timothy Ferrows could bear watching. Would you care to share that task with me?"

I glanced at Holmes, smiling faintly as our hansom came to rest outside our lodgings.

"As always, I am at your disposal," I said.

We were soon settled in our armchairs. I noted that luncheon would be served soon.

"I'm sure that you will have realised, Watson, that Ferrows is by far our most likely suspect," Holmes said through a cloud of fragrant smoke from his old briar. "The manager, Elias Wilton, would hardly have used his own name to summon our client to Goose Street, and the elderly secretary, Miss Hardiman, is less likely still."

"So it would appear, on the face of it, but this wouldn't be the first time that guilt lay in the least-obvious quarter."

"Quite so." He knocked out his pipe after only a few minutes. "But I hear Mrs. Hudson on the stairs, which indicates that lunch is imminent. Come, let us take our seats."

As we arranged ourselves at the table, I reflected that, sorry as I was for Burns' predicament, I was equally glad that it served to dispel Holmes's black mood of late. The spectre that sometimes hovered over me like a shadow, that of his sudden return to the cocaine bottle, had receded once more.

When our meal was over, we conversed pleasantly for the next hour or two. I recall my friend's theory regarding the mysterious disappearance of a Scottish Earl's daughter, a case that Inspector Tobias Gregson had recently been called in on, and his comments on the ever-rising prominence of Imperial Germany.

It was with little surprise that I found myself accompanying Holmes to Hampstead shortly afterwards, since I had anticipated that we would need to be able to recognise Timothy Ferrows and his colleagues by sight. We dismissed the hansom at the end of the High Street and walked slowly past the Green. When we were within sight of the bank, he consulted his pocket-watch and drew me into a coffee shop that stood almost opposite. He selected a table at the far end of the room, positioned so that we had a clear view of the National Agricultural Bank if we craned our necks to look through the smeared window.

"A few minutes," he remarked, "if they leave on time."

There must have been some difficulty, since fully twenty minutes passed before our client emerged from the building. We watched as he hailed a cab that took him out of our sight. Shortly afterwards a lady who could only have been Miss Hardiman appeared and limped off in a different direction.

"She cannot be concerned with this," I whispered to my friend. "She can hardly walk."

"But as you pointed out, it is possible, nevertheless. Or she could simply have divulged the necessary knowledge to an accomplice."

I made no reply, because a stern-looking young man with thick side-whiskers and a tendency to abrupt movement stepped into the street. He spent a few moments searching for a cab with some impatience before strutting away towards a hansom that had just delivered its fare a few paces away.

"Mr. Timothy Ferrows?" I ventured.

"Undoubtedly."

At least five minutes passed before Elias Wilton – his more mature appearance was unmistakable – closed the door heavily behind him and locked it with a key. He replaced it on his person and made off across the street in our direction, but was arrested by an apparent acquaintance with whom he entered the nearby chemist's shop.

"I will watch Ferrows' premises tonight," Holmes stated as we returned to Baker Street, "if you will be good enough to furnish me with his address from your notes."

He said little during dinner, as was his custom when his mind was occupied with his work, and left soon after without specifying when he would likely return. I brought my medical notes up to date and read several journals that had awaited my attention for too long, and was about to retire when I heard him upon the stairs.

"You're back earlier than I expected," I said as he divested himself of his hat and coat.

"There was no need to remain longer. Ferrows is entertaining a lady, and will not leave his rooms tonight."

"Will you join me then, in a glass of brandy before retiring?"

"Gladly," he replied as he draped his thin form across his usual chair.

A telegram arrived before breakfast was over.

As Mrs. Hudson withdrew, Holmes put aside the last of his toast and tore open the envelope with a knife.

"It is from Mr. Burns," he said after his eyes had swept over the message. "I cannot say I am surprised."

He passed it across the table to me. It contained a short introductory phrase from our client, followed by the wording of a telegram he himself had received:

> *You were warned. Further delay will result in dire consequences. Bring what I have asked for tonight at ten.*

"You did anticipate that our adversary might become impatient if our client didn't obey him quickly," I remembered.

Holmes nodded. "He mentions no meeting place, so he apparently intends it to be Goose Street as before."

"So we are to keep the appointment also?"

Holmes stood up and retrieved a pad of telegram forms from his desk.

"Undoubtedly. But our enemy may be cautious. He may show himself only when he has ascertained that our client is present and alone."

He scribbled quickly, then called for our landlady. When she appeared, he gave her the form, telling her to inform the page boy that it was for immediate dispatch.

"Burns should be with us before long," he told me then. "I have addressed the message to the National Agricultural Bank, so he will have to find some excuse to be absent for an hour."

"But you indicated that you had no reason to suspect Timothy Ferrows, so what are we to tell our client?"

"It is precisely because I now believe in Ferrows' innocence that I must see Burns." He picked up the telegram and held it for me to see. "This was dispatched at eight o'clock last night. At that time, Ferrows was at home. By then the lady he spent the evening with had already arrived and

I could hear their voices through an open window from my hiding place. It cannot possibly be he who is threatening our client and his wife, so I must once again ask him if he is aware of any other possibility."

Holmes went to the window and looked out. Apparently, there was little to see, for he turned away quickly, took up his violin and proceeded to play a mournful tune that I recognised as one of his own compositions. I confess to being somewhat relieved a short while later when the doorbell rang and our landlady again announced our client.

We drank tea as Holmes explained his conclusion that none of Burns' colleagues was his mysterious adversary. By the time the cups were cleared away, our client had adopted an expression of deep thought, shaking his head often.

"You can bring to mind then, no other person who might wish you ill?" Holmes asked him. "There is no one who might bear you or your wife a grudge, or who is in a desperate financial position? Is there no one at all who could have somehow discovered that the South African gold is stored at the bank?"

Burns shifted in his chair nervously. "This situation must seem to you impossible, as if I am mad or, for some reason, lying. But why would I do such a thing, Mr. Holmes? I swear I would not. I am a good Catholic and would never – "

He was suddenly silent because he had seen, as I had, that Holmes had become very still.

I was vaguely aware of the sounds of Mrs. Hudson's movements reaching my ears, as she began preparations for luncheon in the kitchen below.

"Have you, by any chance, attended Confession recently?" my friend asked calmly.

Our client looked puzzled. "Why, yes. I believe it was about a week ago."

"Can you recall what it was that you felt it necessary to confess?"

"Oh, my God!" Burns put a hand to his mouth, for he had seen as we had. "I am ashamed to make such an admission, but when I first set eyes upon the gold it crossed my mind how the lives of Ellen and I would be transformed if we owned it. I am not usually given to such fantasies and deeply regretted that it had entered my head. I felt obliged, naturally, to seek forgiveness."

"Kindly tell me the name of your priest."

Holmes's voice held heavy restraint, which I knew resulted from his own failure to have anticipated this possibility, as much as Burns' lack of mention of it. A few moments of tense silence passed.

"But that cannot be!" Our client looked incredulously at both of us. "The Confessional is a sacred place. A priest is sworn to silence."

"It will do no harm to explore the possibility."

A range of tense expressions crossed Burns' face. I could see that his internal struggle was great.

"Father John Mellows," he answered presently. "He has been at the church no more than a few months."

"The church," said I, remembering that Mrs. Burns hadn't needed to take a carriage on Sunday, "is in Hamstead, I take it."

He stared at the floor. "St. Thaddeus, Rosslyn Hill."

"Very well." Holmes expression was suddenly much brighter. "I see that we must make further enquiries. I suggest you now return to your employment, saying nothing of this as I emphasized before, and doing nothing save keep the appointment at ten tonight. I expect the matter to be concluded then, whatever the outcome might be."

Burns left us in a rather glum manner, that was hardly relieved when Holmes reminded him that tonight he would most likely be released from all that he had feared.

At luncheon my friend was in an almost jovial mood.

"What do you say to a drive to Hampstead this afternoon," he asked me.

"I thought Burns' case was all but settled. I had intended to write some long-overdue letters."

"I wish to confirm something. It is always as well to be sure of one's facts."

Not long after, we found ourselves in a hansom, passing Hampstead Green. My friend directed the driver to stop near St. Thaddeus Roman Catholic Church, and we strolled into the churchyard as our conveyance left us.

We were confronted by a gaunt Norman structure, old and in a poor state of repair. Holmes seemed to have little interest in it, his gaze wandered over the stone angels, crosses, and carved books that adorned the nearest graves as I looked on.

"As I expected," he said with satisfaction. "Now there is one more point to confirm before we return to Baker Street."

We made for the tall and rather dilapidated doors with, I thought, the intention of entering the church, but as we drew close to the building two men emerged. One, I saw, was elderly and wore an expression that suggested him to be recently bereaved, and the other was clad in the attire of a priest. Holmes took my arm and guided me away from them. We pretended to study the inscription on the wall of an elaborate family vault, until the conversation ended. The elderly man walked dejectedly towards the lych gate, as the priest re-entered the church.

"That is sufficient. We can leave here now."

"But Holmes, do you not want to speak to the priest?"

"It is unnecessary, since I'm now quite certain that he is our client's enemy. Come, let us see if we can find a cab along the High Street."

"Will you explain to me the purpose of our journey this afternoon, or must I wait until this evening?" I enquired when we were again settled in our sitting room, Holmes having been deep in thought during our return journey. "I saw nothing except the priest, who you could not have recognised as Father Mellows since you have never set eyes upon him."

He looked up from the scrapbook he was busily perusing. "It is all quite simple. You will recall the heavy black curtains that surrounded the room in Goose Street?"

"Of course."

"When I examined them, I saw nothing of significance other than traces of grass cuttings, and long grey hairs adhering in several places. You will recall the smell of newly-cut grass in the churchyard, and the ample evidence of the application of a scythe. Also, that the priest had unusually long tresses of that colour."

I nodded. "And the telegram you dispatched on our return here?"

"To Lestrade. I requested some information about Father Mellows, and asked if Scotland Yard might be interested in our rendezvous tonight."

Dinner-time had approached, by the time my friend had concluded his examination of his index.

"I have found no less than four criminals who have posed as priests during the last five years," he explained. "None of them compare with the appearance of the priest of St. Thaddeus."

"You are certain that he cannot be a genuine priest who has taken a wrong turn?"

"That is the other possibility. In either case, 'Father Mellows' is no more entitled to describe himself as such than I am."

He said little during dinner, though I felt he had a slightly amused air about him. Afterwards, I asked him about other criminals whose careers he had brought to an end, those he mentioned earlier who had profited in the guise of men of the cloth. He was reluctant to speak at first, as he often was except when the mood took him to reminisce, but then he told me a chilling story which I will one day write as "The Adventure of the Rich Parishioner", should he allow me permission. All too quickly, I saw that the time for our departure was drawing near.

Holmes dismissed the hansom in a silent, unlit street.

170

"Goose Street is but a short walk away," he explained. "I don't want our adversary to hear our approach."

We made our way through several grim and poorly lit streets, and found ourselves at our destination some minutes later. Holmes led me into the shadows of a doorway opposite and we listened and watched in silence.

"There is no sign of life," I whispered presently.

"It is now past ten o'clock," he answered out of the darkness. "I heard a clock chime from not far off. Our client and our so-called priest will be in there now, so we must approach stealthily."

On this occasion the door hadn't been locked after Burns, and so we entered and stood in the hallway listening. At first we heard nothing, but then an occasional word reached us. I sensed that my friend had put a finger to his lips to indicate that I should continue to be silent, as I moved with him into the larger room.

A dismal, minimal light leaked in from somewhere – I supposed that the door beyond had been left open to effect escape, if that proved to be necessary – so that we could see Burns standing before the curtain that had been replaced as before.

Holmes and I stood unmoving, as we heard the end of the conversation.

"You can have no understanding as to the difficulties of taking the ingots from the bank," our client protested. "It cannot be done or ordered to a specific time. It is a matter of waiting for a suitable opportunity."

"I have told you," answered an exasperated voice, "that it is imperative that I have the gold in my possession by the end of the week." A short pause followed. Then: "Look, I will allow you one last chance. We will meet here again, three days from tonight. Should you fail to produce the ingots, there can be no guarantee that your wife will live for long beyond that time. Consider that carefully, before you tell me of your problems. Would they not be increased a hundredfold, were she suddenly taken from you?"

Holmes and I had by this time crept towards the front of the room, he along the left wall and I along the right. I saw the dim figure of our client alter its stance, indicating that our presence had been noticed. I took a firm grip on the curtain and wrenched it from its fixture, and my friend did likewise at the same instant, revealing that the screen of metal bars had been installed once more. Behind it stood the priest, portly and with his grey hair bound up behind his head. His long chasuble hung from him like a shroud, and his expression was one of complete surprise.

He recovered quickly. A book – a Bible, I realized – dropped from his pocket onto the floor as he drew a pistol from within his garment.

"I know you!" he shouted with an edge of hysteria in his voice. "You are Holmes, the amateur policeman! It is a bad thing that you are here sir, because your presence ensures my downfall, but first I will without fail destroy this man's wife." He glared at Burns. "Why could you not have done as I instructed? Then both of us could have carried on as before? Now my days are numbered, but so are hers beforehand. That will be my vengeance for your failure."

For a moment I expected him to shoot at us through the bars and drew my service revolver, but he shouted an obscene oath and ran from our sight. I turned to retrace my steps to intercept him, but Holmes placed an arm on my shoulder, and I was still. I assumed that our enemy had left the door of his escape wide open, since the light had increased sufficiently for me to make out the astonishment on our client's face.

"A priest!" he exclaimed. "Had I not seen such a thing, I could not have believed it. Father Mellows has ministered to both Ellen and myself, many times."

"Calm yourself," Holmes advised him. "Unless I am much mistaken, this man is unworthy to be known as such. Ah, but I see that confirmation is at hand. Come, let us leave this place."

I saw that Holmes referred to the silhouette that was framed in the doorway. As we drew nearer I recognised it as that of Inspector Lestrade. He walked with us into the street, where our adversary was being bundled into a police wagon by two burly constables. His screams and the flailing of his arms left me in no doubt that he was quite mad.

"Well, we have a fine kettle of fish here, Mr. Holmes," the official detective said when we had introduced our client. "But I recognised this villain as soon as I read your message. His name is Arnold Crass, and I had a visitor only the other day who told me all about him."

"I will be glad to relate my client's experience of him, so that you can decide upon the charges."

"And I look forward to our interview at Scotland Yard tomorrow morning, when you can do so. But that isn't all. The visitor I mentioned was a bishop, no less. He came to me to unburden his soul." Lestrade laughed at the situation and continued. "Bishop Troughton was blackmailed by this beauty," he gestured towards the wagon, "for nigh on twenty years. It seems the bishop committed some small indiscretion a long time ago, and Father Crass, as he then was, found out about it. That was why Crass was never excommunicated from the church, despite his own many failings. Instead, he was moved to another parish on several occasions. He changed his name often and was permitted to do so, in order that he shouldn't become notorious. The bishop explained that extortion was proved against him more than once, and suspected a dozen times

172

more. This time, however, was different. Cross has lost much of his ill-gotten gains at the tables, and is being increasingly pressed by associated gangs for the payments he owes. When Bishop Troughton heard, from Cross' own mouth, of your client's predicament, he decided that the time had come to put an end to all this, despite the possible consequences to himself.

"We have you and Doctor Watson to thank, Mr. Holmes, for the conclusion of this affair, but be assured sir, the Yard wasn't far behind you."

"The credit for the arrest is yours of course, Inspector," Holmes said with a straight face. "That Burns and his wife are no longer under threat is reward enough for Watson and myself."

At that moment a constable emerged from the door by which our adversary had sought to escape. He approached Lestrade and saluted.

"Anything more, Norgrove?" the little detective asked.

"Only this, sir." He handed him the Bible that Cross had dropped.

Lestrade gave the book a casual examination. "Nothing out of the ordinary, here."

"May I see?" I asked.

"Certainly, Doctor."

I had caught a glimpse of the inside of the front cover, and I turned to it now.

"Do you see, Holmes?"

From his coat my friend withdrew the paper which the boy had given to Burns' wife, and matched it to the torn edge that remained. They fitted together perfectly.

"Well spotted, Watson." He turned to Lestrade. "I can foresee additional difficulties in convicting a priest, Inspector, but should they arise you now have irrefutable proof that Cross was the author of this threatening missive. While not incriminating in itself, it serves to illustrate one of the events contributing to my client's distress." He put out an arm to signal a slow-moving hansom that had apparently delivered a fare somewhere nearby, and continued as it drew to a halt. "I wish you success with the conclusion of this case. But for now, Watson and I will leave you. Doubtless we will continue our discussion at Scotland Yard in the morning."

The Due Debentures
by I.A. Watson

This enigmatic business which is at once the fairest and most deceitful in Europe, the noblest and the most infamous in the world, the finest and the most vulgar on earth. It is a quintessence of academic learning and a paragon of fraudulence; it is a touchstone for the intelligent and a tombstone for the audacious, a treasury of usefulness and a source of distaste . . . .

– Joseph de la Vega, *Confusión de confusiones* (1688),
the earliest book about stock trading

It is seldom that the same client turns to Holmes on more than one occasion, with the exception of those police and private detectives to whom he is a regular consultant. Nor was I accustomed to being disturbed at my breakfast on a Whit Monday, on which all establishments are closed for business, [1] and I might have expected a leisurely day arranging my writings. I was therefore surprised to have my kippers interrupted by the fellow who hammered at the door of 221b Baker Street appealing for our help.

I had not seen Hall Pycroft since the summer of '89, and had thought little about the Mawson and Williams' stockbroker's clerk since then, apart from his inclusion in my accounts of the investigations of my friend Holmes. [2] I remembered him as a young, athletic, fair-haired fellow with an intelligent round face and a light moustache. Nearly thirteen years had passed since then, and I suppose I should not have been surprised to find the broker settled into a comfortable middle age with a spreading paunch and a receding hairline. So time takes its tithe from us all!

He had that same anxious expression that I recalled though, the face of a man who fears that he might lose everything – or might have already lost it.

"You had better come in and sit down, Mr. Pycroft," Holmes advised our pink-flushed, perspiring visitor. "Another pot of tea, Mrs. Hudson, and that will be all, thank you. You could not find a cab, Mr. Pycroft, and have been running all the way from Oxford Circus." [3]

"How did you – ?" our guest panted.

"The splashes on your spats tell it," Holmes advised him. "The sallow skin under your eyes say that have been awake all night. Your newly-bitten nails betray your worry. Your urgent arrival on a general day of rest suggests that you have encountered some critical problem or obstacle that you hope I might address."

"As a doctor," I contributed, "I advise you to calm down and breathe steadily. Have a sip of tea, old chap, and gather your thoughts. It'll be for the best."

Hall Pycroft got a grip of himself. He accepted the cup that Mrs. Hudson brought for him and forced himself to swallow a gulp of its contents. The saucer trembled in his hand.

"You wish to tell us about the contents of your wallet," Holmes prompted him then. To offset more amazement about his deduction he added, "You customarily carry your note-case in your left inner breast pocket, but it is presently swelling the cut of your right outer pocket. You stuffed it there in haste, and perhaps because it is no longer the familiar and comforting weight that you are accustomed to. Tell us your story."

Pycroft took another mouthful of his Lapsang Souchong [4] and set it down. He braced himself and began his account.

"If you can read my travel here by spots of mud," he told Holmes, "then you will certainly have been able to deduce something of my life since last we met. You disentangled me from the ploys of the loathsome Beddingtons when they lured me to a false job so that one of them could report to the offices of Mawson and Williams pretending to be me, their newly-hired clerk, intending to rob the brokerage. Afterwards, the firm was grateful that I had called you in to save them. They felt that I had proved my initiative and perception, and were gracious enough to confirm me in my position.

"I was fortunate in my place, and have worked diligently for Mawson's since that time. I was promoted to Senior Clerk in Derivatives in '93, and to Head Clerk in '95, responsible for keeping track of all the firm's forwards, futures, options, and swaps. By '98, I was a Junior Broker in Debt Securities, handling debentures. [5] Since them my career has progressed until I am now Second Broker in Equities, mostly bonds, deputing for Mr. Walmsley the Senior Broker while he is in New York. This is a responsible post and I am fortunate to have achieved it so young. Or so I thought.

Pycroft swallowed hard. "I thought – I thought I was doing well. I even married this year and took a house in Camberwell. But now I may be ruined – and I may have ruined my employers also!"

The stockbroker pulled out the wallet that Holmes had noticed bulging in his severely-cut black suit pocket. "On Friday night, I had occasion to open my note case, to disburse wages to my cook-housemaid and to pass on money for her to cover household expenses. It was then that

I discovered two other papers had been added to my banknotes – although my wallet had not left my inner pocket all day."

Pycroft first produced a folded foolscap folio [6] certificate printed in red and black with an elaborate oyster-coloured border. It read:

Official Acceptance of Order

The Albion and American Debenture Company
Wall Street, New York

No: SA-20056
Shares: 1000
Date: September 24th, 1900

Mr. George P. Purvis, Bridgeport, Conn.

This is to certify that your request numbered above has been registered, entitling you to TEN- THOUSAND shares in Series A of the Capital Stock of the EAST COAST TELEPOST COMPANY, fully paid and non-accessible (at $10 per share) upon payment according to your application, when the Certificate of Stock will be promptly forwarded to you.

Albion and American Debenture Company
William S. Dawson, President

The paper was rubber-stamped with a red imprint that denoted it as "*Redeemed*".

"This is a standard convertible certificate," Pycroft explained. "It is issued by a debenture company that has acquired a share issue in some promising enterprise and is notification that share certificates are now available to those investors who have reserved them. Albion and American are one of the larger firms on Wall Street who handle such distributions."

He unfolded a smaller certificate, printed on bonded paper with a green ink edging as elaborate as that of a bank-note, and with considerably more detail. The frame was surmounted by an oval engraving of some winged angel, flanked by an issue number, *3470*, and clarification that this was a Series A Class I pressing.

Under the impressive banner was the import of the document:

Certificate of Stock
The East Coast Telepost Company, Inc

Par value $100
Capital $10,000,000 All Common Stock
Full Paid and Non-Accessible

This certifies that MR. GEORGE P. PURVIS is the owner of TEN shares of the Capital Stock of The EAST COAST TELEPOST COMPANY, INC., transferable only in the books of the company in person or by attorney upon the surrender of this Certificate.

In witness whereof the said EAST COAST TELEPOST COMPANY, INC, has caused this Certificate to be signed by its President and Secretary and its corporate seal to be affixed thereto at Trenton, New York this 25ᵗʰ Day of November, AD 1900.

There followed two florid signatures beside a large red wax impression of the company's official seal.

I am not a man with great knowledge of stocks and shares, lacking the resources for such investments, but I knew somewhat of the nature of the impressive paper before me. "This is the Certificate of Stock to which the other paper referred, or such scrip of many," I observed, keener not to show ignorance than to instruct either of the men in the room with me. "It is a promise to pay a fixed sum on presentation to the company that issued it – to pay one-hundred dollars. In fact, which amounts to around twenty pounds sterling." [7]

"The pound is level at four-dollars-and-eighty-six cents," Pycroft told us more precisely, "Or so it was at close of business Friday. That certificate is presently redeemable or exchangeable for twenty pounds, eleven shillings, and sixpence."

Holmes cared little about high finance. "The appearance of these documents alarmed you," he prompted our visitor.

"Oh yes," Hall Pycroft admitted. "You see, these were supposed to be shuttered away safe in Mawson and Williams' strong room, part of a stack of ten-thousand shares in similar ten-dollar Certificates. I had put them in their strongbox myself only two days before. They were secure. Secure!"

"Were they?" I wondered.

"They should have been. Of course, I hastened to find out for certain. I left my Emilie puzzled and alarmed and hastened back to Mawson's offices in Lombard Street.

"You are a keyholder to the strongroom, then?" Holmes enquired.

"Yes and no. I hold one of two necessary access keys. Mawson's takes its security very seriously after that theft in '89, when the lone guard was fatally struck with a poker and bundled into a safe, and the securities carried off. We hold almost a million pounds in common stock, debentures, bonds, and other fungibles alone, not counting all the other margin – that is, collateral deposited with us as a counterparty. Our basement strongroom is as guarded as any bank's vault."

Holmes requested further detail on that point, so Pycroft gave it.

"There is a guard outside the basement vault at all times, but he does not hold a key. Two senior members of staff must be present to open the room, each with a different key. Inside, the various client properties are contained in separate strongboxes, each of which *also* require individual keys *and* a master key. The individual strongbox keys are kept inside the room in metal cabinets, sorted by department, and each department head has a key that accesses only the keybox or boxes relevant to their business. I presently hold one such key to the metal cabinet holding unique keys for each of the accounts that I am managing during Mr. Walmsley's absence."

"But even then another key is required," I recognised.

"That is so," Pycroft confirmed. "Also, all access to the vault is recorded."

"Then to gain access on Friday night – ?"

"I applied to the porter for entry to the building. It was after six, nearer seven, but old Mr. Mawson himself was still in his office, and of course he holds a vault key. Mr. Paggin, my old chief from Debt Securities, was about to leave the premises, but we were able to catch him in the foyer. All three of us descended to the basement to check on the Dennington strongbox."

"Dennington?" I prompted.

"Colonel Rupert Dennington," Pycroft supplied. "The greyhound breeder. He is the client who deposited the stocks with us to underwrite his present capital investments. The Telepost Certificates were his."

I was about to object that his was not the name on the papers until I remembered that such documents were negotiable. They could be exchanged exactly like bank notes. Any holder might present them to the issuing company to cash them in, or might trade or sell them on to some other investor as if they were money. The paper from the broker's wallet might have changed hands a dozen times since it was first circulated.

If the Certificates were stolen but their numbers known, then a hold might be placed upon the issuing company paying out for them, but an unwitting third party might accept the issue in good faith and only learn of its being purloined when he tried to liquidate his asset. By then the thieves would be far away with his money.

"What happened when you checked the vault?" Holmes asked Pycroft.

"Well, first Mr. Mawson consulted the log book to see who had been into the room since Wednesday. There are fourteen men authorised to enter during office hours, department heads or account managers, of which I am the most junior. Seven of these had visited the vault, including myself and old Mawson, but all in the presence of the Vault Manager. The most recent was Mr. Paggin, who had been there from 2:20 to 2:42 p.m. Friday, consulting on some lien detail of deeds for a factory in Belfast.

"Thereafter we all went into the strongroom. It is not a large chamber, wood panelled and tile-floored, perhaps the size of your sitting room here, Mr. Holmes. It is fitted with the new electrical lights and an electrical fan for ventilation. The strongboxes are stacked along two opposing walls. Two floor safes occupy the further end. There is always a large amount of cash on the premises to cover day-to-day transactions. Locked cabinets contain our more confidential account books and audit information.

"I produced my key, and Mr. Mawson has a master key like the Vault Manager's that fits the vault door and any of the boxes, and so we went in."

"I retrieved the correct second key from the Equity Securities cabinet and went to Dennington's account strongbox. It stands against the left wall, about halfway along, third row up. It is about two-feet-by-three-foot-six, and two deep, front-opening, and fitted with excellent Chubb and Son mechanisms. Allen and I opened it.

"It was empty! One-thousand ten-share Certificates like the one in my wallet were gone, representing ten-thousand shares! That is one-hundred-thousand dollar's-worth of Certificates, just vanished without trace, against all possibility. Also gone were some family heirloom jewellery that Colonel Dennington had pledged, opals and rubies in old-fashioned silver settings and a sapphire brooch, which we had valued at two-thousand-four-hundred guineas." [8]

"Remarkable and appalling!" I contributed.

The unhappy stockbroker nodded agreement. "There was only one piece of paper left, a typewritten note," he revealed. "A ransom."

Holmes perked up. "You have it to show me?"

"No. Mr. Mawson would not allow it out of his possession. He has it now. I can tell you what it said."

The detective waved his long fingers to indicate that Pycroft should report the missive's content.

"It read: 'Your reputation is in my hands. It is perhaps worth more to you than the value of the things I have taken. To hear what it will cost to buy it back and recover the things you have lost, send Hall Pycroft to meet with me on Saturday noon at Benton's on Change Alley. Otherwise all is lost.'"

I understood the threat. "If it became known that Mawson and Williams had lost a client's property, had suffered some loss from its own secure premises, then public confidence in the company would plummet, and your firm might even founder."

"Exactly," Pycroft agreed. "You can . . . you understand the consternation and difficulty that the discovery caused."

"You were blamed," Holmes surmised.

"Well, at first. After all, it was I who had received the first evidence of the crime, discovered in my own wallet. I had originally deposited the Certificates in the strong box, in company with Mr. Allen the Deposits Manager who witnessed what I did and countersigned the inventory ledger. And I was named as the man who must meet the thief the day after the discovery. It was natural for some suspicion to fall upon me."

The detective nodded, his eyes fixed on Pycroft like a hawk's on a field-mouse.

The stockbroker looked close to tears. "My suggestion that you should be consulted was dismissed at that time, Mr. Holmes, but I finally convinced Mr. Mawson to give me a chance. If I could meet with the thief, make some arrangement, then the firm's reputation might be preserved. We might recover Colonel Dennington's property and all would be well."

"You attended the appointment at Benton's?" enquired Holmes. Then, recognising that I did not share his extensive catalogue of London locations, he explained. "Change Alley, or Exchange Alley, was the open-air meeting place of London's mercantile community before Thomas Gresham founded the Royal Exchange in 1565. Nowadays it is a narrow passage offering a convenient shortcut between the Royal Exchange on Cornhill and Lombard Street Post Office. Benton's is one of those tiny coffeehouses along the Alley, last vestige of its great coffee houses of yesteryear that were the progenitors of the London Stock Exchange." [9]

"That's rather a public venue to meet a blackmailer," I pointed out.

"I thought so too," Pycroft assured us. "But I attended my meeting, sitting by the window at one of those cramped little bench-tables. I had scarcely settled down and had not even made an order before a runner-lad came up to me and called, 'Please, sir, and I'm to direct you to that there carriage!' And sure enough, there was a covered hansom pulling up outside."

180

Holmes nodded in satisfaction. "Change Alley is too narrow for vehicles to pass each other. It would be easy to spot another carriage following on. It was a sensible precaution against anyone who intended to trail you."

"If that was it, then it worked," the stockbroker told us. "I approached the cab and discovered that the interior was empty. The window-blinds were rolled down. 'Please, sir,' the urchin said again, 'and I'm to tell you to get in and you'll be taken to your meeting. But no peeking. That's all.'

"At that the boy pelted away into the crowd, vanishing as suddenly as he had appeared."

"What did you notice about the carriage?" Holmes asked, but was disappointed when Hall Pycroft had taken little heed of the hansom in which he had been conveyed.

"I was taken out of the City," was all he could inform us. "We rattled along for some time. I did not dare to glimpse out to see what direction we were going. We went for about thirty-five minutes by my fob-watch and finally came to a halt. 'You get out here, sir,' the cabbie told me, and as soon as I had disembarked he turned his hansom and headed off.

"That left me alone on a thickly-wooded country path, surrounded by trees and with no distinguishing sights to help me place my location. I considered walking along the road but I feared that might queer the rendezvous, so I just waited.

"After ten minutes I heard a horse, and a rider came along on a nice chestnut. He wore a dark brown coat and a wide-brimmed hat. A scarf obscured his face across nose and mouth, so I could not see any of his features under the brim of his headgear. He rode well, though, and he spoke in an educated manner."

Holmes required more detail than that. His close-questioning of Pycroft determined that the fellow was around five-feet-ten, that he held his reins in his right hand, that his high boots were polished, and that he carried no crop.

"He bade me good afternoon in a very civilised manner," Pycroft continued on, "as if he was not a d----d thief and a scoundrel who had stolen thousands of pounds. I asked him what he thought he was about, and he answered me.

"'I'm about the business of making profit – which is what all business is for,' he boasted. 'I have Dennington's deposit, and he's not the sort to take well your losing what he entrusted you with. It'll be scandal and ruin for Mawson's, and for you, Hall Pycroft, and don't imagine it won't! Unless your firm does exactly what I demand, that is. Only then can such an end be avoided.'"

"'What do you want?' I asked him, and he laughed.

"'Let's call it sixty-thousand,' he suggested."

"'*Sixty?*' I echoed, dumbfounded. 'Sixty-thousand pounds?'

"'Twenty for the Certificates, twenty for the reputation, and another twenty as handling charge,' he answered, as if he was making a funny joke in a saloon bar. 'I want it in London Stock Exchange first issue three-per-cent Debentures, the five-hundred pound coupons issued by special resolution of the proprietors on 24th April, 1896. And I expect to have it on Tuesday, as soon as business opens – or I shall bring your company down.'"

"That was very specific," I noted. "Could Mawson's lay their hands on such a sum in such a format in so short a time?"

"It turns out that they could," Pycroft revealed. "In fact, that was the exact limit to the debentures of that kind that are held in our Vault. I was surprised that such a collection was at hand, but we have evidently been acquiring them for a client for some time and have not yet assembled the amount for which he asked."

"Which client?" Holmes asked quickly, but Pycroft did not know. Many of the accounts were treated with absolute secrecy and he was still relatively junior.

The encounter had ended there, with the horseman's orders to bring the Debentures to Benton's again at ten o'clock on Tuesday – that was, now tomorrow. Thereafter, on payment of ransom, the stolen Certificates and jewellery would be returned and all would be settled.

Pycroft had thought to ask for assurances about how the materials might be exchanged, and what safeguards would there be that the thief would keep his word, but was not comforted by an answer. "Do or die, Hall Pycroft," was all the stranger told him before riding away.

A short while later a pony and trap appeared along the lane, commissioned to pick up a single traveller and convey him into London.

"Mr. Mawson was grateful for my efforts," the stockbroker recounted. "Mr. Paggin was more suspicious, but he has never liked me, thinking me promoted too soon."

"Who at Mawson's was aware of the amount of Stock Exchange debentures?" Holmes enquired.

"Several of the seniors. Old Mawson, of course, and Paggin and his deputy Hooper, since debentures come under the Debt Securities department. Mr. Kenneal of Currencies and our Senior Accountant Lorrimer, because the purchase had to be funded. I believe that Mr. Harrison of Derivatives, Mr. Clemmens in Risk Management, and my own absent superior Daniel Walmsley had also been consulted on the accumulation at various times."

Evidently the question of whether to pay the demanded blackmail fee and discussion of the consequences of non-compliance has been a knotty one. Pycroft had not been privy to the conversations that must have taken place all through the rest of Saturday and into Sunday, with senior staff and Mawson and Williams' board members being consulted on the dilemma.

"Old Mawson called on me at home late last night, after ten," Pycroft confided. "He told me that my former suggestion had been accepted. That is, I had recommended that the problem be place before *you*, Mr. Holmes, and at last I was granted permission to do so."

"And so you are here," I concluded, but suppressed any comment regarding my interrupted day of leisure.

"Yes. It seems that there is a great mystery. How could those Certificates have been removed from a sealed and guarded vault, from a strongbox requiring two keys held by two people, past vigilant men who would have easily seen a nine-inch stack of papers being removed? Who would know enough of the detail of our company to know exactly what to steal and how much to demand for it? And why am I again made victim of such a crime, threatening everything that have toiled for these long years?"

Holmes studied the documents from Pycroft's note-case. He cradled his fingertips and assayed a small smile. "Those are worthy questions, Mr. Pycroft," he replied. "We shall endeavour to provide the solutions that you require."

Holmes and I had never been to the Lombard Street premises of Mawson and Williams. Our part in the Beddington brothers' plot to infiltrate the eminent stockbrokers firm by impersonating its new recruit Pycroft was to expose the fake Franco-Midland Hardware Company that had offered the real clerk a senior post so that he might be replaced by an impostor at Mawson's. [10] The resolution played out in the fictitious firm's temporary Birmingham office, where the younger Beddington brother attempted suicide rather than be captured. The elder brother was apprehended by the vigilance of City police officers who noticed him departing Mawson and Williams after office hours with a suspicious bag that proved stuffed with securities, but that arrest was no doing of ours.

We therefore entered the august offices of Hall Pycroft's employers for the first time on that bank holiday. Mr. Mawson himself awaited us under the coffered ceiling of the main reception hall, beside a long desk counter. Chalkboard notices of the latest share prices decorated the walls, and a row of tickertape machines stood to receive the latest news from the Exchange.

The senior partner introduced the men with him as Paggin of Corporate Debentures, Allen the Deposits Manager, Kenneal of Currencies, and Dutter, Head Guard. They all seemed flustered and unhappy.

"This is a terrible business," old Mawson mourned. "The thief is right – it might break us! Our whole enterprise depends upon confidence and trust. When that confidence is gone, that reputation lost, then a stockbroker's will fail. This fellow has us! I have consulted with my partner Williams, who is now too sick and elderly to attend upon us today, and we are agreed that if nothing else can be done we must somehow meet the thief's price, although that sum will beggar us."

I tried to reassure them. "You may be certain that if any man can resolve your difficulties, then it is Sherlock Holmes. There are several significant institutions who have reason to value Holmes's intervention and to value his discretion."

Now that Holmes could inspect the typewritten ransom note, he was quick to identify the machine upon which it was made. He discovered not only the type of instrument, but discovered the specific typewriter.

"It was this Blick Number 7," Holmes indicated. "If the key imprints had not distinguished it's type-font stock, then the keystrokes cut onto the ribbon would have."

Alas, the instrument was located in the clerks' side office, so any one of the clerks or managers might have accessed it after hours but before the building was closed, or during a quiet lunch hour. Notepaper of the exact type used for the ransom note was easily available in the clerks' office stationery cupboard.

"You cannot determine the skill or familiarity of the typist by the impressions they leave?" I checked.

"It is an intriguing field of study, worthy of my attention," Holmes acknowledged. "Time will not presently allow such detailed comparisons. Most of the potential typists are enjoying their holiday off. For now we must conduct our investigation along other routes."

Holmes requested an opportunity to inspect the basement vault, which was granted on condition that the Vault Manager and Head Guard were present to observe the procedure.

The basement room was quite gloomy. Its electrical lighting came from overhead, bare vacuum-filled bulbs casting stark black shadows, and the ventilation fan that operated whenever the lights were on had a grating persistent hum.

The lockers were similar to those I had seen before in many banks, of robust composition but not as secure as the two safes in the room. Small card-holders on the front of the strongboxes bore the names and account numbers of the depositors.

"Who has been into this room since the loss was discovered?" Holmes asked Allen and Dutter.

Mawson owned that he and Paggin had entered the vault to verify the theft, and later Mr. Allen the Deposits Manager and Mr. Harrison of Derivatives, while Kenneal had been present to peer into the chamber but had not entered.

"Who has keys for what?" I wanted to clarify. It turned out that old Mawson had a master key which operated many locks, the "*A*" locks suite, one of each two-lock doors including the door to the vault itself. The sickly Mr. Williams had a master key that worked the other half of the locks, the "*B*" locks suite, but that key was secured in a deposit box at Merrow's Bank on Throgmorton Street, and was undisturbed there.

I was shown a useful chart affixed to the wall beside the metal key cabinets that helped me to understand who held what.

> *Mr. Mawson, Managing Director, Master A, Safe Key B*
> *Mr. Williams, Managing Director, Safe Key A, Master B*
> *Mr. Allen, Deposits Manager, Master A, Safe Key B*
> *Mr. Harrison, Derivatives, Vault B, Derivatives Keybox (4 different)*
> *Mr. Farmley, Derivatives Deputy, Vault B, Derivatives Keybox (4 different)*
> *Mr. Paggin, Debt Securities, Vault B, Securities Keybox B (3 different)*
> *Mr. Hooper, Debt Securities Deputy, Vault B, Securities Keybox B (3 different)*
> *Mr. Walmsley, Equities, Vault B, Equities Keybox B*
> *Mr. Wallis, Other Fungibles, Vault B, Fungibles Keybox B*
> *Mr. Kenneal, Currencies, Safe Key A, Vault B, Currencies Keybox B,*
> *Mr. Clemmens, Risk Management, Vault B, Risk Keybox B*
> *Mr. Penwestern, Conversion, Vault B, Conversion Keybox B*
> *Mr. MacLorne, Clearing and Settlement, Vault B, Clearing Keybox (2 different)*
> *Mr. Lorrimer, Accounts, Vault A for emergencies only, Vault B, Accounts Keybox B*

So Mr. Allen, Deposits Manager responsible for basement access, possessed the "*A*" master key to the vault door, to the accounts strongboxes, and to the wall-mounted keyboxes that contained the corresponding strongbox "*B*" keys, but without any "*B*" keyholder, he could not open vault, keyboxes, or strongboxes. He did not remove his master key from the premises. It was instead sealed in a small combination wall-safe in his office after hours.

Each department head like Paggin, Kenneal, and Walmsley, for whom Pycroft was deputing, retained "*B*" keys to the second vault door lock and for specific keyboxes inside the vault that contained individual keys for the second locks of the accounts which they managed or oversaw. Senior Accountant Mr. Lorimer additionally retained a key for the first lock of the vault door for emergencies, which he kept in his office safe and was still sealed up unused. The Chief Guard Dutton held no keys, but kept a register of who had made use of their keys for entry.

Holmes conducted a thorough examination of the room, which included him taking the front off the electrical fan to check its interior venting and testing the roof and wall panelling to be sure there were no hidden surprises there.

"I presume that a check has been made on the other strongboxes to ensure that they have not been emptied out?" Holmes verified.

"It was the first thing we did when the problem became apparent," Allan the Vault Manager assured us. "There are no other empty compartments."

Holmes made no comment, but turned his attention to a close reading of the vault visitation ledger.

When Mawson, Paggin, and Kenneal joined us to see how the search progressed, Holmes requested that each of the keyboxes be opened. Only those with keys held by Paggin, Kenneal, and Pycroft were readily available. The only "*B*" master key was in a bank safe deposit, and the banks were closed. Was that an unfortunate chance or by some thief's design? Whichever, Holmes appalled the staff of Mawson's by simply picking the locks of the other key cabinets.

"Those are supposed to be secure!" old Mawson complained to Head Guard Dutter.

"They are of good quality," my friend assured them. "My chosen vocation requires me to have a familiarity with locks that is equivalent to that of some of the criminals whom I discover. I can assure you from lack of traces on the mechanisms that no opening technique such as this has been utilised to breech these cabinets before, unless one of three men in Britain or four in Europe did the deed, and then they would not have stopped with the contents of one strongbox!"

Having prevailed over the best precautions of Mawson and Williams, he spent a long time inspecting each key therein under his magnifying lens.

"What does he hope to determine?" Paggin whispered to me.

"It is not easy to predict the turns of Holmes's mind," I admitted to the Manager of Debt Securities. "His intellect works like no other's. I have seen him draw conclusions from the slightest of clues and achieve solutions that no one might have believed possible. He is the foremost detective mind of our age, and one of our nation's greatest intellects. Whatever he is doing, be assured that it is of importance to his investigation."

"You offer strong testimonial," Paggin replied gruffly. "I remain uncertain about his involvement, though, and yours. Apart from the fact that it was Pycroft who dragged you into this, there is the matter of your published account about the previous unpleasantness at this institution, and the part that Hall Pycroft played in it."

"My report of Holmes's case regarding 'The Stockbroker's Clerk' obscured the identities of both men and companies. Only those who already knew the circumstances might recognise the original participants."

"It is a mark against you, Dr. Watson. As Mr. Mawson said, our business relies upon public trust. Your popular fictionalisations to promote your confederate risk compromising our reputation."

I decided to be blunt. "You do not like Hall Pycroft?"

"I do not," Paggin agreed.

"And yet you were his supervisor for several years when you had in him on your staff in Debt Securities."

"I had a better opinion of him then."

"Did you object at his promotion to Walmsley's deputy?"

Mr. Paggin snorted. "What would have been the point? Pycroft's future in the company has been *well* secured. Until now."

I sensed something of a sneer in Paggin's statement, so I pressed further. "What assurance does or did Pycroft have that convinced you of his assured employment and advancement, at least up until the present difficulty?"

Paggin sniffed. He kept his voice low and confidential so that only I heard his insinuation. "Hall Pycroft's rise has been swift, don't you think? Remarkable, even. Within a few short years he has found a fiancée, secured a promotion, married, secured another promotion. And now, when twenty-thousand pounds of securities are missing, we are toiling our hardest to find any other culprit than the obvious man!"

"What are you suggesting?" I demanded.

"Why, only that Mrs. Pycroft is a very attractive woman, and the Pycrofts must have hosted *excellent* dinners for Daniel Walmsley and old Mawson." Paggin sniffed again but would say no more.

Holmes's examination at last turned to Colonel Dennington's account strongbox. "The keyholes show no sign of tampering, so keys were utilised," he noted. "The identified card on the door is recently inked. When did Dennington become a client?"

"Almost a year ago," Pycroft supplied. "He was my first significant client when I became Second Broker in Equities."

"But you visited his box only last Wednesday," I pointed out.

"The investment finance that the Colonel required demanded more security. We had already got half of the Telepost stock in guarantee, but I placed the remainder in there at that time."

"Dennington came here?" asked Holmes.

"He came to my office – that is Mr. Walmsley's office – but not to the vault."

"No client would be allowed in the vault," Mr. Allen insisted.

Holmes moved on, inspecting the twin floor-standing safes, paying special attention to their keyholes. These heavy cubes were also key-operated, though different keys from the strongboxes. Mssrs Mawson and Williams had one safe key each, while Mr. Allen and Mr. Kenneal also possessed a key apiece.

"Are you discovering anything?" Mawson asked Holmes anxiously.

"My investigation proceeds apace," Holmes answered him distractedly. "It is a simple enough logic problem, but I should like to have a comprehensive overview of evidence before offering a solution."

He looked up from his magnifying lens and regarded his spectators. "I shall now inspect all of the keys that each of you carries. Perhaps we might move to some room with better light so that I can examine them properly?"

We reconvened in the board room. Holmes took his time with the various keyrings he was shown. After that, he consulted the visitors' books and staff sign-in sheets for the previous week. We had spent over three hours at Mawson's before he was satisfied.

"Well?" Pycroft prompted Holmes, anxious for his reputation. "Anything?"

My friend rippled his fingers to signify that he had made some progress that satisfied him, and deigned to offer one of his gnomic interim statements. "It is of significance that the contents of only one box have apparently been removed. To gain such illicit access, at least two people must have been in collusion."

"Two," Mawson objected. "I find it difficult to credit that even one of our staff might be so underhanded. It is unthinkable, but – We must consider it."

"But who?" Mr. Kenneal blurted.

Holmes held up a finger to appeal for patience. "There is a further question as to whether any of the keys may have been copied. Some of the keys I have just examined are very clean, which is to say they might possibly have been washed down, perhaps soaked in boiling water. Such a procedure is used to remove traces of wax that may have remained after imprints were made so that a locksmith might produce a duplicate. We must therefore seek to determine whether there was any opportunity for a thief to gain some time alone with any of the keys so as to attain such imprints and so cut another key."

"My staff are instructed to keep their keys upon their persons at all times," old Mawson insisted. "At home the keys are to be secured in some locked drawer or bureau, never left in a jacket, brief-case, or document satchel."

"It would be easier for some burglar to sneak into a home and copy a key than to breach security here," I considered. "If it was done slickly enough, then his presence would never even be suspected."

"We must look to such possibilities," Holmes allowed.

"Even you cannot run down all the ways that so many keys might have been handled for duplication," I warned my friend. "Remember, the ransom exchange is set for tomorrow morning. What of that?"

"Must I attend that appointment?" Pycroft wondered.

"If Mr. Holmes cannot find the blackmailer," old Mawson fretted, "then we have to pay!"

Holmes rose from his seat. "When the appointed hour comes tomorrow," he assured the senior staff, "Dr. Watson and I shall have made due provision for interrupting the exchange of debentures for stolen securities. When Hall Pycroft goes to his appointment with the thief next time, we shall be ready for him!"

We accepted Hall Pycroft's invitation to dine with him that evening, so by six-thirty we were sat in his Camberwell house, consuming well-prepared fish in butter and some seasonal vegetables.

"Hall is meticulous in his duties," Mrs. Pycroft assured us as Holmes and I enjoyed our client's hospitality. "He is never careless with his keys. When he is not in his work suit, he secures the ring in a drawer in our bedside dresser, which is kept locked since it also contains our bank book, the deeds to our house, a domestic cash-box, and some few stocks and bonds that he has purchased as an investment on his retirement. The key for that drawer is quite small, and we conceal it in a small gap between the bedpost and bedknob of our martial bed. Any thief must be presumed to have sneaked in as we slumbered, unscrewed the rather squeaky brass knob, opened the drawer, copied the key as you suggested, and then replaced everything without waking us. I doubt it is possible."

"Might any servant know where you keep your valuables?" I enquired.

"We keep only one maid, who is reliable. She knows we have a locked drawer but not how to access it."

Mrs. Emilie Pycroft was resolute in her statement. She was a bright, neat young woman some dozen or so years younger than her husband, with a vivacious manner and a keen intellect. It was easy to see how she might have caught the eye of a rising stockbroker, or how jealous colleagues of a fast-rising executive might ascribe his success to senior men's admiration of her.

"I am new to my present responsibilities," Pycroft reminded us as he finished off his butter-poached sturgeon. "For that reason I am especially careful of my keys, knowing their importance. I cannot believe that anyone might have had access to them without my knowing of it."

"Besides, there must have been at least two men involved in that robbery," Mrs. Pycroft insisted, echoing Holmes's earlier statement. "I am told that it takes two keys to access the vault, and one of the keys has only three copies – legitimate copies – and they reside with the Managing Director and two veteran staff members. I do not suggest that any of them are lax in their vigilance, but somehow one of their keys or a duplicate of it *must* have been used. Moreover, unless the intrusion was timed very specifically, the guard upon the vault door must have been bribed to turn a blind eye to someone leaving with a rather thick stack of papers."

"The guards have been carefully questioned," her husband assured her. "The Chief Guard, Warren Dutter, is very diligent in his office. Have I never told you his history?"

"If you have then I have forgotten it, I'm afraid."

"Well, you certainly know of my previous scrape with a criminal enterprise, of my substitution by the unscrupulous forger and cracksman Charles Beddington and what he did while feigning to be me. He took the vault guard unaware with a poker and murdered him. That guard was Clarence Dutter, Warren's own father. The son has since risen to his present seniority and he has a vehement drive to ensure that no such incident can ever occur again."

Dutton's identity was news to me, but I could see that Holmes had already made the connection during his afternoon's researches away from Lombard Street and Baker Street.

"How might the thief have known the exact amount of debentures to demand from Mawson's?" I wondered.

"I have been considering that too," Mrs. Pycroft responded. "Hall knows what might be at hand, of course, and those men to whom he reports, Mr. Kenneal and Mr. Paggin, right up to Mr. Mawson, But he tells

190

me that he also keeps Mr. Walmsley appraised of such matters by trans-Atlantic telegraph cable. [11] How are those messages sent, Hall? Are they coded?"

"Of course they are," Pycroft insisted. "Such information is confidential and highly commercially sensitive."

"What cyphers are used?" asked Holmes.

"I believe there is some sort of code book. Each message uses up a different page."

"And who cyphers the wires?" I checked.

"It would be the clerks' office, the secretaries," Pycroft supposed. "So . . . *any* one of them might have seen my report to Mr. Walmsley *before* it was encrypted!"

The fish course was cleared and we went on with a fine ragout, with a compote of prunes in custard to follow.

"I hope that you will be able to clear Hall tomorrow, Mr. Holmes," Mrs. Pycroft told the detective. "I understand that you intend to intervene in the payment exchange?"

"That will be the only way to catch the culprit," I knew. "Once the fellow has such a huge sum in easily-transferable securities, he will surely vanish without trace and never be seen again."

"Unless he becomes more aggressive with his blackmail," Pycroft worried. "When I am taken to some remote rural spot with the demanded ransom, what is to prevent him from extracting the debentures from me by force without returning the stolen articles and insisting upon another payment?"

"We shall prevent him," I assured the stockbroker and his wife.

"If the thief uses the same tactics as before, he will send a carriage to wait outside Benton's," Holmes reviewed. "It would be impossible to have another carriage concealed there to give pursuit. But the alley comes out onto Lombard Street, where a vehicle could be waiting and the trail might be picked up there."

"You will have some of your street urchins keeping watch and sending signals," I guessed.

"As you say. Then it is simply a matter of following on until the meeting takes place, wherever that might be."

"You make it *sound* simple," Mrs. Pycroft admitted, "but I fear that something awful might go wrong."

"Will it go wrong?" I asked Holmes as we travelled back to Baker Street after our repast. "It will be difficulty for our driver to keep Pycroft in sight without alerting the other cabbie that he is followed.

"All is in hand, Watson," Holmes assured me. "Did you enjoy your fish?"

"The sturgeon? It was excellent," I judged. "Why?"

"I delivered it to the housemaid myself this afternoon, Doctor, in the guise of a fishmonger at the back door. We got on famously and shared all kinds of scandalous gossip."

Holmes filled his pipe and settled back, formulating his solutions.

Pycroft's pickup was set for ten o'clock. Holmes and I were in position by eight, occupying a covered four-wheeler with a stout pair of horses capable of some speed. We were muffled against an unseasonably chill morning mist, alert for the exchange that had been scheduled.

We need not have been so diligent, since it was not until almost ten-past-ten before one of Holmes's Irregular juniors passed the signal that some unknown youth with *The Sporting News* had entered the coffee house with a message for Pycroft.

"It is beginning," I remarked to Holmes.

"It began some time ago," he corrected me. "There has been at least one fellow watching us since we first parked here. The idler over there is our present overseer, but at various parts of the morning there has also been a boot-black, a fellow with a shovel, and a youth with a hoop-and-stick. We were expected and we have been anticipated."

I didn't like the sound of that. Too many of the staff at Mawson and Williams knew of our engagement and about the intended transfer to be made. "How can we keep after a carriage that knows it will be followed?" I fretted.

Holmes seemed unconcerned. "They have made their provisions. I have made mine."

It was not long before a hansom rattled out of Change Alley and turned away from the City. Holmes's street Arabs indicated that Pycroft was aboard, clutching his brief-case packed with Stock Exchange three-percent debentures.

Holmes called for our driver to follow. "Carefully, though. I expect we shall be interrupted before long."

The detective proved correct. We had scarcely gone two-hundred yards before the hansom we pursued turned up a side-street. As we followed, our way was blocked by a milkman's dray shambling out from a gateway and preventing our passage.

"Move that thing!" I cried to the milkman. He affected to have some trouble cajoling his nag to shift from our path, so that eventually it was three full minutes before he had manoeuvred his cumbersome wagon enough to allow us to continue on.

"You will never be able to prove he was paid to delay us," Holmes advised me to calm my fury. "Pycroft's vehicle will be well ahead of us by now, having made any number of turns to lose us in the time since it vanished from our view."

"Then we are defeated!" I growled.

Holmes was amused. "Hardly. We were never going to succeed in following straight behind that carriage, were we? Even if our adversaries planned no delay to break off our pursuit, it would have proved impossible to trail the hansom along rural roads without our presence becoming very obvious. Another strategy was always required."

"Then what?" I demanded. "How else can we find where Pycroft is being taken?"

"We knew one thing, Watson: That the hansom would halt outside Benton's to admit its passenger. That allowed quite enough time for my young agents to affix an addition to the coach's undercarriage."

"An addition?"

Holmes pointed to the cobbles ahead of us, where a gaudy daub of red stood out on the damp stonework. "A pail of paint, with a small puncturation allowing drops to fall every few seconds. That hansom will leave a clear trail wherever it goes. We need only trace the red signs to reach Mr. Pycroft's destination."

The marks took us past Pentonville, onto the Great North Road at Islington, and over Highgate Hill. We had to pause a couple of times to rediscover the red splotches that betrayed the hansom's route, doubling back until we found its intermittent signs once more.

Our quarry turned off onto Muswell Hill Road, through thickening forest, onto rural lanes that tested Holmes's geographical knowledge. We were now beyond grimy old London Town, into sylvan Middlesex, following on through leafy tracks past villages like Crouch End, Lyttleton, and Finchley.

The modern fashion of street signs had not so far reached this countryside. Even our driver admitted himself somewhat lost, but we did not need to know exactly where we were, only where Pycroft had been taken.

We finally reached a junction where a meandering farm track vanished off between high hedges into a thick copse. We were about to manoeuvre down the single-track way when the very hansom cab that we had been tracing appeared from the other direction, empty of its passenger.

"Let him go, Isaiah," Holmes advised our driver. "We may be sure that Pycroft has been deposited not far up this lane. Remain on the verge here and keep watch. Watson and I shall proceed quietly on foot."

I checked my service revolver, grasped my stout walking stick, and proceeded with Holmes up the rural path. It was not long before we discovered a turnstile where Hall Pycroft waited with his ransom for the mounted thief.

"We shall remain concealed," Holmes told me. "The horseman will not be far off, and possibly his accomplice. When I reveal myself, you should stay back here. I may require you to take the felons by surprise if they turn weapons upon me. Otherwise, keep hidden and bear witness to what is said."

I had scarcely acknowledged Holmes's plan when we heard the sound of a horse approaching. It was a handsome cob colt, sprightly and well turned out, with large empty saddlebags to receive the thick contents of Pycroft's case. Its rider was swathed as before, scarfed and concealed under a broad hat.

He rode up to the stockbroker but did not dismount. "Good morning," he called genially. "You have brought the debentures as requested?"

"They are with me," Pycroft conceded. "You shall not have them until the bonds you took are returned and verified."

"Then we have a difficulty," the thief answered. "As you can see, I do not have the items with me. I would be a fool to bring along evidence that would convict me. However, you have my word as a gentleman that upon receipt of the promised payment, I shall tell you where your lost securities may be found."

"That is not satisfactory," Pycroft insisted. "Do not take us at Mawson's for fools."

"I have already taken you for fools, Hall Pycroft. I have gained the power to destroy you – and I shall. You will not surrender the debentures to me?"

"I shall not. You . . . you must take them from me by force if you intend to have them."

The horseman nodded. "That is admirable – the first admirable thing that I have discovered about you. I am not displeased that matters must end this way. It makes our revenges all the more satisfying."

Pycroft frowned with lack of understanding. "Revenges? What are you talking about?"

The rider chuckled. "It will be my pleasure to tell you. But first I shall have from you the ransom you have brought." He produced a Beaumont Adams service revolver identical to mine. [12] "Let us conduct our remaining business."

Holmes moved out from the treeline, appearing behind the horseman and levelling his own Browning. "Let us indeed bring this business to a conclusion," he told the thief. "What do you say, Colonel?"

"Colonel?" Pycroft echoed.

"Colonel Rupert Dennington, late of the ------shires," Holmes introduced the mystery rider. "His cavalry bearing betrays him, as do his boots and gloves, the slight tension in his left hip where he was wounded in the first exchanges of the Mahdist Uprising, [13] and his choice of weapon. And of course, he is the one outside person who might know the contents of his dedicated strongbox at Mawson's, and the one who would profit from a lawsuit against the firm that lost his securities."

"Dennington?" Pycroft could scarcely believe it. He eyed the horseman, matching the concealed thief to the investor he had met. "But how did he steal back his own sureties?"

"With aid, of course. I am sorry to reveal the name and nature of his accomplice."

"Then allow me to do it for you," Dennington responded. "Do be careful, Mr. Sherlock Holmes. A rifle is aimed exactly at your back."

Holmes did not move. The hedge stirred and another figure emerged from cover. I recognised her at once, and so did Pycroft. "Emilie?"

"Emilie," his wife agreed. Her face was flushed and sullen, suffused with old emotion, but she kept her weapon steady upon the detective. "Lay down your weapon, Mr. Holmes."

"Not yet," the detective replied. "There are points to clarify, and you will notice that my Browning is levelled at your lover. A shot at me, or into me, might cause me to squeeze my trigger and end his life also. Perhaps we should pause and unpack this sorry revenge play before we make any uncertain moves?"

I could scarcely credit Pycroft's bright young wife being tangled in this affair, and neither could the stockbroker. "Emilie?" he appealed. "What is this? Come to your senses! What grip has this man got over you?"

"I love him," Mrs. Pycroft answered certainly. "I have loved him for nigh ten years, since I first became his mistress."

The stockbroker's round face paled. I saw his lips repeat the word "mistress" without sound.

"I was destitute when he first took me in," she revealed to her husband. "If I have manners and poise now, it is because he taught me. And he loves me, or he should not have allowed me such licence in my revenge."

"You had better explain the rest, Mrs. Pycroft," Holmes suggested. "Or shall I?"

"You cannot have the truth of it," Colonel Dennington challenged him.

Holmes snorted. "Your plots have not been as subtle as you imagined. It was clear that some method must have been found to acquire the

195

information and the necessary keys to access the vault and deposit box. Moreover, since no other person's accounts were abused save those of Mr. Walmsley, managed by Pycroft in his absence, it was obvious that one of the keys employed had to be his. Who then had access to Pycroft's keys, and to either Mr. Mawson's set or that of Allen the Deposits Manager?

"There is lurid gossip that Mrs. Pycroft assisted her husband's rise in his company by dallying with certain senior officers. Mr. Mawson has visited the Pycroft home on several occasions, and according to the housemaid, not always when Mr. Pycroft was present. Such an irregular visit might afford Mrs. Pycroft ample opportunity to access and take imprints of Mawson's master key.

"No!" objected Hall Pycroft. "Emilie – !"

The stockbroker's wife seemed indifferent to so scandalous an imputation. "It was no great hardship, Hall," the unfaithful woman told him. "Of no more consequence than going to your bed and playing your loving wife. In fact, it required less effort, since I needed not pretend much affection for a simple carnal transaction. I made a similar deal with Walmsley to secure your temporary promotion."

Holmes continued remorselessly. "Such calls from Mr. Walmsley ensured Pycroft's present advancement to a position where he would be given Walmsley's key during the senior's overseas sojourn. They also offered ample opportunity to learn from Walmsley about the Stock Exchange debentures that were being assembled. The thief knowing that detail added verisimilitude to the suspicion that Hall Pycroft was behind the theft – except that, since Pycroft was so habitually sententious regarding client confidentiality, Mrs. Pycroft did not know that her husband had never been told of the acquisition."

"No . . ." Pycroft repeated, confused and devastated.

Holmes shook his head. "A woman of such shallow morals had no difficulty acquiring the necessary keys," Holmes went on. "She knew from Dennington what securities had been locked away. The next difficulty was gaining access to the vault, and that was another matter of revenge."

"What can you mean?" Pycroft demanded. His anger was overwhelming his shock.

"I refer to the means by which Emilie Pycroft was able to enter the vault. There was always going to be a second person required to gain entry. Unless Allen the Deposits Manager was in collusion with Pycroft to attest that nothing was done to the Dennington strongbox, unless Allen or Mawson were part of the conspiracy, then the only way to extract papers from the vault was for a single person to be in the room with two duplicate keys. Mrs. Pycroft had such keys, but she needed the guard on duty to turn a blind eye to her entry."

I saw the young woman draw a sharp intake of breath. Holmes's deduction had hit the mark.

Holmes continued. "The Chief Guard is Warren Dutter. His father was that unfortunate sentry who was murdered during the Beddington raid twelve years ago. The son was given a position with Mawson's because his father's death left his family with no means of income – but the company granted no other compensation or award for the death of their loyal employee. Dutter had reason to feel that he might be owed something for his father's sacrifice, and that his family had not been well-treated by the rich and prominent stockbrokers' firm in whose service Clarence Dutter had perished. I expect that made Warren Dutter vulnerable to your blandishments, Mrs. Pycroft?"

"Warren was ready to see Mawson's have to pay up for their indifference to his father's death," Emilie admitted. "But there is no proof that it was he who admitted me. There are other guards."

"There is also a full register of shifts, and a visitors' book on reception that records when you came to bring your husband his lunch each day," Holmes pointed out. "It is no difficulty to match the times when you were in the premises with the man who took the watch-shift on the vault. You were therefore also at Mawson's in the lunch hour when the typewriter was available."

"There is still the little difficulty proving how Emilie, or anyone, could have left the building with a substantial stack of bond certificates," Dennington pointed out.

"Nobody did," Holmes replied. "They were simply transferred to another of Walmsley's account boxes. The other boxes were checked to see that they had not likewise been emptied. Nobody looked for additional items in there. Mrs. Pycroft needed only extract the one Certificate that she later placed in her husband's wallet, with the reservation notice for verisimilitude, and they might fold into any pocket. Likewise she could carry the missing jewels out simply by wearing them. The remaining articles could be hidden within the document stacks of fifty other client files. You cannot return the stolen securities even if you wished to, for they have never left Mawson's."

"You seem to have accounted for everything," Mrs. Pycroft acknowledged, "except the why of it – and what comes next."

"You already told me: *Revenge*," my friend reminded her. "Once I looked closely at you it was easy to see. William Beddington, the younger of the larcenous brothers, had a daughter who was ten years old at the time of her father's attempted suicide and his subsequent demise in prison. Her name was also Emilie. As the orphaned child of a convicted criminal, she suffered a dreary and awful life until she found her way into Colonel

Dennington's bed and patronage. Do you blame Hall Pycroft for all your misfortunes because he discovered the ruse played upon him? And did you yearn to take from Mawson's everything and more that your father and uncle had perished failing to steal?"

Pycroft looked deathly. "Emilie . . . You let me court and marry you . . . to pay me out for thwarting your father?" he gasped at his wife. "You did all of that . . . for hate of me?"

"And I shall do more, Hall," Emilie promised him. "You shall disappear today. You and Mr. Holmes, for all his cleverness. It will be supposed that you took off with the debentures, having previously arranged the theft of the Certificates. You will murder Sherlock Holmes to make your getaway. Warren will never be exposed. And of course, your wife will vanish with you."

"And scandal will ruin Mawson's," Colonel Dennington anticipated. "Naturally, I shall seek the maximum compensation from them that the law allows before they are destroyed."

"That would certainly shore up your dubious finances from your greyhound-racing debts, Colonel," Holmes agreed. "Unfortunately, I had already deduced everything I have said now before ever setting out to trail you to this meeting. I have left a full account of it to be delivered to Mawson's and Scotland Yard should I suddenly disappear. As I said, your machinations were not so clever as you supposed."

"Damn you!" the old cavalryman spat. "If that's true, then we shall have to flee after all. But we'll be leaving with sixty-thousand in liquefiable debentures, and Emilie shall still have her revenges on Pycroft and on you!"

I decided that enough was enough. I emerged from my hiding spot, my own revolver trained upon Mrs. Pycroft. "Sherlock Holmes is more valuable than sixty-thousand in promissories," I announced. "You will both lower your weapons now. I am loath to shoot a woman, but Holmes is my friend."

Even then Emilie might have taken her shot, but just at that moment Hall Pycroft collapsed into a heap and began to sob. She turned her rifle on him, a look of demented loathing on her face. Holmes seized the weapon's barrel and diverted it downwards so that her shot buried itself in the turf.

Dennington might have fired too, so I placed a bullet into the bounder's right arm and tumbled him from his seat.

After that, everything was emotional wrapping-up of our forest stand-off, and our driver Isaiah summoning the police.

"I am desolate. Devastated," Pycroft told me that evening, once the police were satisfied with his statement. "My whole life was blighted from the moment that Charles and William Beddington first targeted me with their schemes. That such an entanglement should come back to me in this way now, through my own precious wife, whom I loved dearly . . . ."

"Women are often the coldest plotters," Holmes mentioned. "Why, the most winning woman I ever knew was . . . ." [14]

I was not as indifferent to Pycroft's suffering as was the great detective. Holmes's interest in the case was already waning, his attention moving on to a question of codifying methods of matching typewriter imprints to particular instruments, and the monograph he would publish on them. I was more concerned with the crestfallen stockbroker who had suffered betrayal and heartbreak through no fault of his own.

I cut off Holmes's reminiscence to say, "Your reputation is safe, Pycroft. Your firm has clear proof of your innocence. Indeed, it was only your actions that saved them from ruin."

"And my wife who led them to that ruin," he answered unhappily. "My wife, who was a blaggard's mistress, who cuckolded me with my superiors, and who plotted my disgrace and death. Do you think old Mawson will want me around any more, now that I know of his infidelity with Emilie? Would I *wish* to be around him, or Walmsley, or who knows who else?"

"Warren Dutter has confessed his part in the plot," I went on. "He will turn Queen's Evidence [15] against the others. It is Colonel Dennington who faces disgrace, deregimenting, bankruptcy, and prison, and Emilie Beddington also."

"Dennington may hang for all I care, but I shall never recover from what he has done to me."

"You must face it out," Holmes advised the unfortunate stockbroker. "Your superiors have wronged you in several ways, in their dealings with your wife and by their accusations about your integrity. I daresay they will be ashamed of their behaviour and leery of it becoming known to the detriment of their reputations and that of their company. Dennington and your wife might have escaped prosecution had Mawson's not preferred charges, except for the criminal use of firearms and their intention to take our lives. Mawson's would have preferred that the affair not be bruited in open court. As it is, only your discretion in giving testimony and thereafter can save the public standing of important men and the company they run. I imagine you will find your progression at Mawson and Williams to be steady and assured."

"Why should I – ?" Pycroft began angrily.

"You have worked hard. You have shown your quality. You deserve success," I told him. "Take your licks and stand like a man, Hall Pycroft! You have a future yet, and perhaps pre-eminence in your profession in the years to come. Do not allow your enemies to defeat you. Endure and triumph, man!"

I do not know how much effect Holmes's advice or mine had upon the heartbroken stockbroker, but those who understand stocks and shares and are cognisant of the City's movers and shakers might now recognise and respect the name of him whom I have referred to in my account as Mr. Hall Pycroft.

NOTES

1. Liberal statesman Sir John Lubbock's *Bank Holidays Act* 1871 established Easter Monday, Whit Monday (the day after Pentecost Sunday or Whitsuntide), the first Monday in August, and the first working day after 25th December as public holidays. Good Friday and Christmas Day were already so established "*since time immemorial*". This popular legislation led to the new days off being called "St Lubbock's Days". Since Pentecost is a moveable feast like Easter, Whit Monday in 1902 was the 19th of May, twelve days after Holmes had charted the "*deep waters*" of "The Adventure of Shoscombe Old Place", according to biographer Baring-Gould's chronology.

2. "The Adventure of the Stockbroker's Clerk" was first published in *The Strand Magazine* in March 1893, and was collected into *The Memoirs of Sherlock Holmes* that same year (although publication dated 1894).

3. At the time of their foundation in 1819, Oxford Circus was originally known as Regent's Circus North and Piccadilly Circus was Regent's Circus South, and they were identified by these terms for most of the nineteenth century, even as their more distinctive names came into use alongside them. The opening of the tube station at Oxford Circus by that title in 1900 marked the final transition to the area's modern nomenclature.

4. The Canon mentions tea fifteen times and coffee seventeen times, but is silent upon which blend of tea Holmes drank. Several sources suggest Lapsang Souchong, then a popular choice for its smoky aromatic flavour that went well with strong tobacco. Withered and dried above pine embers, it was recommended with "*English breakfast, light dishes, spicy food, matured cheese, meat and game, and poultry.*" Lapsang Souchong was also Winston Churchill's favourite non-alcoholic beverage.

     Several Sherlock Holmes-themed teas are now available, and at least one Moriarty-themed blend.

5. Since the term "debenture" even occupies the title of our story, it may be worth defining, although English judge the Right Honourable Lord Lindley PC, FRS, FBA, KC (1828-1921) famously declared, "*Now, what the correct meaning of 'debenture' is I do not know. I do not find anywhere any precise definition of it. We know that there are various kinds of instruments commonly called debentures.*" Lindley's seminal *Lindley on Partnership* (1862) is still in publication today, now on its 21st edition.

     Practically, a debenture is a medium-term legal and financial agreement for the issuer to borrow money at a fixed rate of interest. The debenture acts like a certificate of loan, but does not become share capital. Distinctions are made between senior and subordinate debentures, with senior debentures paid off by preference, offering different rates of risk and payoff. Debentures are usually exchangeable and tradable, and so may finally be claimed by someone entirely different from the original purchaser. Many debentures are issued by governments as a way of financing significant projects or meeting debts.

In some countries, the term "debenture" is now applied to mean *any* bond, loan, stock, or note, but a stockbroker of Holmes's time would have been horrified by such sloppy usage.

6. Foolscap was a standard paper size during the Victorian era, measuring 16" x 26" (large enough to fold into the paper cone hat placed on dunces, from which the sheet takes its name). A foolscap folio was half the size, 8" x 13". A *plano* sheet has a half-inch extra in each dimension to allow for printers' trimming.

7. £20 in 1900 would be equivalent to around £3,000 ($3,800) today.

To put this into historical context, Dr. Watson's nine-months' pension after his injuries forced his retirement from military service was 11s/6d per diem or £4/0/6 per week, a sum he felt would not allow him to continue "*living in town*" unless he found shared accommodation. That income would equate to £609.52 or $780 per week in today's currency (considerably greater than the present maximum military disablement pension rate of £220.20 per week, but time-limited not ongoing. Watson's wound would not make him eligible for today's maximum rate). At the time Watson was receiving his disability pension, his daily sum was equivalent to the weekly wage of a heavy agricultural labourer.

8. A guinea is one pound and one shilling, £1.05 in modern decimal sterling. The guinea became a common pricing unit when luxury goods were charged a 5% sales tax, reflecting the cost of the item plus the government's tithe.

9. Seventeenth and Eighteenth Century Change Alley coffeehouses such as Jonathan's and Garraway's were early venues for trading of shares and commodities. Other shops included ship chandlers, makers of navigational instruments, and goldsmiths from Lombardy in Italy. Around the corner at 16, Lombard Street, Lloyd's Coffee House became the forerunner of Lloyd's of London, the Lloyd's Register, and Lloyd's List.

10. Many Holmesians have commented on the similarity of this plot with that perpetrated by the organisers of "The Red Headed League" that Holmes exposed two years previously. These unusual schemes with their complicated diversions have sometimes been attributed to the behind-the-scenes influence of consulting criminal Professor Moriarty.

11. The first official telegram between the United Kingdom and North America was an 1858 letter of congratulations from Queen Victoria to President James Buchanan, but the cable line lasted only three weeks before failing. The first successful, persistent trans-Atlantic cable began operation in 1866. By the end of the nineteenth century there were British, French, German, and American-owned cables linking Europe and North America.

12. The Beaumont Adams revolver was the standard British Army handgun from 1862 to 1880, favoured because of it was the first true double action firearm (cocked by either the hammer or trigger) and delivered a hefty 54 bore, .422-calibre bullet. It was replaced by the Enfield Mark 1 as the army's weapon of choice the year that Dr. Watson was pensioned out.

13. Now preferentially termed the Mahdist War, the rebellion of Muhammad Ahmad bin Abdullah, self-proclaimed "Mahdi" of Islam (the "Guided One")

against the Khedivate of Egypt and later against the British Empire took place from 1881 to 1889. The Mahdi failed, his campaign ending with the establishment of the *de jure* condominium of Anglo-Egyptian Sudan (1899–1956), ceding effective control of the region to Britain.

14. In *The Sign of Four,* Holmes revealed that *"The most winning woman I ever knew was hanged for poisoning three little children for their insurance-money . . . ."*

15. This would be turning State's Evidence in the U.S., referring to a witness admitting guilt and testifying for the state against others, in exchange for leniency in sentencing or immunity from prosecution. Such informants are called *de Kronzeuge* ("Crown Witnesses") in Germany, *Pentiti* ("Penitents") in Italy, and cooperating witnesses, witness collaborators, justice collaborators, or other terms elsewhere in the world.

The Adventure of the
Tall, Slim, Dark Woman
by Craig Stephen Copland

Throughout the nearly quarter-century since I had met him, Sherlock Holmes had an unfailing practice of demanding that clients be entirely forthcoming. Should they dare to deceive him, or even withhold material data about themselves or their case, they were immediately shown the door.

So, you can imagine my bewilderment when, in the winter of 1903, he invited me to join him when he met with a new client.

"Who is she?" I asked.

"I don't know."

"I beg your pardon?"

"I said, I – "

"I know what you said, Holmes, but since when did you agree to meet with a client you don't know anything about?"

"I didn't say I did not know anything, only that she hasn't revealed her name. Other than that small detail, I know enough to conclude she is in desperate need of my services."

"How?"

"From the note she sent me. Here. Take a look."

He handed me a small envelope. I knew straightaway the paper was a select brand purchased from a shop, likely in Bond Street, that catered to the upper class and those who wanted to present themselves as belonging to same.

The note inside was written in a feminine hand that betrayed years in a private school for girls where penmanship was next to godliness. It ran:

Dear Mr. Sherlock Holmes:

> *Kindly forgive my making direct contact with you and failing to seek an appropriate introduction. However, I find myself rather suddenly and unexpectedly in need of your unique services.*

> *Within a week, I shall be falsely accused in the press of having committed a murder in the winter of 1899. I shall be further falsely accused of having participated in an evening of*

204

dissolute, debauched, and unspeakable activities at the soirée *where the murder took place.*

 I have not attached my name or address in this note, as I have learned from previous unfortunate events that no letter or note is protected from curious and possibly felonious eyes. I shall reveal both upon meeting with you.

 I will call upon you tomorrow at your address on Baker Street at three o'clock in the afternoon.

 Enclosed is a sum of money that, I trust, will more than cover your standard fee.

 I look forward to your invaluable assistance.

Yours sincerely

It wasn't signed.

"Where's the money?" I asked.

"It was a substantial amount, and I deposited it in the bank. Ah! That may be her at the door now."

We listened as Mrs. Hudson answered the bell and greeted the unnamed client.

Our long-suffering landlady entered the room.

"You have a guest, Mr. Holmes. I requested her name, but she refused to tell me. Shall I send her away?"

"Not at all, Mrs. Hudson. Kindly send her up."

The visitor ascended the stairs quickly and strode into the room. She had removed her Burberry mantle while on the stairs and now bore it over her arm. She was elegantly dressed in a tightly fitted black dress that exposed her lower calf and ankle, as was now the fashion of the day.

A small, round hat sat on top of her dark hair, and her face was covered by a veil. She was tall and slender, and going by the portion of her lower face and neck I could see, she had a somewhat dark complexion. The mantle was tossed onto the sofa, and she raised her two gloved hands to her head and lifted her veil.

We looked at her beautiful face, with a curved nose, marked eyebrows, glittering eyes, perfectly formed mouth, and the strong little chin beneath it. I gasped and was about to blurt out some words when I felt the cold, tight grasp of Holmes's hand on my wrist. I knew by how he had clamped his fingers like a vice that his reaction was the same as mine.

The woman standing in front of us was none other than the one who had entered the study of Charles Augustus Milverton four years earlier, had sent bullet after bullet into his evil body, and dispatched his soul off to Hell.

Holmes and I had watched her from behind the curtains. We knew who she was.

She did not know that we knew who she was.

Holmes recovered his composure more rapidly than I did.

"Good afternoon, Lady – ." he said. "I recognize you from the photographs in the shop windows. Will you be seated? Some brandy, perhaps? You are facing rather dire circumstances. It might help you to relax. Dr. Watson, might I impose on you for a round?"

[I note that I am continuing to protect her anonymity, which I also disguised in my recently published account of the demise of Charles Augustus Milverton, the worst man in London. For those who are interested, you may find the account bearing Milverton's name in a recent volume of The Strand *magazine.]*

I stepped over to the mantel and filled three snifters from the cut-glass decanter of brandy that had been kept in the same location for years, and had many times proved useful for the same task to which it was now being put.

"Thank you," she said. Her voice was low and resonant. "That is very kind of you to offer. I know, sir, that your time is precious to you as mine is to me, so might we dispense with the idle chat required by social convention and get straight to my reason for needing your assistance?"

"Indeed, we shall," said Holmes. "But permit me to observe that you appear to be exceptionally calm and poised, considering the turmoil your life is now in."

"Difficult situations are nothing new to me, Mr. Holmes. I have faced them before, and I have learned that taking decisive action to rectify a problem is the best – the only – solution."

"I'm sure you have," said Holmes.

I was also sure she had, if firing an entire revolver into your adversary and grinding your heel into his face can be euphemistically referred to as "decisive action".

"Very well, then," Holmes continued, "kindly state your case and what services you require of me . . . and, of course, of my friend, Dr. Watson. We have both read your note. Please explain."

She took a slow but full sip of her brandy, set the snifter down, and placed her hands in her lap.

"Four years ago, the exact date being the thirteenth of January, I was approached by several dear friends of mine and beseeched to join them at a dinner party to be held in north London. It was a cold, frosty winter night, and I had spent my life in isolated mourning for my dear husband, who had died three months earlier. At first, I refused, but then I thought the event might be good for me, and I agreed to go with them."

"Might that event," asked Holmes, "have been held in a fine house in Hampstead Heath?"

The look of shocked amazement on the lady's face couldn't be missed. "Why . . . why, yes, it was. How could you have known that?"

Holmes shrugged. "You said it was in north London, and I am aware that there are some people living within the Heath who have a reputation for hosting dinner parties during the depths of winter for the self-appointed literary and artistic savants. Some of those evenings last into the next morning. Most are highly civil, cultivated affairs, if somewhat pretentious, but some have given rise to stories of behavior that is, shall we say, questionable."

"You are well ahead of me, Mr. Holmes. Yes, the affair to which I was invited began as a delightful evening. A very attentive and very pretty staff of young men and women served us cocktails and champagne to accompany salmon mouse pinwheels, truffled tartlets, and cabin biscuits. The dinner of parsley cream soup, trout almondine, and breast of duck was washed down with as much sherry, white wine, claret, and port as one could absorb. I was cautious with my consumption, as I had plans for later that night. The guests were a sophisticated mix of artists, theatre people, musicians, professors, and politicians who engaged in sparkling, witty conversation that perhaps bordered on competitive erudition. The music started up around ten o'clock. At close to midnight, I slipped out of the house, pulled my winter mantle around me, and departed."

"So far, it sounds like the usual gathering of Oxbridgian snobs in Hampstead," said Holmes. "Wherein is the problem?"

"The problem, Mr. Holmes, is that I learned early the next day that after I had left the party, it descended into a bacchanal of debauchery and immoral behavior of a sort that would make Oscar Wilde, Sappho, Caligula, the Marquis de Sade, and even Lord Byron blush. To make matters much worse, I had been chatting amiably with Viscount Gough-Battenberg earlier in the evening. He had been a dear friend of my late husband and visited often in our home in Kent. It was entirely appropriate that I should chat with him over a glass or two of wine. He is . . . I should say he *was* a jovial fellow and quite the character and *bon vivant*. However, at some time after I had departed, the viscount engaged in some foolish behavior with Lady – . No, I shall not reveal her name. I didn't witness what took place, and only learned by way of the grapevine. But he suffered heart failure and died. Had I not departed the party, I would have restrained him from his reckless behavior."

"I read of his death," said Holmes. "Wherein is the problem?"

"An utterly deceitful, self-serving reporter for *The Evening Star* has acquired knowledge of the evening and the sad death of the Viscount, and

207

has taken it upon himself to investigate the evening. One of the attendees violated the unwritten rule of party-goers in Hampstead – a vow of complete confidentiality – and told the reporter about the events of the evening."

"No doubt for a significant sum," said Holmes.

"Oh, yes, that could be. I hadn't considered that possibility."

"Regardless, you still have yet to explain what this has to do with you."

"He, the repulsive reporter, is about to publish his story claiming not only was I present, but that I engaged in numerous unspeakable acts, and that it was I who caused the Viscount to die. He is accusing me of murder."

Holmes nodded and then shrugged. "But you say you have an alibi that accounts for your being somewhere else when all that took place."

"That is my predicament, sir. I cannot reveal my alibi. Not to anyone. Ever. The consequences to me would be worse than the humiliation and shame that will be visited upon me when the article is published next week. I regret that I cannot even tell you what it is. I can only beg you to believe me and to take on my case."

Holmes leaned back, slowly lit his pipe, and took several slow puffs. The wait was clearly excruciating for the lady, and if I had been closer to Holmes, I would have given him a swift kick for being so inconsiderate.

He gave his pipe a tap on the ashtray. "Fine. I believe you. No need to explain or reveal anything else. I will pursue your case and resolve it in a manner satisfactory to you."

"You will?"

The lady's face was one of bewildered surprise. "That . . . that is wonderful, Mr. Holmes. I must confess, I am amazed by your reaction. I had heard that you would never give the time of day to any client who withheld data from you. I read about how you treated clients like that in all those stories in *The Strand*. Coming to you was an act of desperation on my part, and I must say, I am grateful beyond words."

"My dear Lady – , why be surprised? I believe what you said about your departure from the party, and I believe that your alibi is ironclad. It should prove to be an interesting case. Dr. Watson and I shall get to work on it straight away."

Our newest client thanked him again, rose, pulled on her heavy mantle, and departed.

I glanced over at Holmes. "I must say, my friend, even you weren't expecting that."

"No, I wasn't, but the irony of the arrangement appeals to me. There have been clients who didn't reveal everything they knew to me when presenting their case. Now, I am in the position of not revealing everything I know. I do find it rather amusing."

"Can you solve her predicament? There isn't much time."

"Come now, Watson, getting rid of the reporter is simplicity itself. That doesn't present much of a challenge. But discovering if a murder did in fact take place four years ago and, if it did, who did it is a case that might be of interest to me."

He stood up, walked over to the coat rack, and pulled on his winter coat and gloves.

"Well, don't just sit there," he said to me. "Get your coat on. It's cold outside."

"Where are we going?"

"To Fleet Street. The offices of *The Evening Star*."

We hailed a cab, and it took us into central London.

"This nasty reporter she referred to," he said, "is named Dorian Brewster. He isn't as vile and despicable as Charles Augustus Milverton, but not far off. He also carries on the degenerate practice of soliciting damning letters and accounts from servants, cab drivers, and those set on vengeance. His newspaper pays well for such items."

"Does he blackmail people as well?"

"No, no. He doesn't hold a job as a reporter for the money. No one does. He is obsessed with building his own reputation within his newspaper, earning it greater circulation and gaining the praise and adulation of his peers. He pays for evidence of misdeeds, prints the story regardless of its entire accuracy, helps his employer sell more copies, and receives an award for fearless reporting from his colleagues."

"How are you going to stop him?"

"By giving him the scoop of a lifetime."

The building bearing the name of *The Evening Star* was located at the far end of Fleet Street, almost at the corner of Faringdon. The building was utterly unimpressive, with dark bricks that hadn't been cleaned in a century and windows covered with wire screens to keep both stray birds and stones from enraged readers from inflicting damage.

Unlike the more prestigious newspapers farther to the west, the interior of the building was anything but impressive. There were no marble floors, no grand staircases leading to the offices of the senior editors, and no paintings adorning the walls. Indeed, there were hardly any walls at all, only a large open floor on which sat several dozen desks all crammed together cheek-by-jowl. At some of the desks, reporters in cheap suits were scribbling, some were typing, and some were chatting. The place smelled of orders of now-cold fish and chips that had been brought in for lunch several hours earlier.

Holmes approached a young lady who was seated at a desk close to the door.

"Pardon me, Miss," he said, "I am dreadfully sorry to interrupt your work, as I can see you are busy, but might you be so kind as to direct me to the desk of Mr. Dorian Brewster?"

"That creep? Far corner, back row, two from the end."

She stood up and gazed over the room.

"He's at his desk now. Make sure you get the money he's offering for your story before you leave. Otherwise, he'll welch and lie and say he never agreed to give you anything. We're tired of having people like you come in and start yelling about being cheated. Good luck, whoever you are."

The man at the desk to whom she sent us was hunched over a typewriter, pecking energetically at it with his two index fingers. He was a slight fellow with narrow shoulders and thinning black hair. He didn't notice us until we were standing beside him.

"Mr. Dorian Brewster, is it not?" said Holmes.

"Depends who's asking."

"My name is Sherlock Holmes."

Brewster stopped typing and looked up.

"I've heard about you. What do you want with me?"

Holmes leaned down until his face wasn't more than a few inches from Brewster's. "The matter is terribly confidential. Might you come across the road to The Bell? I assure you, what I have to say to you is of infinitely greater importance than whatever you are currently working on."

Holmes didn't wait for an answer. He started walking toward the door, and I followed him. Brewster fumbled around for a few seconds and then hopped to his feet, grabbed his coat off the back of his chair, and followed us.

The Old Bell Tavern on Fleet Street claimed it had been established by the architect Christopher Wren over two-hundred years earlier as a place to feed and house his stone masons while they were building St. Paul's. As with many such stories from history, it can be neither proven nor refuted. What couldn't be denied was its convivial atmosphere and thoroughly decent offerings of fish and chips and mushy peas, washed down by a constant supply of ale.

At that hour of the afternoon, it wasn't yet filled with its usual collection of reporters, punters, and bankers, and we made our way unobstructed to a small table in the back corner. Holmes took a seat on the far side and indicated to me that I should sit beside him.

Dorian Brewster had followed us and stood at the other side of the table.

"Mr. Sherlock Holmes," he said, "you must tell me what this is about. I'm working toward a deadline to file and – "

"Sit down and listen," said Holmes. "If you aren't interested in what may be the biggest scoop of your life, I can find another reporter who is."

Brewster started to say something but stopped, pulled a chair back, and sat looking at Holmes, his arms crossed over his chest.

"Look here, Mr. Holmes – "

"Barmaid, please," said Holmes. "An ale for my friend and one for me. What do you want, Mr. Brewster?"

"Um . . . an ale would be fine. Now then, Mr. Holmes – "

"Do the names Arthur Balfour, Joseph Chamberlain, George Goshen, Harry Chaplin, and Walter Long mean anything to you?"

"Of course they do. They are all members of Salisbury's Cabinet."

"What I am about to tell you concerns them and other members of the Cabinet. Are you interested or not?"

"If it concerns them – "

"I just said it does. Now, are you interested or not?"

"Very well, I am interested."

Holmes took a slow sip of his ale.

"Good. Then I can make use of your assistance. You may publish the eventual story, but until you do submit it to your editor, you must guarantee me that no one will hear a word about it. Is that agreed?"

"I assure you, I have a reputation for not disclosing any of my sources."

"Good. Then the first question you should be asking me is why I would deign to speak to you and make use of your services."

"That would be – "

"It should be. So, I will answer it for you. I am investigating a criminal scheme involving several members of His Majesty's Cabinet who appear to be involved in an illegal scheme of bribes amounting to several hundred-thousand pounds. The scheme is connected to the construction of ships for the Royal Navy."

Brewster put down his ale and took out his reporter's notebook.

Holmes continued. "As you know, or I assume you know, I have acquired a considerable reputation for my singular skills as a detective. The disadvantage of having done so is that the instant any of the many politicians, captains of industry, and bankers involved in this scheme sense so much as a whiff of my interest, they will move their operations to Switzerland, or Luxembourg, or Uganda, or who knows where, and it will be impossible to expose their malfeasance. Now, do you understand why this issue is important? Do you realize that the future of the British Empire will be at risk? Do you?"

"Um, yes . . . but why me? My expertise is in stories that are more, shall we say – "

"Belonging in the gutter? Dredging up past peccadillos, long-forgotten affairs of the heart, family turmoil, and tragic events? Precisely. That is why you would be useful to me. If you are the one asking questions about an event that took place last weekend, no one will expect it to be about anything of importance to the nation. Their guard will be down and, assuming you have some degree of intelligence, you should be able to uncover the evidence I need to lay the entire case before Scotland Yard."

"Do I get the exclusive right to cover it?"

"From me? Yes. However, I know that other reporters may be interested, and I cannot promise that they will not break the story first if you are too slow."

"If you give me what you know, Mr. Holmes, I will get working on it straight away."

"Excellent. I was aware that you prided yourself on being fearless and accepted threats against you as a badge of honor. You may expect to face determined and dangerous opposition. I already have."

Brewster puffed his chest out ever so slightly. "I have been commended for my courage. That is correct."

"Splendid. Now, take this down. Are you familiar with a select residence in Hampstead Heath called Appledore Towers?"

"I am. It was the location several years ago of a robbery and murder of a chap named Milverton, was it not?"

"I neither know nor care what happened several years ago. I am concerned with what took place there this past weekend. The house is now owned by the nephew of this Mr. Milverton, who rents it out for private affairs. Parties, if you will. The one that took place there on the weekend was attended by ten members of the Cabinet, seven with their wives and three with their mistresses. Several highly placed bankers and industrialists were also present, as were officials of the embassies and high commissions of Germany, the United States, Switzerland, France, and Canada. I discovered that over a dozen, shall we say, *courtesans*, both male and female, were also present. The early portion of the evening was given to making secret arrangements to abscond with large amounts from His Majesty's treasury. After midnight, it degenerated to an orgy of illicit and grossly indecent activities."

Brewster was scribbling furiously. His eyes widened at the mention of orgy and gross indecency. He put down his pencil.

"No offense, Mr. Holmes, but I cannot depend solely on your words. I must find other sources who can corroborate what you tell me."

"No offense taken and perfectly understood. I suggest you start with Lord Snidley of Great Snoring. He is the otherwise anonymous Private Secretary to the Privy Council. He may be visited at the Diogenes Club on Pall Mall between a quarter-to-five and twenty-to-eight. I shall tell him to expect you to call on him tomorrow evening. He is deeply vexed by what is taking place and is willing to violate his oath of confidentiality to see that such villainous malfeasance is brought to an end. The second is the nephew of Mr. Milverton, the owner of the house in which the party took place. For a reasonable sum, he is willing to recount everything he saw and heard. I will not advise him of your plan to pay him a visit tomorrow, as I have discovered that taking him unawares is the most effective way to wring data from him. That is more than enough for you to get going. Please keep me informed so that I may coordinate my activities with Scotland Yard. Good day, Mr. Brewster."

Once we were out on the pavement, Holmes lit a cigarette and smiled smugly.

"The trap is set, Watson. How long do you expect it will be before he publishes his preposterous story?"

"No more than a few days. But Holmes, who are these sources? I've never heard of them. Surely, you aren't expecting your brother to get involved."

"Of course I am. He will be tickled to do so. He's like that. Langdale Pike will play the new owner of Appledore Towers. He will publish a subsequent story in his gossip column exposing the infelicitous greed of Brewster and his newspaper. Come now, we must stop in at Boodles and Diogenes and apprise our players of their parts."

I had first encountered Mycroft Holmes over a decade earlier when he was involved in the incident of the Greek interpreter. It had been some time since I last met with him in the Diogenes Club, and I was pleased to see that his weight had dropped by at least three stone. He remained far from slim, but at least was no longer corpulent.

We met in the Stranger's Room, and Mycroft seemed quite chuffed by the task Holmes had requested of him.

"It should be a rather diverting exercise," he said. "You do know, of course, Sherlock, that you aren't the only one who is capable of disguising himself."

"I humbly acknowledge," said Holmes, "that much of my ability in that regard has come from watching you pretend to be something you clearly are not."

Mycroft ignored the not-too-subtle jibe. "There are conditions to my taking on the role."

"And what are those, dear brother?"

"You shall not censor whatever farrago of lies I tell to this reporter of yours. I plan to be highly creative but never beyond belief. I trust you will not object."

"I have complete faith in your judgment," said Holmes.

Once back out of the pavement, I queried Holmes about the exchange that had taken place between him and his brother.

"What in the world," I asked, "did he mean by saying he refused to be censored?"

"It means that he immediately saw some opportunity to use the meeting with Brewster to further his own plans. He is, however, sufficiently astute not to push them so far as to alert our otherwise gullible and greedy member of the Press. Come now, we need to find Langdale Pike. I expect he will be sitting in the bay window of his club."

And so he was.

He was ensconced in a small armchair with his foot crossed over his knee. A notebook was propped on his thigh, and in one hand he held a pencil and in the other a glass of port.

"Why, if it isn't the illustrious Mr. Sherlock Holmes and the loyal Doctor Watson," he said, looking pleased to see us. "And what delightful jewels of salacious gossip have you come to trade with me today?"

"Not a trade, Pike," said Holmes. "Rather an assignment which, if accepted, you will be able to scribble at least a month of your columns."

"How tantalizingly irresistible. Pray, enlighten me."

Holmes explained how he was about to rent the vacant Appledore Towers from the nephew of the deceased Charles Augustus Milverton. He required Langdale Pike to occupy the premises and pose as the owner. When a reporter from *The Evening Star* came to call and make inquiries concerning a party there on the past weekend, he would be free to regale the reporter with whatever outrageous stories he could imagine. The only restriction on the anecdotes he invented would be that they may not exceed the bounds of the possible. He would then have the first shot at opining on the resulting *brouhaha* in his gossip column.

"And just who was supposed to be attending said party?" Pike asked.

Holmes listed nearly twenty names from the highest reaches of politics, the arts, commerce, and even one from the Church of England.

Pike was rubbing his hands in unfiltered glee. "And you say I may be as salacious as I want, as long as it doesn't require an entire suspension of disbelief."

"You may," said Holmes. "You must convince the reporter that what you tell him is God's truth, regardless of whether or not it is preposterous."

"Oh my, oh my, this does sound like a delightful little adventure! I do enjoy working with you, Sherlock Holmes. Such a pity you don't call upon me more often. Why do you not do that? I am always eager to accept."

To his credit, Holmes laughed and gave the man a friendly clap on his shoulder. "My good man, I am certain that you know the answer to your question."

"Fine. I suppose I do. But I hope that the next occasion isn't far off. This one has more promise than anything going on now in Mayfair or Belgravia. And Hampstead Heath, you say. I have never reported on any social scandal up there before. By jingo, it's an adventure!"

"Two down, Watson," said Holmes as he puffed away on yet another cigarette while we shivered on the pavement of St. James Street. "Fancy a long cab ride up to Hampstead Heath?"

The winter solstice had passed only a fortnight earlier, and the days were still unremittently short. By four o'clock, it was dark, and now, approaching seven in the evening, any trace of glimmer from the sun was long gone.

We took the cab as far as Church Row in Hampstead and then walked for a quarter-hour through the lanes and trails until we reached a big house on its own grounds. It was bitterly cold, and we buttoned up our great coats and wrapped our scarves around our necks.

There were some lights on in the house, and Holmes knocked on the door in a friendly rhythm. As he was waiting for a response, he moved to the side and gazed through the glass panel beside the door.

He turned and shouted to me. "Watson, you'll have to rent it without me! We want it for a fortnight starting tomorrow."

He jumped off the porch and into the bushes.

"Holmes, what in Heaven's name – "

"Don't talk to me. Just get it rented!"

The door opened, and a middle-aged and middle-sized maid greeted me.

"Good evening, sir. How may I assist you?"

I was terribly confused and couldn't imagine what had come over Holmes. I stammered a reply.

"Good evening, miss. I am Doctor John Watson, and I wish to speak to the owner concerning the rental of this house. Is he available?"

"Lovely to meet you, Doctor. I'm Agatha. Please come in. May I take your coat? It's bitter cold out there. Shall I fetch you a glass of sherry while you wait for Mr. Milverton?"

Agatha. Yes, of course. Inwardly, I had to laugh at the situation. If Holmes was curled up behind the juniper bushes, it served him right.

I was led into the parlor, where I sat in warmth by the hearth and chortled to myself. The maid, Miss Agatha, reappeared a minute later bearing a decanter of sherry and a large, full glass. She leaned down in front of me, forcing me to avert my eyes from the obvious exposure of her buxom bosom.

I forced my mind not to think for even a second of what frolicking she might have had with her during her short few days of being betrothed to Holmes. I looked solely at her face and thanked her graciously.

A short, well-made young man of perhaps thirty years of age entered the room and greeted me.

"Good evening, Doctor. Allow me to introduce myself. I am Elmer Milverton. I understand you are interested in renting this house."

"That is correct, sir," I said.

"Excellent. It is available immediately. Renters are scarce during the winter, and we reduced the price. Would you mind joining me in the library? All the appropriate documents are there. Aggie! Please bring the Good Doctor's sherry and decanter. And one for me, if you don't my, my dear."

I followed him down the hall and entered a room I would never forget.

The memory of hiding with Holmes behind the curtain and watching as Lady – executed Charles Augustus Milverton came rushing back to me. I couldn't help but glance at the spot on the carpet to which he had fallen and where Lady – ground her heel into his dying face.

"Doctor Watson . . . Doctor Watson." Young Milverton had been speaking to me, and I snapped my mind back to the business at hand.

"Will you be alone, Doctor?"

"Yes . . . well. No. Not entirely. A colleague of mine will be with me for a day or two starting tomorrow. After that, I shall be alone."

"There is more than enough room for visitors. Now then, the agreement."

"Yes. Yes, of course, the rental agreement. I am sure it will be satisfactory. But I do have one question."

"And what is that?"

I couldn't help myself. My curiosity got the better of me.

"Forgive me, but I seem to recall that there was a rather serious crime that took place here several years ago. Have there been any other such incidents since then?"

"You are referring to the murder of my uncle, no doubt. No, I assure you, nothing like that had happened before and nothing since. There is no danger."

"Did they ever catch the killers?"

"No. They got clean away. All they had to go on was a glimpse of the slower of the two of them as they escaped over the garden wall. He was said to be a middle-sized, strongly built man with a square jaw, thick neck, and mustache. But that was all the police had to go on."

"Not much wonder," I said. "Such a vague description would match thousands of men in London. Why, it might be a description of me."

"It is true," Milverton said and smiled. "If any man matching that description appears during your stay here, kindly give the miscreant a bullet in his backside."

"I cannot blame you for wanting justice. The incident must have been terribly upsetting."

The young fellow smirked. "If you must know, the entire rest of the family was relieved to see him gone. He was a nasty man and an embarrassment to a respectable family. He did, however, leave a bulging bank account, this enormous house, and his vicious dogs that, thankfully, are now gone. We tried to sell it but to no avail. Its unsavory past clings to it like a bad smell. Something of a white elephant."

"Regardless," I said. "It suits my purpose to a *T*."

"Excellent. The maid, Miss Agatha, comes with it. She will be more than happy to look after all your needs."

"Even better."

I departed with a copy of the rental agreement stuffed into the pocket of my greatcoat. Once the door had closed behind me, I whispered into the bushes.

"Romeo, Romeo, wherefore art thou? You can come out now."

He crawled out from the bushes, holding his coat tightly around himself. His teeth were chattering.

"Not a scrap of sympathy for you, Holmes. It jolly well serves – "

"Enough, Watson. Your point is taken. Can we please hurry to the nearest pub so I can warm up?"

It took twenty minutes and several cups of hot tea to thaw him out. When he finally doffed his coat, I asked him about the next step in his plan.

217

"We do nothing for a few days. Langdale Pike will arrive here tomorrow morning. The reporter will call on Mycroft tomorrow evening, and I suspect he will find his way here by the next day. Then we wait for his ridiculous article to appear in his newspaper."

We waited for three days, and then four.

"Holmes, are you quite certain that this scheme of yours is going to work? Don't these reporters try to get their name in print as fast as possible?"

"Of course, they do. But when you are about to accuse the highest elected officials, the wealthiest industrialists, and the most popular celebrities of fraud, espionage, corruption, and immoral behavior, editors and publishers become nervous. Even a newspaper as devoid of ethics as *The Evening Star* must exercise some degree of caution. But worry not. The story will break. It is too great a bombshell to be ignored."

And break it did.

While walking toward 221b early on the morning of the fifth day, my eye was arrested by the full-page headline at the news agent's stall:

Cabinet Caught in Spying, Fraud
and Shameless Acts

The byline was for Dorian Brewster.

As I was staring at it, the chap selling the newspapers laughed. "They're going like hotcakes. They sent me twice as many copies as they usually do, and I'm already running out."

I bought a copy and hurried up the street to 221b. I nearly collided with Langdale Pike coming from the opposite direction and also carrying a copy. He was beaming.

"Isn't it splendid, Doctor? He printed every outrageous thing I told him."

He gave me a not-entirely welcome slap on my back. Mrs. Hudson opened the door, and Pike bestowed a kiss on the dear lady's cheek.

She was shocked, and before she had time to react the two of us sped up the stairs to where we found Holmes sitting with a cup of coffee in one hand and a copy of the paper in the other.

His expression wasn't grinning the way Pike's was, but it was a good yard or two beyond smug.

"I detect the hand of my brother as well as yours, my dear Mr. Pike. The uproar will be heard from here to Shanghai. Watson, did you see what it says about the Assistant Secretary of the Admiralty?"

"I haven't yet read the contents," I said.

"Oh, you really must. It says that Mr. Clement Fairfax of the Admiralty was observed entering a manor house in Hampstead, and he was walking arm in arm with August Friedrich von Spörcken, the First Officer of the German Embassy."

"Why, that would be tantamount to treason," I said. "Does it say that they were engaged in acts that were, well, unnatural between men?"

"Of course not. It only leads the reader to draw that conclusion. And here we see Charles Ritchie, the President of the Board of Trade, and he has the American trade officer on one arm and the man's wife on the other. And on it goes. The suggestions of malfeasance are everywhere. There must be a dozen or more members of the Cabinet named and besmirched."

"Come now, Mr. Holmes," said Pike, "enough of that political nonsense that endangers the Empire. Get on to the scandalous and salacious material I fed him."

"Very well, but it does lead me to blush. All right, you have the wife of the Chancellor of the Exchequer accompanied by a seven-foot-tall African of the Watusi tribe – I suppose that was to make all the German women envious. And, of course, if it were true, it would. And the lady's husband is observed in the company of three pretty, young African women from one of the pygmy tribes. None of them are much above four feet in stature. And . . . Oh, really, Pike, you didn't? Mrs. Akers-Douglas brings a Great Dane, and her husband has a chimpanzee. That really is – "

"Utterly beyond belief," said Pike, "but they printed it."

Holmes read several more lines from the article, the contents of which were beyond my willingness to put into print.

"You certainly exceeded yourself, Pike," said Holmes. "I assume you are going to have a field day treating this news in your own column?"

"In one of what the Good Doctor referred to the 'garbage papers', which cater for an inquisitive public? Of course I am. I already submitted my paragraphs refuting the contents and castigating the newspaper and the reporter. We will scoop the respectable papers on Fleet Street by at least a day. I haven't had such a good time since Louise Bailey was sent to the madhouse."

The three of us were having a jolly good chuckle about our little triumph when the bell on Baker Street rang repeatedly. Mrs. Hudson opened the door, and her greeting was cut short by a female voice. Our visitor ascended the stairs two at a time and stormed into the front room.

It was Lady – . She was clutching a copy of the newspaper and seemed highly distraught.

"Mr. Holmes!" she said, throwing the newspaper down on the coffee table in front of him. "You said you were going to do something about this man, but look what he gets away with exposing. If he can do that to

219

members of the Cabinet, what is he going to do to me? My story is bound to come out within a week. You promised me you would help me, but I am undone!"

Holmes stood and faced the woman. "My dear lady, allow me to assure you that you have nothing to worry about. The story you hold in your hand is entirely a confection orchestrated by yours truly, with the help of an unnamed trusted accomplice and this fine gentleman you see here with us."

Langdale Pike leapt to his feet. "A pleasure to meet you, Lady – . Newspaper columnist extraordinaire Langdale Pike at your service. Anytime you need to generate a maelstrom of outrageous gossip to suit your purposes, I am your man. My card, Madam."

Lady – 's face was a portrait of bewilderment. "Are you saying that this entire story is a hoax? And that you perpetrated it? And you did so for my sake?"

"Guilty on all counts," said Holmes. "Whatever story about you this Brewster miscreant was going to publish will never see the light of day. No newspaper in Britain, the Empire, or even in America, will ever allow him to cross their threshold."

I stood and stepped over to the mantel, poured a full snifter of brandy, and presented it to Lady – . Although the hour was still early in the morning, I thought she looked like she needed some liquid courage.

She took the brandy, guzzled the entire glass, and collapsed into an empty armchair. Then she laughed.

"Oh my, I haven't had such a delightful surprise in years. Thank you, Mr. Holmes, and you too, Doctor, and Mr. . . . What was your name? I am going to take a walk in the park and revel in my newfound freedom. Thank you."

"Enjoy your freedom, my Lady," said Holmes. "Your adversary has been taken care of. There is no need for you to . . . Well, who knows what you would have to do? Track him down in the middle of the night, take out a revolver, and shoot him dead? Or worse? No need at all. Enjoy your walk."

For a second, she stared at Holmes in disbelief, and Holmes put on his all-innocence face and smiled as if he were just making conversation.

She shook her head and departed.

The garbage newspapers containing Pike's disparaging rebuttal of the story in *The Evening Star* appeared in the late afternoon and evening of the same day. The following morning, the newspaper ran a subsequent story, also penned by Dorian Brewster, proudly denouncing Pike and going on about the great dangers faced by the stalwart reporter in securing his exclusive exposé.

At noon the same day, the Prime Minister, the Right Honorable Arthur Balfour, rose in the House of Commons. His face, I was told, was red with rage, and his hands, usually so reliably calm, were trembling.

For an entire fifteen minutes, he called *The Evening Star* every vile name known in the English language and several in French, which are too vulgar to be translated. Not only was the story a complete farrago of lies, but no such event could have taken place, for on the very night claimed for the debauchery, he, the Prime Minister, hosted an evening for all members of his Cabinet and their wives at Number 10. He called upon the major newspapers, the respectable denizens of Fleet Street – an epithet he wasn't known for using – to advise the public that they should have nothing to do with *The Evening Star*, that degenerate newspaper. They should cancel their subscriptions and withdraw their advertising.

The leader of the opposition, Sir Henry Campbell-Bannerman, subsequently rose and repeated the same sentiments, attempting to be even more outraged than the Prime Minister, as was expected of his position.

By the afternoon, all others named or insinuated in the now-infamous article had announced that they were suing the paper for libel and defamation. Mr. Elmer Milverton, who had been quoted as the owner of the house who had observed all the leaders of the nation deshabille and *in flagrante delicto*, issued a statement asserting that he had never spoken to the reporter, and that every word attributed to him was an outright lie. His maid, a pleasant, buxom woman of a certain age named Agatha, was asked if she knew anything about the interview the reporter claimed to have held at the Appledore Towers house. She said that she had been given the day off and was having a picnic with the local plumber at the time in question.

The following morning, *The Evening Star* had a different full-page headline.

We Are Sorry

The text, under the name of the owner and publisher, apologized for their mistake and went on to claim that they, trusting souls that they were, had been the victims of a horribly dishonest reporter who had been terminated and would never work for the noble enterprise of the press ever again.

By the close of the stock market, the paper's share value had dropped in half. Investors astutely assumed that the subscriptions, newsagent sales, and advertising revenue would never recover.

Justice had been served.

Or so we thought.

It was yet another bitter, cold morning a week later. I had bundled my great coat and scarf around me and walked up Baker Street to join Holmes for breakfast. The hearth was ablaze, and we were sipping on yet another cup of steaming coffee when the bell rang.

We recognized the voice.

"Good Heavens!" I said. "What in the world does Lestrade want on such a miserable morning?"

We felt a blast of cold air sweep up from the doorway below, followed by the muffled sound of footsteps from heavy winter boots. Our longstanding colleague entered the room, doffed his police great coat, and helped himself to a brandy from the mantel. All this he did without so much as a good morning.

Holmes and I kept sipping coffee, knowing Lestrade would pontificate within the next minute or two, which he did.

"Mr. Holmes, my sources tell me that a couple of weeks back, you had a meeting on Fleet Street with a reporter, a man named Dorian Brewster. That true?"

"It is true."

"Are you not going to ask me why I am asking you?"

"Why do you ask?"

"Because around midnight last night, he was murdered. It would appear that one of the parties he slandered and libeled took exception to what he wrote and did him in. Now, I cannot prove it, Mr. Holmes, but I wasn't born yesterday, and I have a strong suspicion that every name that appeared in the horrible article was quite possibly supplied to that reporter either by you or that pompous oaf of a brother of yours, or by your favorite tattle-tale, Mr. Langford Pike. That true? No . . . don't answer. I can tell by the look on your face it is, or close to it."

Holmes was silent for a long time.

"It is possible," he then said, "that one of the accusations made landed close to the truth, and someone took exception. I suppose that might have happened. If you and your fine men interrogate those whose names appeared, I expect you will unveil the one who had the motive to kill the man."

"We could, but that isn't what is going to happen. Since you already know all there is to know about the contents of the article, you, sir, will carry out a thorough investigation. Your standard fee will be applicable. Please report to me on a regular basis. And thank you for the brandy."

He got up, pulled on his coat, and departed.

I looked over at Holmes. He was staring, glassy-eyed, into the hearth and as still as a statue.

"Holmes? . . . Holmes?" I said. "Are you quite all right?"

"That reporter was a vile, despicable wretch of a man. But now he's dead. He is dead because of the oh-so-clever scheme I concocted. I wanted him to be disgraced. I didn't expect to be responsible for his death."

"Come, now, my friend, you couldn't have – "

"No, Watson. I am Sherlock Holmes. I should have anticipated the possibility of something like this."

I had known Holmes and worked alongside him for over two decades now, but I was hard-pressed to remember a time when I saw him so deflated, so depressed. As he lit his pipe and stood up and began to pace, his movements were slow and labored. After several minutes of moving back and forth across the floor, he turned to me.

"You will forgive me, Watson, if I decline your company for the next few days . . . possibly a week or more. I have no choice but to solve the murder of that reporter, for which I am the immediate cause. I will find the culprit and see that he is punished. It is the only thing I can do now to atone for my failure."

He strode over to the coat rack, pulled on his winter coat and traveling hat, and descended the stairs. The door opened, and he vanished into the cold.

I had not expected to see him for some time, but the following day, I had a note from him.

> *Would you please meet me this evening at half-past six at the Diogenes Club? I would find it valuable to have you there while I interrogate my brother.*
>
> *Holmes*

I couldn't refuse him, and I appeared a few minutes before the stated time at the familiar address in Pall Mall and was led into the Stranger's Room.

Holmes was already there.

"Thank you, my friend," he said, putting his hand on my arm. "Your assistance is greatly appreciated. Forgive me for not thanking you enough for the many times I have come to depend on you."

I was moved by his expression of sentiment, but it was uncharacteristically strange. The look on my face must have conveyed my surprise.

"Please, Watson, you do not have to be shocked. In the past, you have gone so far as to call me a calculating machine for my abhorrence of allowing emotions to cloud my reasoning. But you are the only man on earth who has been able to see past my outward pretense of scientific deduction and discern the feelings I do my best to suppress. I don't have to tell you that I have been deeply troubled by what has taken place in this case, and the horrible failure of the scheme that I concocted for assisting Lady – and her feared humiliation in the press. I wanted that reporter, Brewster, and his newspaper to be shamed and ridiculed. I didn't imagine that he would be murdered directly as a result of my devious plot against him."

"My dear Holmes, I do believe I have sat and listened to you tell clients who feel a great sense of guilt for the tragic loss of a loved one that the only person who ever deserves the blame is the one who committed the act. In your case, it is the murderer who must be judged, not you."

He looked at my face and forced a small smile. "True, and applicable to every client I have ever assisted, but I cannot bring myself to apply that insight to myself."

"You will feel better when you catch the killer and drag him to the bar. Now then: How can I help?"

My offer elicited a larger and unforced smile. "Good old Watson! You can listen and help me as I question my older brother. Interrupt whenever you think necessary, especially if you detect I am allowing my emotional turmoil to take precedence over my clear reasoning."

I was about to say more, but it was at this point that Mycroft Holmes lumbered into the room. He dropped his large frame into an armchair and took an immediate gulp of the select sherry the porter had set out for him.

"Well done there, Sherlock," he said. "That diabolical scheme of yours worked beyond anything I had imagined. I hear that your reporter got what he deserved. There will not be a civilized man or woman on earth who will shed a tear for him. Yes, well done indeed, Sherlock."

"He deserved to be shamed and forced out of the press and of any respectable social circle," said Holmes. "He did not deserve to be murdered. It is now incumbent on me to solve the crime and see that his murderer is hanged. I am the one responsible for his death,"

"Oh, come now, you are no such thing. You do not have a client who is asking for your help finding the killer, do you? You will not receive a farthing for your troubles. Why not leave it to Scotland Yard? They – "

"No, Mycroft. I have blood on my hands, and I need your help to cleanse them. Can you not understand that?"

For a brief second, I caught a flash in Mycroft Holmes's face of something approaching compassion. He looked at his younger brother for a moment with what could only be called brotherly love and concern. He recovered his facial appearance straight away, but he softened his voice.

"If you say so, Sherlock. Very well then, what do you need from me?"

"You did a masterful job of acting as Lord Snidley of Great Snoring and convinced Brewster that corruption, treason, and goodness knows what all was going on behind the doors of the Cabinet. Was there any truth in what you led him to believe and then print? Was there anyone who might have had a motive to murder him?"

Mycroft took another gulp of his sherry and then refilled his glass. "You might say, yes and no."

"Please, Mycroft, I am not in the mood to play our one-upmanship games."

"No, and neither am I. By my answer, I mean to say that I provided a long list of well-known names in politics, commerce, the universities, and other fields of endeavor who I knew were being tempted to engage in unscrupulous behavior. To date, not one of them has yet succumbed. Their names in print with the innuendo that they were engaging in malfeasance has, to the best of my knowledge, frightened everyone of them to their marrow, and they have all moved quickly to put the temptation well behind them, and to act only with the honor and trust that has been given to them. The one exception was the chap from the Admiralty."

"The one Pike had entering holding hands with the German diplomat?"

"Yes. That one. The German was recalled to Berlin this morning, and our boy has requested a transfer to Argentina. But he'll be back, and he is vulnerable."

"Ah, so you used it as a warning? To him and all the others?"

"Precisely."

"And not one of them was already engaged in wrongdoing and thus fearing he would be further exposed?"

Mycroft scowled and, after another swallow, replied. "Not yet. Mind you, all my data comes from my network of agents – "

"You mean, your spies."

Mycroft shrugged. "Would you prefer I called them my *Irregulars*? They aren't one-hundred-percent reliable, but I have no reason to suspect any of them would either mislead me or pass on data that was questionable. I will have them report to me again and inquire more rigorously if that would help you. But I suspect that your expert in social gossip might be much more likely to have touched a nerve. While his prurient descriptions of what went on at the non-existent gathering were enough to make a sailor blush, it is possible something he said hit a little too close to home. That is all I can suggest. If I think of anything else, I shall let you know forthwith."

Holmes thanked his brother, and we departed the Diogenes Club. Once out of the pavement, he lit a cigarette and gazed down Pall Mall.

"Holmes," I said, "you know that if I can help in any way, you have only to ask."

He put his hand on my shoulder. "No, my friend, unless you wish to soil your soul by investigating every conceivable immoral vice practiced by the elite members of English society. Even if you were to so offer, I would have to refuse. You don't belong in such a disgusting underworld. I shall do whatever is necessary in that nefarious sphere and find whoever feared being exposed by Brewster. Until then, my friend."

He turned and marched away from me, hailed a cab, and vanished in the direction of Trafalgar. I pulled my coat around me and walked home.

I neither saw nor heard from Holmes for the following two weeks. The weather had descended into the depths of winter, and I confined myself to my surgery, hearth, and home. I was somewhat concerned, but it was far from the first time Holmes had vanished into the investigation of the case, and I knew he was determined, compelled to solve this one.

On the fifteenth day, however, I received a note from Mrs. Hudson. It ran:

Dear Doctor Watson,

You must come as quickly as possible and attend to Mr. Holmes. He has slept in his bed less than half of the past fortnight. He is not eating properly and is getting by on tobacco and chocolate. I saw him this morning, and he looked like death warmed over. Please, do see what you can do.

I hustled through my remaining patients, closed my surgery early, and took a cab directly to Baker Street. Mrs. Hudson met me at the door.

"Oh, Doctor, thank you, thank you! I'm worried sick about him. For the first week, he was miserable and cantankerous, but we're all used to that. But for days now, he has hardly said a word. He comes and goes, and when he's here, he does nothing but pace and smoke. He looks . . . he looks sickly . . . like he should be in hospital. Please see if you can do anything to get him to at least eat something. I can make up some soup. He – "

"Yes, my dear," I said. "I'll see what I can do.

I ascended the stairs, only to find Holmes apparently in utter exhaustion and tottering back and forth in his customary armchair.

226

"Hello there, Holmes!" I said and walked over to him. "You said I might help if I was willing to join you in the depths of depravity. Well, here I am. What have you got for me? Come on, man. Speak up!"

He gave his head a shake and took several deep breaths.

"Nothing, Watson. Nothing. I have toiled all day and all night for days and have come up with nothing."

His voice was weak, and the tone of abject sadness was heartbreaking. I continued to play the cheerful helper.

"I'm listening. As you would say, kindly state your case. Try to be both concise and precise, and leave nothing out."

He wearily lit a cigarette.

"I have chased down every person named in Brewster's outrageous smear. I have infiltrated every gambling room in the back of every men's club, every den of iniquity, every brothel and Molly house, every opium basement, and every low-rent hotel that is used for immoral purposes. And what have I discovered? Nothing. I acquired no end of incriminating data about all sorts of horrid activities in the dark underbelly of London, but nothing – *Nothing!* – that is remotely connected to the murder."

"Did you speak directly to the poor dukes and earls and rich he slandered?"

"Every one of them. And I was quite aggressive and confrontational. That gained me a blast of indignation and orders to go away on several occasions."

"But what did they say about what he wrote?"

"They were, to a man – or to a woman for that matter – initially apoplectic with rage. But when the lies were exposed and the reporter and the newspaper exposed and shamed, they were giddy with *schadenfreude*."

"Even about his murder?"

"More so. Scotland Yard has, for good reason, refused to release details on how he was killed, and so these people, these esteemed paragons of civic virtue, exulted in imagining how he was done in. Some hoped he was flayed alive, others that he was impaled in the manner of Count Dracula, and others yet nibbled to death by rats."

"You horrify me!"

"As would I have been, had I not been at loose ends to find even a trace, an iota of possibly useful data. But . . . but nothing. I confess, my friend, I do not know where to turn next."

He retreated into silence, puffing on yet another cigarette. Imagining myself following the example of Job's comforters, I sat in silence with him. Very well, I was quiet for about five minutes, and then a thought came to me.

"I do recall you saying, more times than I can count, once you eliminate the possible . . . ."

He waved his hand at me to make me halt.

"Yes, yes, Watson, I have said that. But what else is there, improbable or not?"

"What if . . . what if the murder had nothing whatsoever to do with the article Brewster wrote? Could it have had some other source? Maybe some other bloke had it in for him for a completely different reason. Maybe it was something in the past? Years ago. What about that?"

I knew I wasn't making much sense, but I was desperate to get him away from feeling he was the immediate cause of the murder. If I could get him to pursue another line of investigation, it would likely not lead anywhere, but it would at least divert him from his feelings of utter failure.

He said nothing, but he stubbed out his cigarette and stared at me.

"There are times, my friend, when your otherwise frivolous comments are useful. Yes, it is possible, however remote, that there was no connection. All right then, what else do we know about his enemies from the past?"

"What about Lady – ? She said he was going to accuse her of participating in a similar scandalous party four years ago and to accuse her of murdering her friend, Viscount . . . Viscount, oh, what's his name?"

"Viscount Gough-Battenberg. Yes, we do know about that, but we also know that she is entirely innocent of those accusations because we know precisely where she was at the time. She was busy shooting Charles Augustus Milverton. But, perhaps . . . perhaps there was someone else who could be accused of the viscount's death if the whole thing were to be reopened. That is a possibility."

"Worth pursuing?"

I didn't harbor any faint hope that he would now pursue a new set of activities, but it would get him out of the house and get his mind off his failure to unearth anything related to the party that never happened.

He started pacing.

"Watson, if a man died at a house party in Hampstead Heath four years ago, where would they have taken him? What hospital?"

"The nearest one is the Highgate Hill Infirmary, over beyond the cemetery."

"Do you happen to know – ?"

"Indeed, I do. One of the surgeons also served in the army. That was years ago, but we old boys are still a rather tight lot."

The next thing I knew, he was pulling on his coat.

"Come, Watson. No time to lose. It will take us a half-hour or more to get there. We should be able to make it before your old colleague leaves for the day."

A cab took us almost directly north to Highgate, around the cemetery, and to the entrance to the small hospital.

"I need to confer with Doctor Gareth Barry," I told the woman at the reception desk. "Would you please let him know that Doctor John Watson is waiting to speak with him?"

The middle-aged and middle-sized lady looked up at me and beamed a smile.

"Are you the Doctor Watson what writes all those tales about Sherlock Holmes?"

"I am indeed, Madam, and I am an old friend of Doctor Barry. Would you mind sending someone to let him know we're waiting for him?"

"I absolutely adore those stories. How did you ever make up that odd detective, Sherlock Holmes? You must have a marvelous imagination."

I was about to disabuse her of the notion that Sherlock Holmes was imaginary and point her to the man standing directly behind me, but time was of the essence, and I merely thanked her and reminded her one more time to kindly fetch Dr. Barry, which she finally did.

"John Watson!" a voice boomed from across the hospital lobby. "What a surprise! You don't have to tell me what you've been up to. I've been reading all those stories you publish in *The Strand* about that character, Sherlock Holmes. My, but you do have a splendid imagination to come up with such a bizarre – "

"Lovely to see you again, too, Gareth," I said. "Allow me to introduce my friend, Mr. Sherlock Holmes."

Dr. Barry's mouth dropped open.

"Oh, my goodness. He's . . . he's *real*? I didn't think anyone that odd could be a living human being. Well, now, that just goes to show you – "

"What we need to be shown," I said, "is the report on a death that took place about this time of year, four years ago. We were hoping you would find the file for us. Would you mind, Gareth?"

"Of course not. What was the name?"

"Viscount Gough-Battenberg. He died in a house in Hampstead Heath, and I assume he was brought here, as you are the closest hospital. I expect the report is in your file room."

"That it is, but it might not be necessary to run and fetch. I remember him quite well. I did the autopsy. What can I tell you about him?"

"What was the cause of death?"

"Well, do you want what was on the death certificate? Or do you want my opinion?"

"Both. The official version first, please."

"Heart failure. The man exerted himself a little too strenuously, and his heart seized."

"That is a common thing to happen with men of his age. Why does your opinion differ from what went into the report?"

"I don't know if you know, but the details of when and where he died and what he was doing at the time were, well, you might say, rather scandalous. His family didn't want all that released to the public, and there was nothing to be gained by not adhering to their request. So we put down heart failure and left it at that."

"And your opinion?"

"Well, his heart had most certainly stopped beating. But it didn't look like a normal heart attack."

"In what way?"

"He also had all the symptoms of having been poisoned."

"Did he now? What did you observe?"

"Me? Nothing. But a maid accompanied his corpse to the hospital. She was with him as he died. She told us he had been happy as a lark throughout the early portion of the evening, but at some time after eleven, he seemed dizzy and confused, and then he vomited. He began gasping for breath, and he lost consciousness. He lay gasping for a minute and then stopped breathing."

"He didn't die from heart failure caused by vigorous activity while unclothed?"

"No. I'd say someone slipped some cyanide into his drink, and he swallowed enough to kill him, but the laboratory analysis was inconclusive, and all I had to go on was the maid's account."

"Do you, by chance, remember the name of the maid? Or anything about her?"

"I do. Friendly girl. She was loaned to the hosts of the party by a neighbor down the lane. I don't think I ever knew her family name, but her first name was Agatha."

Holmes, who up until that time had said nothing, quietly gasped. Then he posed a question.

"Pardon me, Doctor," he said. "Would you mind describing this maid? We may have to have a word with her. Can you remember much about her?"

"A little. Friendly. Indeed jovial, which seemed strange seeing as she was delivering a dead body to a hospital. Middle-aged, but passably attractive in the sort of way women of a certain age are. I remember asking

230

her why she seemed so happy, given the circumstances. She told me that she was about to get married and that her fiancé was a handsome devil and as clever as they come. Brown hair. Never looked close enough to tell the color of her eyes. Beyond that, can't tell you much more."

"We thank you for your time," said Holmes.

"Oh, there is one other thing that may be of interest to you," said Dr. Barry.

"And what might that be?" asked Holmes.

"Several weeks ago, a reporter came here and asked the same questions you did about the death of Viscount Gough-Battenberg. Then I read that he had himself died of a cause that was unknown, or at least not revealed to the public."

A row of cabs stood outside the main entrance of the hospital.

"Shall we have a cab take us to Appledore Towers?" I asked Holmes. "Like it or not, my friend, your past has come to haunt you, and you're going to have to face up to your breach of promise."

"That will prove to be an interesting meeting. I don't have time to disguise myself, but I'm sure she will recognize my voice and face, regardless of whatever costume I put on. Yes, this will be an interesting interview . . . No, wait."

"For what? It's already seven o'clock. She's only one street away, and she might not be present if we delay going there until later in the evening. We can grab some dinner later. The Bull and Gate pub is close by. We could – "

"No, we couldn't. We need to go straight away to Scotland Yard and have a chat with Lestrade."

"Isn't that somewhat premature?" I asked.

"Maybe not. But tell me, my dear Doctor, is it possible to ingest opium in a gelatin capsule?"

"Certainly. It's one of the most common ways of doing so, particularly amongst those who don't like inhaling smoke. Why do you ask?"

"I'm curious. Now, tell me, is it possible to pull a gelatin capsule apart and replace the contents with another substance?"

"Simplicity itself. The most common is to empty out the useless crushed herbal concoction and replace it with powered laudanum. Some more adventurous types will stuff the capsules with opium, or even heroin. Why are you asking?"

"I am merely pursuing another line of a highly improbable possibility."

231

He said nothing more and sat in silence, scribbling notes to himself until we reached the Embankment and entered Scotland Yard.

"Lestrade is a diligent sort," he said. "It isn't unusual for him to work through until near midnight. I expect he is still at his desk or berating his men to work harder. Come, we'll pay him a visit."

His face had become animated, and I saw the familiar twinkle in his eye when he was following the scent and closing in on his quarry. I welcomed the change but there was no apparent reason for it.

Lestrade was still in his office, and he welcomed us brusquely.

"What do you have for me, Mr. Holmes?" he said.

"For now, only a question. More later."

"Not much to show for over two weeks' work. All right, what's your question?"

"What was the manner in which Dorian Brewster was murdered?"

"We chose not to make that public. It was a bit on the gruesome side, and we didn't want to inspire any imitators. But since you ask, he was – "

"Stop. Allow me to guess. Might he have been shot five times in the torso at close range, then once at point-blank range in the head after he had fallen? And was his eye socket destroyed by his assailant grinding the heel of a boot into it?"

Lestrade gave Holmes a sideward look. "Enough of your being clever. Yes, that is what happened, and clearly, you are on to something. Out with it."

"Kindly give me an hour or two, and I shall deliver the murderer into your capable hands. And, by the way, this is the name of the chap in the Admiralty who you need to keep an eye on. He is susceptible to being turned toward treason."

He handed Lestrade the note he had scribbled in the cab on the way.

"I'll worry about spies tomorrow, Mr. Holmes. For now, I'll be waiting for you to deliver."

Holmes rushed me out of Scotland Yard and into a cab.

"Holmes, are you sure of this? You think Lady – killed the reporter?"

"I am reasonably certain."

"But how? Why? She was safe after the fraudulent story was exposed. He was put out of business. He – "

"My dear Watson. You have a grand gift of silence. Kindly exercise it."

I wasn't about to put up with that order this time around. "No. Explain yourself."

"Not necessary. Within an hour, she will do so herself. Driver! Mount Street in Mayfair, and quickly, please."

Fifteen minutes later, we stopped in front of an elegant terraced house. The lamps were on inside, giving the windows a warm glow. Outside, it was still bitter cold and windy, and I welcomed being inside, regardless of what events might transpire once we were there.

A maid opened the door cautiously and asked us to identify ourselves. A minute later, Lady – appeared and bade us enter.

"Oh, Mr. Holmes and Doctor Watson, what a lovely surprise. You were on my list to send a note expressing my gratitude. Ever since that insane story appeared and Brewster and his ilk were shamed, I have been so relieved. I am finally free of anything that can destroy my life. Do come in. What can I offer you? Brandy? Claret?"

Holmes glanced around the entry and the parlor before answering.

"Are we celebrating your departure from England? I see only cheap prints on your walls. You have disposed of all your fine art. The breakfront case is void of valuable plate and stocked only with bric-à-brac. Where are you going?"

She put her finger to her lips. "*Ssshh!* Please. My maid is new, and I am not yet comfortable having her hear all my personal plans. Come. We can speak privately in my husband's study."

She turned, walked toward the back of the ground floor, and opened the door to a small room in which there was a desk and a few chairs. The bookshelves and the walls were bare.

"We can chat in here," she said. "There is brandy on the credenza. A glass for each of you?"

"That will not be necessary," said Holmes. "This won't take long. After all that has been said and done, I have one question that is bothering my mind."

"Ask me anything. I am an open book now, finally."

"You told me that Brewster was going to accuse you of murdering Viscount Gough-Battenberg, did you not?"

"Yes. To think that that horrid man would stoop so low as to accuse me of harming one of my husband's dearest friends. How beastly of him."

"You said he was often a guest in your home. Was that here?"

"Oh no. He stayed with us several times in the manor home down in Kent."

"And was that where he found your indiscreet letters, which he sold to Charles Augustus Milverton? He needed the cash from Milverton to do what? Pay off gambling debts? He, your trusted friend, betrayed you and your husband, and that is why you slipped him the capsules you said were stuffed with opium. You said it would help him have more fun at that party. But you had filled them with cyanide, hadn't you? It took an hour for the capsules to dissolve and the poison to be released. By then, you were long gone over to Appledore Towers. You took revenge on him just as you did against Milverton. That was my only question. You may answer it now."

I expected her to fly into a rage or perhaps rush out of the room. She did neither.

"Oh, Mr. Holmes, I am surprised it took you so long. And now, I suppose you think I am going to accompany you to Scotland Yard, where you will hand me over to the police."

"With the free advice to find yourself the best barristers and solicitors you can. I was willing to let you get away with murdering one evil man, but I'm afraid that killing three is somewhat beyond my limit. So, shall we go?"

"No, Mr. Holmes, I am not going anywhere with you. And you and the doctor aren't going anywhere at all. You are, no doubt, aware that I know how to use this little thing."

She had drawn a little gleaming revolver and was pointing it directly at Holmes.

"No, Mr. Holmes, I will not stay around and stand trial for executing three despicable, evil men. They all deserved to die. I had expected you to discern my actions much faster than you have. I discerned yours over a week ago. Shall I tell you how?"

"I am all attention."

"I always wondered who the two men were that night four years ago. They watched me send that hound off to Hell, and they let me get away with it. The police reported that one of them was tall and slender and a bit too active. But the second was a middle-sized, strongly built man – square jaw, thick neck, and a mustache. I had no idea who they were until I met with you the second time in Baker Street. At our first meeting, I told you my alibi for the night of the viscount's death was ironclad, and you believed me right off. I have read all those stories about you, and I knew you never allow your clients to withhold data from you. Yet you believed me. Then you couldn't resist tossing that little nugget of my not needing to track down Brewster in the middle of the night and shoot him dead? That set me wondering, and it came to me that you and the doctor must have been those two men."

"I am not entirely prepared to believe your account," said Holmes. "The leaps in your deductions are somewhat beyond belief."

"Oh, did I leave something out? Yes, I did. I neglected to mention that the lovely young Lady Eva Brackwell is a member of my badminton club, and we have become great friends. Being women, we share all our secrets. She told me how you had saved her reputation. She suspected it was you and the doctor who burglarized Milverton's house, but she was unsure. I was not."

234

"You could mount a case of self-defense. A good lawyer would get you off with a minimum time in prison. Five years at the most. I can recommend an excellent law firm or two."

"And have my life ruined a second time? No, Mr. Holmes. That isn't going to happen. I have already liquidated my property, and all my assets and my funds, which are considerable, are no longer in England. I shall start a new life in . . . Oh, I don't know. Perhaps New Zealand, or maybe Cairo. I'm told that in California, no one cares what you did in the past as long as you are passably attractive and rich. Any suggestions?"

"The arm of the law is long and relentless. You cannot escape forever."

"Forever? I don't care about forever. But ten years seems a reasonable amount of time before having to reinvent myself again. Until then, gentlemen. Oh, by the way, there are biscuits in the credenza, and that door leads to my dear husband's private lavatory. I gave the maids the evening and tomorrow morning off. They will return at noon tomorrow. I trust you will be comfortable until then. Allow me to bid you a good night."

She rose and walked backward toward the door, all the time pointing the revolver at us. As soon as she was past the door, she closed it, and I heard the lock snap shut. I leapt to the door and tried the handle.

"Holmes, can you pick this lock? We have to get out of here."

He sauntered over, knelt down, and took a close look. "The latch is simple to undo. But I noticed that there was a padlock a foot above to handle when we entered. It cannot be undone, and this door is solid oak. We cannot break it down."

"Then we are stuck here until noon tomorrow? You are going to let her get away?"

Holmes sighed. "No, my friend. I have some sympathy for those who take the law into their own hands, having done so more times than I can count myself. But killing three men – all deserving of their fate – is more than I can allow."

"But she'll be on a ferry and over to the Continent by the time we get out of here."

"A part of me would be glad if she were. But no. That will not happen. Lestrade will have read my entire note, and he and three of his men are sitting in a police carriage directly in front of this house."

The Perfect Spy
by Martin Daley

Chapter I

It was a grey late morning in the early days of December 1910 as Sherlock Holmes stood in the tiny churchyard with a handful of other mourners. They watched as the coffin was being lowered into the ground. Mrs. Hewitt had lived all her life in and around Fulworth and, for the last seven years of her life, she had acted as Holmes's housekeeper at his isolated cottage on the Downs following his retirement. Her final resting place looked out onto the Channel. It could be pretty when the sunshine glinted like millions of diamonds on the azure, blue sea, but it was cold and bleak on a day such as this with the prevailing wind whipping across the tops: A perfect day for a funeral.

Once Reverend Hornby had delivered his final blessing, Holmes turned to leave and became immediately aware that any thoughts he may have had of spending the rest of the day in quiet solitude were to be denied him. Under the two overhanging yew trees that framed the wrought iron gate stood two men, apparently waiting for the brief ceremony to end. One was the burly figure of Inspector Bardle of the Sussex Constabulary. Beside him was a smaller, dapper man who – like Bardle – stood with his hat in his hand, out of respect for the deceased. He had an extraordinary domed head, fringed around the back with dark hair and matching pencil-thin moustache. It was clear to Holmes that the two men were waiting for him.

"Good morning, Bardle," said he, walking over. "It isn't often we see you in this isolated corner of the county. What brings you and your colleague from Scotland Yard here on such a sad occasion? Not the passing of my old housekeeper, I would wager."

"Good morning, Mr. Holmes. No, you are correct. I must apologise for our intrusion. I was contacted by Inspector Reynolds here – " The small man nodded by way of introduction. " – who asked if I could help him locate you. I had no idea that your housekeeper had passed away. It was only when we arrived and I asked Anderson in the village that we were informed of your loss and where we might find you. Condolences, I'm sure."

"Thank you, Bardle. Mrs. Hewitt was indeed a fine housekeeper and someone who I will miss greatly. But your business?"

"How did you know I was from Scotland Yard?" Reynolds spoke for the first time.

"It wasn't difficult to deduce, Inspector," replied Holmes. "A well-turned-out man such as yourself, in the company of a local police inspector, arriving in the area at such an hour? The obvious suggestion would be that you are a policeman yourself who has probably made a two-hour journey to be here, as that is approximately the time it takes to travel from Victoria Station, I conclude that you can only be from Scotland Yard, seeking me out in order to ask for my help with some matter."

The two policemen stood in silence for a few moments before Reynolds spoke.

"I sought advice from our retired Inspector Gregson regarding the matter. He told me of your powers of observation, Mr. Holmes, and how you've helped the Yard in the past. I see he didn't exaggerate."

"Ah, good old Gregson," replied Holmes. "Please pass on my regards when you see him next."

"I will."

"But you will know, Inspector, that I *myself* am retired."

"I am aware of that, sir, but we have a difficult problem requiring your help, and I've come in person to ask for your assistance."

Holmes was silent for a few moments before saying, "Well, I suppose the least I can do, following your trip, is to offer you some refreshment. I'm sure that in Mrs. Hewitt's absence, even I am capable of making us all a cup of tea."

The three men walked the half-mile or so to Holmes's small villa.

"It's a beautiful place, Mr. Holmes," said Inspector Reynolds, looking out of the window at the spectacular views as his host arranged some refreshment.

"Yes, I'm quite settled here. I enjoy the solitude. I find that being at one with nature is good for both mind and body."

"I noticed as we entered that you keep bees?"

"Are you an apiculturist yourself, Inspector?"

"No," said the Scotland Yard man, "but my father was. I do see the attraction, having witnessed him spending many an hour among his hives."

Holmes set the tray down on a small table in front of the fire and invited his guests to sit.

"Hardly a gentle activity associated with the noise and pollution of the metropolis, I would have thought."

"No, I grew up in a small town in Kent. As you infer, very different from London."

"And here you are. So, tell me: What is so important that you have sought me out in my humble hideaway?"

"Well, Mr. Holmes, no doubt you have read in the press about the ongoing disruption caused nationally – but particularly in the capital – by the so-called 'Suffragettes'."

Holmes chuckled noiselessly. Reynolds ignored his host's mirth and continued.

"It seems for some years now that the police have done nothing more than contain whatever disruption these women have caused. But now, it would appear that they are becoming increasingly well-organised, and the information they are obtaining is causing great embarrassment amongst the authorities. It's as though they are always one step ahead of us."

Inspector Bardle, who had sat silently through his colleague's narrative, threw his head back and emitted a loud booming laugh from his large frame.

"I can't believe you London types have been given the run-about by a bunch of women!" he said in his strong Sussex brogue.

Again, Reynolds remained calm. "I wouldn't have come all the way down here if it wasn't serious enough to ask for Mr. Holmes's assistance."

"You want someone to infiltrate the Suffragettes?" asked Holmes. Taking Reynolds' expression as a sign of assent, he further stated, with a smile, "I'm not sure even my talents of disguise could be *that* convincing! Surely, you would be better employing a female in the role?"

"We thought of that, sir, but we don't have any female agents we could rely on for such a task. It was during my conversation with Gregson when he mentioned you used to have a network of men, women, and children you could use in assisting you in your cases. I was hoping you would still have your contacts and could act for us as a type of go-between. There are a few women I could approach myself, but once they smell the official force, I reckon they would run a mile."

Holmes thought for a while before replying. "Well, whereas I typically refuse to make a habit of disturbing my retirement to assist the authorities, it so happens that I do have business in London next week, at the request of my brother, Mycroft. While I'm there, my old friend Watson has invited me to stay with him and his dear wife for a few days. I suppose an extra day or two won't make any difference."

"That's wonderful news," said Reynolds. "Thank you. I only hope you are as good at your little detective work as Gregson claimed."

Holmes let a silence hang in the air for a while as he reminded himself of one of the main reasons for leaving London: Dealing with inept, ungrateful authority figures. He looked up slowly at Reynolds.

"Well, it is obviously my *little* detective work that has brought you to Sussex in the first place, Inspector. Seeing as you have a long journey back, I won't delay you any further. I shall contact you in due course and visit you at Scotland Yard, sometime next week."

With that he retrieved the coats of the two policemen and made to usher them towards the door.

"I . . . I . . . am extremely grateful for your assistance, Mr. Holmes," spluttered Reynolds on his way out, apparently realising he may have caused some offence.

"Indeed," said Holmes, smiling yet gesturing them to leave. "I shall speak with you next week."

Chapter II

Following a telegram to Inspector Reynolds, Holmes arrived at Scotland Yard eight days after their initial meeting at his Sussex home. In his wire, he didn't invite Reynolds to suggest an alternative date and the policeman thought better of suggesting one. Instead, the inspector left a message with his desk sergeant to expect his visitor at eleven o'clock.

"Good morning, Sergeant MacPherson," announced Holmes as he entered at the appropriate hour. "I see you finally achieved the promotion you so richly deserved."

"Mr. Sherlock Holmes!" exclaimed MacPherson, who had first encountered the private consulting detective over twenty years earlier during the Godolphin Street affair. "As I live and breathe! Inspector Reynolds said he had a visitor, but he didn't tell me who it was. It's wonderful to see you again, sir, after so long."

"Yes, I moved away from Baker Street some years ago, but it seems my services are still required every so often."

"I'll be retiring myself next year, sir. Thirty years, man and boy."

"Well done, MacPherson, I hope you and your good lady wife enjoy a long and happy retirement together."

"I don't know about that, sir. The wife's already complaining about me being under her feet."

"Just like you are at work," said another voice.

A lady had appeared behind the counter with a mop and was hurrying the sergeant out of the way. Sergeant MacPherson wore the expression of a defeated man.

"Bullied at home, Mr. Holmes, and bullied at work. Will no one protect me from these women?"

Holmes watched on, amused, as the big man hopped uncomfortably from one foot to the other while the cleaner attempted to mop the floor around him.

"Steady on, Lizzie!" MacPherson cried. "I'll be out of your way in a minute."

"Well, what can you expect?" complained the cleaner. "I'm on my own today."

The desk sergeant rolled his eyes as he turned back to address Holmes. Before he could do so, however, a commotion was heard outside and the doors of the station were almost knocked off their hinges as two constables manhandled a young woman into the station. The young lady was well-dressed, if a little dishevelled after such rough treatment, and was struggling to relieve herself from the policemen's grip. No sooner had the doors swung back shut behind the unusual trio when they burst open again in similar fashion as a single, burly officer literally carried another female, kicking and screaming, into the station. There then followed a procession of eight or ten similar groups of constables and women, some of whom wore coloured sashes with the legend *"Votes for Women"* emblazoned across them.

"All the other stations are full up, Jock!" said one of the constables to MacPherson as he struggled with his prisoner.

"Get your hands off me!" she shouted. "Have you no shame? No sense of decency?"

The constable ignored the women's protestations and resumed his explanation to the desk sergeant. "We're gonna have to use some of the cells here."

The noise from the entrance hallway caused other policemen to appear from the various offices along an adjacent corridor. Among them was Inspector Reynolds who – amid the commotion – had been distracted from expecting his visitor.

"What is all this – ?" he started as he appeared and immediately interrupted himself, when it became clearly obvious to him what the disturbance was. "I feared as much," he said, almost to himself.

"Right," announce MacPherson to the room. "Let's start booking them in."

In his distraction, Reynolds hadn't seen Sherlock Holmes, who was standing back beside Lizzie, the cleaning woman, observing the unseemly spectacle that was being acted out before them. Holmes sidled round the melee.

"Perhaps now is an inconvenient time, Inspector," he said.

"Mr. Holmes!" Reynolds raised his voice above the din. "I didn't see you come in. This is exactly what I asked to see you about. Things are getting more and more out of hand as the months go by. This was a demonstration that we actually *knew* about, and look at the result."

"Your inference is that there are demonstrations and gatherings that you don't actually know about?"

"Exactly." Reynolds attracted the attention of MacPherson, who indicated that he could supervise the situation from here. He turned back to his visitor. "Follow me, Mr. Holmes. Let us find somewhere a little quieter."

"What exactly do you want me to assist with, Reynolds?" Holmes asked, once they were seated in the inspector's office.

"It seems the organisers of these events are always one step ahead of us."

Holmes smiled inwardly but refrained from any barbed comment he would have instinctively made in the past concerning the abilities and foresight of Scotland Yard.

"To what type of events are you referring?" he asked instead.

"Well, they started off with unauthorised gatherings. Then there were demonstrations, and then they led to sinister attacks on the homes of police and government officials. Now we see these marches, like the one this morning that has ended with more disruption and arrests." Reynolds rubbed his bald head and mumbled resignedly, "I don't know why they just don't give them the vote and have done. It would make my life much easier."

Holmes chuckled. "So you believe that there is someone in the Suffragette movement who has access to information proper to the authorities that is being used to facilitate the protesters' movements?"

"Yes, that's right," agreed Reynolds. "There must be someone in the corridors of Whitehall who is feeding information to the organisers, which is stretching our manpower to its limits. This morning's march was an exception. We knew all about it and managed to deploy an appropriate number of officers to the scene, but even then – Well, you have just witnessed the aftermath for yourself."

"And my role?" asked Holmes. "How can I succeed where the authorities have failed?"

"Well, I was talking to old Gregson," said the policeman, "and he was telling me about your – shall we say – *unorthodox* methods? Methods that those of us in official positions don't have the benefit of. What with your connections in Whitehall and your network of contacts – " Reynolds hesitated and cleared his throat. " – elsewhere, I was hoping that you may be able to uncover the spy."

"Ha! A spy indeed! You afford me too much credit, Inspector, and as for my network of contacts, as you put it, it has been seven years since I left London. I'm not sure if many of them will still be in operation. However, as I'm here now, I may be able to afford you a little time."

"That's excellent, Mr. Holmes. Thank you."

"Tell me, what makes you believe this mysterious secret agent is within the corridors of Whitehall? Why not here in Scotland Yard?"

It was as though the inspector was quite affronted by Holmes's question.

"The thought of a member of my force imparting information to someone intent on causing criminal damage and injury is ridiculous! Operational security is of paramount importance, and all of my men understand the need to carry out their duties with the utmost integrity."

"I'm sorry, Reynolds," said Holmes with a thin smile. "I didn't mean to offend."

Suitably placated, the inspector offered his guest some refreshment.

"Would you like a cup of – ?" he began before he was interrupted by a knock at the door.

It was Lizzie, the cleaner. "Sorry to disturb you, sir, but can I empty your bins while there is all that carry on going on outside?"

"What? . . . *Erm* . . . yes," replied the inspector, distractedly. Before he could resume his offer to Holmes, there was another knock and a constable put his head around the door.

"Sorry to disturb you, sir, Sergeant MacPherson would like a word. Apparently, one of the ladies arrested wants to speak with someone in a higher authority."

"I'm sorry, Mr. Holmes," said Reynolds, rising from his chair. "I'll have to deal with this. If you need anything to help in your own work, please don't hesitate to contact me."

"Certainly, Inspector," said Holmes making to follow him out of the room. "I may need access to Scotland Yard again, but I will keep you informed."

Reynolds was a little baffled by the comment, but shook it off as he entered the corridor once more to be greeted by the increased noise level. As he made his way behind the counter to join Sergeant MacPherson, he was further confused as he saw Holmes out of the corner of his eye, waiting a while before speaking with Lizzie the cleaner who followed them out of the inspector's office. He couldn't hear what was being said above the din, and his attention was quickly drawn to the rather officious lady that stood in front of the counter.

"Now then, Madam," he asked, "how can I help you?"

Holmes left the inspector and his men to their task at hand and took a hansom to Queen Anne Street, where he was to stay as a guest of Watson and his wife. As Watson had his morning surgery, Holmes had travelled straight from Victoria to Scotland Yard. They had then arranged to have lunch afterwards at Watson's home.

"You look well, old fellow," said the doctor, shaking his friend vigorously by the hand.

"As do you, Watson. It is good to see you again."

Holmes's comment was another sign that his once sullen, indifferent approach to any form of affection had lessoned somewhat since his retirement to a more relaxing environment.

The maid took Holmes's hat, coat, and carpet bag containing his few essentials, and Watson took him through to the sitting room where his wife was seated, sewing by the fire.

"Mr. Holmes," she said rising as the two entered. "How lovely to see you again."

"Mrs. Watson. Thank you once again for your kindness in offering me a place to rest."

"Oh, it's our pleasure. Isn't it, John?"

"Indeed it is, my dear."

Before they had a chance to sit down, the maid entered. "Lunch is ready, sir, if you would like to go through."

The three entered the dining room and sat down to a hearty meal of cold ham and boiled potatoes.

"I see you took my advice in publishing the Cornish Horror," said Holmes. "A most accurate narration, as opposed to the rather imperfect account published in the newspapers at the time, if my memory serves me well."

"Thank you. It isn't often that you have complimented me on my writing."

Holmes threw a glance at his old friend. "Well, since I've been doing more of my own writing, perhaps I realise that it isn't as easy as I once thought."

"John didn't tell me why you are in London, Mr. Holmes," asked Mrs. Watson.

"The original purpose was to visit my brother on some government business he wants to discuss, but I've also been asked by Scotland Yard to look into an issue regarding the so-called 'Suffragettes'."

"Oh, don't let us start on that subject!" interjected Watson.

"Why ever not?" questioned his wife. "Women constantly demonstrate their talents and efforts just as much as men, and yet they aren't afforded the same rights. We boast a free democratic society while excluding half the population from voting, simply based on their sex?"

"I doubt if a stronger case could be put forward in Parliament, Mrs. Watson," said Holmes as his old friend rolled his eyes.

"Parliament?" she replied with a laugh. "I very much doubt it. Women may well write bestselling novels. They may travel abroad with our armies to tend the wounded on the battlefield. They may even reign over an empire spanning half the globe for more than sixty years. But if a woman can't even get a vote, I doubt the day will ever come when she will be allowed to speak in Parliament."

"Well said," replied her guest.

With that, Watson subtly changed the subject as the three carried on their lunch.

Chapter III

The following day, after a morning meeting with his brother and lunch at the Diogenes Club, Holmes returned to Scotland Yard shortly after three o'clock.

"Any luck so far, Mr. Holmes?" asked Inspector Reynolds as he was shown into his office.

"Not yet, Reynolds but I hope to have some news by the end of the day."

"Oh, really? That *is* promising. Did you speak to your brother on the matter? Did he help with some information about possible culprits within Whitehall?"

"The issue of the Suffragette disturbances did come up in our conversation, but it was never suggested that government officials would be colluding with the perpetrators of the various disruption."

"Why ever not?"

"Because I have reason to believe that whatever information is being passed to the criminals is coming from within the police force itself."

Reynolds was aghast at the comment. He rubbed his bald head, agitatedly. "I find that hard to believe, Mr. Holmes. Why would one of our own feed pieces of information to people who are intent on making our lives as awkward as possible?"

Holmes ignored the question and instead asked, "Would you have any objection to me spending the rest of the day here, Inspector?"

"Well . . . no . . . I don't suppose that would be a problem. I do feel a little uncomfortable, however, if you are proposing to go round the building questioning my men."

"That won't be necessary. I shall just stay here for the remainder of the afternoon and into the evening, if that's all right with you?"

"Into the evening? I'll be leaving around six o'clock. I didn't tell Mrs. Reynolds that I would be late, and she will have my supper ready."

"Oh, there will be no need to upset Mrs. Reynolds," said Holmes with a chuckle. "I'll remain here on my own after you've left, if you have no objections."

Reynolds was more confused than ever. "Well . . . I suppose so, if you think it will help."

"Thank you."

Holmes sat patiently for the next three hours, most of the time spent with his eyes closed. Reynolds came and went from his office, wondering what the consulting detective was up to and beginning to wonder about the glowing reference given about him from his old colleague, Gregson. Shortly after six o'clock, he announced, "Well, I'll be going Mr. Holmes. Do you need anything?"

"No, I'll be fine, Reynolds, thank you, providing you have no objections to me waiting in your office?" Reynolds nodded. "And if you could refrain from telling anyone I'm here, it would be greatly appreciated. I may have some information for you in the morning."

The policeman looked sceptically at his guest. "Very well," he said, reaching for his hat and coat. "I shall look forward to it and bid you good evening."

Once Reynolds had left, Holmes moved his chair to the far corner and seated himself in a partially obscured position behind the coat stand. There he waited. It was shortly before seven when his patience was rewarded.

The office door opened and a cleaner entered with a mop and bucket. She was a different woman to the one identified as "Lizzie" the previous day and with whom Holmes had spoken before he left the building. Walking with a slight stoop, this woman appeared older, and had a general air of somnolence about her. This initial appearance altered dramatically however when she closed the door quietly behind her after doing a final check of the corridor outside. The woman put down her bucket and raised herself to her true height. Her demeanour instantly changed and, from his hiding place, even Holmes could see an alertness in her eyes that made him smile inwardly.

Completely unaware that anyone was near Inspector Reynolds' office, let alone hiding in a corner, the woman proceeded to first take papers from the wastepaper basket and lay them out on the desk. She scanned them before apparently deciding they contained nothing of interest. She placed them in a bag that was tied to her bucket. She then turned her attention to the inspector's desk, opening the drawers and inspecting the contents. Again, Holmes smiled at the carelessness of Reynolds in leaving both his office and his desk unlocked. With nothing of apparent interest, the woman replaced the contents and sat back thoughtfully in the inspector's chair.

"A fruitless search this evening, I presume?" said a voice from the far corner of the room.

The woman visibly leapt in fright. "Who's there?" she blurted out after a few seconds.

Only then did Sherlock Holmes appear, as if he had walked through the wall. The woman's face was a picture of betrayal and guilt.

"I should actually thank you, Madam," said Holmes. "Rarely have I had a case when I didn't have to move or do any work."

The woman was speechless. Holmes continued.

"I was asked by Inspector Reynolds to look into various pieces of information that were being passed to women in the Suffragette movement. He thought there was a spy in the corridors of Whitehall, but it turns out that any information about police whereabouts, available resources, and personal details of government officials was stemming directly from his own office."

The woman – still in a state of shock after being caught red-handed – again said nothing in response.

"My name is Sherlock Holmes. I am not part of the official police force. You can speak freely with me. Perhaps you could explain who you are and why you're taking such action. Then I will decide what to do about the matter."

After taking some time to compose herself after such a shock, the woman finally spoke and told her story . . . .

Martha Grice was born in 1853. Her earliest memories were of being brought up in a workhouse in Aldershot, Hampshire. She didn't know what happened to her parents and was never told. She received the most basic of schooling and, when she entered adolescence, was taught to sew and spin in the yarn room. Determined to make something of her life, she left at the age of nineteen, but quickly found that a child of the workhouse wasn't an attractive candidate to fill positions in seamstress or tailoring establishments. As a result, she had to lower her expectations and find work as a char and cleaner to make ends meet.

Being a military town – like many in the area – Martha gravitated towards the regimental depots, and it was when she got a job as a cleaner there that she met a corporal in the Rifle Brigade, Fred Brooks, who was two years her senior. Love blossomed between the two and, with his regiment's consent, they were married in 1875. In the early years of their marriage, Martha had to endure her husband being abroad on campaigns.

246

She, meanwhile, continued to work at the depot and whatever free time she had, she spent reading and improving her education.

Her life was changed with the outbreak of the Boer War in the final year of the century. Fred – newly promoted to sergeant – was once again called to action and duly travelled to the Dark Continent with his regiment. But when the war was over, he wrote to his wife expressing his wish to remain on the Cape. He explained that there were opportunities in the South African Constabulary, a paramilitary force set up to keep the peace in British-controlled areas. The climate was good and the income was attractive to a Non-Commissioned Officer who was approaching his retirement from the army anyway. He asked that Martha join him, as married quarters were also included in the role.

Martha therefore left England and travelled out to the Northern Cape, where she would spend the following six years. While there, she enjoyed being part of the foreign community of peacekeepers, and particularly became friends with Helga Müller, the wife of a German Missionary. The two women spent much of their spare time together and Martha – with her enthusiasm for learning and adventure – gradually learned to speak German.

Tragedy struck in 1908 when her husband Fred was killed in a training accident. With no means of support, no veteran's pension, and little opportunity for the widow of a foreigner, Martha reluctantly made the long journey back to England. For the three years prior to her meeting with Sherlock Holmes, she had reverted to her role as a char and cleaner in various establishments in London.

"And apparently aiding and abetting illegal activities," commented Holmes when the woman had finished her story.

"England was a very different place to the one I left, Mr. Holmes. I had a husband, security, and a certain standing. I returned with nothing. No social standing, nothing. There may have well been social reforms with pensions and a minimum wage, but I was too young for one and too old for the other. The authorities seem more interested in building up arms to fight more wars than to look after its people.

"There is injustice everywhere, no more so with the plight of the English woman. She has always been a second-class citizen, and things are getting worse. If you are in the lower classes like me, you don't stand a chance. The government makes decisions that send men away to war, never to return. It puts people out of work. Create social injustice, and yet half of the population don't even have a say in who makes the decisions."

Holmes looked at the woman, admiring her stoicism and warming to her point of view. She had logical thinking, and an ability to articulate an argument that was wasted simply by her social status.

"You are the second woman in as many days I have heard voice such a sentiment. As with the other lady of which I speak, I believe you would be a wonderful orator in Parliament itself."

Martha laughed. "Parliament? The chance would be a fine thing!"

"Again, a sentiment expressed by the lady in question. Tell me how you came to be passing information to the Suffragettes."

"I have only worked here for three months. When I saw how those women were treated when they were brought in, I thought it was disgusting."

"And that is when you decided to offer your help?"

"It so happens that one of the activists stays in the same boarding house as me. When she discovered I did some cleaning here, she asked if I could find pieces of information that would help them in their cause. I told her that I wouldn't provide addresses of people who could be placed in danger, but I could see how many officers were available at various times. That way, the protestors could arrange several demonstrations at various locations while there wouldn't be enough police available to supress them."

"That approach appeared unsuccessful yesterday, judging by the number of women that were arrested."

"I couldn't do anything about that. That was a national rally with women traveling from all over the country to be here. It was well-known that the march was taking place, and extra police had been brought in to deal with it."

Sherlock Holmes thought for a while before asking, "You say that no one has been identified or hurt as a result of the information you have passed to your fellow lodger?"

"No, sir. I see the injustice and I want to help, but I am not supporting violence."

"I see. Perhaps there is a way out of this that could benefit us all."

Martha looked at Holmes with a questioning expression.

In the hour or so in which they had spoken, Holmes had been impressed by the woman's honesty when speaking about her position, and the series of events that had led her to this point and the course of action she had decided to take.

"How do you feel about moving back to the south coast?" he asked, after a while.

Martha was dumb-founded, and several seconds passed before she could splutter, "Sorry, sir, I don't know what you mean."

"I think I have a solution to the problem with which Inspector Reynolds has tasked me that could prove beneficial to us all." In response to Martha's astonished expression, Holmes continued. "The inspector asked me to find an individual he believed to be passing information to the Suffragettes. I have now found that individual, and therefore ensured that any inappropriate disclosures will cease.

"For my part, I am in need of a housekeeper. It seems, Mrs. Brooks, that you are in need of regular employment and somewhere to stay. I live in a little villa on the South Downs, and I propose that you come and work for me. From what you've told me, there is nothing to keep you in London."

Martha was still trying to come to terms with what her discoverer was saying.

"But won't you have to tell Inspector Reynolds about me?" she asked after some thought.

"I'm sure I can reassure the inspector that the matter has been resolved satisfactorily and there will be no repeat of any unfortunate breaches of information."

"I don't know what to say," said Martha.

"A simple *yes* would suffice, although I must point out that my habits are thought by some to be a trifle . . . *singular*. Some may even say infuriating, although I can't see it myself."

"I'm sure I'll cope, Mr. Holmes. I've dealt with plenty of men in my time who think they are different."

Holmes burst into a roar of laughter and had to quickly compose himself for fear of alerting someone else in the building.

"Tell me, Mrs. Brooks, did anyone see you come in this evening?"

"No, sir. No one ever notices the cleaner."

"Indeed," he mumbled to himself. "The perfect spy." Then back to Martha. "In that case, if you've a prepared to accept my suggestion, it may be wise to slip away unseen, and we can make arrangements for you to return to Sussex with me."

"Won't it seem a little – " Martha hesitated, embarrassed at what was running through her mind. " – *unusual*? Even inappropriate?"

Holmes smiled at her insinuation. "I assure you, Madam, that my proposition is perfectly genuine. If you would like me to provide references as to my character, I'm sure that can be arranged. As for whatever neighbours I have in my isolated corner of England, they all know that I need a housekeeper after the unfortunate passing of my dear Mrs. Hewitt a couple of weeks ago."

Martha laughed noiselessly. "I'm sure that is the first time in history that a man has interviewed a woman for a job and offered to provide references without asking for any in return! You have been more than fair with me. It seems as though I have nothing to lose in coming to work for you. If you're sure, then I accept your offer."

"Splendid!" said Holmes. "I'll return here in the morning and speak with Inspector Reynolds, assuring him that the matter has been resolved. As there will be nothing else keeping me in London, I'll return to Sussex tomorrow afternoon. You can either join me at Victoria Station at two o'clock, or make your own way there at a later time and date."

"Tomorrow will be fine, I suppose," said Martha, still stunned by the events of the last hour. "I won't have to give any notice at the boarding house."

"Until tomorrow at two o'clock then," said Holmes, bringing their interview to an end.

They both left separately out of a back entrance.

The following morning, Sergeant MacPherson showed Holmes into Inspector Reynolds' office. The consulting detective wore an expression of chagrin.

"Good morning, Mr. Holmes. Have you any news?"

"I do, Inspector, and I'm embarrassed to say that I owe you a heartfelt apology."

"An apology?" repeated Reynolds.

"Yes. I have to report that you were right all along. I believe the perpetrator was indeed a member of the domestic staff at the Home Office. One of my *network*, as you called them, informed me that they knew of a woman who was accessing information and then passing it on to the would-be protestors. Apparently, this lady had performed a similar task when she was employed at the Chancery aiding fiscal criminal activity. When I made some enquiries there yesterday, I found that our bird had flown once more. Always one step ahead of the authorities, it seems.

"I repeat: I apologise for too hastily dismissing your suggestion that the individual originated among the masses of Whitehall."

Reynolds adopted a self-assured air. So pleased with himself, believing he was now cleverer than the great detective Tobias Gregson had spoken so highly of, he completely overlooked the obvious questions: What was the name of the individual involved? To where had the woman fled, and when did she leave? If she had already been suspected or discovered at the Chancery, why wasn't she brought to the attention of the police *then*? Instead of all this, Reynolds just sat back in his chair, wearing a smug grin.

"Well," he said, "we can't be right all the time, I suppose."

"I suppose not," agreed Sherlock Holmes, maintaining his air of defeat.

"Wait a minute!" cried Reynolds suddenly. "Why did you remain in my office last night if you knew the culprit was at the Home Office?"

"I just wanted to re-assure myself that there was no accomplice working here in Scotland Yard."

"Ha! Not very likely. There isn't much goes on in here that we don't know about."

"Indeed not. Well, Inspector, if you have no further need for my services, I will bid you good morning."

"Certainly Mr. Holmes. Thank you again for coming, although I now see we could have resolved the affair ourselves."

"No matter, Reynolds. No doubt we have all benefited from my visit."

With that, Holmes left the policeman, who sat at his desk somewhat baffled by Holmes's last comment.

Chapter IV

Martha Brooks had been working as Holmes's housekeeper for two years before another unexpected visitor to the South Downs would ultimately lead to a hitherto unimaginable disruption for them both. Each had been enjoying their lives under the same roof, but independent of one another. Holmes had his bees, his writing, and other hobbies. Beside her own room, Martha had a tiny compact space where she could read or sew quietly.

Holmes kept up with the outside world by continuing to read the newspapers. He noted that German belligerence was leading to an increase in arms production in both England and on the Continent. War had already broken out in the Balkans and Europe was looking increasingly unstable.

It was in the early spring of 1912. Holmes was tending to his small allotment when Martha called from the house. He looked up and through the dark netting of his veil could see an unmistakable figure standing beside his housekeeper: His brother Mycroft. Beside him stood a thinner man who Holmes didn't immediately recognise, but he somehow knew what the two men wanted.

"Sherlock, my dear boy!" said the older brother, as Holmes approached while removing his protective hat and gown.

"Mycroft. I would calculate that the likelihood of you leaving the confines of your lodgings or the Diogenes Club for the purpose of a pleasure trip to this secluded corner of the country would be precisely zero. It can therefore only be business."

"Indeed it is, Sherlock, indeed it is." In the process of turning to the man beside him, he added, "May I introduce the Foreign Secretary. Sir, this is my brother, Sherlock."

"I have heard a lot about you, Mr. Holmes. I'm pleased to meet you, and hope you can help us."

The merest glance towards Martha suggested she make some refreshment, and they all followed the housekeeper inside.

"Before you begin, Mycroft," said Sherlock as he offered his guests a seat, "I should remind you that I am retired and not available, or need I say interested, in undertaking any government activity."

"I understand your position perfectly well," replied his brother. "I am in exactly the same position myself."

Martha broke the tension somewhat as she brought a pot of tea through to the sitting room. With a nod from her employer, she poured the three men each a cup and then retired to the kitchen.

"It is the most serious of situations, Mr. Holmes," said the Foreign Secretary. "We first approached your brother for advice, and he pointed out to us that there was only one man capable of solving the most delicate of problems."

Sherlock looked at his brother.

"Well, it's true, Sherlock!" Mycroft replied in response. "You have always been the one with the energy, and I am hardly in the best physical condition to carry out such a task."

"I must decline, gentlemen," said Holmes, without waiting to hear what the task *was*. "I am fifty-eight years old and enjoying my retirement. You need a younger man."

"You don't know what we're asking yet," said the Foreign Secretary.

"Given your position in government, Sir Edward, I would postulate that it is something to do with the escalating tensions with Germany. Perhaps someone is passing secrets to Berlin? Or our armaments are being sabotaged in some way? Whatever the issue, I'm afraid I can't help."

Sir Edward looked at Mycroft and then again at Sherlock. "You are as perceptive as your brother indicated Mr. Holmes, which is all the more reason why I am asking for your help. If I could at least speak confidentially for a moment and explain.

"We believe there is a German spy at the heart of the British establishment. There is evidence of information gathering regarding naval installations and the movement of our vessels. It seems as though the Germans are aware of our every move. In the strictest confidence, Mr. Holmes, we're about to move our fleet from the Mediterranean to the North Sea to guard against possible naval attack as a result.

"It's imperative that we identify this individual or individuals, which is why we have come to you."

Holmes sat politely listening throughout the official's narrative.

"I have to say that it's a situation of your own making."

252

Sir Edward was taken aback by the comment and bristled with indignation. "What do you mean, exactly?"

"It is common knowledge that numerous notable personages and courtiers from the great Houses of Europe regularly mix with their counterparts in this country. His Majesty has played host to many a foreign dignitary at his various estates, and I'm aware that the Kaiser himself has been hosted by his cousin, the King, as well as his friend Lord Lonsdale in Cumberland. It would be like looking for a needle in a haystack!"

The Foreign Secretary could barely hide his fury. "I must say, Mr. Holmes, I am extremely disappointed in your attitude! We came here asking for your help, and all you have done is sullied the reputation of those who should be beyond reproach."

"I have no wish to insult anyone, Sir Edward. I am merely pointing out that the upper classes of our country wouldn't suspect your man of espionage, as they are blinded by his good company at the card table or the drinking club.

"For my part, I must express my own offence at being asked to supplement the deficiencies of the authorities – the same authorities who have allowed such a situation to manifest itself through their own carelessness."

The Foreign Secretary bristled with anger at Holmes's words. It took all his self-control to refrain from shouting at his host. For his part, Holmes sat there, quite impassively, thumbing some tobacco into the bowl of his cherry-wood pipe.

"Well, there is little more to say," said Sir Edward at long last. "We shall detain you no more."

With that, he rose and left, without waiting for Mycroft or to be shown out. Before joining him, the tall portly figure of Mycroft Holmes turned to his younger brother and spoke gravely. "The matter is extremely serious, Sherlock. I urge you to give it some thought."

"I cannot promise, Mycroft. All I can do is wish the Foreign Secretary well in his quest."

The little cottage was silent for several minutes following the departure of the two officials. Holmes sat with his eyes closed, sucking on his pipe. He sensed a presence in the room.

"You disagree with my response to our guests' request, Martha?"

The housekeeper had quietly entered the sitting room to remove the tray. She stood for a while, not wishing to disturb Holmes.

"It isn't for me to agree or disagree, sir."

"I would welcome your opinion."

253

She was slightly taken aback by the comment. "Well, sir, I think it shows how highly you are thought-of, if such a senior statesmen would visit you in person to ask for your help."

"Did you hear what was said?"

"I couldn't help but, sir. Everything can be heard in our small abode, and when voices are raised in such an excited manner, I couldn't help but be party to what was being said."

"And?"

Martha paused before giving her opinion. "Well, sir, having seen war – or at least the aftermath of it – first-hand, and seeing the death and destruction it causes, not to mention the effect it has on those who survive it, I firmly believe it should be avoided at all costs. Anything that can be done by you or anyone else should be explored."

Holmes smiled. "I seem to recall that when we first met, I suggested your oratory wouldn't be out of place in Parliament. In the two years since then, I must say that nothing has changed my initial view."

Martha smiled at the compliment. "Whether such oratory in that House will ever come from a woman in my lifetime is highly unlikely, sir. But I also recall that when you were asked to look into the information finding its way to the Suffragettes, it didn't take you long to find that I was the culprit. You described me as 'The Perfect Spy', given that I was operating right under the noses of the people who were looking out for me. Using that same principal, I believe you would be one of the few people who could uncover the Kaiser's agent. If that would prevent a war between us and Germany, then surely it should be explored."

"We shall see," was Holmes's enigmatic reply. "Perhaps I *could* look into the matter and see if there are any obvious candidates."

Martha didn't reply. She simply cleared away the tea tray and retired to the kitchen.

For the next three weeks, Holmes scoured the newspapers and poured over his extensive library, as well as paying regular visits to both London and Southampton. Finally, he sent his brother Mycroft a telegram. It simply read:

Von Bork is your man. – SH

Mycroft replied:

I am visiting you next week. – MH

When Holmes's brother returned, he was once again accompanied, but not this time by the Foreign Secretary. Martha stood, dumbfounded for a moment, disbelieving the figure who was now gracing her employer's little hideaway. After taking a little time to compose herself, she showed them both into the sitting room.

"Now, Sherlock," said Mycroft, without any greeting and with a solemnity which demonstrated the importance of the subject. "I hope this proves how serious we are about this matter."

Following him into the room was none other than the Prime Minister. "Sir, may I present my brother, Mr. Sherlock Holmes."

"Welcome, Prime Minister," said Holmes, not the least bit surprised or overawed by his presence. "Martha? Some refreshment please."

The housekeeper took their coats and disappeared into the kitchen as Mycroft lowered his large frame into the seat opposite his brother. The Prime Minister took the sofa, set back from the fire, between the two.

"Mr. Holmes," said the Premier, "your brother tells me that you have being looking into the problems we have been having with our German friends. The name you passed to him is someone who is trusted and has been welcomed into the highest circles."

"That is exactly the reason why he has gone unnoticed, Prime Minister. I believe he has hunted with the King himself." He turned to his brother. "If you return a third time with His Majesty, I will tell him the same thing. It is Von Bork who is your spy. He has the means and the motive to go about his business virtually unmolested."

"Well, what do you suggest we do, Mr. Holmes?" asked the Prime Minister. "We can't just arrest the man because you have identified him. Where is our proof?"

It was Mycroft who moved to support his brother's conclusion. "I must say, Sherlock, there was part of me that wasn't surprised when you named this chap. He has been in this country for two years and, not long after he arrived, it was noted that some sensitive information concerning our international treaties had found its way back to the German Chancellor. The information had originated from a cabinet minister who held a weekend gathering at which Von Bork was invited. As he was the only German present, it was thought by many that he couldn't be trusted. I believe he was given the benefit of any doubt, considering it was the minister who was at fault for speaking so indiscreetly to a foreign national."

"Again!" cried Sherlock, not attempting to hide his frustration. "An example of the authorities creating a problem for themselves."

"That is as may be, Mr. Holmes, but this problem is now clearly very serious. What do you propose we do?"

"It occurs to me that Von Bork's tactic is to elicit intelligence in small quantities. A chance indiscretion here – as you have just alluded to, Mycroft – or a memorandum there. Such a strategy takes time, and no doubt he has spent his years in England building up a network of followers. In short, it is a long process, and in order to catch him and his gang, it will take an equally long process. If you wish to break the whole ring of espionage, I believe it will be necessary to do exactly what Von Bork has done to the British establishment: Attack his spy ring from within."

"You mean we would need to implant a sort of counterspy into his gang?"

"A good way of putting it, Prime Minister."

At that point, Martha entered with the tea tray and poured the three men a cup. It provided a suitable pause before the obvious question was asked.

"Would you perform such a task for your country, Mr. Holmes? I can think of no one who possesses the necessary skill and experience to undertake such an important mission?"

"I must concur with the Prime Minister, Sherlock," added Mycroft.

The younger brother thought for a while. "If we undertake such a task," he said at last, "I think it would be beneficial for us both to be involved."

"I don't have the energy to undertake such matters," said Mycroft.

"I'm not referring to you." His two guests looked at him. "I am referring to Martha."

"Martha?" repeated Mycroft. "Who is Martha?"

"She is the lady who has just served you your tea!"

The two men instantly looked round at the housekeeper.

"I'm sorry, Mr. Holmes," said the Prime Minister. "Is this some sort of joke?"

"Far from it, sir. I suggest Martha would be the perfect agent in such a circumstance." He indicated for his housekeeper to take a seat and join them before continuing to address the two men. "You have just proved how effective she could be. We have been holding what some people would see as a highly confidential conversation, all within earshot of someone you didn't even notice. I can inform you that Martha speaks fluent German and would be ideally suited to acting as a member of Von Bork's staff. A spy to catch a spy, you could say. Besides, there would be no work for her here."

"Why, where will you be?" asked Mycroft.

"I think the best way to infiltrate Von Bork's gang would be through another member. That way, there would be no suspicion that Martha and

I came into his employ at the same time. There would be no indication that we even know each other."

"What do you propose?"

"I'm aware that one of the German's agents is an American called Jack James. The man is a complete imbecile, and I should have little difficulty in ingratiating myself with him. He will then lead me to Von Bork himself, as well as sharing with me the names of his colleagues.

"One of Von Bork's tactics appears to be to create confusion amongst the British authorities while fuelling sectarian unrest in Ireland. This causes enough of a distraction to allow him time and accessibility to information that is duly passed to Berlin. If war is declared, Germany's enemy will be stretched on two different fronts, increasing their chances of victory.

"If I could align myself to Jack James, in the guise of a supporter of the Irish Republican Movement, I should be able to not only establish their nefarious activities, but adopt a tactic of counterintelligence by giving them false information."

"That is a brilliant plan, Mr. Holmes!" said the Prime Minister.

"I assume you have no objection to all of this, Martha?" asked Holmes, addressing his housekeeper for the first time regarding the matter. "After all, anything that can be done by myself or anyone else should be explored."

Martha smiled at Holmes using her own words against her. "Very well, sir," she said.

"Excellent!" cried Holmes, and then, turning back to his guests, he added, "Well, gentlemen, let us get to work!"

The Swapped Names
of the Saviour
by David Marcum

Yesterday, I read in The Times *that Reverend Rayford Chinnor Longwick had died at Gallipoli. When the war began, he volunteered immediately as an Army Chaplain, and from what I've heard, he never hesitated to place himself where he could do the most good, even at the greatest personal risk to himself. I was greatly saddened by the news that he is lost, and now, four years after we first met, I'm still shamed at my first reaction to this brave man, when I initially thought him to be nothing more than a pompous, ineffectual, and silly* poseur. *This, in truth, was the same hero who raced into a contested plaza, the bullets flying like maddened hornets, to lead out a mother and child who were trapped in the deadly crossfire. Only when he knew that they were safe did he allow the thread of his life, nearly severed by the four bullets he'd taken from the Turks' Mausers, to fray and drift part, and he went to his reward, so I'm told, with a smile upon his face.*

– JHW
6 June, 1915

An adage that never loses its efficacious wisdom is that one shouldn't count upon the weather. The seasoned traveler understands this, and heaven knows that I – nearing the middle of my seventh decade as I recall these events – am certainly one of those. However, on that day in early autumn 1911, my planned holiday to Beachy Head, on the Sussex coast where I would spend a few days visiting in the cottage of my friend Sherlock Holmes, had established itself in my head with visions of bright blue skies and bracing walks across the countryside. Despite the accumulating daily evidence to the contrary, I continued to picture it with high anticipation, even as London, seventy-five miles nearly straight to the north from that piece of coastline, settled further into an interminable repetition of dank and foggy days.

I knew better, of course, with each day's weather predictions, but still my imagination would drift toward that idyllic image, even as the facts negating it mounted. The newspapers reported that the same conditions were in place in Sussex – deteriorating, and likely to remain so for a week or longer. Still, each morning, and each day closer to my short holiday, some primitive part of my brain fooled me into thinking that circumstances could possibly still improve even as the glass was falling.

My practice in Queen Anne Street had, by that point, become rather reduced, as I only saw a handful of old patients – by then it might hardly have been called a practice at all. My wife was away for a visit to a long-time friend, and it had seemed to be a perfect solution to my daily malaise when Holmes had invited me to journey south. (I found out later that my wife had wired him and suggested it, should it be convenient to Holmes's schedule.) I needed the change, and amongst my traveling bags I had packed some of my notes, hoping to question my friend regarding a few points concerning his past investigations with the possibility that the narratives might someday appear in *The Strand* – which, it cannot be denied, was always a useful supplement to my income.

I'd convinced myself early on that I would hazard the journey in my automobile, and had made sure beforehand that it was adequately prepared for the trip – fuel tank filled, rubber tires pressurized, and lamps in good condition – but as the day approached, I understood that these plans were also doomed to failure.

The night before my departure, it began to rain in earnest.

Notifying the garage that I wouldn't be taking the car after all, I instead entrained at Victoria Station and settled into a private first-class compartment, thankful at least that I was on an express. It was no use looking to either side as we progressed – the weather made sure that none of the usual pleasant scenery was visible. Instead of daydreaming the journey away by watching raindrops streaking along the windows, or sleeping – The temptation for that bled away too much of my time already! – I settled in with the last-minute editing of the manuscript that I was preparing for publication within the next couple of months – that of the rescue of Lady Frances Carfax from the clutches of the thoroughly despicable "Holy" Peters. The story hadn't ended quite as well as the version I'd recorded – as Doyle insisted on a "happy ending" – and the lady had suffered from terrible and crippling recurring nightmares after being nearly buried alive in a coffin, sidled up alongside another dead body, but there was no need to subject the poor woman to worse scrutiny than she'd received from the press at the time.

The train arrived on time, and I was soon ensconced in a rackety old cab and rattling west along the narrow road to East Dean. The weather was breaking up for just a little while, and at times I could see glimpses of the angry churning sea in the distance. I knew the driver, Beauchamp, from previous journeys, and he told me of some of the recent local flooding, including a wash-out on one of the roads upon which I would have driven. I had made the correct decision to leave my automobile in London.

We turned south at Crapham Hill and soon passed the old inn and then the coaching establishment before veering back west, with the ground sloping dramatically upward on our left to the edges of the high chalk cliffs. Meanwhile, the road itself was steadily dropping toward Birling Gap, with its limited access to the sea at the Coast Guard station. However, before we reached it, Holmes's small farm – a "villa" as he liked to call it – came into focus on the right, a rectangular plot of five acres, surrounded by a low wall made from the local quartz, with open fields stretching behind it to the north, used only by those locals walking from here-to-there and the many sheep that dotted the nearby landscape.

Beauchamp delivered me right to Holmes's door, which was thrown open before I reached it by Mrs. Hudson. At the time of Holmes's retirement, she had initially thought to stay in London, but as time passed, she agreed that her days would be better spent in the countryside instead of the smoky and unhealthy capital. (It was a lesson that I hadn't seemed to learn.) At the time of her relocation, Holmes had arranged to purchase her lease of 221 Baker Street, to use as a base of operations whenever he needed to return to the capital – for his "retirement" was more often than not a convenient fiction used to cover his activities as he went all over on errands for his brother Mycroft, preparing for the ever-certain impending war with Germany. (In fact, within a year from the events that I describe, Holmes would take on his identity as the mysterious "Altamont", a bitter and disaffected Irish-American willing to spy for the Germans. But that is a tale I'll reserve for another time, when the end of this war is in sight.)

At that moment in time, a war with Germany seemed much more likely after the previous April's Agadir Crisis, and finally the common-folk were beginning to understand a bit more about what was coming, although none could realize to what extent. I had the benefit – or curse – of both being a veteran of and a witness to a particularly terrible battle, and also the keen insight of both Sherlock and Mycroft Holmes to explain just what a modern conflict with so many entangled nations – and such modernized weaponry – would be like. We had worked long to avoid it entirely, but now it was clear that such a more-pleasant outcome wasn't possible. We could only hope to delay the war's inevitability, and to place ourselves on the best possible footing when it arrived.

But none of that was on my mind when I entered Holmes's warm cottage that day and hung my coat and hat to dry. I chatted with Mrs. Hudson for a moment before she bustled toward the back of the house to finish up lunch, which she promised would be something special. Leaving my bag at the door until later, when I would carry it to my room, I wound through the house to Holmes's study, where I found him, standing near one of his shelves, a book opened in his hand.

"Have you read the new *Britannica* article on recidivism?" he asked, looking up, his tone critical, as if we were continuing a conversation already begun that morning. "It refers to '*some ardent reformers*'" – and he glanced back at the book, reading, "'*recommend a system of indefinite imprisonment or the indeterminate sentence, by which the enemy once caught is kept perpetually or for a lengthy period, and thus rendered innocuous. Habitual offenders, it is argued, should be detained as hostages* – ' Note that phrasing, Watson. ' – *until they are willing to lay down their arms and consent to make no further attempt to attack or injure society. The theory is sound and has been adopted in part in several countries, especially in the United States.*'" He looked up while closing the book. "A bit harsh, don't you agree?"

"Indeed. Besides the idea that such a system would basically encourage a prison industry, how would one determine who is an '*habitual offender*', worthy of an open-ended sentence – perhaps for life?"

Holmes shook his head and returned the volume to the shelf. "The United States adopted such a system two or three years ago. Here in England, we've been much more tentative about it, but the procedure is in place to add '*habitual offender*' to a criminal's charge. Of concern is the fact that this decision is likely left up to the local police."

I nodded. "You're thinking of that constable in Bostock, back in the eighties, who framed several of his rival suitors."

"Which goes to show that even our noble law enforcement officers are still just men, with all the faults that are possible as such."

"We were quite lucky," I replied, "that so many officers with whom we worked – Lestrade, Gregson, Bradstreet, and such – were men of honor *and* little imagination."

"Yes. Thankfully, it never would have occurred to Lestrade to frame one of his enemies. Lack of imagination is sometimes a blessing."

We continued with our discussion, with one topic passing easily to another, uninterrupted through Mrs. Hudson's excellent lunch, featuring one of her fine pork roasts. Although it had only been a month or so since I'd last visited, I felt very much the guest of honor – and also quite sleepy afterwards. Rather than let me slide into an afternoon of wasted dozing, Holmes suggested a walk along the Downs. I had some wariness when considering the recent weather, but I agreed, retreating to my room long enough to change into more appropriate boots and then grab my coat and hat.

Within fifteen minutes, we'd made our way across the narrow road and then up the meandering paths that wound back and forth through the gorse, rising to the cliff-top. Both of us were canny enough to stay well back from the edges, which were always dropping way in great chalky chunks, and especially likely with the ground so saturated, the rain reaching deeply into the countless cracks we crossed. Many was the time that one would take a walk and find the perch from the night before, where the view of the sunset had been most beautiful, simply gone – dropped away into the water hundreds of feet below. Even well back from the cliff, the ground was striated with fissures extending to unknown depths, certainly filled with groundwater which would freeze and expand in winter, and indicating where some future fracture would inevitably occur.

We walked west, and the stiff sea breeze finished chasing away any of the sleepiness that I might have retained. In the distance, we could see the dip the cliff line where the Cuckmere reached the sea, and beyond it the Seven Sisters. Much closer and more accessible was the small settlement at Birling Gap. As we passed the old abandoned lighthouse and started down the slope, I could make out, at the far end of the Gap, the distinctive corner tower and slate roof of The Gables, where the Bellamy family had once lived. I'd had occasion to meet them on several occasions, including a few times after Holmes had related to me the events of their tangential involvement in a schoolmaster's death by way of an encounter with a misplaced creature of the sea. The young lady of the house, Maud, was quite the beauty, and I was unsurprised to hear that she had since married and moved to London.

At the Coast Guard barracks, we repeated our familiar discussion – wondering why they were located at that spot, a location where the sea could only be reached by a makeshift and occasionally shifting staircase (as the natural gap where the land sloped down to the ocean had long since vanished as the cliffs receded) and no boats could be moored. It was always a puzzle that such a station wasn't re-located to Eastbourne, or perhaps at the nearby mouth of the Cuckmere River. As always, we had no solution, and Holmes, his interests elsewhere, had never bothered to pursue an answer.

The barracks were where the road turned north, and in another mile we were in East Dean and passing through the low door of the Tiger Inn, a favorite visiting spot. We were both greeted with warmth and spent the next couple of hours in conversation, sometimes just the two of us, and at other times joined by various patrons. A portion of our visit was spent with a fellow named Patrick, manager of farm not far north of Holmes's villa, discussing a number of Satanic symbols that had been maliciously chalked on various buildings. He'd apparently consulted Holmes about it the previous week, and Holmes was able to confirm that his investigations had revealed the culprit to be the owner's eleven-year-old daughter, half-British and half-American, who seemed to have an unhealthy preoccupation with religion. The introduction of symbols had recently stopped as the family, who traveled more often than they were in England, had departed on another journey. Holmes recommended that the child see an alienist before she progressed to killing animals, but Patrick shook his head, agreeing that she "wasn't quite right," yet feeling unable to relate such a recommendation to his employer. As he shuffled heavily away, Holmes shook his head. All too often after his advice was ignored, the result of which was nearly always tragedy for someone. This matter would come back to pester Holmes greatly in a few years, but neither of us could knew that then.

By late afternoon, with the threat of rain returning, we hired a local named Steed to drive us back to Holmes's farm. We were soon returned to his door and, as we approached, Holmes touched my arm and nodded towards the building. The lamp in the front parlor was lit – which wasn't always the case – and we could see the shadowed silhouette of a visitor perched on the front of a chair near the large front window.

I glanced toward Holmes, thinking that he might evince some of his enthusiasm of the old days in Baker Street, when we would return to our rooms to spot a similar image outlined against the pulled shades in the sitting room windows above us. His reaction then would run the gamut from barely suppressed excitement to impatience that he might have missed the opportunity for a new case by being away unnecessarily. But now I could perceive that he was the least bit irritated. Clearly he didn't need the stimulus of new problems as he had in the old days – or more likely, he didn't need *this kind* of problem, whatever it turned out to be.

As we placed our hats and coats to dry on the hooks by the door, Mrs. Hudson joined us from the back of the house, handing Holmes a card and explaining softly that his visitor had come all the way from London.

Holmes glanced at it and then passed it to me. *Rev. Rayford Chinnor Longwick, BD, DD*, it said, with a Mitre Court address.

"Poor man," she murmured. "He seems most distressed, and he berated himself terribly when he found that you weren't here and that he'd neglected to send a wire asking for an appointment." She lowered her voice even more. "He must be quite absent-minded. He suddenly became concerned that he'd misplaced his umbrella, looking from side to side as if it might have dropped at his feet, never noticing 'til I told him that he still held it gripped in his left hand." She shook her head. "He's only been here for ten minutes or so, and I've served him some tea – he wanted nothing stronger. Now I'll go finish fixing something warm for all of you."

We entered Holmes's study to find a tall stork-like man in minister's garb, standing in the center of the room, facing away from us and apparently listening to something that wasn't perceptible to my ears, nor to Holmes's from his expression. Normally when one spends time waiting in a strange room, activities range from sitting quietly, perhaps smoking or sipping something, or if in a location as interesting as that one, examining the various objects sitting haphazardly on shelves and table-tops, or possibly perusing one of the many eclectic volumes on the densely packed shelves. But not this fellow.

He appeared to be about my age – nearly sixty – and his hair, though silvered, was thick and combed from his left to right. His matching eyebrows were tangled and tufted, perched out on a rather prominently ridged brow. He had a pair of *pince-nez* sitting upon his notably long nose, deeply grooved lines running on either side of his small dark-lipped mouth, and a prominent chin that left his similarly jutting Adam's apple in shadow, although quite visible over his clerical collar. His voice was high, and unfortunately unpleasant and quarrelsome when he spoke.

"Do you hear her?" he asked softly, turning toward us, his tone rather stressed.

"No," I replied, sounding sharp against the silence. "She is in the back of the house, preparing some refreshments."

"No, no!" the curious fellow snapped. "Not the housekeeper. It's the lady's *shadow* – the woman from *before!*"

I glanced at Holmes and saw the expression I'd expected: One corner of his mouth pulled slightly to one side, and the opposite eyebrow lifted in skeptical irritation at Mrs. Hudson for admitting some spiritualist crank who thought that he could communicate with ghosts. He'd had enough of that foolishness the previous spring, when Doyle and his wife wanted to pick a fight with anyone who dared doubt that she wasn't receiving messages from the crew of the *Wiln* after it sank in the Bristol Channel, and had dragged Holmes in by thoughtlessly mentioning his name in a newspaper interview.

Holmes opened his mouth to speak, but the man quickly raised a hand, forefinger extended, and cut him off. "She is a *Gray Lady* – I see a gray bonnet and dress. She lost her child – crib death, I expect. She wanders here in despair – and has done so for nearly half-a-century I would guess. What do you know of her? Have you seen her?"

"I've seen no one," Holmes snapped. "If this is why you've traveled all the way from London – "

"*I've* seen her," said Mrs. Hudson, entering with a tray. "The Gray Lady. Sometimes she passes at the end of the hallway, or occasionally I come upon her in the small room upstairs. I've also sensed that she's looking for a child that died, and she cannot rest. I just let her be – for I believe that she does not see me. She only sees the shadows of the cottage the way it was when she lived here."

Observing Holmes's scowl, she set her mouth and scowled back. My friend and I had learned over thirty years earlier that Mrs. Hudson was not a woman to back down from what she believed. I suspected that this topic, curiously avoided until now, would be a source of much discussion between the two of them, some of it possibly even polite, and I hoped that they would refrain until I'd departed.

"Nevertheless," said Holmes, turning back to his visitor, "if this is why you've traveled to Sussex, Reverend – " He glanced at the card, still in his hand to refresh his memory. " – Longwick – "

"So sorry," said the fellow quickly, seemingly jumping back into his skin from a great distance, and now with an amiable smile in his eyes and the harshness completely vanished from his tone. He pulled another card from his pocket and handed it to me, stating, "Reverend Longwick. I have a small ministry in No. 7, Mitre Court, off Fleet Street, leading through to the Temple. No, no – it isn't a church. Rather, my efforts are spent preparing and distributing religious materials and providing them to the various immigrants that continually wash ashore in London." He glanced my way. "You must be Dr. Watson. I'm so fortunate that you're here as well." Then, accepting more tea from Mrs. Hudson, and indicating that he simply couldn't say no to a piece of her lemon seed cake, he sat where indicated and continued speaking.

"No, I'm not here about anything related to restless spirits. It was only when Mrs. Hudson placed me in this quiet room that I couldn't help but become aware of your ghost – although I do so hate to call them that. I've always had a gift, you see. I choose to call it a gift, although there are times . . . I can sense them, particularly when they are unable to move on due to some unresolved grief. That's what afflicts the poor woman here at your farm, Mr. Holmes – unresolved grief."

"I've neither heard nor seen anything," Holmes rather growled, glancing at Mrs. Hudson, who met his gaze firmly while departing. "If you aren't here about ghosts, then – "

"Yes, yes. It's something much more prosaic than that. You see, I publish various foreign-language versions of the Bible for immigrants, and after many years of creating a system that works quite well, I've become aware that the works have recently been altered – not necessarily in a bad way. Nothing like changing the meaning of the text entirely to something that welcomes the Antichrist or the insertion of naughty words. No, it's more subtle than that, and I'd like to know why."

"You didn't say you'd like to know *who* did it – perhaps because you already know?"

"I think so. I'll get to that in due course."

As we settled more comfortably, partaking further of the tea and cake, the wind and rain increased, and I could only imagine conditions out upon the Channel, just a few hundred feet away from where we sat – sloping up to the top of Beachy Head, and then dropping abruptly over five-hundred-

265

feet straight down to the water. Although I knew better (because it really was too far), I liked to think that on a clear day I could see France when standing at the cliff-top, but now, visibility would be negligible – up there one might be hard-pressed to see the very edge of the precipice – and I was thankful, for the benefit of others who needed it, that the great lighthouse at the base of the cliff was there. It had been commissioned in 1902, just a year before Holmes had retired to this area, replacing the old Belle Tout lighthouse on the rise just to our west. I knew that the old light had never worked as planned, often being obscured by sea mists, which required its replacement. I could only imagine when it was still functional, and its beams would have doubtless cruelly illuminated the windows of Holmes's villa whenever it was lit.

Holmes, his mood now more relaxed after learning that the reason for the minister's visit was earth-bound, settled back and asked for more details.

"As you probably know," Longwick began, "there are different versions of the Bible – various translations besides our own King James version, and different arrangements of the ancient texts. The Protestant Bible has sixty-six books, the Catholic has seventy-three, and the Orthodox eighty-one. Some of those included in the Catholic version are part of the Protestant *Apocrypha*.

"Years ago, I had the idea of publishing the Biblical books separately as individual pamphlets, in different languages, to be handed out among the London immigrants like periodicals. Now, I know what you're thinking, and many have pointed out to me before that wouldn't it be better just to print Bibles in the different languages in their entirety, instead of in the manner of monthly installments, but this format actually has its uses. A number of Bible study groups have been established across London through the years, and having the books presented in this more-digestible manner tends to be less overwhelming for some, and breaking the narrative into small pieces, so I'm told, ensures that the participants return regularly to the meetings, becoming used to studying one isolated and less-formidable portion of the scripture at each session.

"We use translations of the Protestant version, sixty-six books, and some of the shorter works like *Second* and *Third John*, or *Philemon* or *Jude*, being just one chapter each, are combined in pamphlets with longer books so that we publish fifty-two issues per year, one per week, and start all over again in January. Initially, I thought about dividing the Bible evenly by the number of chapters – there are nearly twelve-hundred, not counting the Apocrypha – but dividing by fifty-two caused some awkward arrangements, breaking one book at a crucial point and joining it to something completely unrelated." He looked at both of us over his *pince-*

nez, as if giving good advice. "If you're going to set yourself a schedule to read the Bible once per year, as many do, three or four chapters a day is a good plan."

Longwick gazed upon each of us for another few silent seconds to make sure that we were following. We both nodded, and Holmes added, "I recall seeing a number of your publications over the years, when passing through various East End sanctuaries for immigrants – coffee-shops and churches, and the back rooms of pubs. You'll be happy to know that your influence has penetrated into the worst of the East End Hell-holes, populated with some of the most angry and revolutionary types to walk upon our shores."

The minister seemed intrigued. Leaning forward like a long-bodied water bird with a black body and gray top-knot, he said, "Knowing some about your past work, Mr. Holmes – I've read a number of your stories, Doctor – gives me some sense of just where you've been when you say 'Hell-holes'. The Bar of Gold, for instance, in Upper Swandam Lane just off Upper Thames Street. I won't ask you to elaborate upon why you were in such places, beyond what was shared in *The Strand*, but I thank you for letting me know about my little volumes. I, too, have been in those places as part of my ministry, but going in as a minister does not provide the same perspective as one who is disguised to fit in with those needing guidance. I've learned that even the darkest of hearts may be reached – but the effort must be ventured or nothing will be gained. I feel that the work of the publications has done some good, and that's why I'm angered that someone has been altering the texts."

"In what way?" I asked. I had been inclined to first think the man something of a fool, but as he spoke, I was reassessing my initial impression.

Longwick finished his tea and set the cup aside. Recrossing his long legs, he explained. "Just as there are many books of the Bible, and alternate versions with more or less books, each language also has different ways of spelling our Lord's name. In English, and German and Portuguese, it is *Jesus* – as we have known all our lives. But this isn't the universal spelling. In Albanian it's *Jezu*, Turkish is *Isa*, Romanian and Russian is *Iisus*, and in Croatian and Serbian it's *Isus*." He spelled each, and pronounced them so we would understand the difference. Some were quite similar, but there were small variations. "Italian is *Gesù*, Ukranian is *Icyc*, and Slovak is *Ježiš*, spelled with accent marks upon the *Z* and *S*." He illustrated these accents with a flick of a finger.

"The list goes on and on. Years ago, when the idea for this ministry was first conceived, we – and by 'we' and 'our', I mean myself and whichever staff member I'd hired at the time – went through the process of having the Bible translated into a number of different languages, and then setting up each of the individual pamphlets. It was a great deal of initial effort, but once the system was in place, we've been able to print as the need demands ever since. For instance, I simply have to place an order with the printer, with whom I've worked for years, telling him that I need so many copies of a certain month's booklet in Turkish, and he prints what's required for distribution. That way, we don't have to store a massive amount of already-printed materials. Basing the printing on the demand is really a revolutionary and valuable idea, and the greater publishing industry would benefit from taking a look at it.

"However, having done this work so long ago, I became rather complacent, thinking that aspect of the operation need not ever be reviewed again. Therefore, it was with some surprise that I was stopped on the street two days ago by a man named Josef, a long-time associate who is employed in distributing the pamphlets. He informed me that the latest set of booklets – we're late enough in the year to now be publishing *The New Testament* – had an error. In the *Italian* edition, where Jesus' name is supposed to read *Gesù* on page 92, it now said *Isa* – the *Turkish* spelling."

He reached inside his coat and pulled out several pamphlets, all about eight inches high. Each was folded once, long-ways, and when opened, they were about five inches wide. He opened one of them to a page marked with a folded corner and handed it to Holmes. I rose and looked over his shoulder, observing the word in question, circled in red ink. It was as the minister described, but I would have to take his word for it that the word had been swapped.

I sat back down, but Holmes continued turning the pamphlet this way and that before noting, "The printing plate has been altered," he said. "Adequately, but not without certain peripheral and careless flaws. The letters spelling *Isa* look a bit ragged and don't quite line up, and the spacing to each side is incorrect. " He laid the pamphlet on the table beside his own empty teacup. "I assume that you investigated further."

Longwick nodded. "I did. Not having any pamphlets stored at the office, I began visiting the different distribution sites located throughout the city. Not only did this month's version have the substitution of Jesus' name to the Turkish spelling in the Italian edition – and from what I can tell, only once, on page 92 – but it was the same way in the German and Russian editions, and also only on that particular page. And I found that last month, the spelling in those three editions – Italian, German, and Russian – Jesus was spelled with the Albanian *Jezu*, but this time on page 84. You can imagine that researching this took some time – flipping through each version to see when an incorrect usage appeared."

"But there were no changes in other printings?" asked Holmes. "Romanian or Croatian, for instance?"

"None that I could determine – and I made a careful examination of all of them! But you didn't let me finish. I also found that two months ago, in July, the spelling of Jesus in those three language editions was the Serbian version – *Isus*.

"And before that? How far back does this go?"

"Only those three editions – the current, and the previous two months – July and August. Nothing beyond July that I could find – and I checked all the way to the beginning of the year."

"And what page did the error occur two months ago?"

"On page 77."

"Do you have any idea as to how this happened?"

"I do," said Longwick, now sitting forward upon the edge of his chair, his long legs and bony knees supporting his folded arms as he leaned forward. "I went 'round to the printer – a friend named Millhouse that I've used for years – and we looked at the plates for this month together. We found that each one of them has been repaired, and now all of them once again have the correct word in the correct language for *Jesus* on page 92, Millhouse could see where the plates had been altered. We looked back at the August and July issues as well, and they have also been repaired."

"You said that you knew who had done it," I said, puzzled at the apparent senselessness of such an obscure action.

"That's correct, Doctor," said Longwick, now leaning back and crossing his arms. "About four months ago, I hired a new assistant. It's always just me and a single assistant – it's been that way since the beginning. I take care of the ministerial side of things – visiting the locations where the pamphlets are placed, and seeing the people where they live, and particularly raising the funds to support this endeavor – and the assistant deals with Millhouse, as well as seeing that the orders and deliveries are made, and paying our office rent and the printing and delivery costs." He looked from one to the other of us. "I tried to keep my investigations discreet about what the alterations, but my assistant seems to have discovered that I was asking questions. He didn't come to work this morning, and when I went to his lodgings, the landlady said he'd abruptly packed up and left."

"And who was this assistant," asked Holmes.

"A fellow named Fred Curll – with two *L*'s. There was once a famous British publisher named Curll, but my assistant isn't British. He speaks English very well, but he has some sort of accent – German or Dutch, if I'm correct. I'm usually good with languages, but I had a difficult time working out just where he was from. I never did, as a matter of fact. I didn't want to ask him about it, as he kept to himself and wasn't easy to get to know – very much different than my last assistant, Ian Murchison, who left last summer when his gout became too much to manage."

As Longwick explained about his vanished assistant, I saw Holmes's attentiveness increase from the usual curiosity he displayed during the description of a puzzle to sudden keen interest. I had no idea why, but the answer to his next question seemed to fix an idea in his mind.

"Tell me, Reverend Longwick: Was your former assistant – Curll – well-dressed, and with somewhat long hair combed down beside his thin face, oversized bad teeth, a large red nose covered with tiny broken capillaries, and similarly lined red cheeks? Does he have an arrogant expression with odd light-brown eyes, and with the whites around the pupils discolored and bloodshot, as if each entire eyeball is a solid muddy marble?

Longwick's jaw dropped in surprise. "How do you know that, Mr. Holmes?" He leaned forward again. "That is so specific! That's Curll to a *T*!"

When Holmes waved away an answer, Longwick continued. "When I discovered this matter, it concerned me more and more, although I'm not sure why. Perhaps I've been more nervous than normal – I'm always a nervous fellow – because lately there has been growing unrest among the immigrants. I talked it over with Millhouse, and he suggested consulting a detective. I've been hearing good things about a young fellow near Paddington – since he set up shop three or four years ago, they've been calling him 'The Sherlock Holmes of Praed Street' – but I became convinced that I should actually seek out the *actual* Sherlock Holmes. I'm most grateful that you took time to see me and hear my story without an appointment, and from your reaction, I believe that there is more to this than I previously suspected . . . ."

He paused, his last words almost a question, waiting for Holmes to provide some explanation, but instead my friend simply answered, "I believe that I'll need to return to London with you." He cocked his head at the sound of the still-rising storm. "This is a terrible night to travel, although I understand that the worst of it will pass before morning. Will you stay for dinner? Then I can put you up overnight so that we can travel back together early tomorrow."

Longwick immediately accepted, and when Mrs. Hudson had shown him to his room in order that he might prepare himself for dinner, Holmes turned to me, asking, "I hope you don't mind running back up to London for the day."

I shook my head. "Not at all. Apparently you see something serious in this business."

"Quite possibly – although . . . Of course, I could just be imagining things, but . . . ." He shook his head. "No, I don't think so. Do you recall the aborted riot last week in the East End? By Turkish immigrants? It took place on the second."

I nodded.

"There were similar Turkish riots on that same day in Berlin and Rome and St. Petersburg – and they were brought under control much more violently than our local version was. I believe that our home-grown riot was suppressed before it ever really started. The previous month, on the fourth of August, Albanian immigrants rioted here – again, a small affair hardly worth reporting, but also much worse in St. Petersburg and Berlin and Rome – particularly the latter. And on 7 July, it was the Serbians that were rioting in London and the other three capitals – again just a skirmish here, but quite ugly upon the Continent."

"I don't understand."

"I don't either – not yet – but it can't be coincidence that on the 7th of July – which might be written as '7-7' – there were Serbian riots in the capitals, and the alteration in the July edition of Longwick's monthly Bibles – on page *77* – was a *Serbian* spelling in those printings. The next month, on 4 August, the error was the *Albanian* spelling – on page *84*. As in August 4th."

"But we write August 4th as '*4-8*'."

"But in Germany they write that date with the month first, as '*8-4*' – as they do September 2nd: '*9-2*' – the same as page *92* of the most recent edition, which had Jesus spelled in the *Turkish* way . . . and this time it was the Turks who rioted."

"Hold on," I said, raising a hand. "I'm trying to understand this. Loosely pieced together, it seems as if a man with a vague foreign accent, Fred Curll, took a job as the latest assistant at Reverend Longwick's ministry, wherein he was in charge of the printing and business side of things. Soon after, small changes were made to the long-standing printing plates, altering the language of the word *Jesus* to fit with certain groups that have been rioting in London, Rome, Berlin, and St. Petersburg, and that the dates of these riots correspond with the page numbers on which the errors appear."

Holmes smiled. "Essentially, yes."

"That's quite a stretch."

"True, but you'll recall that it's no more so than the messages that Maybrick was placing in the newspapers during late August '88."

I nodded. "You were also able to describe Fred Curll – 'to a *T*' as Reverend Longwick put it. How did you know who he is?"

"I didn't *know*, necessarily, but his name is something of a clue. The Reverend was very perceptive when he said that Curll's accent sounded German or Dutch. The latter is correct."

"You've heard of him. Is he mentioned in your scrapbooks?" I asked, nodding toward the shelf which held the many and varied volumes, brought down from London when Holmes retired."

"Yes, but not under that name. This fellow took the name *Curll* – or rather, it was assigned to him – as something of a little inside joke – and I happen to be in the group that would understand it. As the Reverend mentioned, there was a famous eighteenth-century publisher named Curll – Edmund Curll – who became synonymous with many unscrupulous practices like publishing accounts of scandals and pornographic materials, and generally anything that would make money. Calling this fellow *Curll* has always held an element of irony.

"You seem to already know what's going on."

"To a great degree, although there are still edges of the painting to fill in. But by tomorrow, you and I will know what's happening – although I doubt that we can share the true story with Longwick."

The next morning, Holmes telephoned for the local cab, and Beauchamp had us in Eastbourne with time to spare for the first train back to London. The night before, dinner had been an interesting exchange of ideas, as Longwick explained more about his mission, comparing notes with what Holmes had seen in disguise throughout the poorest parts of London as compared to Longwick's experience visiting there as a recognized man of the cloth. The minister was fascinated and somewhat saddened, and rather surprised as well, to learn that in many cases, the people he'd met over his many years of service didn't behave the same with him as they did when he wasn't around. The knowledge actually left him rather shaken, as if a rug had been pulled from underneath him. At the end of the meal, he thanked Holmes for the information, stating that aside from the help he was receiving in determining who had altered and then repaired the printing plates for his pamphlets, what Holmes had conveyed to him about his "flock" was worth more than he could repay.

He appeared to have been affected by learning that he hadn't truly connected in quite the way he'd always thought, and he excused himself after the meal to rest and get his thoughts in order. He promised to be up on time and, as he'd left us, I noted that Holmes had successfully distracted him so that he hadn't been asked to elaborate on what might have taken place in the minister's operation. Likewise, the minister had shown the good sense to avoid mentioning the spirit he'd sensed haunting Holmes's villa. I myself had never seen her, and I didn't see her that night, but my

272

many varied experiences over six continents had given me an open-mindedness to such things that Holmes refused to acknowledge within himself.

I thought that Longwick had retired, but later that night, I passed down the hallway and saw that he and Mrs. Hudson were having a discussion over cups of tea. I wondered if the topic was the cottage's supposed spirit, or if they had more in common, and whether Longwick might became a somewhat-regular visitor at the villa – although not to confer with Holmes.

When we arrived at Victoria Station in the middle of the next morning, Holmes led us outside and waved down one of the newer automobile cabs. There were still hansoms and growlers about, but less of them, it seemed, with each passing week. Although I could see the sense of the automobile on that rainy morning, I think I would have preferred a four-wheeler, as it was roomier than the three of us trying to fit into the tightly constructed metal contraption. It was one thing to have your own automobile, as I did, and to be in control of where it went and how many souls were crammed into it, but I found that the sudden unexpected accelerations and stops associated with such *taxis*, when in the hands of a stranger, were a much more unnerving and unpleasant experience.

Holmes had explained to me that, while he knew much about what was going on, he had to make a show for the minister of carrying out a full investigation, not wanting to reveal anything too soon. I was beginning to have the sense that before the day ended, we would probably end up in Whitehall or Pall Mall.

Holmes asked that we first be taken to Millhouse's printing establishment, located in an unmarked passage off Chancery Lane, not far from Longwick's Mitre Court office. We found the printer to be a solid and bluff man in his mid-fifties, his sleeves rolled up on his great forearms, and ink stains of long standing up and down his fingers and wrists, underneath his short nails, and across his high brow and unto his thinning hairline. He could tell us very little beyond confirming what we'd already heard.

"This Curll was in and out of here quite a bit over the last three or four months, several times a week, since the time he was hired, but that ain't unusual, is it? All of the Reverend's assistants have checked in the same way over the years, keeping track of each month's printings. No, it would have been easy for Curll to get in after hours if he'd wanted. The Reverend and I have an arrangement, seeing as he's my oldest and steadiest customer. His Ministry has a key so that the Reverend's man can drop in anytime and pick up the printed pamphlets directly here, instead of me sending them over to the Mitre Court office. It saves him some money by not paying for delivery, and me from not needing to hire delivery people. That's right – it's no secret where the plates are kept, and anyone who had tolerable skill to make the changes could alter them and then just as easily fix them back again."

Holmes turned Longwick and asked about the key's whereabouts.

"I don't know," he admitted. "It's normally in the assistant's desk at the office. I didn't think to check that. We can go look, if you'd like."

Holmes nodded, but first he and Millhouse examined the plates, each making a series of comments that elicited nods of agreement from the other. Then, thanking the printer, we walked down to Fleet Street and across, and so through the passage leading into Mitre Court. I glanced just south, toward where our old friend Thorndyke lived, where the Court opened into King's Bench Walk, and was considering suggesting that we ask if he'd noticed anything unusual about the minister's curious assistant, but Holmes, seemingly reading my thoughts, shook he head, stating, "5A is too far away through the passage to expect that anyone there might have seen Mr. Curll, and in any case, I happen to know that Thorndyke is away right now – some dire business at the Chelmsford Police barracks."

How Holmes kept up with these things while in Sussex was a mystery, but that he did so didn't surprise me. Though supposedly retired, he still had any number of strings in hand leading to who-knew how many unlikely spots.

A quick search of Longwick's office showed that everything was in its place, including the key to access Millhouse's printing operation. In fact, the assistant's work area was so tidy that Longwick commented on just how unusual that was.

"Curll wasn't the neatest of men, although he could always lay a hand on any invoice when I asked. The fact that he left everything cleaner than he found it means to me for sure that he's gone. But what could making these alterations have accomplished?

What indeed? I wondered. While I had a dim grasp of what Holmes had explained to me, I could find no purpose to it. And yet, we continued our investigation, with Longwick walking us eastward to the missing man's lodgings in Fore Street, almost evenly situated between the Guildhall and Moorgate Street Station. His landlady, a very fat and wheezing woman named Mrs. Evans, was limited in what she could tell us.

"He showed up yesterday afternoon," she said, catching her breath, "early home from work and all het up about something. He went upstairs and came down with two bags – I guess it was all that he had – handed me the key, said he had business that was calling him away urgently, and left.

He still has two weeks left on his rent, but it sounded as if he won't be back, so I've already advertised for a new lodger."

She agreed to let us see the room, which she informed us hadn't yet been cleaned, and she fetched the key from somewhere in her own chambers and sent us upstairs on our own. We ascended the two narrow flights, and I could only imagine the poor landlady trying to do the same. I doubted that the room would be ever be cleaned if she was the one required to do it.

Holmes made his usual systematic search, but the room had apparently been swept clean, for there was neither scrap nor crumb to give any indication about the previous occupant – except for one object left precisely centered upon the desk: *The Strand* magazine from the previous April, which had featured my most recently published story, "The Red Circle".

The magazine was open to the first page of the story, and the first line had been altered. Originally reading: "*Well, Mrs. Warren, I cannot see that you have any particular cause for uneasiness,*" the words *Mrs. Warren* had been crossed out and *Mr. Holmes* written above it in red ink.

"What does it mean?" asked Longwick, his eyes widened. "What is going on?"

"It means that your Mr. Curll is sending me a message – that he knew you intended to seek my opinion, and that since his scheme was discovered and he was forced to move on, possibly sooner than he expected, he wanted to gain my attention when we searched this room."

"But for what purpose? None of this makes any sense!"

"It does, Reverend Longwick – but I'm afraid that we cannot share with you the reasons why. I'll need to confer with someone about this, to see what needs to be done." He looked around the room once more, seemingly deciding that there was nothing more to discover. Then he refocused his gaze upon the minister.

"You said that you tried to keep your investigations discreet, but somehow Curll found out. What did you do to make him suspect?"

Longwick looked as if he'd been caught doing something shameful and was loathe to admit it. "When examining the back issues for alterations, I didn't seek his help, for he wouldn't know what to look for – or so I supposed. But as I found altered pamphlets, I set them aside, and he would have certainly seen which issues I'd pulled – and if he was the one who changed them, their significance would have been obvious. Then, when I decided to seek your help, Mr. Holmes, I made a telephone call to a fellow that I knew in divinity school – Dr. Thorneycroft Huxtable. I recalled from seeing his name in *The Strand* some years ago and, knowing you were retired, I wondered if he could tell me where. He has kept up with you, and was able to point me toward your Beachy Head cottage."

"And no doubt," I said, "Curll put all these pieces together and knew that his scheme was discovered, and he absconded."

"Perhaps that word is a bit strong," said Holmes, "but we shall see." With that, he led us back outside. Thanking the rather confused minister, we abruptly left him standing there with a promise to let him know what we could. Then we hailed a cab heading west.

I made a point of pulling out my watch. "Too early for your brother to be at the Diogenes. Are we going to one of his offices?"

Holmes's eyes widened with surprise, and then he gave a bark of a laugh and slapped his knee.

"Oh, Watson, you are well-and-truly caught up, aren't you? Well done!"

"Not all the way," I assured him. "Your knowledge of this Curll fellow, and the message to you in 'The Red Circle', and this scheme's relation to riots in foreign countries, gives me some sense that Mycroft must have a finger in the pie somewhere – or if he doesn't already, he probably should have. We're either going to ask him some questions, or to relay information top him."

"The former – for Curll is one of Mycroft's agents. I have some vague sense of what might be happening, and if I'm right, it's a very fragile construct, and I hope that our involvement, by way of Longwick's tumbling to what's going on, hasn't spoiled anything. But be prepared, for I suspect there's an ugly shade to this whole business."

But our visit to the man who sometimes *was* the British Government was unexpectedly delayed as – to our great surprise – we found that not only was Mycroft Holmes not in his most-likely office, but he wasn't in the others as well. Nor would we find him in his Pall Mall lodgings, or in the Diogenes Club across the street. "Urgent business," we were told by his secretary, and not even Holmes's brotherly connection, and the knowledge that he often carried out the most confidential tasks for Mycroft and The Crown, could get the man to provide any additional information. He did, however, state that Mycroft should return that same day, and we received the promise that we would receive a message at my Queen Anne Street home when Mycroft was available.

Outside, Holmes stated that he would continue to fill in the edges of the painting while checking with me throughout the day about Mycroft's availability. "If you don't mind spending the day here in London," he added, "and interrupting your holiday."

I assured him that the change in plans was not a difficulty, and he replied that he would be in touch. Then he walked away while I found a cab.

I puttered the rest of the day, answering some old correspondence, and considering what new story that I might prepare for publication, having left my notes of the nearly-finished Lady Frances Carfax matter with my luggage in Sussex. I had a plethora of material from which to choose – an overabundance of a plethora – and despite his earlier attempts to disassociate himself with Holmes's adventures, my literary agent had come to recognize the continuing financial value related to their occasional publication, and he was constantly pressing for another one – although too often he wished for those that seemed to have some supernatural bend, and when the solutions were solidly down-to-earth (as they always were) he too-often tried to insist that they be edited – "punched up" as he called it – in order to add false spiritualistic aspects, satisfying some broken need within himself. I could only hope that he never heard the story of the Gray Lady at Holmes's cottage, or he and his wife would be on the first train south to set in motion one of their ridiculous séances – no doubt claiming that Phineas, Lady Doyle's spirit "guide" and their resident pet phantasm, was along with them.

Although well able to keep myself occupied, the house felt lonely when my wife was away, and at some point I gave up on my efforts and settled down for a nap – planned, and not an accidental dropping-off where I would wake confused, and vaguely irritated that the afternoon had slipped away. I had awakened not long before the doorbell rang. Beating the maid to the door, I opened it to surprisingly find Holmes – along with his brother, and an ugly man who could only be Fred Curll.

"I came across Mycroft as he was returning to Whitehall," Holmes explained, "and since he was already untethered from the temptations of his nest, I suggested that we come here, rather than asking you to get back out and journey to us. We stopped along the way to collect Mr. Curll."

"Pleased to meet you, Doctor," the curious man said. I understood what Longwick had meant about his puzzling accent. Dutch, as I'd been told, but there was something else that was odd about it. However, all was soon explained when the fellow spit forth an appliance from his mouth – a construction of bad and distracting false teeth that covered his own, while also affecting his manner of speech. "There, that's better," he said. Fortunately he'd caught the false plate in his left hand, as it was his right that he offered to me. We shook, and then Holmes suggested that we adjourn to my study.

After brandies and whiskies were shared, and chairs were claimed – including the settee for Mycroft – Holmes's brother looked my way. "Of course, Doctor, what we're about to discuss is not for sharing."

I agreed, as he knew that I would. He was still somewhat nettled that I had mentioned him in print without consent back in 1893, nearly two decades earlier, when publishing my earlier efforts to memorialize my supposedly dead friend. My wife, Mary, had died by then, and writing seemed to be the only way to fill my empty hours and avoid following the grim destructive paths of my late father and brother. With Doyle's encouragement – "The public will eat up the idea that Holmes had a brother!" – I had given no thought that such a revelation might shine an unnecessary light on just what it was that Mycroft Holmes did . . . and was still doing, apparently, since this entire business had turned out to be one of his many schemes.

Sherlock Holmes took the reins. "Correct me if I'm wrong, Mycroft," he said. Then he looked my way. "I've refrained from asking any questions." Back to Mycroft: "This is some convoluted intrigue that is designed to provide legitimacy to one of your agents infiltrating German Intelligence."

Mycroft nodded. "I'm rather proud of it. There were seven other ways to go, but Longwick's monthly Bible books presented the easiest path forward."

As usual, I had to raise a hand for attention, as if I were politely drowning off-shore while the two Holmes brothers stood on the beach having a discussion about politics without sparing a glance my way. "Can we begin at the beginning?"

Holmes smiled and nodded to his brother.

"We have an agent who has penetrated German Intelligence. He has found a path to a very integral position – a nexus of several of their interconnecting data-gathering agencies. But he needs to retain his value to keep that position, so occasionally he must bring some grist for their mill – something useful and unique to win their trust and admiration. Recently he was able to predict riots in London, Rome, St. Petersburg . . . and Berlin."

"Riots planned and instigated by you," interrupted Holmes.

Mycroft nodded. "With varying levels of intensity. Those in London were quite minor – essentially stopped before they began. Rome and St. Petersburg were somewhat more . . . escalated. And the Berlin riots – as foretold by our embedded agent – were lessened due to the knowledge that our agent provided from his 'secret' source."

"That source being you," I said.

"That is correct. After I identified Longwick's monthly Bible books, and their translation into various languages and how they were spread throughout the immigrant community, I saw a way to insert coded messages. We manipulated events so that only Curll applied to become Longwick's new assistant – by preventing Longwick's advertisement for help from actually being published – and then, when he was in place, Curll set about making the alterations.

"However, having a coded message without anyone being able to read it was useless, so word was spread throughout the immigrant community that the coded messages would reveal the location of the next riots – Serbian immigrants in July, Albanians in August, and most recently the Turks. Then, our other agents in the different capitals arranged for those riots to be planned and to actually occur, providing legitimacy to the coded messages, and for our agent who was seemingly able to predict them, based on information from his mysterious source. His reports allowed his German masters to diminish the riots, while they observed that the London, Rome, and St. Petersburg riots also occurred – exactly as prescribed by the coded messages."

"The codes had already served their purpose," continued Curll, "and I was due to leave Reverend Longwick's employment soon in any case, and in a more orderly manner, so as not to inconvenience him. But then he found out what was happening, and I could tell that he suspected me. When I overheard him trying to find you, Mr. Holmes, I vanished – but I left a copy of *The Strand* in my room for you to find, knowing that you'd certainly head in the right direction."

Holmes nodded, and Mycroft finished his brandy, setting the small glass upon the nearby table. He was clearly finished and ready to go, but I had one further thought – for both Holmes brothers.

"Longwick cannot know about this."

Mycroft looked as if I'd said something stupid. "Of course he cannot. It is a State secret, and the operation is still ongoing. Our agent in Berlin cannot be discredited."

I shook my head. "No. I mean that some legitimate-sounding tale must be contrived to satisfy him. He is owed that. And it must have no aspect related to the riots being planned from his periodicals – no half-truths about that included to make the lie more believable. I'm aware that the London riots were very small, and quelled before they really began. Am I also right that the Rome and St. Petersburg riots that you fomented were larger, and more violent?"

Sherlock Holmes turned his head toward his brother, cocking it to one side as if the question hadn't occurred to him, and now he wanted an answer too. Curll dropped his eyes to the whisky glass held in both of his hands.

Mycroft's lips tightened and he nodded. "That is correct. Both of those riots quickly spiraled into full-scale street battles – rather along the lines of Bloody Sunday. And before you ask your next question: Many were injured – both rioters and police – and three were killed in Rome, and four in St. Petersburg . . . including a mother and child trampled by the crowd."

My gaze darkened. "A crowd that you stampeded."

I had known Mycroft Holmes by then for nearly a quarter-century, and I had gone from being curious about Holmes's rather idiosyncratic brother, to awe at his power and position, to something approaching friendship as the years passed and Holmes and I worked with him in the nation's interests. But I never let myself forget that he was much more of a cold calculating machine than his younger brother, and that he had no compunction about making cold calculating decisions. I knew that he was a good man, and that the death of the mother and child weighed upon him, but at that point in his life, a thousand-such decisions were already upon his broad shoulders, and Atlas-like, he showed no signs that his stamina was failing now after the thousand-and-first.

"That is correct, Doctor." His voice softened. "And it will always be tallied against me, Watson. But hopefully, for the greater good, it will have been worth it."

I could only nod, but my agreement had varying levels of nuances, which was understood by the others sitting there in the waning daylight.

We found Longwick later that night, and Holmes gave him some story about how Curll was a known trickster who had an arrest record at Scotland Yard as long as the minister's skinny shanks. That explained how Holmes knew of the man, while completely avoiding the reasons that nothing more could be revealed.

Longwick shook his head. "I must be more careful." Then he proceeded to tell us of other times when other assistants had also violated his trust, and it took too long to extricate ourselves, leaving the man with another learned lesson – which I could tell wouldn't count for much.

Earlier that afternoon, at the conclusion our discussion when Mycroft and Curll were preparing to depart, we were standing up prior to moving toward the front door. "What happens if you run across Reverand Longwick once again?" I asked Curll. "He's bound to recognize you. After all – " I stopped myself without mentioning the man's unfortunate and notable ugliness.

He smiled and held up the false plate of crooked teeth. "These aren't the only part of my disguise, Doctor," he said, the curious Dutch accent now completely gone, and replaced with another that implied that he was a lifetime resident of Yorkshire. I'd occasionally heard hints of these same tones and pronunciations from both Sherlock and Mycroft Holmes, as Yorkshire was the land of their birth, but mostly they never gave any indication of it, as they had both traveled abroad for much of their formative youth, and each had later worked hard to homogenize their way of speaking to something that might be called "British Neutral".

"I think that it's about time Fred Curll retired. Don't you, sir?" he asked Mycroft, who nodded.

"He has earned that, I suppose – but more importantly, he is becoming too recognizable. I have an idea about his successor. Be in my office tomorrow morning to discuss it."

The man known as Fred Curll grinned, slipped the false teeth back into his mouth, nodded my way, and turned to depart. It suddenly crossed my mind to wonder if I'd met the man before, in some other guise, but before I could stop him and ask, Mycroft looked at us both. "Would you join me for dinner at the Diogenes? I have an idea that I wish to run by the both of you. Never fear, Doctor," he added for my benefit. "It will involve a small trip to Staffordshire in the morning, and then you'll back to your Sussex holiday by the weekend."

Later, when Mycroft explained what he wanted, I thought that he might be right – a short but essential errand, and then back to my interrupted plan. But on Saturday night, when Holmes and I were hidden in the hold of a ship crossing to Calais on stormy tossing seas, with the likelihood that our upcoming rendezvous at the Au Calice brasserie on the Boulevard Jacquard would shunt us even further eastward, I suspected that Mycroft had deliberately misled us – for surely a man with his undisputed omniscience had known when he recruited us the previous week that this mission had no easy solution.

Holmes seemed to read my mind, and when we heard the rough tone of the boat's engines change their pitch, indicating that we would soon be docking, he smiled. "Once more unto the breach?" he asked.

Reflecting that, were we not here at this moment and in this place, we would have likely spent the rest of the week wandering the Downs near Holmes's villa, or too much time imbibing in The Tiger Inn, I nodded.

I had to admit: This holiday had turned out to be much better than I'd imagined, and there was no end in sight.

The Ghost of Mycroft Holmes
by Paul Hiscock

The funeral of Mycroft Holmes was a quiet affair. Nobody seemed surprised that it was sparsely attended. Mycroft had never sought out nor encouraged close friendships. I imagined that he might be missed at the Diogenes Club. Its manager was present, but the members of that venerable institution would not venture beyond its walls, even for Mycroft. I wondered if they would raise a silent glass to him from their chairs, or would their strict rules would mean that his departure would pass entirely without acknowledgement?

There were no tears during the service, and an outsider might have considered Holmes's eulogy for his brother perfunctory at best. However, those who knew Mycroft understood that he had been a deeply private man. It was right that the story of his life should remain a closed book in death, just as it had been in life.

After the service, our small party processed behind the coffin, out of the church, and across the frosty graveyard to his final resting place.

"We therefore commit his body to the ground. Earth to earth, ashes to ashes, dust to dust, in sure and certain hope of the resurrection to eternal life."

The vicar hurried through the burial prayer slightly faster than might have been deemed proper, but nobody commented on it. Like him, we were all anxious to get inside, out of the cold, and, having watched the coffin being safely lowered into the grave, most of the mourners dispersed quickly.

"My condolences. He was a great man."

The man in front of us spoke in a thick Prussian accent. He shook Holmes's hand then swiftly departed. Just the last in a procession of strangers. I had been surprised by how many of them spoke with foreign accents. It was a reminder that while Mycroft's close friends been few, his connections had been extensive, not just in London but around the world.

I was about to suggest to Holmes that we should leave too when one last mourner came over to us. I was surprised and pleased to see a familiar face.

"Mr. Melas," I said as I shook the hand of the elderly Greek interpreter. "I didn't realise you were here."

"I was sitting at the back of the church – Well, not quite the back. There was a terrible draft near the door and my old bones do suffer in the

282

cold – Do you find that too? I did not wish to intrude, but I was hoping that I might have a few moments of your time, Mr. Holmes? It does concern your brother."

Holmes nodded but did not speak. I had seen little of him recently, and although it was a sad occasion, I had hoped that his return to London for the funeral would provide an opportunity for us to catch up. However, aside from the eulogy, he had barely uttered a word all day. Every man grieves in his own way, but I will admit that I found his silence disconcerting.

We adjourned to the nearest public house and while Holmes and Mr. Melas found a quiet table in the corner, I bought a round of drinks. Once I had sat down, I raised my glass.

"To Mycroft Holmes," I said.

The other men echoed my toast, then Mr. Melas took a long drink.

"I was sorry to hear that Mr. Holmes had passed," he said. "I have felt like I was in his debt ever since the three of you helped me all those years ago, but now I will never be able to repay him."

"There is no need," I said. "We were all happy to help."

"That is kind of you to say, Dr. Watson, especially since it was your medical attention that saved my life."

"I am just pleased to see you again, but I got the impression in the graveyard that you were hoping to do more than offer your condolences."

"Indeed, but it is a sensitive matter. We are all practical men, are we not? Not prone to flights of fancy or seeing things that aren't there."

"I like to think I have some imagination," I replied. "I find it helpful as a writer. However, Holmes is the most logical and practical man I have ever met. The only person to match him was his brother."

"Then please appreciate that I racked my brain for any other explanation to what I have witnessed before coming to you with this disturbing report. Even now I struggle to credit it, and must resist the urge to tell you it was nothing. Yet you deserve to hear it, Mr. Holmes. The spirit of your dead brother is restless and haunts his rooms in Pall Mall."

"Nonsense," snorted Holmes. "How many times must I explain to people, ghosts do not exist. Every supposedly supernatural phenomenon is either a tall tale, intended to fool the guidable, or can be explained by scientific enquiry. Besides, even if a spirit were to return to walk the Earth, it would certainly not be my brother's. He barely saw fit to move around in life. He certainly will not do so in death."

"It does seem rather unlikely," I said. "Can you tell us exactly what you witnessed?"

"As you are aware, for many years now I have lived in rooms above Mycroft Holmes in a house in Pall Mall."

"I knew you had been neighbours at one time, but I didn't realise you still were."

"I never felt the need to move. Marriage and children passed me by – I have some regrets about that, but not many. Still, it meant that I never needed to seek larger accommodation, and since my rooms were conveniently located and comfortably appointed, I never felt the need to move. I believe Mycroft felt similarly."

"Mycroft never countenanced any change to his routine without a most pressing reason," said Holmes. "Having found rooms that suited him, I had no doubt that he would keep them until the day he died."

"I certainly couldn't imagine him retiring to the countryside, as you have done," I said. "Mycroft was a creature of the city, through and through."

"As his neighbour," Mr. Melas continued, 'I grew accustomed to Mycroft's habits. I would hear his alarm sound at precisely seven o'clock every morning. The sound of his footsteps as he moved about his rooms performing his morning ablutions provided a counterpoint to my own lonely routine. When I would hear his door slam at half-past-eight, it was the starting gun that marked the beginning of my own working day. Even in retirement, I kept my routine synchronised with his. I don't think it was a conscious decision. It is only now that I look back that I realise how comforting I found his constancy in the face of this ever-changing world.

"Then, last week, everything changed. The faint ringing of his alarm couldn't be heard. There were no footsteps from the room below me, and come half-past-eight, the door to his rooms neither opened not slammed shut. I didn't think too much of it, as while my neighbour was undoubtedly a creature of habit, very occasionally, maybe once or twice in a decade, he would be forced to go away for a day or two. Therefore, it was still quite a shock when, later that day, I learned that Mycroft had died."

"It is hard to believe," I agreed. "It is akin to the ravens leaving The Tower of London. A harbinger of some catastrophic change."

"Please refrain from such superstitious clap-trap, Watson," said Holmes. "You know better. Mr. Melas, please tell us exactly what it is that makes you believe you have seen my brother's ghost."

"Very well, Mr. Holmes. I know you don't believe me, but I promised myself I would tell you everything. It was two days ago. I awoke to the sound of footsteps in the rooms below. When I happened to meet my landlady on the stairs by his rooms, I asked her, 'Have you let Mr. Holmes's rooms already?'

"'Gracious, no!' she replied. 'I have received instructions from his brother that they are to remain as they are and that nobody other than himself is to enter. I haven't seen him since he gave that instruction, and since the rent is fully paid until the end of the year, I have no reason to defy him.' She rattled the handle. 'See? They are locked up tight.'

"'That is strange,' I said. 'I could have sworn I heard someone moving about in there this morning.'"

"I can confirm that I wasn't in the room," said Holmes. "I haven't been near the premises since the day after my brother's death, when I collected some of his clothes. Neither have I given the keys to anyone else."

"I had other business to attend to and I gave this small mystery no more thought for the rest of the day. However, when I returned home later that night, I looked up at the windows and saw that the lights were on in Mr. Holmes's rooms. Even more astoundingly, there was the man himself, standing by the window."

"How could you be sure it was him?" I asked. "Did you see his face?"

"No, the figure was turned away from me. It seemed slightly insubstantial, yet it was wearing Mycroft's favourite smoking jacket and held one of Mycroft's cigars in his hand.

"I ran into the building and up the stairs. When I reached the landing, I found that the door was still locked. I banged hard upon it, but there was no reply. Even then, I might have dismissed the whole thing as a figment of my imagination. Looking through the keyhole, it appeared that the room was dark again and there was no sign of movement. However, the distinctive aroma of Mycroft's cigar hung in the air, confirming that what I had seen was true."

"It was just your imagination," said Holmes. "You were tired, or had enjoyed too much to drink that evening. Either way, your mind conjured memories from before my brother died and you imagined them to be real."

"When I woke the next morning, my first instincts were in accord with yours," admitted Mr. Melas. "I had been drinking the night before and had to accept that my vision might have been caused by decidedly un-supernatural spirits – ouzo is quite potent. But then, just as I was about to forget the whole matter, I heard him walking across the floor below me again. I have listened to that sound every day for years and immediately recognised the squeak of his shoe leather and the strike of his heal. You will remember, I am an interpreter by trade, and while my other senses might have begun to deceive me as I have grown older, my hearing remains as sharp as it ever was."

"Have you seen the apparition again as well?" I asked.

"Yes, every night. Never quite as clearly as that first time, but still distinctly enough. Yet every time, when I get to his door, the room is dark and silent. And no, I am certain that these later sightings haven't been drunken delusions. This is the first drink I have touched since that first night."

So saying, and having finished his story, Mr. Melas finished what remained in the glass in front of him.

"Should we investigate, Holmes?" I asked. "It sounds like there is some mystery to be solved here."

"Absolutely not!" Holmes's command was emphatic. "My brother must be left to rest in peace. I can state with absolute certainty that whatever trick of the light you might think you have seen, it wasn't him, and I would ask you not to share this ridiculous story with anybody else. Mycroft prized his dignity above almost everything else. He would be horrified to hear such stories associated with his name."

I was shocked at this outburst. I had seen Holmes greatly angered in the past, but this was different. Usually, when people presented him with poorly thought-out arguments or fabricated stories, he would use logical reasoning to take apart their statements, piece by piece. However, today he seemed frustrated, as though he wanted to present a counter argument, but couldn't find the words to express it.

"I think we should leave him alone for a moment," I said to Mr. Melas and guided him away from the table. "He can pretend to be emotionless, but it is a façade. This has been a very difficult day."

"Of course," replied Mr. Melas. "I shouldn't have intruded on such an occasion. It is just that it was the only place where I could be certain to find him."

"I understand. Why don't you stay and have another drink with me. Maybe after a little time alone, Holmes will become more sociable again."

"Thank you, Dr. Watson, but regrettably I must decline. There is other business requiring my attention today."

"Then please take my card and call on me some time. I would enjoy an opportunity to catch up properly."

"As would I," said Mr. Melas. "Until then." Then he turned towards the table, where Holmes still sat. "Goodbye, Mr. Holmes. Once again, I am sorry for your loss."

I took a moment to buy another drink before returning to the table. I was cross at Holmes for being so dismissive and even cruel. He had never had much patience for stories of ghosts and spirits, and I knew he was mourning the loss of his brother. Still, he should have acknowledged that Mr. Melas was in mourning too, and that his ghost story was probably a manifestation of that grief.

"I know Mr. Melas's story was outlandish," I said when I sat down again, "but did you have to treat him like that?"

Holmes didn't reply. He had retreated into silence again, and I decided it was best to leave him to mourn in his own fashion.

It had been decided that Holmes would stay the night with me after the funeral. So it was that he was present when Mr. Melas called while we were having breakfast the next morning.

"This is a surprise," I said when the maid brought him into the dining room. "I hadn't expected to see you again so soon."

"I am so sorry to disturb you, Dr. Watson. I wouldn't have dreamed of doing so – although I had intended to accept your invitation to call in maybe a week or two – but there has been a most distressing turn of events. The dead body of Mycroft Holmes, which we buried just yesterday, is now lying in the middle of the living room floor in his rooms on Pall Mall."

Holmes turned pale. I'm not sure I have ever seen him quite so shocked.

"Are you certain? This isn't just another phantasm that you have dreamed up?"

"No, I am quite certain. When I returned home last night, I did see that spectral figure at the window again, and I heard more movement in the rooms below as I tried to settle down to sleep. Yet, I was resolved to respect your wishes and did my best to ignore them. However, in the morning, I found myself accidentally slipping into my recent habit of looking through your brother's keyhole as I pass his door, in search of some sign of movement. It was then that I saw your brother, lying face down on the floor.

"I called for my landlady. At first she refused to open the door and disobey your instructions, Mr. Holmes. However, when I persuaded her to look through the keyhole for herself, she saw why it was necessary. She let me into the room and I hurried over to check the body for signs of life. However, it was immediately obvious that he was dead and had been for some time.

"We locked the room again, leaving everything exactly as we had found it. My landlady wanted to call the police, but I knew that you would want to see the body first, Mr. Holmes."

"Thank you, Mr. Melas, for your kind thoughtfulness and consideration. I apologise for how I reacted yesterday and for not taking your story more seriously. It was a mistake, and one that may have incurred a steep cost. Still, it is too late to undo the past. We can only deal with what is. Come, Watson. We have a body to examine."

Although I knew where Mycroft had lived, I had rarely visited him there. Most of our encounters had taken place in the Stranger's Room at the Diogenes Club, that peculiar space which is the only place in the building where one is allowed to hold a conversation.

Mr. Melas's landlady was all of a fluster when we arrived. She still wanted to call for the police, but Holmes persuaded her to wait a little longer. She lacked the resolute composure of Mrs. Hudson, and wouldn't have coped with everything we asked that remarkable woman to handle while we lived under her roof. We left her downstairs in her kitchen, and Holmes let us into Mycroft's rooms with his own key.

When I had first visited, I was surprised to find that Mycroft's rooms were smaller than the ones Holmes and I had shared in Baker Street. I had imagined that a man of his stature would have chosen to live in more opulent surroundings. However, it made sense when one considered that Mycroft had spent almost all his free time in the silence of the Diogenes Club. The chief advantage of these rooms for him wasn't their size, but their location.

The body lay face down on the floor in the middle of the room, just as Mr. Melas had described. I went over and automatically bent down to check for a pulse, even though I was certain I wouldn't find one. I could see the large pool of blood spreading from underneath him. I noticed that the clothes seemed to be loose on the body, and when I went to turn it over, the corpse was far lighter than I had expected. The dead man might have been wearing Mycroft's clothes, but he was of an average build and didn't share the same corpulent frame as Holmes's brother. When I looked into the dead man's face, the eyes of a stranger stared back at me.

"It is not Mycroft," I said.

I thought that Holmes looked relieved, although I couldn't imagine that he had suspected anything else. He came over and squatted down next to me to begin his own examination of the body.

"Oh, it wasn't a ghost," said Mr. Melas. I wasn't sure if he sounded disappointed or relieved. "But what is he doing here, and why is he wearing Mr. Holmes's smoking jacket?"

"That is what we must discover," replied Holmes.

"Should I call for the police now?" asked Mr. Melas.

I began to say, "Yes," just as Holmes said, "No."

"Holmes," I said, "there is a dead body here. The police need to be informed."

"One cannot keep a secret in Scotland Yard. The press will get hold of the story within hours, and the scandal will attach itself to my brother's name, since he isn't here and able to defend his reputation. No, we will solve the case first, then present it to the police."

I knew our friends on the force wouldn't have approved had they been there, but Holmes had solved enough cases for them over the years to earn a lot of leeway.

"What do you see, Watson?"

"Well, there is little to be learned about this man from his clothes, as they obviously don't belong to him. I don't know why he would choose to wear the clothes of a much larger man, but I cannot help but feel there is some significance to his superficial resemblance to Mycroft."

I peeled back the bloody jacket.

"Obviously this isn't a natural death," I said. "The blood appears to have come from a single wound to the chest. A knife, or some other sharp object, was plunged straight into this man's heart. I cannot see the weapon, so it's likely that the killer took it with him."

"That is a good start," said Holmes, "but you need to look deeper. There is more clothing to be examined."

I unbuttoned the man's oversized borrowed shirt and saw that Holmes was correct. Beneath it, the man was wearing a tattered and threadbare jumper. Beneath that, there were more layers of clothes, all grubby and worn.

"It is cold outside at the moment," said Holmes. "Those unfortunate souls who live on the streets wear as many layers of clothing as they can get their hands on in order stay warm."

"I've seen it for myself. They gather under the railway arches and huddle together for warmth."

"It appears this man found a more comfortable place to get warm," said Holmes.

"He must have found out that these rooms were empty, moved in, and decided to take advantage of what he found. That is why Mr. Melas heard and saw someone moving around as though Mycroft had returned."

"Exactly. As I've always maintained, ghosts do not, and have never, existed."

"He must have known that he would get caught eventually."

"Of course, but every night in here was another night out of the cold."

"That explains why he was here," I said, "but not why he was murdered."

"No," said Holmes, and I realised he still looked worried. Although the dead man was a total stranger, the association with his brother was obviously affecting him. Or perhaps the connection was stronger than that?

"You never told me how Mycroft died," I said. "Knowing the state of his health and his lifestyle, I assumed heart failure, and you didn't contradict me. But I realise now that you didn't confirm it either."

"What are you thinking?" asked Holmes, gravely.

"I follow the news. International tensions are higher than I can ever remember. We also both know that despite Mycroft's apparently indolent lifestyle, he was a person of considerable influence in the affairs of our government. Is it possible that another country had him assassinated?"

"And this man?" asked Holmes, clearly expecting me to follow my train of thought to its logical conclusion.

"As we surmised, he came in here to get out of the cold and decided to put on some of Mycroft clothes. He was then seen in the window by Mr. Melas, but also by the assassin, or one of his accomplices. They thought their previous attempt had failed and came back to finish the job."

"Assassins? Oh my!" said Mr. Melas. "Are we safe?"

I remembered the poor interpreter's ordeal at the hands of Latimer and Kemp. He knew all-too-well how innocent people could suffer when they got drawn into criminal conspiracies.

"You are safe here with us," I told him. "Besides, I really think now is the time to call for the police."

"And cause an international incident?" asked Holmes. "Can you imagine the uproar there will be if detectives from Scotland Yard start knocking on the doors of foreign embassies, accusing them of conducting assassinations on British soil? It could be the act that starts a war. However, there are people who should be alerted to this possibility, although unfortunately the protocols for contacting them are more complex than simply picking up a telephone. I may be gone for some time. During that time, keep searching these rooms, and make sure no one calls the police."

As he hurried out, I realised that he had never confirmed how Mycroft Holmes really died.

Holmes never said where he went, but it was clearly not far as he returned within half-an-hour. During that time, Mr. Melas and myself discovered numerous signs of the murdered man's occupancy of Mycroft's rooms.

There was a pair of worn boots by the door, which he had exchanged for a pair of Mycroft's brogues. There was a fresh indentation in the bed of a thin man that fitted comfortably within the impression made by Mycroft's much larger body. There were also impressions left in the arm chairs, two brandy glasses on the table, and a couple of cigar butts left in an ashtray. The man had clearly been taking full advantage of Mycroft's home.

There were also notable gaps. There was an empty case in Mycroft's bedroom with spaces for a dozen pairs of cufflinks. On the mantelpiece, there were four small round holes in the dust, which I suspected corresponded to the feet of a carriage clock. Most notably, there were two unfaded rectangles of paint on the wall where pictures had obviously been hanging.

Holmes considered all our discoveries carefully upon his return, and noted several other missing items that he knew should have been there, including a gold pocket-watch, a silver-topped cane, and a large crystal decanter. I thought he would be upset that so many of his brother's mementos had been taken, but instead he seemed excited.

"You have done splendidly," he told us. "Now we have a trail to follow."

He went to the window and raised his hand. A moment later, a boy knocked at the door. It did not surprise me to learn that he had instructed one of his Irregulars to wait for instructions. Since his retirement to Sussex, Holmes relied upon his band of young informants more than ever to be his eyes and ears in London.

Holmes sent the boy away with a list of the missing items and instructions that the Irregulars were to scour the pawn shops of London, starting with the least reputable ones. Then he invited us to sit down and wait with him.

"At least they didn't finish Mycroft's good brandy," he said as he poured us each a generous glass.

I wondered how long we would have to wait there. It wasn't that Mycroft's rooms were uncomfortable. It was just that it was unsettling sharing the space with a dead man. I could see that Mr. Melas was even less happy about the situation than I was. I did suggest that he could return to his own room. After all, he had done his part by alerting us to the crimes that had taken place here. However, he insisted that he should stay and see it through, for Mycroft.

Luckily for us, Holmes's Irregulars were still as efficient as they had ever been. After less than twenty minutes, a younger boy arrived with news that he had spotted a number of the missing items in a pawn shop just off the Strand.

The shop was a seedy-looking establishment in a dark alleyway. The boy must have run all the way there and back to return so quickly, as it took us almost as long just to walk there. We certainly wouldn't have found it without his expert local knowledge, and I felt that he had thoroughly earned the shilling which Holmes gave him.

Inside, a thin man with a face that resembled a weasel stood behind the counter. He looked surprised and concerned to see the three of us enter at once. I spotted him surreptitiously trying to move a tray of items below the counter and out of sight.

Holmes had noticed this too. He strode over to the counter and reached behind it to retrieve the hidden items.

"Here, you can't do that!" protested the weasel-faced man, but Holmes ignored him. He called over Mr. Melas and myself.

"Look, here we have three of the stolen pairs of cufflinks and the pocket-watch."

"Are you the law?" asked the proprietor. "You don't look like police. You should have just said. I've been looking after these items. Liberated them from a known thief. I was planning to hand them in at the station just as soon as I got a chance."

It was a brazen lie, but that was unimportant.

"Who was this 'known thief'?" asked Holmes. "I need his name and description."

"They call him Jimmy the Eel, partly on account of his ability to slide into places."

"He's a balding man of medium build," I stated. "About five-feet-seven in height?"

"I don't know where you got that idea. He's much taller than that, skinny as a rake, and has horrible greasy black hair. He's a slippery fellow all round."

"And do you know where we might find him?"

The weasel-faced man hesitated, considering his options.

"I'm not sure I should say. Jimmy has a temper. He won't be happy if he finds out I've been talking to you."

"I could get some uniformed men down here to spend some time going through your stock," said Holmes. "How many more stolen items do you think they might find that you're looking after?"

The proprietor looked around, considering the items for sale in his shop.

"No, that won't be necessary. You can probably find him drinking at The Bucket of Blood."

I racked my mind, but couldn't think of a pub by that name anywhere nearby."

"Do you mean The Lamb and Flag?" asked Holmes.

"Yeah, that's its proper name, but like I said, Jimmy thinks of himself as a fighter."

I knew where he meant now. A pub in Covent Garden that had hosted bare-knuckle fights in years gone by.

"There hasn't been a fight in the courtyard there for years," I said.

"Not official-like, but Jimmy's started a few brawls. He calls it 'Keeping tradition alive.' Like I said, he's a violent man."

292

"I am sure we can handle him," said Holmes, confidently. However, Mr. Melas looked scared, possibly regretting his decision to join us as we made our enquires.

Holmes picked up the items that had belonged to Mycroft. "We will take these, and anything else you bought from Jimmy at the same time."

"There's nothing . . ." the weasel-faced man began, before having second thoughts. "That is to say, there is nothing else out here, but if you will wait a moment, I might have a couple of other items out the back."

He scuttled away and returned a few moments later with a small bag that clinked as he put it into Holmes's hands.

"That's all, I swear."

Holmes gave him a hard stare, but it seemed like he had nothing more to give up. When Holmes nodded and turned away, he collapsed like a puppet whose strings had been cut, slumping backwards onto a stool behind the counter.

There was nothing about the façade of The Lamb and Flag that spoke of violence, in the present or in the past. Nevertheless, Mr. Melas opted to wait for us outside.

Inside it seemed crowded but congenial, Holmes made enquires at the bar and was pointed towards a table in a shadowy corner. We went over there, and I immediately recognised the thief we were seeking from the pawn-shop owner's description.

"Jimmy the Eel," asked Holmes.

"Who wants to know?" asked Jimmy, standing up to confront us.

He was tall, and clearly used to using his height to intimidate people. However, Holmes didn't give him the chance. Before he had finished standing, Holmes shocked me by hitting him in the jaw with a viscous uppercut. Jimmy dropped heavily back into his seat, dropping the switchblade he had been holding in his hand as he did so. I picked up the knife, then quickly examined the man. He was still breathing, but out cold.

I looked around the bar. It was quiet and everyone had turned to stare at us, but nobody did anything. The bartender shrugged, and the other patrons seemed to take that as their cue to return to their drinks and conversations.

Holmes and I sat down at the table opposite Jimmy.

"I am sorry, Watson," said Holmes. "That was uncalled for."

"I understand. I saw the knife."

"It isn't just that. This affair has me on edge."

"You are grieving," I reminded him. "Times like this are difficult, for anyone. You can talk about it."

"I would like that," he replied, "but I cannot. Not yet, and certainly not here."

"Whenever you are ready."

"Thank you for your patience. I will be glad when this is over."

There was a groan from opposite us, indicating that Jimmy was coming around.

"Easy now," said Holmes. "I don't want to have to put you down again."

Jimmy rubbed his jaw. "You might try, but I won't be falling for a sucker punch a second time. Besides, this isn't the place. You want to fight me, we'll go out to the courtyard. The Bucket is the place for fighting, not the bar."

"I want to talk to you about this," said Holmes, and he took out Mycroft's pocket-watch.

Jimmy studied it. It was the expert appraisal of a professional who could calculate the worth of an item in an instant, and the amount that he could get for it.

"That's a nice piece," he said, "but I'm not really in the market for buying. Now if you are proposing to put it up as collateral against our fight, then I could be interested."

"You stole this watch from a home in Pall Mall just a few days ago, along with a large number of other items."

"I don't know what you are talking about."

"You don't remember the watch?" said Holmes. "Well, do you remember stabbing the poor innocent man who was living there and leaving him for dead."

"Innocent? Is that what he told you?" In his anger, Jimmy forgot he was meant to be denying everything. "Henry was there robbing the place, too. That little wretch. I should have stayed and checked he was good and dead."

He thumped his fist on the table, then looked at our expressions and realised what he had just admitted to.

"He didn't tell us anything," I said. "Is this the knife you used?"

I held up the switchblade and Jimmy nodded.

"I don't understand," I said. "You say he went there with you to rob the place, but he had obviously been living there for a few days?"

"We had a nice little scam going. Henry kept his ear to the ground, listening for news of lonely rich folks passing away. He'd check out their homes, make sure they were empty. Then, while the dearly departed's loved ones were preoccupied with preparing for the funeral, before the will was read and they came to pick over the spoils, I'd sneak us in and we'd clean the place out. It's worked great for ages, only this time Henry decided to get comfortable. Overheard the landlady saying the place was staying locked up indefinitely and decided he could stay there for a while. When I found out, I went back and I told him not to be so stupid, but he was between accommodations and didn't want to go back to sleeping on the street in this weather."

"An understandable desire," I said. "It is bitterly cold and only likely to get worse with December around the corner. Why did you have to stab him? You could have just left him there."

"It wasn't his decision to take. It didn't just affect him. What if he had been discovered? There had already been people knocking at the door thinking that they had seen something. He knew I couldn't take the chance that he might get caught and tell the police everything. Still, I didn't want to kill him, just scare him into doing the right thing. It just happened."

I was sure he meant what he said, but I had seen this man's temper and imagined that such things "just happened" quite often.

"You ran out of there, leaving him bleeding out on the floor, not even certain he was dead."

"What was I supposed to do? I couldn't carry him out of there, dripping blood everywhere. I'd have been spotted in minutes. No, he knew the rules. Self-preservation first. Worry about anyone else later."

So it was among the criminal classes. I was glad I didn't live in their world. It seemed a cold and lonely place.

I went over to the bar, and told the landlord to send for the police. He frowned at me, as a number of his other patrons seated nearby decided they had other places where they urgently needed to be. However, he did as I instructed and I went back to the table to wait with Holmes and our prisoner.

Holmes had instructed Jimmy to make a list of the other places where he had sold items from Mycroft's rooms. A number of items were still unaccounted for, including the two large paintings.

"Mycroft would be angry with me if I didn't recover all his property."

It seemed an odd thing to say. I knew Holmes didn't believe that Mycroft would be expressing his displeasure from beyond the grave. Still, the dead cast a long shadow, even for a man as logical as Holmes.

We didn't have long to wait before a policeman arrived. Holmes quickly explained the situation, and Jimmy the Eel was led away. We followed them outside, where we found Mr. Melas, still waiting for us.

"Is it over?" he asked. "Is that the killer?"

"Yes, he has admitted to everything," I told him, before giving him an account of our encounter in the pub.

"So, it was just a falling out among thieves?" asked Mr. Melas, when I had finished. "Not about Mr. Holmes at all?"

"It would seem that way," I replied.

"The violence of these criminal types. I don't know how you can bear to be around such dangerous people. I couldn't do the work you do."

"It is necessary that someone should," said Holmes, "to protect the rest of society from their depredations."

"Quite so, quite so, and I thank you for your sacrifice. After Mr. Kratides, I had hoped never to see another body again, yet so it is. Speaking of which, what will you do about the body? I'm not sure that I will be able to sleep comfortably while it lies there in the room below me."

"I told the police that I would follow them to the station to explain everything," said Holmes. "I will instruct them to deal with it post-haste."

"Thank you. I feel happier now, knowing that you will handle everything, and that my friend can finally rest in peace."

One week later, I received a message from Holmes asking me to meet him at the Diogenes Club. In the past I would have thought nothing of this, but now it seemed odd. Why would he want to meet there, now that we no longer had to accommodate Mycroft's sedentary tendencies?"

The manager admitted me and led me to the Stranger's Room, where I found Holmes waiting for me.

Once the door had closed, I said, "It is good to see you so soon, but why did you want to meet here? You could have come to the house. Have you decided that the buzzing of the bees in your hive is too loud and decided to return to London and fill Mycroft's vacant chair."

"My brother is welcome here any time, as he well knows, but that seat is taken."

I hadn't even heard the door open behind me. The silence of the Diogenes Club extended to its fixtures and fittings, not just its members. One can therefore imagine my extent of my shock at hearing the voice of the recently deceased Mycroft Holmes.

I turned around, and there he stood. Not a spectre, nor an apparition, but the solid and substantial form of the man who I had thought we had buried just one week earlier.

Mycroft walked across the room and helped himself to a drink. Then he sat down in his habitual chair, quite casually, as though there was nothing out of the ordinary.

"My dear Watson," said Holmes, "please take a seat and we will explain everything. Can I get you a drink to steady your nerves? It looks like you need one?"

He stood up and poured me a large measure. As he placed the glass in my hands, I saw that they were shaking.

"Don't coddle the man, Brother! I'm sure he has no need of explanations. I sometimes think you underestimate the Good Doctor's intelligence."

"The reports of your death. The funeral. They were all a sham."

"Quite so," said Mycroft. "I knew you would understand."

"And you knew all along?" I said to Holmes.

"Yes. I am sorry to have kept you in the dark so long. It wasn't what I wanted. However, Mycroft insisted that I speak to no one, even you, before this point, out of concern for the nation's security."

"You are a good man, Watson," added Mycroft, "and I have nothing but respect for you. However, you aren't adept at hiding your emotions, and I worried that you might not be able to feign grief suitably at my funeral. An exaggerated reaction might have given away the truth. However, it turns out that I should have been more concerned about my brother. His withdrawn demeanour veered too far in the opposite direction and risked attracting the wrong sort of attention."

"I admit that I found it harder than I had expected to play the role of the grieving brother," Holmes said. "I will endeavour to do better when you actually die.

"It is obvious what has happened," I said, trying not to show in my voice the anger and sense of betrayal I felt. "It isn't the first time that one of my friends has faked his death."

"Indeed," said Mycroft. "In fact, the success of that deception inspired me."

Holmes rarely regrets anything, firmly believing that he consistently makes the best and most logical decisions based upon the information available to him. Nevertheless, I thought I might have seen a small hint of shame on his face at the reference to his disappearance, all those years before.

"However, that doesn't explain why you did it."

"Dr. Watson," explained Mycroft, "you know more about the role I play than most."

The statement surprised me. I had been granted glimpses of the work he carried out on behalf of the country, but still didn't really understand what he did, or what position he held within the hierarchies of power.

"I have always toiled in obscurity, but over the years, rumours about me have spread. It used to be that if someone mentioned my name, people wouldn't recognise it, or think that they must have meant my brother. Yet now my name is whispered in the corridors of Whitehall. Not just in the Cabinet Room, but throughout the Civil Service.

"I had come to accept this, though I wasn't interested in recognition. However, now a crisis is upon us. I do not exaggerate when I say we stand on the brink of a conflict on a scale unlike anything the world has ever seen. Yet, still there remains a small chance that this disaster can be averted, or its scope mitigated, if the right people act now, in secret!"

Mycroft picked up his glass to take a drink, and Holmes took over the narrative.

"There was a meeting that needed to take place. Nobody could know that was happening, and it could only take place if Mycroft was there to act as broker. He knew that the movements of all the parties involved were being watched and scrutinised."

"Including my own," said Mycroft.

Holmes nodded. "It was necessary to create an unimpeachable reason for all the parties involved to travel to London at the same time. A funeral was the obvious choice, but not just any funeral. The funeral of the only man who could have brokered such a meeting and persuaded them all to co-operate."

I thought of the man with the Prussian accent who had offered his condolences after the funeral.

"All this for one meeting?" I said.

"More than that, I hope," said Mycroft. "With my death, I am able to return to the shadows, where I belong, Although I cannot return home at present, it barely inconveniences me. I have simply taken a room here. The strictures of this club ensure that even if someone might wonder at seeing me alive, decorum ensures that they will never mention it."

"So, since you are now telling me this, I assume the meeting has taken place."

"Yes," said Mycroft. "It was scheduled for the evening of the day after my funeral."

"It was imperative that no one should enquire into the circumstances of Mycroft's death, lest it reveal some trace of our deception. Once the funeral was over, he should have disappeared from everybody's minds into obscurity. However, then Mr. Melas came to us with his story of a ghost haunting Mycroft's room, and it threatened to turn the spotlight back onto him. I did what I could to dismiss Mr. Melas, but even I couldn't overlook a body."

"You seemed genuinely concerned by my theory about the assassin, or was that all an act too?" I asked.

"No, I was gravely concerned. While I knew that Mycroft hadn't been assassinated, the idea that somebody might have tried to kill him, especially after his death was the worst news possible. It would have meant that someone thought he was still alive."

"Worse," said Mycroft, "it suggested that someone might know about the meeting and be taking steps to prevent it."

"I reported everything we had found to Mycroft and left him to plan his contingencies. However, upon my return to his rooms, I realised my fears had been unfounded. The evidence uncovered by yourself and Mr. Melas told a different story. The multiple used glasses and smoked cigars spoke to two intruders who knew each other, and the nature of the items taken suggested common thieves. Once the pawnbroker confirmed that there was indeed a second criminal involved, I knew that there was no reason to worry."

"I am cross about that, Brother," said Mycroft. "You of all people know that one must never try to reach a conclusion before one has all the facts. I wasted precious time and effort on your theory."

"I make no apologies for warning you. If the case had gone the other way, those preparations would have proved vital."

"I am just glad that you are safe and alive," I said. "However, from the way you have been speaking, it sounds like you don't intend to make your return public?"

"Certainly not. That meeting has taken place, but there is plenty more that I can accomplish more easily if people believe I am dead. Now, if you will excuse me, one of the distinct advantages of being dead is that should be able to spend less time in this room speaking to people. If you have more questions, Dr. Watson, I am sure my brother will be able to answer them. Good day, gentlemen."

And with that, Mycroft Holmes departed from us and entered into his own personal heaven, the eternal silence of the Diogenes Club.

The Ebony Bastet
by Roger Riccard

Chapter I

It was late November 1918, and the United Kingdom was recovering from the effects of the Great War. Much of my work in hospitals with wounded veterans was coming to an end, as they were either being discharged to return to civilian life to cope as best they could, or transferred to facilities for the permanently catastrophic disabled.

One case of mine was that of Lt. Colonel Nathaniel Forrester, who had lost a leg in a battle along with other serious injuries. It was particularly sad because I knew the gentleman. He was the son of Mrs. Cecil Forrester, a former client of Holmes and employer of my late wife Mary Morstan when she was a governess, back in the late eighties.

While the amputation of his leg had stabilized and gangrene had been avoided, he had suffered other internal injuries that required multiple surgeries and extensive rehabilitation efforts. I and other doctors had been able to keep him going for nearly two months, hoping he might see the end of the Great War for which he had fought so gallantly and possibly make it to Christmas. However, on 13 November, two days after the Armistice, he succumbed to his injuries.

He was buried with full military honours and I found myself standing next to his mother, who held on to me for support as she was in her seventies and unsteady on her feet for long periods. The sight of the two of us, at our ages, holding our canes and leaning on each other, brought her son-in-law to our aid. After assisting as a pallbearer in delivering the casket to the gun carriage that would transport it to the cemetery, the fifty-year-old Major Davies came to our side and was of great comfort. I sincerely appreciated his assistance in caring for this kindly soul of a woman. He escorted his mother-in-law, his wife, Kathryn, and Nathaniel's widow, Nadine, to the car that would accompany the deceased to the graveside. I and his other surgeon, Dr. Youngblood, who had assisted in Forrester's care, followed in a separate vehicle.

After a moving prayer by the vicar and a three-volley salute [1] at the gravesite, the mourners went their various ways, and I was given a grateful hug by the grieving mother who whispered, "Thank you for letting him see the war's end, Doctor."

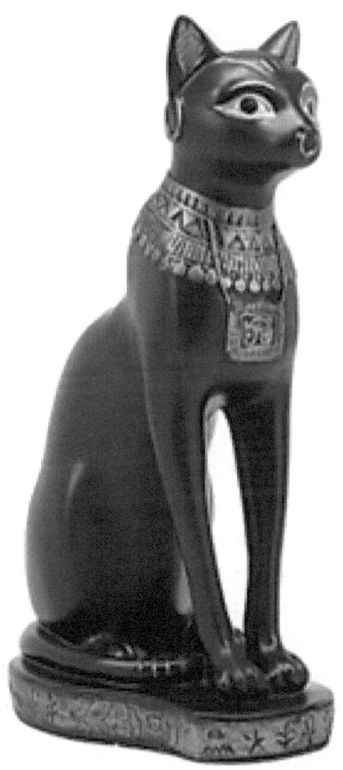

The next day, I was at home setting mousetraps in the kitchen against what appeared to be at least a pair of the meddlesome creatures when a messenger arrived with a package. Inside it, wrapped carefully in what appeared to be Egyptian cotton, was a statue of a cat. It was just over a foot tall, and at first I thought it to be made of basalt, as it must have weighed at least a stone, [2] and black as coal. Upon further examination, however, I realized it was a dense and highly polished ebony with gold trimming in the ears and eyes, and a thick gold necklace about its neck from which hung a golden pouch that exuded a faint scent of peppermint. A note inside was addressed to me by Mrs. Forrester:

Dear Dr. Watson,

This was among my son's belongings as a keepsake from his time in Egypt. As that was where he received his wounds, however, neither Nadine nor I wish to have it as a reminder of his death. I have no idea as to its value, but would much prefer you to have it in gratitude for your long friendship and service to my family. I have enclosed some reference material that Nathan had obtained regarding it.

Bless you, sir,
Sincerely,
Morna Forrester

I recalled from my days serving in Her Majesty's Army in Afghanistan that cats were considered clean and highly valued in Islam, but were not worshipped there. This creature before me, however, was a different story, as the included note explained:

Bastet: One of the Main Goddesses
of the Egyptian Pantheons

☐ *A goddess of cats, the sun, the East, fire, love, intoxication, music and dancing, joy, celebration, fertility, secrets, magic, and sex.*

☐ *However, she was also a goddess of war, known for her wrathful vengeance.*

☐ *She protected households and individuals from disease and evil spirits, and guarded pregnant women and cats.*

☐ *She served as the divine nurse and mother of the Pharaoh.*

☐ *Due to Bastet meaning "she of the ointment jar", she also became known as a goddess of perfume, and was called the "perfumed protector".*

☐ *Bast/Bastet was the protector and guardian of Lower Egypt.*

☐ *She was the patron goddess of fire fighters because the Egyptians believed that a cat running through a building on fire would draw the flames out.*

☐ *She was also one of the goddesses who was known as the "Eye of Ra" – the sun. In this aspect, she symbolized Ra's feminine counterpart and was sent out to take vengeance on his enemies. The "Eye of Ra" was both a part of Ra and a separate being from him, and was considered his mother, sister, wife, and daughter simultaneously. She had life-giving capacities, both protective and destructive.*

□ *Cats were sacred to Bast and were treasured pets in many Egyptian households. (In addition to their religious association, they were highly valued for their vermin-killing abilities!) In the homes of the wealthy, cats wore gold jewelry and were fed lavishly from their owner's table. People deeply mourned their departed cats and dedicated their mummies to Bastet. At the height of Bastet's popularity, the penalty for killing a cat – even by accident – was death!*

After reading this cornucopia of facts regarding this creature, I recalled that, in my native Scotland, if a black cat appears on your doorstep, it is seen as a sign of prosperity. Thus I took this gift as a good omen. Impressed by its beauty, I found a place for it in the sitting room, which is adjacent to my kitchen. It is also where I craft my stories about my friend Sherlock Holmes, and I felt a "goddess" with such powers certainly couldn't hurt my writing process. Not that I am superstitious, mind you, but I do tend to be more open-minded about these things than Holmes. [3]

Chapter II

The following Monday, I returned from my morning round of house calls and immediately noted something odd when I opened my door. It sounded as if my house had been invaded by jazz musicians. I brought my cane up into a defensive position and moved toward the room I used as a waiting room for patients. I surreptitiously peeked around the corner and beheld the figure of Sherlock Holmes lounging before a fire in a chair next to a small table where I usually keep a reading lamp. He had set the lamp aside and had placed a Decca Dulcephone in its place, where a record was spinning and sounding off a cacophony of noise including a clarinet, horns, piano, and drums.

"Holmes!" I shouted to make myself heard. "Whatever are you doing here?"

In response, he, thankfully, turned off the machine and said, "Listening to *Tiger Rag* by The Original Dixieland Jazz Band. Quite invigorating, is it not?"

"That's one word for it," I replied, shucking out of my overcoat and bowler and setting them on the sofa. I approached my old friend and shook his hand. "I meant what are you doing in London, and what is this contraption doing here?"

303

"I have been in London for some weeks now, quite busily obtaining information for Mycroft to use in his recommendations for the terms of the Armistice and the future peace treaty." He looked at me with pursed lips, "Unfortunately, those in charge and the other countries involved are ignoring the majority of his proposals. Everyone is out for German blood and cannot see the dangers an overzealous punishment will entail. I fear not a generation will pass before Germany rises again to throw off what they will perceive as their oppressors."

He gave a quick sigh then turned to the machine with a smile. "However, on a happier note, this, my friend, was a gift from a grateful client and, as you know, I have an excellent gramophone down in Sussex, so I thought it might help your patients while away the time in your waiting room."

"Well, thank you," I said wincing at his pun, but appreciative for his thoughtfulness. "Speaking of gifts from grateful clients, come look at this."

I led him to the sitting room to show him the Bastet statue, but was surprised to find it on the floor beneath the shelf where I had placed it. It was standing upright and facing the same direction as it had before.

Holmes, in an attempt at humour, observed, "An odd place for a doorstop, but it is a beautiful piece of workmanship."

I grimaced at him, picked the statue up, and replaced it on the shelf. "It was up here when I left this morning. It is a gift from the Forresters."

Holmes came over to examine it. Placing a hand upon it, he asked, "Do you mind if I take a closer look?"

"Be my guest," I replied, always anxious for his opinion.

He picked it up noting its texture. "Did you know that ebony is such a dense wood it doesn't float in water?" He hefted it to test its weight. "This base is quite heavy. It isn't impossible that the statue fell from the shelf and landed right side up. The question is, 'How did it fall?'"

He examined the item with his lens and then the shelf upon which it had sat. He shook his head. "You are obsessed with cleanliness. You obviously cleaned this shelf before you set the Bastet upon it. There are no signs of any creature that may have dislodged it."

"The only creatures in the house are some mice in the kitchen," I replied. "Do you think it possible one of them knocked it over?"

"No mouse could have moved an object this heavy," he replied. "Not even a rat would have that capability."

"I am certain there are no rats," I replied. "The mice only appeared a few days ago, and I've set out traps for them in the kitchen."

He set the statue back in its place and stepped toward the kitchen. He stopped short at the doorway. "It appears your traps are no longer needed."

There on the floor were the chewed-up remains of two dead mice.

"Well, those certainly weren't there when I left this morning," I said. I swept up the remains and dumped them into a trash receptacle behind the house.

In the meantime, Holmes observed, "They were killed by a predator that somehow made its way into your house, old friend. Likely a cat, but I wouldn't rule out a dog, or even a squirrel. You must have left a door or window open."

"That would be unlikely. We have observed the two doors since my return, so unless you found one open when you arrived, they couldn't have entered in that way."

"The front door was locked when I came on the scene. I was sure you wouldn't mind if I waited for you inside on such a cold day, so I used the key you provided me years ago."

We then went throughout the house and verified that the windows were all shut and latched, even on the upper floors. Returning to my waiting room and taking seats by the fire, I queried my friend. "Do you suppose some creature could have come down one of the chimneys?"

"Only if you've recently had your chimneys swept," he observed. "Otherwise, any creature should have left its footprints tracked in soot across your floor."

"The top floor bedroom my wife used for her sewing has had its chimney swept and the room closed off since her passing. The maid opens the window to air it out once a week while she's cleaning the rest of the house, and then locks it up at the end of the day."

"Given that all other avenues appear to have been latched tight, that would appear to be the point of entry," suggested Holmes. "If you ensure that the dampers are closed on the fireplaces you aren't using, it should solve your problem."

We left the subject at that and I put together a cold lunch of bread, meats, and cheese. As we ate, Holmes shared what he was allowed to regarding the peace treaty terms being debated and I gave him my opinions. Having seen the horrors of war firsthand in Afghanistan, and again through the ruined lives of the wounded veterans I was treating, I'm afraid I wasn't as liberally minded as he. I could well understand the vehemence that England and her allies wished to visit upon an enemy who stooped to the use of poison gas as a weapon and who raped, pillaged, and slaughtered hundreds of civilians in Belgium, despite having signed an agreement guaranteeing Belgian neutrality. German *U*-boats had sunk hospital ships and German troops were complicit in atrocities related to mass extermination throughout Eastern Europe and the Ottoman Empire.

The anti-German sentiment was such in Britain that even King George V had the British royal family name changed from "*Saxe-Coburg and Gotha*" to "*Windsor*". My exposure to German atrocities was such that I'm afraid at this time I was among those whom Holmes considered the ones crying out for blood-lust revenge and punishment so severe that Germany would never think of going to war again.

I could see his point regarding the danger, and given enough time, I might come around to his way of thinking. However, for the time being, my Hippocratic Oath meant little, and I longed to "do harm" to those who had caused so much harm in the world.

Chapter III

After this invigorating discussion and spartan meal, we were forced to go our separate ways. Holmes back to Whitehall to confer with Mycroft, and me to make rounds with homebound veterans I had been treating.

An afternoon of seeing patients who had lost limbs and lungs to German ambitions didn't improve my mood. When I returned at the end of a long and depressing day, I proceeded to my sitting room where I could stir up the fire and enjoy a brandy to warm my insides and relax my brain. To my surprise, the fire Holmes had started as he awaited me at noon was yet burning. I had expected possibly a few embers to which I could add kindling, but there was still a small blaze throwing heat into the room, and so I merely added more coal, and soon had a proper evening fire going.

I settled into a chair in my sitting room with the afternoon mail. There was an enquiry from my literary agent, Doyle, as to when he might expect a new Holmes adventure now that the war had ended. I had sent him what I believed would be the final story of my friend, "His Last Bow", the previous year. There were many more cases among the notes still in my dispatch box, although not every one was suitable for publication. Besides, they were all regarding pre-war incidents and I wasn't convinced that a war-weary public would be interested. However, he was adamant that *The Strand* was willing to pay a hefty price for a new story, and the figure he named was beyond generous. I smirked at the number and raised my gaze toward the Bastet statue, saying to myself, "*Maybe there is something to that old proverb about black cats and prosperity.*"

There was also a letter from my stepson, George Savage. [4] The cavalry unit to which he had been attached as a veterinarian was returning to England and he was due to muster out at the end of the month. He was well, and hoped I would join him, his wife, and his sister's family for Christmas dinner at his brother-in-law's equestrian estate. It was welcome news on such a day as this had been, and the thought of spending the holiday with George and his sister Marina, was a pleasant distraction. Marina had married the well-known horse breeder Joshua Morgan and produced four children of her own, so I could imagine what a lively holiday it would be.

My mood, now somewhat lifted by these cheery correspondences, was such that I decided to rummage through my case notes in response to Doyle's suggestion. I put a pot of leftover stew on the stove to warm up for dinner, then returned from the kitchen, sat at my desk, and reached for the bottom drawer where my dispatch box lay with its myriad of notes. As I did so, my eye caught the list of Bastet's attributes, which still lay where I had left it.

As I gazed upon the document, I was suddenly struck by the similarity of recent events to the attributes of this Egyptian goddess. In addition to the dead mice in the kitchen, there was the fire which had continued to burn longer than normal. The new source of music that Holmes had brought. The promise of celebration with my step-children for both George's safe return and the upcoming holidays. The secrets Holmes had shared with me regarding the peace negotiations – and also the feelings of wrathful vengeance I had towards Germany.

I had to admit these occurrences seemed more than coincidental in light of the fact they happened after my receipt of the Bastet statue. This realization brought me up short. I had witnessed many strange things during my adventures with Sherlock Holmes, and I recalled what he had once told me:

"My dear fellow, life is infinitely stranger than anything which the mind of man could invent. We wouldn't dare to conceive the things which are really mere commonplaces of existence. If we could fly out of that window hand in hand, hover over this great city, gently remove the roofs, and peep in at the queer things which are going on, the strange coincidences, the plannings, the cross-purposes, the wonderful chains of events, working through generations, and leading to the most *outrè* results, it would make all fiction with its conventionalities and foreseen conclusions most stale and unprofitable." [5]

Despite this seeming openness to the possibility of the supernatural, Holmes had never accepted anything less than a logical conclusion to the cases we had worked together. I was sure he would somehow explain away what I was thinking. However, I vowed to take notice of events in the coming days that might bolster the reputation of having Bastet in my home.

Chapter IV

Going through my case notes, I found a dozen or so that I felt had enough material to turn into a new story for *The Strand*. There were others for which the world was not yet ready, and still more where promises had been made to hold publication until after certain persons were deceased.

I ate my dinner as I was going through these. Eating alone was one of those mundane tasks which seems all the more so when you have no one to share them with. I had spent most of the last three decades in the company of Sherlock Holmes, or my wives, Constance Adams, Mary Morstan, and Adelaide Savage. The death of Mary, during the time when Holmes was presumed dead, had been the low point of my life and I had delved dangerously close to alcoholism.

Holmes's resurrection and my return to our Baker Street lodgings eventually snapped me out of my doldrums, after seeing a performance of Dicken's *A Christmas Carol* during one of our cases, and I realized how much like the old Ebenezer Scrooge I had become. [6]

Still, eating alone was boring, and I often skipped meals. When I did eat, I found that reading while doing so at least relieved me of some of those feelings of loneliness. Thus, I entertained myself with the reminiscences of these adventures with my old friend as I consumed my stew.

After my meal, I stacked the dishes in the sink for the time being and returned to the sitting room to finish reading. It was well into the night before I narrowed my choices down to three. "The Problem of Thor Bridge" presented some good examples of observation and deduction. "The Mazarin Stone" offered a chance to see Holmes using technology and stealth to fool and capture the thieves. "The Creeping Man" was a study of man trying to outwit nature to rise above himself and the dangers of playing God.

Still, I was unsure which I should submit to Doyle and decided to seek out Holmes's opinion for any preference he might have. I piled those three bundles of notes atop my writing desk and put the others back into my dispatch box in the drawer. It occurred to me as I did so that perhaps, due to the private nature of several of these cases, I should consider removing the box to the safety of a bank vault, and I decided to look into the matter the next time I visited my bank, Cox and Company at Charing Cross.

It had been a long day of rising and falling emotions, and I fell asleep almost as soon as I hit the pillow. What dreams I had I don't remember, except that there was a cat involved, and the house had seemed to shake. I had never had a cat as a pet, though with Adelaide we had a dog for a few years. Down on Holmes's bee farm, he had both a dog and a cat for company. When I awoke the next morning and began my trek down to the kitchen, I noticed a familiar odor coming from Adelaide's dressing room. I stepped in and found a bottle of her favourite perfume lying on its side, much of its contents having spilled into the sink. I set the bottle upright and splashed some water into the basin to wash the smell down the drain. I didn't need that constant reminder in my nostrils that she was gone. I checked the window to see if some creature had gotten in and knocked the jar over, but it was latched. For now, I put it down as the bottle being too close to the edge of the sink and falling over due to the house settling. Perhaps that was the shaking I remembered from my dream. Sometimes, a strong gust of wind would make the house rattle as well.

At any rate, I thought no more about it until I reached downstairs and passed through my sitting room on the way to the kitchen. Bastet was again on the floor, as were two of the three bundles of notes I had set aside the previous evening. Only the case of the Mazarin Stone remained on top of my desk. I also felt a breeze and turned to see the window was open. I examined the latch and found it appeared to have become cracked over time, judging by the tarnished brass, and finally broke. I remembered giving that window a tug the day before when Holmes and I were checking all the windows and it had some play to it. At the time, I thought it merely worn from old age. Now I realized I must have brought it to the edge of breaking and perhaps it was the wind gust that shook the house during the night that made it give way. With the window open, a breeze could have blown those papers off the desk, and allowed some creature in that knocked Bastet off the shelf. That animal could also be responsible for the perfume bottle incident.

But the fact the statue was once again on the floor, right side up, sent a little chill down my spine. After setting the statue back on the shelf, I picked up the list of Bastet's attributes. It was then I noticed that she was also the goddess of perfume.

Chapter V

While there must have been a logical explanation for those coincidences, there was that primal instinct that I believe all men have for belief in the supernatural. I remembered reading an article by a doctor in the relatively new field of psychology that implied a human need for beliefs in something outside the realm of normalcy, in order to explain what they could not understand.

While I wasn't ready to attribute recent developments to this ancient Egyptian goddess on my shelf, I was curious to learn more. I resolved to take some time that afternoon to stop by the British Museum and confer with a historian I knew who had previously assisted me in research.

I did stop by my home briefly for lunch while on my house calls and found a telegram from Holmes inviting me to dinner at Simpson's that evening at eight o'clock. I scribbled out an affirmative reply and dropped it at the post office on my way to the Museum. It was a mild autumn day with no threat of rain as I entered the imposing structure where so many of the Empire's treasures are stored. Yet, once inside and walking through the Egyptian exhibit, I felt like I was in the heat of the Sahara Desert, observing the statues of crouching lions guarding ancient tombs. There were several statues of pharaohs, queens, and other nobles. Also a number of mummy cases, mostly of the reddish clay of the land, but some painted in vivid colours. Surpisingly, I passed by a display of cat mummies of various textures and designs.

At last, I reached the office of Professor of Egyptology, Rhys Roberts. He was a stout fellow with a body shaped like a barrel, slightly shorter than myself, and a short black beard with no sign of grey despite his forty years of age. He had already led two expeditions to the land of the pharaohs, and was responsible for many of the finer items on display in the Museum.

He stood upon my entering and bellowed, "Watson, dear chap! Welcome! Please have a seat. I got your note that you wished to discuss the Egyptian goddess Bastet. Is this another case for Mr. Holmes?"

"Not yet," I replied, causing a raised eyebrow from the professor.

"That is to say," I continued, "that I need more information. You know how Holmes is a glutton for data." I went on to explain how I had received the Bastet statue and all the strange events since doing so.

He sat in rapt attention, his large hands folded atop his desk. When I finished, he leaned slightly forward and said in a low tone, "This Bastet you received: Would you describe it, please?"

"It is just over a foot tall. It is so heavy that at first I thought it to be made of basalt, but upon further examination, I realized it was a dense and highly polished ebony with gold trimming in the ears and eyes, and a thick gold necklace about its neck. There is a golden pouch on the end of it that gives off the scent of peppermint."

He nodded and asked, "It is the body of a cat sitting on its haunches, not of a woman with a cat's head?"

"Yes," I replied. "Were the coat not so smooth and polished, it could almost pass for a real cat."

He leaned back and hooked his thumbs into his braces. "Dr. Watson, I should very much like to examine this statue for myself."

I shrugged my shoulders and replied, "Certainly, if you wish. I could bring it by tomorrow."

He held up a finger and gave me an expression I couldn't quite read. "Actually, if convenient I would like to come by your house tonight."

I was a bit caught off guard by this request, but replied, "I'm having dinner with Holmes later, but if you could come by between six and seven that would work."

"I can be there at six-fifteen if convenient."

"That will be fine," I replied. Then I added, "If you don't mind my saying so, you seem somewhat affected by this statue. Is there something I should know?"

He gave his head a slight shake. "As your friend would say, I would rather not speculate without sufficient facts, but there is a possibility you have something significant on your hands. Does anyone know you have it, other than the sender or Mr. Holmes?"

"I'm unaware if Mrs. Forrester told anyone she was giving it to me. I haven't mentioned it to anyone other than Holmes and you."

"Just as well you keep it that way for now." He stood and reached out to shake my hand. "Until this evening then?"

"I'm looking forward to it," I replied.

Chapter VI

I was home from my house calls by five o'clock and fixed up some tea and biscuits for myself, and to have on hand for Professor Roberts' later arrival. There were no new incidents regarding Bastet. It remained on the shelf where I had replaced it that morning. The papers I had originally left on the desk, were neatly tucked in the top drawer, where I had moved them. The fire in the hearth consisted of glowing embers as expected, and not ablaze as it had been the day before after my afternoon absence.

I did find that a box of biscuits in the pantry had been knocked over and chewed open. I assumed this meant that not all the mice had been eliminated as I had supposed, and I set out more traps.

The Curator of Egyptian Antiquities was prompt. A couple of minutes early in fact, and I welcomed him in heartily. He removed his hat and threw his scarf into it and onto a chair, but was too anxious to remove his overcoat. "Where is it?" he asked excitedly.

"This way," I replied leading the way to my sitting room.

He stopped short when he saw the ebony Bastet on the shelf. He took a quick glance at me and I waved him onward. He approached the statue almost reverently. As it was just below eye level, he bent his knees slightly and leaned in to get a closer look. He tilted his head this way and that, then took out a magnifying lens to study its surface and gold trimmings.

Looking back at me and reaching a hand towards it, he asked, "May I pick it up?"

"By all means," I replied. "Perform as thorough an examination as you like."

He took great care to hug the heavy object to his chest as he removed it from the shelf so as not to risk dropping it. He set it upon the desk and sat in my chair with his lens, examining it from top to bottom. He sniffed the golden pouch and asked, "Did you add the peppermint?"

"No, it came to me that way."

After several minutes of intense scrutiny, he turned to me. "This isn't one of those mass-produced decorative statues that pretentious people or cat lovers place in their homes. I'm quite sure this is a genuine ancient relic, possibly three-thousand years old, or more."

I gaped in amazement. "But it is in such pristine condition. Surely something that old should show signs of its age."

Professor Roberts shook his head. "There are still active cults who worship the goddess Bastet. If this has been passed down through the generations, they would have taken special care of it as a revered symbol. It would also explain why the peppermint odor still lingers. It was probably refreshed right before Forrester took possession of it."

I had sat in one of the chairs to the side of my desk and narrowed my gaze at Roberts. "Are you saying he stole this idol from some Egyptian cult?" I couldn't reconcile such a thought with the man I knew, but then war does strange things to men.

Roberts shook his head. "'Stole' is such a provocative term. We've no idea how he came upon this. It's quite possible that he rescued it from plunderers who would have taken it after the sacred place it was being kept in was bombed. He may have had every intention of turning it over to the Museum. There was nothing in his private papers regarding it?"

"I didn't have access to his papers or any journal he may have kept. If there is such a thing, it likely went to his wife."

"I should be very interested to see if he wrote down the provenance of this find," said Roberts. "Could you arrange an introduction for me?"

I hesitated, then replied, "I could certainly do so, but I prefer Nadine have a proper mourning period. The Lt. Colonel was only buried a few days ago."

The professor had the good graces to look abashed. "Of course, of course. I'm sorry. You are quite right. I'm afraid I let the significance of this find carry away my manners.

312

"May I suggest, if its provenance turns out to be what I believe, you have a valuable piece of artwork here. Would you consider selling it? Or at least depositing it with a bank for the time being?"

He named a significant price and I pondered his statement. It was a handsome piece and a gift from a friend – not something one easily discards. However, if it was truly an ancient artefact, it should be shared with the public rather than having me as its sole admirer. "I shall give your offer due consideration, Professor. I've been considering a visit to the bank to deposit some other valuables, so I could certainly add it to my bundle for now."

"Do you have somewhere in the house where it would be safer in the meantime?" he asked, with some trepidation.

I recalled some previous cases with Sherlock Holmes where he quoted a story by Edgar Allan Poe, and I asked Roberts, "Have you ever read the tale 'The Purloined Letter'?

He shook his head. "I have not. Is it relevant?"

"It basically comes down to hiding an object in plain sight," I continued. "If I put the statue in an odd location such as a closet or some other out-of-the-way place, a burglar who finds it would believe it must have some worth for me to go to the trouble of hiding it, and likely add it to his pile of booty. Whereas if I leave it where it is, he would assume it is just there for décor and of no great value."

He started to object, but I raised my palm to forestall him and said, "I promise, I will go to the bank tomorrow and arrange to place it in their keeping until we get to the bottom of the matter. For now, I'm afraid I must get ready to meet Holmes for dinner. I'll check in on the Forresters and let you know when it will be convenient for you to meet with them."

He left, reluctantly, and I prepared myself for an excellent meal at Simpsons, and an evening of stimulating conversation with my oldest friend. What I wasn't prepared for was what was about to happen.

Chapter VII

I arrived at Simpson's about ten minutes early and strode through its high-arched entrance to intake the delightful scents of what P.G. Wodehouse had called "*A restful temple of food*". I was shown to the table the staff had reserved for Mr. Sherlock Holmes and ordered a sherry while I waited for my friend.

He wasn't long in coming and arrived promptly on the hour. Unfortunately, it was with distressing news. "I'm afraid we must delay our dinner. I just received a message at the Diogenes Club from Scotland Yard. There has been a burglary at the Forrester home."

313

I stood and followed him out to the cab he had waiting. "Are Morna and Nadine all right?" I asked. I knew that, in Morna Forrester'sdvancing years, she had moved in with her son and his wife, and it seemed a suitable arrangement while the Lt. Colonel was deployed overseas.

"Yes," replied my friend. "Fortunately they were visiting her daughter and Major Davies, and weren't home when the burglars struck."

As we traveled, I told Holmes of my meeting with Professor Roberts and his estimation of the value of the Bastet statue. "That is very interesting," he responded but didn't elaborate as our trip was a short one, with little traffic at that time of night.

We arrived at the Forrester home in Chelsea. The arched wrought-iron gate opened on a short walkway to the front door, flanked by two white columns. The ground floor was clad in white wood siding, while the two upper stories were of tan brick. All the windows were framed in white, and the overall appearance of the house was clean and crisp in the light of the nearby streetlamp.

A young constable in front of the door stood aside when Holmes presented his card. "A pleasure to meet you, sir. Sergeant Wyles is inside with the family and is expecting you. They're in the parlour to the right."

He opened the door for us and we stepped inside, removing our hats and overcoats, and setting them on a nearby table as we made our way to the parlour. I have to admit I wasn't prepared for what greeted us. Of course, I recognized Morna Forrester and her daughter-in-law, Nadine, sitting on a sofa before a warm fire. What took me aback was the person opposite them in an Edwardian leather club chair. Standing upon our entrance, the uniformed person spoke. "Gentlemen, thank you for coming on such short notice. I am Sergeant Lillian Wyles, Women's Special Police. [7]

She stepped forward and put out her hand as Holmes introduced us.

"We are happy to be of any service we may, Sergeant. May I see where the break-in occurred?"

After ensuring that the Forrester women were all right, I followed Holmes, and we were led to a back door that opened to the kitchen. "I made a cursory examination of the lock," Sergeant Wyles explained, "which you can see was jemmied by some tool with a curved blade. I also noted the footprints on the path, but chose not to step out to measure them as I was made aware you would be coming to assist in the investigation and would want the least possible contamination. As there was no danger of weather washing them away, I felt the wait would be inconsequential, and possibly vital to your gathering of facts."

Sergeant Lillian Wyles

Holmes gave a nod of satisfaction to the lady and replied, "Thank you, Sergeant. You have been most considerate."

He examined the damage to the door with his magnifying lens and measured the width of the dent in the wood caused by the jemmy. Then he stepped out and around the tracks left on the dirt path, kneeled, and measured the size of the feet and the length of the strides.

I noticed something peculiar about one of the shoeprints and asked Holmes if it might be significant. "The pointed toe of those tracks: Could that mean this was committed by a woman, or are you leaning more towards a foreigner, such as an Egyptian?"

"Very good," he said. "While I do not necessarily rule out a woman, it is much more likely these are the prints of two men. As you see, the depth of the prints indicates someone of a weight more conducive to the average male. For a woman's print to sink that deeply, I would have expected a much longer shoe befitting a rather stout female.

"No, we have two gentlemen here. One was approximately five-foot-seven, wearing a size nine shoe or sandal, of significant age as it was heavily worn on the outer side of the heels, indicating a fellow who walks with his toes pointed slightly outward rather than straight ahead. The other was much taller and wore a heavy-soled, size eleven boot."

I nodded in agreement and noted that Sergeant Wyles was taking meticulous notes. I took the opportunity to ask, "Was anything stolen, Sergeant?"

She turned to me and replied, "According to the ladies, nothing appears to be missing. Whoever these fellows were, they made a fairly thorough job of it, turning out drawers and going through closets and cabinets. Odd thing was, they didn't touch the jewelry boxes or take any money from the box in the desk where the Forresters keep their spare cash. It appears they were after something specific that wasn't here."

I looked at Holmes at the same time he whirled his head toward me at her statement. We both turned on our heels and made for the parlour with a startled policewoman in close pursuit.

I'm afraid we burst in upon the ladies with something of an appearance that startled them. I was about to apologize when Holmes asked the question of Morna Forrester that had occurred to both of us: "I need you to think carefully, Mrs. Forrester. Did you ever write down what you planned to do with the Ebony Bastet you gave to Dr. Watson?"

She looked confused for a moment, then recalled, "Oh, you mean the cat statue? No, I didn't make a note of it." She looked to Nadine who also shook her head, then back to Holmes. "Nadine and I discussed it and agreed we didn't want that symbol of the country where Nathan received his fatal wound to be here as a constant reminder of his death. But we only talked about it. We didn't put it in writing."

Holmes put a finger to his lips and pondered that a moment, then asked, "Where were you sitting when you wrote out the address label for the package?"

"Over there." She pointed across the room. "At that desk."

Holmes rushed to the desk and searched the papers atop it and then stopped short and gazed at the blotter. There in faint impressions were several words from items she had written recently. Among them, my name and address.

Turning to Sergeant Wyles, Holmes ordered, "Call Scotland Yard immediately and have them dispatch officers to Dr. Watson's home, as well as Dr. Youngblood's." He pointed to the addresses on the blotter and we sprinted for the door to hail a cab while she picked up the telephone receiver.

In the cab, Holmes stated, "We are fortunate that there were several addresses on that blotter, Watson. Our hope lies in that it may take some time before the thieves gets around to yours."

Chapter VIII

When we pulled up in front of my home, a constable was guarding the front door. He immediately informed us that another officer was watching the back and that there had been no sign of a break-in.

Relieved, Holmes and I entered, the policeman at our heels. I immediately went to my sitting room and found the Bastet in its place on the shelf. "Well, if this is what they're after, at least we beat them to it," I said, picking the statue up and looking it over to see that it hadn't been substituted.

Holmes gazed about the room, assuring himself nothing had been disturbed and that the policemen's arrival hadn't caused a thief to go into hiding. Then he posed the hypothesis we had both been thinking.

"If the members of the cult to which that statue belonged found out it was Forrester who took it, they would certainly attempt to get it back. It is obviously an idol to their god, Bastet, and with the war's end, they would attempt to regroup and continue their worship."

"I still cannot believe Nathaniel Forrester would steal such a thing!"

"We should request permission to go through his papers and journal. He may have had a very legitimate explanation for rescuing this artefact from danger."

I nodded. "That's exactly what Professor Roberts suggested. I advised him to wait a little longer into the mourning period for the Forrester women before questioning them, but this invasion of their home puts a much more urgent light on the matter."

We agreed that we should return to the Forrester house and examine Nathaniel's papers immediately so that we might be better prepared to take appropriate action.

Before we left, Holmes made another suggestion and to fulfill it, I brought along my medical bag. We arrived back at the Forrester's just as Sergeant Wyles was speaking to the constable out front. She looked upon us with curiosity as we exited the cab, but seemed welcoming.

"Gentlemen, I was just about to dismiss the constable back to his normal duties. I intend to stay the night as a precaution and provide a sense of security so the ladies might get some sleep. Is there something else you need?"

Holmes explained our desire to go through the Colonel's papers as they might give us a clue to the culprits and she readily agreed to support our request to the widow.

Nadine Forrester was happy to oblige us, as she was anxious for this incident to be solved and put behind them. She led us to the lumber room and pointed to her husband's trunk on the floor in a back corner, under a canvas tarp.

"I'm not ready to go through his things yet and didn't want it in our room, constantly beckoning to be opened. A lieutenant from his unit retrieved his dress uniform for the burial before we put it away. Otherwise, it hasn't been opened."

Holmes and I carried the trunk to the dining room where we could spread the papers on the table as we went through them. The two Mrs. Forresters went to bed, knowing that they were well-guarded.

The Colonel's journal was easily found, tucked between two stacks of neatly folded clothing. There was also a tin dispatch box filled with papers – some official, others personal. Holmes took the journal while I went through the papers. Sergeant Wyles stood in the doorway where she could keep an eye and an ear out for any disturbance, though it seemed unlikely the burglars would return that night.

It didn't take long for Holmes to find what he was looking for. He had concentrated his search on the latter pages of the journal and found the following entry:

> *13 September, 1918 – 19:30 hours Port Said. B Company spent the day rooting out snipers and rebels in the southern section of the city. Enemy casualties: 6 killed, 4 wounded, 11 captured. No British casualties. One particular building where several were captured appeared to be set up as a cult worship center. It was not Moslem, but some ancient sect. I have requested Egyptologists to translate the hieroglyphics found on the scrolls and the walls. There were no valuables of gold or silver. I have retained an ebony statue of a cat, which I believe to be this cult's ancient goddess. I intend to bring it home to turn over to the British Museum. Meeting with Eygypologists tomorrow at 13:00 hours to discuss the translation of hieroglyphics and ascertain what they know about this cat-goddess.*

It went on with more mundane news, but we had found what we were looking for. "That meeting must be where he got the information he included with the statue," I observed. "He suffered his wounds just four days later and was shipped home."

Holmes nodded. "It also proves his intent to turn it over to the Museum as an ancient artefact, and that he didn't steal it for mercenary reasons."

"Professor Roberts will be happy to hear that," I answered. "He was most anxious to purchase it from me. Now that I know it was meant for the Museum all along, I shall gladly turn it over to him."

Holmes looked at me curiously. "Knowing that you received it as a gift, Roberts didn't ask you to donate it? How much was he willing to pay?"

I named the amount and my friend pursed his lips and squinted his eyes in thought, shaking his head slightly. I presumed he was surprised at the figure. Then Sergeant Wyles, having overheard the conversation asked, "Just what was he willing to pay such a small fortune for?"

Holmes looked at me and said, "Go ahead and show her. I think it would be wise for you to have multiple witnesses of your possession."

I was unclear as to why he made that statement, but I opened up my medical bag, removed the heavy Bastet idol, and placed it on the table for the policewoman to see. She came over from the doorway and bent down to examine the statue.

Straightening back up she said, "It's certainly beautiful, but how can it be worth that much money? I'm sure you could commission a craftsman today to make one just like it for one-tenth the price."

"To paraphrase an old saying," Holmes replied, "'Value is in the eye of the beholder'. When something is new, its price is high. When it's used, its price drops. When it's old it's often considered worthless junk, but when it's *very* old it becomes a valuable antique worth more than its original price. When it's ancient, and a cultural artefact to boot, it becomes priceless."

Wyles just shook her head, then asked, "Why are you carrying it around with you, Doctor?"

Again my friend answered. "That was my suggestion, Sergeant. When we noticed that Watson's address was imprinted on the desk blotter in the parlour, we thought the burglars may have noted it as well and could be planning to strike his house next in their search for the statue."

"How do you know they were looking for the statue?" she asked.

"Process of elimination," he replied. "Since they took none of the valuables here, it implies they were looking for some particular item. The most valuable thing that used to be in the Forrester's possession was the Bastet statue. Also, one set of footprints was of pointed-toed footwear. It is possible that someone from Egypt is attempting to reclaim the statue "

"Do you know who we're talking about, Mr. Holmes?" enquired Wyles.

"Someone who knows that Lt. Colonel Forrester had the statue. It could be a member of his staff, though I find it unlikely that they would turn to burglary. I would be more inclined for it to be members of the cult

319

from whom it was taken. In wartime, there are spies everywhere, and they may have discovered it was he who took possession. Now that the war is over and travel restrictions are more lax, they could have come to England and found where the Forresters live."

"So now you'll turn it over to the Museum?" asked Wyles.

Holmes looked to me and I replied, "I will call Professor Roberts first thing in the morning. I'm sure he'll be ecstatic."

"I'm certain he will be," Holmes commented. "I would like to make a suggestion, however . . . ."

Chapter IX

The next morning, I called the Museum and spoke to Rhys Roberts. I explained that I was willing to sell him the Bastet statue, but my patient load was too heavy for me to leave my practice that morning. I asked him if he could come by at noon when I would have about a half-hour to spare.

He readily agreed and the stage was set. At five-minutes-to-twelve, a ring and a rapid knock came to my door. I opened it to find the Professor and two other gentlemen. I invited them in, saying my last patient of the morning had just left, but they were a couple of minutes early.

"Does that matter?" asked one of his companions impatiently. He was a swarthy young fellow with a trimmed black beard and moustache. The other, a tall, clean-shaven older man with curly black hair, stood by, stoically silent.

I looked at the speaker with a scowl at his rudeness and turned to Roberts. "And who are these gentlemen, Professor?"

"They are guards I hired to ensure the safe transfer from here to the Museum," Roberts replied.

I frowned, but nodded and said, "Very well. If you will come with me, I will explain."

Upon entering the sitting room, Roberts saw the empty shelf and exclaimed excitedly, "The Bastet! Where is it?"

"Patience, dear fellow. Take a seat."

The professor sat in one of the stuffed chairs by the fireplace. Anxiously he perched on the edge waiting for my explanation. His companions chose to stand behind him on either side. I sat at my desk and swiveled my chair around to face them.

"I told you I was to have dinner with Sherlock Holmes last night. However, our plans were interrupted when Scotland Yard advised us that the Forrester home had been burglarized."

A look of confusion and fear seemed to cross Roberts' face. "That's terrible! Are they all right?"

"Yes. Fortunately, they weren't at home. Holmes and I assisted the police in searching for clues, but found little to go on." I couldn't help but notice a quick glance from the swarthy fellow at his companion who remained passively still, giving away nothing.

"However, Holmes is fairly certain that they were after the Bastet, since nothing else was taken. Mrs. Forrester had inadvertently left my address on the blotter when she addressed the label for the package to me. So we rushed back here and found it still in place. Recalling your concern for its safety and the value you had assigned to it, we felt the safest action was for Holmes to take it with him to the Diogenes Club where he is staying while in town."

Roberts looked aghast. "He took it to his club? What made him think it would be safer there?"

"The Diogenes Club is one of the safest buildings in the city. Its founders ensured it so."

"How?" asked the professor.

"I don't know all the details," I said, keeping what I did know to myself. [8] "But Holmes assures me it would be as secure there as in any bank vault. He'll be bringing it by any minute now so that we may complete our transaction."

As the clock was just then striking twelve, the bell for the front door rang. I went and opened it, admitting my long-time companion and two other people, a fashionably dressed woman and a burly, red-haired fellow carrying a camera. They followed me into the sitting room. Professor Roberts, though surprised at the presence of these extra visitors, still minded his manners and stood when the woman entered. I noticed, however, that his guards visibly tensed at the sight of these extra people, especially the cameraman.

The lady took the other stuffed chair while Holmes made introductions. "This is Miss Wyles. She is a reporter for *The Daily Telegraph*, and wants to do a story on the Bastet Cult. This is her photographer, Mr. Olsen. He's here to photograph the transfer of the artefact so it can be published with the story."

Holmes had set a Gladstone bag on my desk and gathered the reporter and the photographer around, whispering something to them. Miss Wyles then turned toward Professor Roberts and said, "Let's get the photograph first. That way Mr. Olsen can have it developed so that it's ready when I return with my story.

"I think the fireplace, will make a nice background. Professor, why don't you stand here? Dr. Watson, if you would stand to his right – that's it. Professor, I presume you have a bank draught to hand over?" Roberts reached into his coat's inner breast pocket and pulled out a check.

"Excellent!" she said. "I think I'd like to get a couple of different shots. First a group photo, and then one of just the two of you. Gentlemen," she said, speaking to Roberts' companions, "why don't you stand behind the professor on either side? Mr. Holmes if you would stand behind Dr. Watson next to them. There, that's fine."

Holmes had removed the Bastet from the bag and handed it to me, to pass along to the professor. I took the heavy object with both hands, my left around its neck and my right under its base.

She turned to her photographer. I noticed he was using an older model camera with a magnesium flashlamp and I commented on the fact. He replied good-naturedly, "Oh, I've been using this for years, Dr. Watson. I know there are some fancier cameras out there now with light bulbs, but this has always served me well. This old dog doesn't need any of those fancy new tricks to do the job."

Miss Wyles then moved to a position just out of the picture on Roberts' side and said, "All right, gentlemen, here we go. Professor, if you would hold out the check, and Doctor, you take hold of it so you both have your hands on it. That's it. Now, Dr. Watson, hold the statue toward the professor, and Mr. Roberts, reach toward it, but don't actually grab hold of it yet. You would have to turn too far and we want to get a good angle of the expression on your face. That's right. All right, Mr. Olsen, you may proceed."

What happened next was a blur. Holmes had told me to be ready to move when he did, but hadn't indicated when that might be. I'm sure he had to improvise based on the presence of these two 'guards'. Olsen triggered the flash powder on his camera and a burst of light went off like a lightning bolt. The Bastet slipped from my hand and fell onto the foot of the younger guard who had flinched from the blinding light, and now fell to the floor in pain from a broken foot where the heavy statue's base had landed on his thin Egyptian shoes. Holmes was on top of him in an instant, his knee into the fellow's kidney and gun to his head. I remembered to pull my gun from my coat pocket and covered both Roberts and the taller guard. Olsen and Wyles stepped forward to add their strength to our numbers. Olsen and Holmes handcuffed the two guards and sat them down on the hearth. Sergeant Wyles pulled out her warrant card and identified herself and Olsen as police officers who were placing Roberts and his cohorts under arrest.

Professor Roberts was aghast. "Why are you arresting me?" he cried. "I've done nothing wrong!"

"Suspicion of conspiracy in a burglary, and suspicion of a conspiracy to defraud the British Museum for starters," the sergeant replied. "We'll let the Crown Prosecutor decide exactly what to charge you with."

"I didn't know they were burglarizing the Forrester home at the same time I was visiting Dr. Watson. I hadn't spoken to them since the day before, when they told me they were looking for stolen antiquities from their country and were willing to pay to get them back. They were particularly interested in the Bastet statue."

"So," Holmes declared, "you're admitting that you were misrepresenting yourself and not acting as Curator of Egyptian Antiquities, but rather a broker for the sale of this statue."

Roberts grimaced but replied, "I never said I wanted it for the Museum. I only asked if the doctor was willing to sell it."

"You can make your case in court," Wyles said. "In the meantime, all of you, march out. There's a police van out front waiting to transport you to Scotland Yard."

The older guard who had remained silent to this point finally spoke out. "What of the Bastet? She is a symbol of our god and must be returned to Egypt!"

"The disposition of the statue will be up to Lord Balfour, the Foreign Secretary," Holmes replied. "As a British protectorate, the Sultanate of Egypt falls under his jurisdiction – but as you can imagine, with peace treaty negotiations underway, he's quite busy at the moment. There is also the issue of the Egyptian Revolution. While you have been over here, Saad Zaghloul and the Wafd Party are pushing for Egyptian Independence and demanding to be recognized at the Paris Peace Talks. It's likely this statue will become a pawn in the negotiations."

"This is intolerable!" cried the Egyptian.

I spoke up at that point and declared, "So is invading a widow's home to burglarize it! If you had gone through proper channels, this whole situation might have been avoided. By your criminal actions, you have brought disgrace upon yourself and your god!"

Holmes made one last statement before Wyles and Olsen marched them out the door: "In the meantime, it was Forrester's wish that it be displayed at the British Museum, so it will reside there for the time being."

As I actually had no patients scheduled for that afternoon, Holmes suggested we take the Bastet to the Museum and then go to Simpson's for lunch to make up for the meal we had to forego the night before. We handed the Bastet over to the Director and explained the situation regarding Roberts, and that the statue's provenance was still in question. Also, we indicated that he might have to return it to Egypt someday. He was shocked at Robert's behaviour, but grateful for the artefact, even if was only to be on display temporarily.

As we enjoyed our aperitifs at Simpson's while awaiting our lunch, Holmes complimented me on my actions in the arrest. "That was an excellent step you took to drop the Bastet on that fellow's foot. It quickly removed him from effective resistance. Well done!"

I set my glass on the table and replied, "Thank you, but I must admit, it wasn't intentional. The brilliance of Olsen's flash surprised me and the statue virtually leapt from my hand like a scared cat. I presume he doubled the amount of flash powder to create that distraction?"

"Yes, that was the instruction I whispered to him. I had taken into account that Roberts might bring someone with him, but I was surprised that both the burglars were there. Tactically they should have only sent one and kept another in reserve for any trouble. Roberts and one cohort could dissuade you, should you balk at the deal. Having both of them there was unnecessary."

I took another sip and pondered all the circumstances surrounding me since the Bastet had arrived in my home. The elimination of the mice, the generous offer from my publisher, the celebration with my family, the music from Holmes's gift, the long-lasting fire, the spilled perfume, and finally the vengeance with which it struck the burglar's foot. I mentioned these to Holmes, who shook his head.

"You are forgetting the chewed-open cereal box. You'll agree that a statue cannot eat, and that it could also not kill the mice we saw. Allow me to hypothesize, Watson: When your maid aired out the upstairs sewing room and left it unattended, a cat came in through the open window. When she closed it up again, the animal was trapped inside. You now have a predator who could have killed the mice, knocked over the statue and the perfume bottle, and chewed open the biscuit box seeking food. The message from Doyle was bound to happen with the war's end, as was the letter from your stepson regarding celebrating Christmas, now that everyone had returned from the hostilities. The long-lasting fire was due to the fact I had picked out the densest logs from your pile. The secrets I shared with you were also a natural occurrence at war's end. Finally, as you held the statue in your left hand, which is your weaker side due to your old war wound, it slipped at the startlement you experienced with the overpowered flash."

"I don't know," I replied. "It all seems too coincidental."

He grinned. "That is because cats are such noble creatures. They inspire us with their beauty, grace, and skills. It's natural for us to admire them, and even for the ancients to worship them. I believe our former client, Samuel Clemens, said it best: *"If man could be crossed with the cat, it would improve man, but it would deteriorate the cat."*" [9]

NOTES

1. The three rifle volley consists of no less than three and no more than seven rifles firing three volleys in memory of the fallen. Typically three fired cartridges are placed into the folded flag prior to presentation to the next of kin. The cartridges signify "duty, honor, and sacrifice".
2. One stone equals fourteen pounds.
3. For an example see "The Curious Case of Charlotte Musgrave" in the *Sherlock Holmes Alphabet of Cases Volume One* and *The MX Book of New Sherlock Holmes Stories – Part VIII – Eliminate the Impossible: 1892-1905.*
4. Per the Granada Television *Sherlock Holmes* series, George was the son of Victor Savage, the victim in the story "The Dying Detective". Notes discovered by the author have concluded that Watson married Adelaide Savage, Victor's widow, in 1902 after they were reunited during *The Case of the Twain Papers* (Baker Street Studios, 2014)
5. From "A Case of Identity".
6. "The Seventh Swann" in *Sherlock Holmes Adventures for the Twelve Days of Christmas* (Baker Street Studios, 2015).
7. Born Lilian Mary Elizabeth Wyles in 1885, Wyles was the remarkably gifted daughter of a Lincolnshire brewer who hoped his daughter would consider a career as a barrister. She served in the First World War as a nurse, and enlisted in the Women's Special Police Patrols on her return in 1918. This was meant as a temporary force in the face of the nationwide manpower shortage, but Wyles proved herself a survivor, escaping the disbandment of the Women Police to become an attested officer of the Criminal Investigations Division.
8. Per Ian Fleming, creator of James Bond, the character '*M*' was named for Mycroft Holmes. In his notes for this story and others, Dr. Watson infers that the Diogenes Club is a front for MI6.
9. See *The Case of the Twain Papers* (Baker Street Studios, 2014).

The Intrigue of the Torn Treaty
by Shane Simmons

The War was won. Not by any great battle or mighty cavalry charge that shattered the enemy lines, but by attrition. The Germans simply couldn't keep up their end any longer. An army does not fight well on an empty stomach. A starving army will not fight at all. Just like that, it was all over. Not with a shout, but a whimper. Snipers on either side took their final shots, spilled some more blood, and added a few extra dead to a total that ran in the millions. And then, at precisely eleven o'clock, on the eleventh day of the eleventh month, the front fell silent. The ceasefire that had been agreed upon held, and nobody else had to die a miserable death in the mud.

The war was won sure enough, but there was a hard fight to be had deciding what the peace would look like.

"Mercy is the prerogative of the victor, and the default position of a wise one," Mycroft Holmes told me seven months later in Paris. "Unless, of course, you plan to salt the earth and leave not a single man, woman, or child alive. We are not as vindictive as that. Even so, the peace treaty we have agreed upon is a punishing one. Such humiliation will not sit well in Germany."

"Well, I suppose they had it coming," was what I said to that.

He sighed deeply, as though he had heard that same sentiment too many times.

"Such is the prevailing opinion of the allied forces. The Germans were not consulted and will have to accept the terms as presented. It is not a formula for lasting peace."

"They started the war," I said.

"Perhaps," Mr. Mycroft wondered aloud. "Or did they get swept up in the tide of madness that rolled in following a single assassination in distant lands? Regardless, the terms for peace being thrust upon them will likely assure they start the next war. May none of us live long enough to see that."

I hadn't spoken to Mycroft Holmes in months. The whole time he had been in Paris, in or around the French Foreign Ministry, never more than a couriered note or local phone call away from the negotiations happening inside. I didn't know what part he played in those debates, but it was important enough for him to have been relocated from his favourite chair in the Diogenes Club and planted in French soil longer than any self-respecting Englishman would ever care to be. I had been stuck in London for the duration, collecting his mail and forwarding the vital bits. The work was undemanding, and the whole stretch of time felt like a vacation. Longing for action, I was pleased to catch the first boat out the moment I received word that Mr. Mycroft wanted me at his side.

"Let us greet my brother," he told me within an hour of my arriving at the hotel he'd been housing himself in.

"He's here?" I asked, looking around as though Sherlock Holmes himself might dramatically burst out of the armoire.

"Fetch him," said Mycroft Holmes. "You'll find him along the Quai d'Orsay, if he has kept to our schedule."

"I'm sure the other Mr. Holmes will be precisely on time," I said.

"We are not young men anymore, Wiggins. Inevitably, we all lose a step. Hopefully that moment will not come before we have seen this war through to its conclusion."

It isn't difficult to spot an Englishman in Paris at the best of times. When one considers the lanky stature and distinct profile of Sherlock Holmes, he may as well have had a neon discharge tube pointed at him, lighting up the banks of the Seine. It's a wonder he got away with so many of his disguises over the years. I easily spotted him from several streets' distance.

Approaching from behind, I was unable to get a single word out before the detective exposed me.

"Wiggins," he said from the riverside bench, not even bothering to turn around to confirm my identity. "I didn't know you were in France, but your presence is most welcome."

"How did you know it was me?" I asked.

"An Englishman in Paris stands out," he said.

"I was thinking just the same thing when I spotted you. But you didn't even see me."

"I heard you coming."

"I said nothing before you greeted me."

"Your shoes squeak," said Mr. Holmes. "Still wearing those old Grensons?"

"I could use a new pair," I admitted. "But many shoes squeak."

"Yours do so in a distinct *C*-sharp," he said, rising and offering his hand.

We shook as old friends might, though I couldn't help but still see him as a boss, and myself as an employee. He was the first man to ever pay me a wage.

"I see Paris has come through relatively intact," he said, as we walked along the river. "Zeppelin raids notwithstanding."

There were still monuments and landmarks cushioned by stacks of sandbags that had yet to be removed. In some areas it felt like the people weren't yet convinced that the bombings had stopped for good.

"Most of them tried their luck over London," I said, recalling the nights of air-raid sirens and terror. "I expect the Germans were holding out hope that one final breakthrough at the front would let them capture Paris intact."

"I can scarcely recall the last time I was in either city," said Mr. Holmes. "Mycroft has certainly kept us busy these last few years. All for the good of the nation, of course. Even now, months since the fighting has ended, I see there remains one more problem for us to resolve."

"Do you know what he has in mind?"

"I will know better when I see him myself. Unless, of course, Mycroft wishes to conceal it. He is the only one who has ever been good at keeping secrets from me."

Mycroft Holmes met us in the lobby of his hotel. A private sitting room had been reserved for us in advance. As such, the two brothers reunited with only an exchange of curt nods. It wasn't until we were alone, sealed together in a lavish room, with a selection of seats and refreshments, did the long-awaited conversation come to life.

"You look even more out of place here than I do," said Sherlock Holmes to his brother. "When was the last time you stepped outside of Britain? It must be years."

"Not as many as I would prefer," replied his sibling.

"I suppose Paris is pleasant enough, though they might have moved the negotiations to the Riviera for the sake of the council."

"The Germans have been pushed out, and France is for the French again," said Mr. Mycroft. "They can have it. I look forward to the wet and gloom of home."

"And yet, for the time being, here you remain."

"Officially, I am not here at all. Unofficially, however, I have been the fly on the wall, the ear to the keyhole. Present and unacknowledged, but on hand for consultations and debriefings between rounds of negotiation. The diplomats represent politicians and political parties, governments and policy. I advocate for Britannia herself, and have been deferred to accordingly, with the papers and transcripts of historical record none the wiser."

"Your advice has not been heeded to your satisfaction," said Sherlock Holmes.

"Wiggins has briefed you, I see."

329

"He has remained loyally discreet and has said nothing," was the response in my defence. "It is your expression, dear brother, that tells the tale. I count no less than six new lines in your face. The sort of creases that appear not through age, but through much frowning and consternation. The content may have been agreed upon, but your disagreement with the specifics is written into your flesh as legibly as the articles within the treaty."

"I have been fixed to this spot since January, with little to show for it," said Mycroft Holmes. "They failed to heed my warnings before the war, and they continue to do so in its wake."

"I clearly recall your advance notice about the unfortunate undertaking in Sarajevo," said Mr. Holmes of his brother's early efforts. "Eleven days. Enough time to save a certain archduke if action had been taken."

"Not that the world needs more heirs apparent to one throne or another," said the elder Holmes, "but the first domino might have never tipped if minimal steps had been taken."

"You knew an assassination was in the works?" I interjected.

"An obvious conclusion once the evidence was considered," said Mycroft Holmes.

"In this case," his brother elaborated, "the evidence of a single leather glove, a chipped snuff box, three tacks, a bottle of expired ointment, and a taxidermied marmot."

"Child's play when it was laid out end-to-end."

"Did you see it coming, too?" I asked the detective of the family.

"I merely discovered the clues," he said. "Their meaning was better divined by Mycroft, who is well attuned to all the moving pieces upon the international stage, be they party factions, social agitators, or anarchist groups."

"The Black Hand has already played their role in starting this last war. Pray their ilk doesn't succeed in rekindling it now that it is done."

A secret military society out of Serbia, such political agitators had busied themselves assassinating a variety of targets who hampered their goals since the turn of the century. Their more notorious royal successes had been a matter of public record for years, but the murders didn't end there, as certain insiders knew well enough.

"The Black Hand has backed many a revolutionary," said Mycroft Holmes. "Young Bosnia and *Narodna Odbrana* are but two groups to have bloodied themselves in the name of their masters. Always young men with grand ideas and the passion to see them through, regardless of how wrongheaded or manipulated they are."

"What good would it do Serbia to push for more war?" I asked.

330

"None whatsoever. Nor will it serve anyone else. Not even The Black Hand."

"Then why?"

"Because I believe The Black Hand, holding the strings of these various radicals, is itself being puppeteered at a higher level still. The ultimate agenda has nothing to do with the well-being of Serbia, nor the world at large. It serves one man alone. And that man is here, in Paris, massaging and moving the treaty negotiations to his own ends."

"You have proof of this?" asked Sherlock Holmes, ever in the mindset of a sleuth.

"None whatsoever," replied his brother. "And yet I feel this man's presence in all that has gone wrong since these talks began. He never signs his work, but there is a lingering aftertaste to every misfortune that suggests his hand in it."

"He sounds like a ghost story," I commented.

"You'll think I am jumping at spirits making things go bump in the night," said Mycroft Holmes with a grim smile.

I can't say I ever heard him sound so unsure of himself, but the younger Holmes didn't hesitate to place his unconditional trust in the intuition of the man he believed dwarfed his own considerable intellect.

"Not at all," said Sherlock Holmes. "I have my own experience with a master manipulator who pulled many a string before I was able to expose his direct involvement. It took many months of hard labour, and much damage was done in the interim, despite my best efforts."

"Your Napoleon of Crime," said Mr. Mycroft.

"Indeed," was all his brother said, but I thought I could detect the smallest of winces at the foul memory. Beyond that, he betrayed nothing.

There was a heavy silence in the room and I could feel the gravity of the matter. Any man who could so rattle Mycroft Holmes was a worthy opponent. And most assuredly a dangerous one.

"This man," continued Sherlock Holmes. "Let us call him your Caesar of Subterfuge. Does he have a name?"

"His aliases are many," said Mr. Mycroft, "though Niccolai Kobelansky is the name best associated with his machinations and most likely to be the original."

The detective didn't prompt him, but instead waited for his brother to further elaborate in his own good time. After a sip of tea to moisten a mouth that had gone dry, he did.

"He is the tainted tincture that has poisoned many moments in the history of this new century, swinging pivotal events towards terrible outcomes. He was likely the one who convinced the Bolsheviks to turn the Romanovs from hostages to murder victims, ending three-hundred years of dynastic rule in a hail of bullets. We know for a fact that he pushed for Japan to begin bombarding the Far East Fleet several hours before their declaration of war was delivered to the Russian government. Only a few years before that, he funded his war chest selling arms to the Chinese Boxers, escalating their rebellion from swords to rifles. There has hardly been a conflict he has failed to swing to his favour, or profit from."

"And here he is now," said Sherlock Holmes, "lurking in the shadows, planting the seeds of the next war in the open grave of the one we have just ended."

"We are on the very eve of showing him our vulnerable underbelly," said Mycroft Holmes. "Dignitaries of the highest order have been arriving all week from lands far and wide. This peace treaty, such as it is, will be signed tomorrow in Versailles. There will be much pomp and circumstance. Photographers and press will abound. Security will be tighter than it has been for any event in recorded history. This is where and when Niccolai Kobelansky shall stick his knife in."

"It does seem an irresistible target," agreed Mr. Holmes.

"It's a royal palace and a national treasure," I said. "With all these mucky-mucks showing up at the same time, you couldn't get a mouse in there without every gendarme in the country putting their boots to it."

"Most certainly not," agreed Mycroft Holmes.

"Which means he has already made his move," said Sherlock Holmes. "Well in advance of the signing."

"We cannot afford to assume otherwise," his brother concurred.

The detective rose from his seat at once, with all the energy of a coiled spring.

"Then I shall leave as soon as I am equipped."

"Anything you need will be provided," vowed Mycroft Holmes.

"What I require then is as follows: A precise duplicate of the treaty, a loaded revolver, a selection of fresh pastries, two train tickets to Versailles, the highest conceivable level of security clearance, Wiggins of course, and complete discretion until the moment of our arrival."

"The exact details of the treaty aren't yet open to the public," Mr. Mycroft cautioned, though he didn't deny a single requested item. "Any draft is considered a secret of the first order."

"Rest assured I have no intention of reading a single word of it," replied his brother.

"It is a dull document that wouldn't pass time on the train well."

"I will be preoccupied with other matters."

"Your shopping list suggests you have a solution in mind."

"Merely a premise. I hope we will arrive sufficiently armed to deal with the problem and prevent catastrophe."

"Then I suppose you need only specify your choice of pastry."

"Croissants will suffice."

"Of course," agreed Mr. Mycroft, as though he understood perfectly. For my part, I didn't understand much of the list – My being on it least of all.

"Let us see if our efforts can guide this war to a successful resolution before the sun rises again. Perhaps then I can return to Sussex in peace."

"Sherlock and his bees!" Mycroft Holmes declared. "They've done well enough for millions of years without your constant administration, Brother. Surely they'll survive this war and the peace yet to come, even if it kills off the rest of us."

We were en route to the train station within the hour. I was put in charge of the pastries, as well as a service revolver which I hid under my coat to avoid alarming the other passengers. The copy of the treaty was delivered by hand from one Holmes to the other.

"It is a perfect match with the one to be signed tomorrow?" said Sherlock Holmes.

"Down to the letter," confirmed Mr. Mycroft. "It is one of three emergency backups should anything untoward happen to the signing copy. They will be burned once the master has been archived with its collection of signatures."

"I cannot guarantee the return of this loaned copy," said Sherlock Holmes. "I can only swear I will see to its destruction myself before anyone else lays eyes upon it."

"I might normally object to those terms," replied his brother. "However, given the level of security I have arranged for you, you are now authorised to act with impunity befitting an international emergency. Your clearance expires in twenty-four hours. Use it wisely."

"At least wisely enough to keep anyone else from knowing there was ever an emergency of international scale," promised the detective.

And then we were off, with a loaded gun in my pocket, fresh pastries cooling in a box, and a stack of papers destined to end one war and potentially start another.

"I'm glad you're here, Mr. Holmes," I said before our train was no more than a hundred yards down the track. "I have no idea what we're heading into, or whether the threat is real or not."

"We must proceed as though it is, Wiggins," he replied, as he began leafing through the pages of the treaty that was due to become official in less than a day. "Failure to do so would be to invite disaster. If this Niccolai Kobelansky is half the threat Mycroft believes him to be, he won't miss the opportunity that stands before him."

"I can hardly wrap my head around such political maneuverings," I confessed. "Even after working for your brother all these years, I try to keep my nose out of it."

"As do I," said Mr. Holmes. "I avoid involving myself in politics, except for the intrigues of politicians that must be swept up after the fact. Blackmail, adulteries, the occasional murder. Our elected officials often seem to be touched by as much crime as the worst of their constituents."

"And yet you have been on call throughout the war."

"There are moments in history of such import that we must all do our duty. Thwarting spies and exposing enemy plots hasn't always presented me with the mental stimulation I crave, but when the stakes are so high, with so many lives on the line, I must set aside my personal preferences for a greater good."

"What about this problem we have on our hands?" I asked. "Is this enough of a poser to get the juices flowing?"

"It presents certain unique challenges," said Mr. Holmes. "Not the least of which is a lack of any evidence whatsoever."

"Maybe you'll turn some up once we get to the palace."

"With good fortune," he replied. "But there is no time for that. I must arrive at a hypothesis now, based on no data at all, if we are to have any chance of catching up with the moves Kobelansky has made in the weeks and months leading up to this day."

"How can you possibly manage that?"

"By asking myself how I would do it. If I were to turn my mind to a great act of evil, how best could I seize this opportunity to harm as many heads of state as possible in one fell swoop and get away with it?"

"Mow them down with a machine gun?" I suggested.

"It would never get past security, and someone would have to pull the trigger and face capture and interrogation."

"A time bomb!"

"I can assure you bombs of any sort are being hunted for most diligently. And a timing device would have to be set too far in advance to count down to a precise moment sometime tomorrow – a moment that may be subject to delays and other unpredictable elements."

"I suppose you could just poison the water supply."

"All well and good until the first person takes a sip and suffers an adverse reaction, likely a member of the serving staff. The whole scheme will be foiled before anyone of importance needs to quench their thirst."

"How about something slower acting in whatever food they're serving?"

"That would involve kitchen staff and more interrogation. Food tampering will be high on security's list of suspect possibilities. No,

334

Wiggins, it must be a multi-tiered attempt. Different elements, each innocuous in and of itself, but deadly once combined. And this combination must be inevitable in nature, correct in its timing, and require no direct involvement from Niccolai Kobelansky, who will want to be safely removed from danger."

"He must have deduced some sequence of events that will involve all those dignitaries directly."

"As have I."

"Is the answer in that treaty?" I asked.

The document lay open on Mr. Holmes's lap. We were in a private compartment, so there was no worry of someone trying to read the contents over his shoulder.

"I believe so," said the detective. "Deeply ingrained, in fact."

He had out one of his magnifying glasses and was studying the page he was on closely. I thought at first he was only reading it with aging eyes that might not have been as sharp as they once were, but then he cast the glass aside in frustration and seemed to give up.

"If only I had the fixings of my old laboratory at Baker Street!" he lamented. "The right compounds and a powerful microscope would be of critical assistance at this moment."

With a sweep of his arm, he tore the treaty page in two. I thought he might crumple and shred the whole document in a fit of rage as the impossibility of our task got the better of him. It seems, however, that he was only procuring a sample for further examination.

Gripping the torn edge between thumb and index finger, Mr. Holmes carefully ran the paper between the two, feeling the texture.

"Is there something about the parchment it's printed on?" I asked.

"Perhaps," was all he would say. And then, to my surprise, he licked the bisected page from bottom to top in a single long stroke. I could hear him clicking his tongue against the back of his teeth, carefully considering the taste like a wine connoisseur might savour an initial sip of a promising vintage.

"Or possibly the ink," he added.

"I can't wait to hear how a box of croissants factors into this investigation," I said.

"The purpose they serve is lunch. A trip to France without partaking of their pastries seems a terrible waste, and I could use a cleansing of the palate after that last study."

The grounds of Versailles were thick with military men of many nationalities. Everyone had a stake in the signing coming off without a hitch. Yet even after fighting side-by-side for four years, there wasn't

335

enough trust between allied nations for them all to not have at least a few of their own uniforms keeping an eye on things. Once we arrived, there was much time wasted on papers and identifications. No less than six telephone calls were made to high-ranking authorities before the security detail was satisfied, we were who we said we were, and granted the necessary permissions to poke about.

Belmont was the name of the sergeant-at-arms who was assigned to give us the tour and open doors that were otherwise under lock-and-key. The whole ordeal only confirmed it was impossible for Niccolai Kobelansky or one of his surrogates to get anywhere near the palace or the dignitaries for the purpose of mischief. If he was indeed plotting something for the event, he would have done it already, long before anyone had a mind to stop him.

"It is Holmes and Watson, is it not?" said Belmont, when he was informed of our credentials.

"It is Holmes and Wiggins today," he was told. "The doctor has retired."

"Are you not retired as well, Monsieur Holmes?"

"Not as much as I should like."

"Your business here must be of great importance then. No one is dead and nothing stolen, I hope."

"It is a routine security check," Mr. Holmes assured him. "We are merely addressing the concerns of a few men in high positions who trust my suspicious mind to spot any holes."

"Then you need only tell me where you wish to begin," said Belmont.

"Show us where the signing itself is to take place," said Mr. Holmes. "It may prove to be our beginning and end."

I had seen picture postcards of the Palace of Versailles before, but to see it in person was so far out of my experience that I could hardly hold it in my mind. Riches had crossed my path before over the course of my duties safeguarding or recovering them, but this was opulence at a level that escaped my wildest imaginings. I came from the gutter. Having a solid roof over my head and a proper bed to sleep in was no longer a novelty, but such simple amenities would never seem so familiar that I could ever take them for granted. Stepping foot upon those grounds, never mind inside the palace itself, felt like I was trespassing – like a condemned sinner squeezing between the bars of the Gates to Heaven. I had to keep telling myself I was in my rights to be there. More than that! It was my duty to intrude upon this realm of the highest of high society, despite coming from the lowest of the low. I was there to preserve it, even if it wouldn't have had me under any other circumstances.

Mr. Holmes seemed less impressed. He didn't see the world in the same terms as I did. To him, it was nothing but problems to solve, no matter if they came from the top or the bottom, so long as he found them interesting.

The gallery we were brought to was a long hall of marble and mirrors, with enough frescos stretched across the vaulted ceiling to fill a dozen museums at once. Towering windows looked out at the gardens behind the palace, with pools and fountains and greens as far as the eye could see.

Looking around with my mouth agape and my jaw hanging off my face, I had to ask, "What do you call this hall with all the mirrors?"

"It is the *Galerie des Glaces*," said our guide. "'The Hall of Mirrors' in English."

I must have looked disappointed.

"The creativity and artistic ingenuity of such monuments rarely extend to the naming of them," Mr. Holmes told me. "Nevertheless, it was here, Wiggins, in this very room, that the German Empire was proclaimed nearly fifty years ago. And it is here it will be ended."

"For good?" I wondered.

"For better or for worse," said Mr. Holmes. "I would suggest worse. The terms are most punitive, and the Germans will not accept such humiliation well. Excluded from the negotiations entirely, their signature will be made with a figurative gun to their head. This treaty may punctuate The War to End All Wars, yet I fear it will not be a period, but rather a comma awaiting an addendum."

"You said you wouldn't read it."

"I may have glanced at it," the detective confessed. "Mycroft was quite right. It is a dull document. How often do terrible things in this world spring from the banality of bureaucrats, I wonder? At any rate, it is our duty today to stop the terrible things that might spring from the violence of a political radical and profiteer."

Belmont permitted us to compare notes in privacy and offered us ample space to conduct our inspection. Mr. Holmes seemed most interested in the long table that had been brought in for the occasion. With so much signing to do, a suitable platform was in order, with matching chairs that would not seem out of place in their palatial setting.

"Fancy," I said of the new additions.

"Down to every detail," said Mr. Holmes, walking around the grand piece of furniture and looking at each station that would seat a signatory come the morning.

Set up in front of every chair was an ink blotter, a bottle of ink, and a fountain pen. The detective took one of the bottles, uncapped it, and sniffed at the contents. He then seized one of the pens and scrutinised the parts. The pens on the table were pristine and specially constructed to order for the occasion, with engravings and seals designating their historic importance. No doubt they were meant to find their way back to each dignitary's country of origin and put on display somewhere to commemorate the event.

I imitated Mr. Holmes's moves, having my own sniff at an ink bottle and rotating one of the fountain pens between my fingers so I could look at it from every angle. It was certainly the finest writing instrument I'd ever seen, befitting the stature of whoever would end up wielding it in a matter of hours.

"Very fancy indeed," I said. "In my Irregular days, I'd have been tempted to nick one for myself. Let a couple of the big men share if they don't keep spares."

"You might find yourself dissatisfied with your prize, Wiggins. Look closely and tell me what is amiss."

Sherlock Holmes was quizzing me to see if my detecting skills were up to snuff. I looked at the pen in my hand again and wondered what I would find lacking if I was one of those big men in charge of armies and nations and lots of money.

"The nib is bronze," I observed.

"So it is."

"I'd figure it should be gold. At least plated."

"And yet it is a mere alloy."

"Well, there's quite a lot of them," I said, looking at the collection, each element precisely placed. "Maybe somebody was trying to save a few francs. The war cost a pretty penny, after all."

"We stand in a palace, Wiggins. This isn't the place for frugality."

"Then they're all bronze for a reason," I said. "Someone must have pulled strings to keep them from going for gold."

"Belmont, a word," said Mr. Holmes, waving over our guide.

Belmont came over at once and put himself at the detective's disposal.

"When were these pens substituted for the originals?"

"Ah, you were told about that, were you?" replied Belmont.

"Not at all," said Mr. Holmes. "This is the first I've heard of it."

Belmont made one of those confused faces I'd seen so many times in the presence of Sherlock Holmes.

"Then how did you . . . ?"

"He just does," was as much as I bothered to explain. Time was short, and there were enough French reprints of Dr. Watson's stories for him to read up on the specifics of deductive reasoning.

"We received the replacements three weeks ago," said Belmont. "Such accoutrements are always being second-guessed on these occasions. Someone important decides they don't care for a certain colour or style, and minor details that were set in stone for months are changed at the last minute."

"Are the original pens still present?"

"They were put back in their cases and stored in an empty chamber."

"Then they must be retrieved and set out in place of these pens at once."

"As I have said, last-minute changes aren't unusual, but I couldn't do that on your orders alone, Monsieur."

"Wiggins, fill the pen in your hand from one of bottles on the table and join us outside," said Mr. Holmes, leading the sergeant out the door to the gardens.

I did as instructed, dipping the nib of the pen in the ink and pulling back the lever on the side of the casing to draw a full supply into the body. Joining Mr. Holmes and Belmont, I found them situated on the vast patio between two enormous pools of water overlooking the rest of the grounds. The gardens only got more elaborate in design and scope the farther you wandered, but closest to the palace the layout remained simple enough to give Mr. Holmes the space he needed to demonstrate whatever he had in mind.

Setting his copy of the treaty on the gravel underfoot, he opened it to a random page and stepped well back from the document. At his prompting I handed over the pen and watched as he carefully adjusted the draw lever until enough ink was expelled to gather at the tip – a single drop that dangled precariously but lacked enough volume to fall of its own accord.

With a flick of his wrist, Mr. Holmes flung the excess ink towards the pages of the treaty lying several paces away. The liquid broke apart in midair into multiple droplets, but enough of them reached the document to spatter it with a disfiguring line of pinpoint marks. At once, the pages erupted into violent flames with an audible pop as the fire hungrily consumed fuel and oxygen alike. The bonfire burned hot and fast, and the entire document was reduced to embers in moments. Ash came free in the slight breeze and languidly circled the devastation, caught in the currents that blew between the raised sides of the bracketing pools.

Belmont and I stared blankly at the scorched spot where the treaty had once rested. We had both withdrawn from the sudden conflagration, but now stepped forward to better appreciate the shocking results.

"And now?" asked Mr. Holmes of our liaison.

"I shall arrange the substitutes immediately," Belmont dutifully reported, turning back towards the palace to see about it.

"The ink as well, if you please," Mr. Holmes called after him.

"Of course," agreed Belmont, bowing his head.

"Not a word of this to anyone," he was cautioned. "The signing tomorrow must go off without delay. I will personally report this development to those awaiting word."

Belmont had his orders and was on his way to fulfill them. Alone again, Mr. Holmes explained what I had just witnessed.

"Two chemical compounds, separately harmless, but highly volatile when they come into contact. All that is required is for a pen to introduce one ink to the other."

"There was ample blank space to sign," I said. "Surely there was no guarantee the inks would mix."

"Have you ever seen the signature of a head of state? Great swooping strokes and no end of flourishes! They would call it confident, bold. I might suggest narcissistic. Inevitably someone would cross a line, mingle the chemicals, and ignite page and pen alike."

"So Kobelansky meant to set fire to a few diplomats and burn the treaty in the process," I said.

"Far worse than that," said Mr. Holmes, handing me back the pen and offering his glass. "Observe the casing."

I looked at it as closely as I could. Once my eyes adjusted to the magnification, I detected a checkered pattern, slight but distinct. It was too bland to be a decorative design, and too hard to spot to be an intentional flourish. It had to be a practical feature of the casing construction itself.

"Funny that," I said. "Those big squares aren't for show. They look built in."

"Does it put you in mind of anything in particular?"

"It isn't so plump, and maybe I just have war on the brain after the last four years, but I was thinking I've seen grenades that look quite like it."

"A pattern scored into the casing to better allow it to break apart and send deadly shrapnel everywhere. Each fragment made of an additional explosive material, I expect."

"It's been coated to make the surface feel smooth, but I reckon you're right," I said, running my finger across the length of it and feeling not the slightest irregularity.

"Once ignited, a chain reaction would follow," said Mr. Holmes. "Not like a single bomb going off, but more akin to individual sticks of dynamite, each acting as a fuse to the next. So many powerful men with their own fountain pen close at hand, and all of them brimming with a compound awaiting the slightest provocation. The results would be cataclysmic."

I tucked the pen away for safekeeping, hoping none of the explosive residue had come off on my fingers.

"Will it be safe if the signing copy was printed the same way?"

"Marked with regular India ink, the lone accelerant will be quite inert. As for the rigged pens, they must be boxed up and removed from the premises at once. A bomb squad can see to their destruction in more controlled circumstances."

"You said yourself you had little to go on. How could you have known what Niccolai Kobelansky was planning?"

"Chemistry has always been a fascination of mine," said Mr. Holmes. "So much of the destruction we have seen in these recent years can be boiled down to a series of chemical reactions. Wartime innovations are primarily about creating bigger and better explosions. As a dealer of arms and devastation, I expect Kobelansky has a similar outlook, and would be likeminded when considering how best to spoil a signing ceremony. I only had to put myself in his place and imagine the inevitable moment of interaction between elements. As for the precise chemicals involved, there are at least a dozen possibilities, and I shall be keen to test samples for myself, though the preference to conduct the reaction through a bronze nib as opposed to gold is suggestive."

It sounded like a puzzle that could keep Mr. Holmes occupied for the coming weeks, if only to satisfy his curiosity after the fact. For the moment, however, disaster had been averted.

"I'll never know how you can deduce so much from so little," I said.

Mr. Holmes waved away the suggestion like it was an irritant. He wasn't cross with me so much as frustrated by shortcomings of his own I couldn't appreciate.

"This was no great feat of deduction," he fumed. "I guessed! I set my mind to criminality and this is what I arrived at. I despise guesses and prefer to act on certainty, but when time is short, it is the last resort of the desperate."

"I'll take an educated guess from Sherlock Holmes before anyone else's certainty," I told him, and my faith seemed to lighten his mood somewhat.

"Come, Wiggins," he said, resting a hand upon my shoulder, "there is still much to do."

"What about your copy of the treaty?" I asked of the pile of ash resting atop a blackened mark on light stone base.

"I think a dustpan and broom will sufficiently keep its secrets now. I'm afraid we have a far greater concern on our hands."

Only then did I realise what he was referring to.

"Niccolai Kobelansky? He's here?"

"No," said Mr. Holmes, pointing at the thousands of acres of woodland and gardens that lay behind the palace. "He's there."

"You sure?" I asked, as though Sherlock Holmes was relying on another wild guess.

"How could he resist watching his handiwork blow the back out of Versailles and kill so many of his enemies who would make peace and cut into his profits? The man thrives on chaos, and there is a veritable forest of meticulously manicured shrubbery to lose himself in. He need only pick a vantage point from which to watch the show with a pair of field glasses. No number of guards could possibly cover gardens this vast. He is out there, somewhere. I can feel his presence now, as assuredly as Mycroft did. He could never walk away from his trap after spending so long setting it. He must see it sprung with his own eyes. That is how we catch him."

The open spaces of lawns and fountains were mostly contained within a wide strip that ran down the centre of the gardens, but they were surrounded by woods. Not a forest of natural growth, but a very orderly one, with full grown trees, generations old, evenly spaced and so very tidy. The planting pattern made it easier to see through the rows of trunks and spot things that might otherwise be obscured by a regular thicket.

The grounds seemed endless, but with so many open spaces and lines of visibility, I had hope that we might find the man we were looking for in the outer limits of the royal playground, far from guards and security patrols. That hope faded with the afternoon. We had already been losing the light when Mr. Holmes incinerated his copy of the treaty. Now night was falling fast, and the shadows were multiplying Niccolai Kobelansky's potential hiding places by the minute.

Sherlock Holmes stuck to it, stalking him like a bloodhound, following tracks I couldn't see, and finding hints of footsteps in the grass I would have overlooked even if you pointed my nose right at them. Some of the trails seemed promising, only to taper off to nothing or become too muddled with other recent footsteps to suggest which lead was our best bet. Any of them could have belonged to some innocent gardener or arborist rather than the villain we were hunting, but Mr. Holmes persisted, inexhaustible and resolute in his belief that Kobelansky was close. I, however, was losing confidence.

"We'll never find him at this rate," I complained after we had been at it for three solid hours with no firm direction. The dark of night was upon us, and without lanterns to show the way, the race was lost.

"I'm afraid he has found us," said Mr. Holmes, rising from the last set of tracks he had been fixed upon.

As he stood straight, he continued to lift his arms, elevating his hands to signal surrender. I looked over my shoulder, wondering what Mr. Holmes had perceived that I had missed. Several paces behind us, there was a man standing with a pistol trained at our backs. It could only be one person.

"Eyes forward and hands up," he told me.

The gun barrel was pressed into my back as Niccolai Kobelansky pawed through my coat and came away with the revolver I had been armed with for just such an occasion. With my only weapon in his charge, we were at his mercy. Mr. Holmes was given similar rough treatment, but the only thing of interest Kobelansky found was the torn page of the treaty that had been stuffed in his pocket since the train ride.

He ordered us to turn around and demanded, "What is this?"

The paragraphs on the page, truncated by the tear, weren't immediately obvious in the dark.

"It is evidence," said Mr. Holmes.

"To convict me?" Kobelansky laughed in our faces.

"To disappoint you. It is evidence your scheme with the exploding fountain pens has been discovered and thwarted. Peace will be made tomorrow, despite your best efforts."

News of his months-long plan ending just short of the goal inspired no more than a momentary sneer from Kobelansky. The game he played was a long one, and a single missed turn had no impact on the many other moves he had planned upon the board.

"Peace is never made," he said. "It is momentarily tolerated. The men who sign that worthless document will look for any excuse to be at each other's throats before the ink dries. Even now the White Russians wage civil war against the Red Army. How simple would it be for me to tip other nations into direct conflict with the Bolsheviks? If I am denied one war now, I will arrange for another tomorrow – one that might occupy the attention of the Holmes brothers even longer than this last."

"I see no introductions need be made, Mr. Kobelansky. If that is your real name."

"Real enough, Mr. Holmes," said the man with the gun directed at us. "My aliases are so many, one loses track. I know of you, your brother, and this fool you both employ as fits your needs."

I couldn't bite my tongue at the insult.

"You should thank us for stopping you," I said. "It's seven years bad luck if you break a mirror. You blow up the Hall of Mirrors and that's a run of bad luck that will last you to the end of the century, and a few more past that."

"Isn't it entirely appropriate?" he asked me. "Imagine the arrogance of signing that abomination in the Hall of Mirrors. I can't fathom how a single one of them is so shameless as to be able to look at himself in a mirror, let alone at an entire hall of them, built by the excess of monarchy with wealth stolen from peasants. The entire allegory makes my stomach churn."

"As your cynicism does mine," said Mr. Holmes.

Kobelansky could only scoff at us.

"Such a lecture from an old detective who never served on any police force, and a would-be soldier who never spent a day in uniform," he said.

He raised his pistol as he turned towards me, and I figured who he meant the first round for.

"What did you expect to accomplish out here?" he wondered. "Did you think you might capture me? Shoot me? Kill me? You who sat out the greatest war in history running errands for the Holmes brothers?"

I had friends who died in that bloody war. Good men. Young men. If I'd had my way, I would have been in the trenches right next to them, but fate and Mycroft Holmes himself had other plans for me. Other uses. Had my contribution to the war effort been any more substantial working behind the lines than it might have been at the front with a rifle in my hand? It was impossible to say, but I had passed through the Great War having never fired a shot, nor killed a single enemy. And here I was, disarmed once more, with no means to strike out against the enemy before me.

Well, perhaps one.

Kobelansky had been so pleased to disarm me of the revolver, he had missed something in one of my other pockets. As I slowly lowered my hands, acting like I was resigned to my fate, I inched closer to the contents of my breast pocket. It was where I had stowed the trick fountain pen Mr. Holmes had entrusted to me hours earlier. All but forgotten, I remembered it now, and employed it as best I could.

I was no circus knife-thrower, and what I was throwing was no knife. It wasn't properly balanced to be an effective projectile, but it was sharp enough and I was angry enough, and that fit the bill. With a forceful fling, I threw the pen at Kobelansky as hard as I could in the same moment that I snatched it out of my pocket. It was pure chance that it struck him tip first, imbedding itself in the page he was still holding and pinning it to his chest. Between the layers of paper and clothing, it barely managed to break his skin, or cause him any significant injury, but it caught him by surprise.

I wish I could say it was a brilliant tactic on my part, but I was only thinking I might cause the bastard some small pain before he executed me on the spot. What I hadn't anticipated in the moment was that the pen penetrating him would leak some of its chemical compound upon impact. Although the nib had imbedded itself in a blank space upon the page, the resulting trickle of ink slowly ran down towards the print that had been designed to react with it.

Mr. Holmes knew at once what was about to happen and tackled me to the ground, seeking cover behind the nearest tree. The last I saw of Kobelansky was him staring down at the point of impact with a look of dismay before the page ignited. It burned no more than a couple of seconds before the explosive pen performed as it was designed to and burst with enough force to separate the arms dealer from his black soul, and most of his limbs from his body. When we dared look up again, his feet were still planted on the spot he'd been standing, but the rest of him was to be found elsewhere, strewn about the woods in gruesome disarray.

"Quick thinking and a quick hand, with unerring accuracy," said Mr. Holmes, helping me up. "Wiggins, we may have done a grave disservice to the nation by keeping you off the lines."

"All skill and no luck at all," I said with a wink. "Though I suppose we've failed our mission. Kobelansky and his plan may have been taken care of, but this will surely disrupt the signing tomorrow."

Mr. Holmes was making calculations in his head as he looked back towards Versailles and the men stationed there overnight. We had come far, and it was an awfully long way off.

"It was a sizeable bang," he concluded, "but one muted by the trees, and too far distant to be heard back at the palace. It seems Kobelansky may have been dealt with subtly enough to avoid disrupting tomorrow's festivities. If we can keep this incident from becoming general knowledge for another day or so, the vital moment in history may yet pass without disruption."

"What if some groundkeeper finds him like this?" I wondered, looking about. "Or worse, what if one of those heads of state decides to have a nice stroll in the gardens and trips over a bit of him?"

"Steps will have to be taken to prevent that. Given the amount of care land such as this requires, there must be a least one tool shed in close proximity. See if you can locate a shovel and torch so that we may, at least temporarily, sweep Niccolai Kobelansky's nefarious schemes under the rug. Or beneath the grass, as it so happens."

Heroics can be a dirty business, as I was to discover over the course of the rest of the evening. I insisted on taking care of the cleanup myself. Sherlock Holmes was better dispatched elsewhere, confirming that the trap laid by Kobelansky had been dismantled and that everyone in the chain of command who was on a need-to-know basis was in the know. I was done with the unsavoury business by first light. Once I returned the gardening tools I had liberated to their shed, I took the opportunity to rest for a moment, well removed from the hive of activity that was building up around the palace.

Sleep must have overcome me. When I was discovered and awakened with a jolt, it was the afternoon sun that streamed into the hut to blind me. My eyes came into focus as a large figure stepped into the open doorway, casting a long shadow.

"Sir!" I said, leaping to my feet.

Mycroft Holmes looked me up and down. Filthy from my duties, soiled head to toe, I wasn't presentable in polite company, let alone at a palace.

"Making mud pies, Wiggins?" he asked.

"Cleaning up a mess, sir."

"It looks like you've gotten your hands dirty in the process," he concluded, once he'd made enough deductions from my appearance to have figured out exactly what I must have been up to.

"Haven't we all," I said.

I saw his lips tighten in a moment of reflection before he issued his orders.

"Wash up. There are sandwiches and tea. We'll see if the French, for all their cuisine, can get that much right."

"The treaty – " I began.

"Signed and sealed without incident."

"So the war is truly over at last."

"As the historians will claim, for however long that stands," said Mr. Mycroft. "With luck, our work here will not even merit a footnote."

"And Niccolai Kobelansky?" I asked, stepping outside into a glorious summer day.

"I have no recollection of any such man. Do you?"

"Never heard of him," I confirmed, and that seemed to satisfy Mycroft Holmes.

In that moment, it came to pass that one of the most dangerous men in the world – a man who had made so much history – was erased from history entirely. It made me wonder how many secrets were kept out of the history books by silent editors who got to decide what we were all better off not knowing.

Enough to double the size of every volume, I expect.

The Adventure of the Surprises

by Dan Rowley

"Obviously, this was supposed to have been a surprise."

"Sherlock, I tried my best to dissuade Watson, but he was determined to try."

I sighed and smiled at the Holmes brothers. "Your brother did warn me, and I had scant hope we could surprise you. But I know you do not care for a fuss, so I determined on this course of action."

"I appreciate the thought, Watson, but really – a telegram that you required my assistance with a story about the Garrideb matter, and that your war wound was bothering you and you would appreciate my presence here in London to avoid having to travel to the Sussex Downs – the conclusion was obvious. You rarely ask my assistance for your tales, and indeed did not do so for your most recent effort, which you so colorfully entitled 'The Adventure of the Sussex Vampire'. And, despite the recent snowfall, the temperature on average has been approximately ten degrees above the coldness that typically aggravates your wound. I was suspicious already, but sent a message to Mycroft to see if he could have dinner with me. His evasive reply was uncharacteristic. Add to all that you suggested a private room at Simpson's as a venue in the month of my seventieth birthday, and it was manifest you were planning a surprise party."

"You came nonetheless, for which I am mightily pleased. Shall we go into the room to see the other guests?" Sherlock Holmes, his brother Mycroft, and I proceeded down the oak-paneled hallway to the private room I had arranged. The Holmes brothers could not have presented a more striking physical contrast. Where my friend retained his slim, angular features, his brother seemed stouter than even. Both, however, had similar facial features, even if those of Mycroft were somewhat softened. And the two pairs of eyes were searching, quickly taking in everything.

Inside the private room, there was a circular table with five place settings of the finest china, crystal, and silver. The hearty fire in the corner warmed the room and cheerily reflected off the gleaming wall panels. The other two guests had already helped themselves to claret from the decanter on the sideboard, and quickly rose when we entered.

347

"Mister Holmes, congratulations. I was so pleased when Doctor Watson asked me to attend. And former Inspector Lestrade asked me to convey his regrets. He is not as fortunate as am I with his health."

"Gregson, thank you for coming. Please assure Lestrade that I understand his predicament. I will enjoy reliving some of our old cases during the course of the evening. And is that Wiggins I spy behind you, looking prosperous and fit? I suspect your days in the streets are long past."

"Thanks to you, Mister Holmes. I'm now chief clerk at a brokerage house in the City. And may I echo the congratulations."

I had thought long and hard about the composition of this gathering. I knew Sherlock Holmes would not want too many in attendance. His brother was an obvious choice. Although at times he been rather hard on former Inspector Tobias Gregson, whose once fair hair was now white with age, Holmes did have somewhat of a soft spot for him. At one point, Holmes told me that Gregson was the smartest of the Scotland Yarders, although he was too conventional for Holmes's taste. He and Wiggins, the former head of the crew of street urchins Holmes had called the Baker Street Irregulars, had both been involved in the first story I published about my friend. It was not widely known that Holmes had paid for Wiggins' education and commenced him on the career that had now brought him to the solid middle class, a shining example of the opportunities that our Empire afforded those willing to apply themselves.

After some further pleasantries, we assumed our places at the table. A staff of tuxedoed waiters with starched white aprons served us an excellent repast of roast beef, Yorkshire pudding, winter vegetables, and broiled potatoes *au jus*, finished off with *crepes flambé*. Once sated, we gathered around the fire for brandy and cigars. I felt this was the right moment.

"Holmes, I trust you will not mind that we pooled our resources to acquire a small token of our esteem."

"Unnecessary, Watson. The companionship of the evening has been more that satisfactory acknowledgment that I am now seventy."

"Thank you for that. Perhaps this will remind you of the evening whenever you peruse it." I went over to the sideboard, opened a drawer, and extracted an aging pamphlet, which I brought over to Holmes. "We hope you enjoy this as much as I enjoyed finding it."

Holmes examined the title page. "Quite interesting. Robert Huish's *A Treatise on the Nature, Economy, and Practical Management of Bees*. I know of the book published in 1815 by that name, but I am not sure I was aware it ever came out in pamphlet form."

"Yes. As you can see, it was published in that form in 1813 in London by Samuel Barton, Clay, and Smith. I have here the papers relating to the provenance of the pamphlet. Clay eventually formed his own publishing firm, and his son made a gift of the pamphlet to a friend. The papers trace all that down to the dealer from whom we obtained it."

"Excellent! I shall cherish it as a true gift of friendship."

We discoursed for some time and then decided to take our leave of one another. Holmes and I made arrangements to meet for lunch at a small French bistro near where he was lodging for the night.

My friend was already waiting for me when I arrived at the bistro. We ordered a light meal of consommé, roasted squab, watercress salad, and a white Bordeaux. When the waiter departed, Holmes reached into his overcoat, pulled out the pamphlet, and placed it on the table. "Watson, I did not wish to disrupt the festivities last evening, but this pamphlet is a forgery."

"What! How? Why – ?"

"As you may recall, I have made a study of printing as relates to the criminal underworld. I have in mind a monograph, but there are at least several *indicia* here of forgery. First, the font used is French Ionic, which didn't come into use until 1870. Second, I believe a proper scientific analysis would show that the paper consists of wood pulp rather than rag, which entered commercial use in late 1850's. Third, I held the paper up to the light in my room, and that revealed a watermark of the so called light-and-shade variety, which was invented in 1848 by W. H. Smith. The pamphlet also is in remarkably pristine condition for something allegedly produced over a century ago."

The look of dejection must have been manifest on my countenance, for Holmes continued before I could say anything. "Watson, I believe we have an opportunity for another adventure, perhaps even another of your stories. Let us examine the papers related to provenance and see if we cannot determine who the forger is."

I took the papers from his hand. Although I had previously only skimmed them, I now intently scrutinized them. "It says here that the pamphlet was initially a gift by the author to his publisher, Clay. His son, also a publisher, must have inherited it, because he in turn made a gift of it to his acquaintance, William Worthington. Then in 1880, Worthington's estate sold it."

"Quite right. Let us pause there. One of the documents in the provenance packet is an inventory of Worthington's estate, signed by the executor. The inventory lists the pamphlet, along with a number of other rare books and manuscripts. There is also letter attached to the inventory signed by a 'Richard Sampson', stating that the pamphlet was a gift from Clay to Worthington. Sampson appears to have received this information from Worthington."

"Here it is. The executor's name is Samuel Edgeworth, Esquire."

"Correct. I consulted a directory at my hotel this morning and learned that there is a solicitor by that name with chambers near the Inns of Court."

"Surely Edgeworth cannot still be practicing law. That sale was almost forty four years ago."

"You may be correct, but I suggest we start our search there."

We settled the bill, went outside, and hailed a cab. We soon were passing Staple Inn with its picturesque black-and-white timbered frontage, punctuated with oddly placed gables and lattice windows. We soon were on Gray's Inn Road, and stopped before a red-brick building that lodged a number of solicitors. Holmes paid our driver and then proceeded to inspect the brass plaque affixed next to the oaken entrance door.

"Here we are, Watson. Edgeworth is on the third floor." He led the way through the door and up the worn staircase. I must admit I became a bit winded by the climb, but Holmes, despite his age, went up them with ease and no effect on his breathing or facial colouration. On the third floor, another brass plaque announced that we had found Edgeworth. We entered and were met by a slight man in his thirties, who must have been a clerk. When my friend explained that Sherlock Holmes and Doctor Watson were here to see Mister Edgeworth, the young man couldn't keep the astonishment from his face. "Do, do, do you m-m-m-mean you're . . . ?"

"Yes, yes. That Holmes and Watson. Please convey our presence to your employer." The young man rushed off, and Holmes gave me a baleful glance. "You and your stories, Watson. I cannot understand their popularity."

Before I could defend myself, the clerk returned and motioned us down a hallway. At the end, we entered an oak-paneled room lined with bookcases filled to overflowing with legal tomes and papers. A portly man in his mid-sixties rose from behind the massive desk, his bald head and the glasses perched on his nose both gleamed from the fire going in the fireplace near the desk. "It is quite an honor to meet both of you. Doctor, I recently read your vampire tale and quite enjoyed it. How may I be of assistance?"

Holmes, as was his custom, didn't acknowledge my literary efforts, but rather went straight to the point of our visit. "We wanted to ask a few questions about the provenance of one of the items from the estate of William Worthington, which was probated in 1880. By your age, I assume you were not the executor."

"No, indeed. That was my father. At the time I was training for the bar here in his chambers and at Gray's Inn. I have a vague recollection of that case, because my father mentioned to me that Worthington was an avid collector. As a result, my father had to ensure adequate documentation of the provenance of the various items to maximize their sale value, which of course as executor he was obliged to increase if he could."

"We are interested in particular pamphlet related to beekeeping. Might you have any records related to the estate?"

Edgeworth chuckled. "I am sure we do. My father was extremely meticulous. Allow me to instruct my clerk to retrieve the relevant file. Might I offer you some refreshments while we wait?"

We politely declined. He bustled from the room and shortly returned. Then he and Holmes exchanged views on proper ways to enjoy retirement after Edgeworth indicated his wish to do so in the near future. Soon, there was a timid knock on the door, and the young clerk who had met us entered with a file. He kept glancing at my friend with an awe-struck look, placed the file on Edgeworth's desk, mumbled something, and scurried from the room.

Edgeworth opened the file and began to search through its contents. He smiled and extracted a folder. "I knew I could count on father. He has a separate folder on the books, pamphlets, and manuscripts in Worthington's collection. Please have a look at it."

Sherlock Holmes took the folder and began to intently study the contents. When he was done, he closed it and looked up at Edgeworth. "It appears from this that most of the cataloguing was done by Richard Sampson, who I take it was Worthington's personal secretary. Do you know how we might contact him?"

"He was one of our clients. Unfortunately, he passed away in the influenza epidemic after the war. I was his executor, and I don't recall anything in the estate relating to Worthington's estate."

"That is unfortunate. What is your impression of Worthington and Sampson."

"Both of them were solid, upright men. They were devout Anglicans, and gave freely to many charitable institutions."

"I noticed also in the file that a Jonathan Baylor sorted through some of the relevant estate materials."

"Ah, yes, I had forgotten about him. I believe he sold some items to Worthington, and my father asked him to examine those items. Baylor has actually subsequently become quite famous in rare book circles. Perhaps you have heard of him."

"The name sounds familiar. I notice you have a copy of Black's updated version of *Who's Who*. Might I consult it?" My friend's keen eyes obviously had been scrutinizing the room while he and Edgeworth were chatting. His ability to perform multiple tasks simultaneously was only one of the amazing facets of his powerful brain.

"Certainly. Please be my guest."

Holmes rose from his chair, went over to the bookcase, pulled out the volume, and paged through it to the entry on Baylor. "Here it is." After a moment, he handed to me and I read:

> *Baylor, Jonathan Wesley (b. 19 July, 1859, Gravesend).*
> *Matriculated City of London School. Oxon, M.A. (hon.). Hon.*
> *Fellow, Worcester College. Member, Consultative Committee*
> *of the Friends of the Bodleian. Pres. Bibliographical Society,*
> *1922- .*

"Quite a resume. There is more about his marriages, business interests, political activities, and so forth, but that is the relevant portion for our purposes. Perhaps we shall pay him a visit. Do you have a *City Directory*?"

"Of course. Please ask my clerk on the way out. Is there anything else I can do for you?"

"One last question: The records indicate that the estate sold the pamphlet to a certain Richard Grant. Do you know anything about him?"

"I am afraid not. Is that all?"

"Yes. You have been very accommodating. We will leave you to your work."

We shook hands, and, thankfully, Holmes was out the door when Edgeworth asked if he would appear in one of my stories. I replied that it was too soon to tell if this would merit that treatment, but assured him that, if it did, he certainly would be featured. When I returned to the main entrance, Holmes was consulting the directory, while the clerk was staring intently at him. My friend motioned that he was ready to depart, so we went down the stairway, found a cab, and proceeded to Baylor's office, which was in the City. Holmes was deep in thought, so I refrained from expressing my puzzlement as to the motive for the forgery. When we pulled up at the address, Holmes broke his reverie, paid the driver, and led the way to our destination, which was a formidable granite building with little decoration. In the lobby, there was a board with office numbers. Fortunately, the building had a lift, as the office was on the top floor.

We entered the outer room of the office, in which sat a young woman working efficiently on a typewriter. The war had changed so much, and I still wasn't quite accustomed to such a sight. Holmes explained our business, and the woman left and then returned to inform us Baylor would see us. She opened a door off to the side, and we went into a large corner room furnished with mahogany and Oriental carpets. Several stands punctuated the room with open manuscripts and books on them. A thin, wizened man wearing an old-fashioned wing collar and cravat came over to meet us. After introductions, he indicated we should take chairs around a circular table in the center of the room. We again declined tea, and Holmes began.

"Thank you for taking the time to see us."

"My pleasure. It isn't often one has the opportunity to meet a famous detective. How may I be of assistance?"

"We shall not be here long, I'm sure. Doctor Watson has run across an old pamphlet and, knowing your vast expertise, we thought we might explore a bit of its history with you. We wanted to ask some questions about William Worthington. Do you remember him?"

"Indeed, I do. He was one of the very first people to whom I sold a few items."

"You must have been quite young back then."

"I was. I actually began collecting when I was a schoolboy. I would take my pocket money and scour the barrows in Farringdon Road. When I was fourteen, I began as a clerk at H. Rubeck and Company, a dealer in essential oils. I quickly became a salesman, and in that capacity met several of the firm's wealthy customers, and Worthington was one. We learned of our mutual interest in book collecting, and I began to act as his agent in locating books he was desirous of owning. I performed a similar service for others – all of course disclosed to my superiors at the firm."

"Do you recall what you obtained for Worthington?"

"Let me see, I think it was a few pieces of eighteenth-century poetry and drama, which was particular interest of mine back then. I hadn't been doing it for very long, perhaps a year or two, before he passed away."

"Yes. His estate was finalized in 1880. You would have been in your early twenties."

"I would have been twenty-one at that time."

"And you assisted the estate in establishing provenance of the collection."

"Yes, the items that I had sold to him. The rest was handled by his secretary, whose name I cannot recall. You might want to talk to him."

"He has passed away, but there is a letter in the estate files that states the pamphlet in which we are interested was a gift to Worthington by the son of the publisher, Clay."

"I know of the Clay publishing firm, a very reputable concern. I didn't know Worthington was acquainted with them, but that isn't surprising. He had many connections in the book trade due to his collecting activities."

"The pamphlet in which we are interested was sold by the Worthington estate to Richard Grant. Do you know him?"

"Not personally. He was a lesser-known author of historical romances and some bits of maudlin poetry. He must have had some interest in collecting as well."

"You said 'was'."

"I think he passed on, but I am not positive."

"I have nothing further. Watson – as an author, do you have any questions?"

"I would be interested to hear how remunerative your collecting activities have been. I am always fascinated by how people make a living from the literary side of life. It is something my literary agent and I frequently discuss."

Baylor smiled. "I must confess I made my money through commerce. I rose to become the lead salesman at Rubeck. Then, in 1906, I cofounded my own essential oils company. But I have been fortunate to act as agent for several collectors, such as the American millionaire John Henry Wrenn, and some other British collectors and minor authors."

"Very interesting. Holmes, I think we may depart. Thank you for your time." Holmes had risen and started for the door. Seeing Baylor's startled expression, I indicated this was normal behavior for him and rushed to catch up with him. Once in the cab, Holmes pulled out the provenance papers that had accompanied his present. "Well, Watson, I will confirm Grant is indeed dead, so that leaves only Coddington, the collector who bought the pamphlet from Grant, and Benjamin James, the dealer from whom you acquired it. I suggest we commence with them in the morning, as I would like to return to my hotel and smoke a bit to mull this over."

We parted at the Savoy, where he was staying, and I returned to my residence. The next morning, we met as arranged in front of Coddington's home at eleven o'clock. Holmes was waiting outside for me. "Watson, Grant is indeed dead. I sent messages to Coddington and James, and they both replied that they would be glad to meet with us. So let us begin, my friend."

We rang the bell at the Mayfair townhouse, which was of Palladian design with red brick, white cornices, balustrades, and columns. The door was answered by a stately butler who told us Coddington was waiting for us in his study at the back of the ground floor. He led us to yet another richly furnished room with heavily polished wood and brass, and the inevitable bookcases that I was coming to associate with this species of

354

collector. Here, however, there were many empty shelves. Their owner, a slight man with sharp features, reddish hair with specks of grey, and a luxurious mustache was waiting by the door. He welcomed us and we took our seats, two chairs flanking a sofa on which he sat.

"Your note indicated you wanted to talk about an item in my collection. Which one?"

"The pamphlet *A Treatise on the Nature, Economy, and Practical Management of Bees* by Huish."

"It is my misfortune that I no longer own it. Between the inflationary situation created by the war and these infernal taxes imposed by Lloyd George and his cohort, I have found myself in somewhat straitened circumstances."

"Yes, we are aware of your sale of the pamphlet. Might we go back though to when you first purchased it. Can you give us some detail about that?"

"Just a moment, I still have my files." He went over to a large oaken cabinet in the corner of the room and began rummaging about in it. "There we are. Let me see . . . . Yes, I purchased it from Richard Grant in 1903. He was a rather minor author who had fallen on hard times and was likewise forced to sell. My notes say that he went to a dealer by the name of Bashor, with whom I was acquainted. Bashor called on me, told me of several items held by Grant that might interest me, and so I met with Grant. He showed me the materials, and I offered him one-hundred pounds for the lot. Must admit that was a bit low, but the Empire wasn't built on sentimentality."

"So you met directly with Grant. No one else was involved or inspected the documents?"

"Did it all by myself. The notes indicate that Bashor hadn't looked at the documents and offered to verify them – for a fee, of course. Told him I didn't intend on paying any fee."

"Would you mind looking at this letter, which was included in the provenance papers?" Holmes handed him the letter from Richard Sampson, Worthington's secretary, which stated the pamphlet had been a gift.

"I remember this. It was included with the pamphlet when I purchased it from Grant. Of course, I passed the letter on when I sold the pamphlet."

Holmes then gave him the pamphlet. "And this is the item you owned, correct?"

Coddington examined it closely. "That is it. May I ask what your interest is in this?"

"The pamphlet was a kind present to me. Watson and I thought it might be enjoyable to have more information about its journey to my hands than the dry recital of facts in the papers that accompany it."

Coddington chuckled. "That's right. In those stories, you always go on about the need to have facts. Glad I could be of help."

We thanked him and went outside to find another cab. Holmes's eyes had that familiar gleam, which I knew meant we were near the end of our search. We arrived at Charing Cross Road, where Benjamin James had his store. The dusty windows were full of his stock in trade. When we entered, the front room was crammed with books and manuscripts. From the back came a tall, thin man in his seventies with white hair, ruddy cheeks, and a monocle dangling from a ribbon attached to the linen coat he wore to keep the dust from his suit.

"Oh dear, oh dear. Doctor, I trust there isn't a problem with your purchase. I was barely able to sleep last night. A telegram from Sherlock Holmes! My oh my. I hope to never . . . ."

My friend made a slight bow. "Please put your mind at rest, my good man. This is merely a case of two old bloodhounds amusing themselves by putting flesh-and-blood on the dry history of this delightful pamphlet."

With a sigh of relief, James led us to his back room which, if possible, was even more chaotic than the front. He cleared three chairs of the books piled on them and bade us sit down. Holmes smiled. "We understand you purchased the pamphlet in 1922 from Thomas Coddington."

"Coddington is a bit of an odd duck, I must say. Has a reputation in the trade of being difficult to deal with."

"What do you mean by 'difficult'?"

"Well, as long as this stays between us – ?" Holmes nodded. "This pamphlet is a good example. He often buys and sells – Or I should say *used* to buy and sell? – in lots. Would demand that a seller or buyer take it as an all-or-nothing proposition. The result was that you might get some gold or silver mixed in with dross. He could be very high handed and, I must say, inclined to sharp practices."

"Why, then, did you buy from him?"

" My specialty is seventeenth-century political pamphlets, especially from the 1640's and 1650's. He had some excellent pieces from that period, particularly a few works by Gerard Winstanley, one of the founders of the True Levellers, or 'Diggers' . . . ."

Thankfully, Holmes gently ended what promised to be a rather long digression. "I see. Very interesting I am sure. So the Huish pamphlet wasn't what attracted you to the lot."

"Good Heavens, no! I frankly didn't know what to do with it. After a little over a year, I took out an advertisement in our trade sheet listing

356

several items that were out of my purview. When the Good Doctor approached a colleague about any rare beekeeping items, he remembered my advertisement and directed the doctor me."

I interjected. "That is correct. I wasn't looking for the Huish pamphlet in particular – didn't even know of its existence. I felt quite lucky to have found you and it."

Holmes smiled at James. He then proceeded to have him verify the Sampson letter and the pamphlet as we had done with Coddington. Thanking him, we left and went outside. Once in a cab, Holmes turned to me. "Watson, what do you make of all this?"

"Frankly, I am most perplexed about motive, given the facts we have uncovered. *Cui bono*? you might say."

"An excellent question – Who indeed benefitted?. You haven't forgotten my methods as regards facts. Please continue."

"I will start at the beginning. There are four people. I dismiss Baylor because he only was involved in the items that he sold to Worthington, which were drama and poetry, thus completely unlike the Huish pamphlet. Likewise with Clay, mainly due to the fact the pamphlet was a gift, and I don't see how he would benefit from making a gift of a forgery.

"I suppose Worthington or Sampson could have sold the original pamphlet and substituted a forgery in its place. Based on what Edgeworth said, however, that seems inconsistent with their characters. And their charitable donations would indicate that they weren't in financial distress.

"The case is different with respect to Grant and Coddington. We know both had financial difficulties, and both had connections in the book trade, which could have included sources that knew how to procure a forgery. Either could have wanted to sell the pamphlet, and other items, twice – one genuine, and one false. The same could be said of James, although we have no basis to suspect a financial need, and his area of interest is political material from the mid-sixteenth century, about as far as one could get from beekeeping one-hundred-fifty years later."

"An admirable summary. I see by my pocket-watch that it is now almost four. I need to check on a few things, so will part company here at Trafalgar Square. Shall we meet at the American Bar at the Savory at, say, six?" He tapped on the roof of the cab with his walking stick and alighted at Nelson's Column. I decided to continue on and take a stroll along the Strand before our meeting.

After a pleasant walk, and resisting the urge to enter Simpson's in deference to the need to restrain my waistline from further expansion, I came to the Savoy. I walked past the theater and entered through the main doors of the hotel. Passing through the sumptuous lobby, I turned to the left, and ascended the short flight of stairs leading to the American Bar.

To my surprise, former-Inspector Gregson was seated at a table in the corner, gesturing for me to join him.

"Gregson, what a pleasant turn of events! I didn't expect to see you again so soon."

"Nor I you. I received a telegram about an hour ago from Mister Holmes requesting that I meet the two of you here."

A waiter approached, and Gregson and I decided to have an American-style cocktail, which had given the bar its name. Knowing that Holmes would disdain them, I ordered a dry sherry for him. Just as the waiter was serving our drinks, my friend strode through the door and came to our table. We toasted one another and waited for him to speak, as I knew Gregson's presence signaled that his fertile brain had, as usual, solved the mystery.

"Gregson, thank you for coming. I realize you are retired, but assume you still have connections at the Yard. The tale I am about to tell you may warrant notifying them, but I will leave that to your discretion.

"Although I sincerely appreciate the sentiment behind the gift, *A Treatise on the Nature, Economy, and Practical Management of Bees* is a forgery. I immediately noticed that due to the typeface and paper and the pristine condition of the pamphlet. Watson and I have spoken to everyone still living that had something to do with the transmission of the pamphlet into Watson's hands. Have you had occasion to examine the provenance papers? No, well a short summary will assist you in following my reasoning.

"The pamphlet was first sold by the estate of William Worthington to Richard Grant, an author. There is a letter from Sampson, Worthington's secretary, that the pamphlet was a gift to Worthington from the son of the publisher of the pamphlet, Clay. Grant then sold the pamphlet to Thomas Coddington, who sold it in turn to Benjamin James, the dealer from whom Watson acquired it."

Gregson's keen eyes showed he was following Holmes's recitation closely. "So it is possible that someone in that chain sold the original pamphlet and substituted the forgery."

"Watson had the same thought – that financial gain might be a possible explanation. It seems unlikely that was the case for Worthington or Sampson, or Clay for that matter. But Grant and Coddington had financial difficulties, and so may have James. Added to that, the specialized nature of the collecting interests of some of these men make it a bit less likely they would decide on Huish's work as a target.

"As I thought about the matter further, I began to question whether we were dealing not with one forgery, but *two*. There were other peculiarities about the pamphlet that I did not mention. For example, there is no inscription by Huish on the pamphlet, which would be a common practice if Huish presented it to Clay's father. Nor are there any signatures by Clay and his son, again a common practice. Not conclusive, but suggestive.

"Allow me to take a slight digression into printing practices in the last century, a topic I may include in my monograph. It was quite common for a work to be published in pamphlet form before it was printed as a book, which was one way of determining the demand for the more expensive version. Or an author might publish as a pamphlet to circulate for comments and suggestions. Huish's book was published in 1815. The title page of the pamphlet says it was published in 1813 by Samuel Burton, Clay, and Smith, the Clay being our Clay's father.

"After I left Watson this afternoon, my first stop was the nearby Diogenes Club, where, as you know, my brother is a founder. They have an excellent but rather esoteric library, which includes a history of printing in London. I consulted it and learned that Samuel Burton, Clay, and Smith wasn't founded until *1817*. Obviously Clay wouldn't have made a mistake like using a date four years before his Father's firm existed. So that ruled out Clay or his father as the forger."

I was beginning to see where his reasoning was headed. "You said there were *two* forgeries. Do you mean the Sampson letter?"

"Capital, Watson! Yes, the letter also must be a forgery, most likely by the forger himself. I don't believe Sampson would be so foolish as to use his own name, so let us provisionally eliminate him."

Gregson then spoke up. "But how did Worthington come to possess the pamphlet? I don't see him forging both a pamphlet and a letter from Sampson, who might see the forged letter bearing his signature during the course of his duties. "

"Correct, Gregson. Let us separate the two forgeries in time – one before Worthington's death and one after. Let us say the forger is at an early stage of his criminal career. He sells the falsified pamphlet at a trifling sum to Worthington just to determine if he can get away with it. He does, perhaps because he has sold other items to Worthington, earning his trust, or Worthington likes a young man on the rise.

"Then, upon Worthington's death, our forger sees a chance to further his art, if I may call it that, by creating a bogus provenance for the forged pamphlet. He then sits back and watches with satisfaction as his initial foray goes undetected for forty-four years."

I spoke up. "Never suspecting that one day the materials would become the property of Sherlock Holmes. You can only be describing Jonathan Wesley Baylor. He was young at the time and had sold a few items to Worthington. He assisted with the inventory of the estate, and thus could have slipped the Sampson letter into the pamphlet without Sampson realizing it."

"And we only have his word that he only sold poetry and drama to Worthington. He also cleverly insinuated Worthington knew Clay without directly stating that."

Gregson, deep in thought, looked over at Holmes. "What was his motive Mister Holmes? Money?"

"Perhaps at first. I suspect, though that, over time, it was the sheer enjoyment or feeling of power it gave him as he became more and more prominent in the field. Imagine how it felt when he uncovered someone else's forgery. He also may like the ability both to fool someone with a forgery while retaining the original for his own pleasure. When we visited his office, I took note of several manuscripts and books on display. My other stop this afternoon was at Sotheby's, where there is a senior manager for whom I performed a service in connection with a stolen Grecian urn at a time when it might have ruined his promising career. With his assistance, I determined that several items in Baylor's office were auctioned by the firm. The records also revealed Baylor was involved in these transactions, usually as an authenticator of the work."

I interjected. "The Yard will need to consider the ramifications of this case, Gregson. Baylor is quite influential and has received many honors and positions. He also has likely duped some prominent and powerful people who might not desire potentially embarrassing publicity."

"Quite so, Watson. Gregson, if someone at the Yard wishes to speak to me, I would be glad to do so. I also will have a word with Mycroft, as his diplomatic and political skills might be useful to the Yard if they so wish."

Gregson thanked us and left, with a look that was a cross between admiration for my friend and relief that the decision on how to proceed was not his to make. I signaled to the waiter for another round of drinks, which quickly arrived.

"You haven't lost the touch, Holmes, which I never doubted for an instant. I must apologize, though, for giving you a forgery for your seventieth birthday."

"Nonsense, Watson! Having a new adventure with you is the best present I have ever received. Cheers!"

The Case of the
Purloined Pistols
by Mark Mower

"I really must begin to tidy some of these files," said Holmes, wearily. "Even by my standards, these records are looking disorderly. It's taken me a good five minutes to find the information I needed. Ordinarily, I can locate most things within two."

It was a rare admission. But the curious arrangement of bookshelves, boxes, folders, and stacks was not the most efficient archival system I had ever seen. Set within a corner of Holmes's spacious sitting room in his cottage on the south coast, it contained a lifetime of invaluable information and intelligence on all manner of subjects and people that had come within the purview of the world's first consulting detective.

"A-ha! At last. My file on snipers, shooters, and gunmen." He held the thickly filled manilla folder in both hands, contemplating it with evident affection as an orchidologist might regard the acquisition of a previously unknown flower.

I was staying with Holmes for a long weekend as my wife had made plans to attend a reunion of her school friends at an hotel in Brighton. Having driven her to the seaside watering hole in my Crossley 20/25, I had then motored back inland some fifteen miles to reach Holmes's smallholding on the South Downs. It was already balmy on that June day, and with our breakfast completed Holmes was keen to get to work on a new assignment which had been presented to him by our good friend, Solar Pons, a renowned detective in his own right.

"There are some familiar names in here, Watson!" said he, flicking through the alphabetically arranged papers. "Most notably, Colonel Sebastian Moran . . ."

I shuddered at the memory of the vile man who had once made it his mission to assassinate my colleague.

". . . and yet, the bulk of the men and women in this folder are individuals whose crimes and misdemeanours have been largely overlooked, or even lost to history. Now, here's the example I seek – Carlton Anstruther."

"Certainly not a name I recollect."

"No. But in his day, this man was every bit as cunning and capable as the late Colonel. I will tell you more when Pons arrives. Our good friend has some information about Anstruther which he is keen to share."

We had just enough time to finish our coffee and cigarettes before hearing the unmistakable sound of a Triumph 10/20 touring car pulling up on the verge beyond the stone wall of the cottage. It was driven by Dr. Lyndon Parker, an excellent medical practitioner, and Pons's close confidant.

Holmes and I walked down to meet them, and we spent some minutes catching up on all that the pair had been up to in the four months since we had last seen them. Thereafter, we ambled back up the drive and around to the back of the farm, where Holmes proudly showed off what was new with his impressive collection of bee hives. Pons was enthralled, and the pair spent twenty minutes discussing the benefits and challenges of tending to the apiary. Parker and I were content to chat about cars, golf, and football.

When we were at last seated within the sitting room with some tea and biscuits provided by Holmes's housekeeper, my colleague turned the conversation around to the subject of Carlton Anstruther. Pons was happy to oblige.

"Parker and I are currently engaged in a kidnapping case involving the daughter of a wealthy city banker. Two nights ago, we had cause to visit an East End pub which I know to be a point of rendezvous for those wishing to hire criminal associates.

"Would that be The Ten Bells?" ventured Holmes, with a knowing smile.

Parker laughed. "That's the one!"

I too knew of its reputation as one of the capital's most notorious drinking dens. At the corner of Commercial Street and Fournier Street in Spitalfields, the public house was said to have been frequented by two of the victims of Jack the Ripper.

Pons continued. "In recent years, the pub has become a brokerage for contracts and commissions in the London underworld. If you need a forger, burglar, or assassin, the chances are you'll find one through the middle men who operate from the establishment. They take a tidy percentage of the fee that you're willing to offer the hired felon to complete your task. You benefit from their extensive range of contacts, without having to interact directly with the criminal fraternity."

"Sounds delightful!" said I, imagining the sort of characters likely to frequent the place.

"Indeed. We were there trying to track down a man who was seen driving the car used for the abduction. One of my contacts had agreed to meet us there at seven-forty-five to provide us with his name. Now, as we were sat with our pints of stout, attempting to pass ourselves off as London cabbies, a tall, muscular, man entered the bar and proceeded to sit at a table behind us. This was already occupied by a small, bearded, and bespectacled fellow called Stanley Westhall, who is a concierge at the Dorchester Hotel. With our backs to the pair, it was difficult to discern much of the short conversation which followed, for the bar was rather lively that evening. However, what I did hear the small man utter was 'rare pistols', 'will be stolen as requested', and 'cash on delivery'. The only audible response to this was '. . . early Saturday evening, a week from today'.

I was intrigued by one minor detail. "How did you know the name of the concierge?"

It was Dr. Parker who responded. "Pons and I had agreed to meet at the pub just before seven-thirty. I was a few minutes late and arrived at the same time as Westhall. As he was about to enter the bar, I saw him remove his Dorchester lapel badge, which displayed both his name and position. He looked embarrassed as he realised that I had seen this, but carried on regardless. I mentioned it to Pons as we ordered our drinks."

Holmes interposed. "And you believe the other man to have been Carlton Anstruther, the so-called 'Marksman of Maidstone'?"

"I'm certain of it. I was in the public gallery on the last day of his murder trial. While that was a little over twenty years ago, the man is still recognisable. If you remember, he was only thirty when convicted."

"Yes. And I will say that I was a little surprised at his conviction. Despite my testimony, which focused purely on what I discovered at the scene, I thought the prosecution's case was weak and largely circumstantial in nature. It didn't help that Arthur Quirrell, the defence barrister, did a very poor job of representing Anstruther. The man himself always maintained that he was in Oxford at the time of the murder, but had no credible witnesses to corroborate it."

I asked Holmes to tell me more about the trial, as it wasn't one I recollected from our earlier years together. As we each enjoyed a cigarette after our tea and biscuits, he sought to explain.

"Anstruther was something of an enigma. The press frequently referred to him as 'The Marksman of Maidstone', simply because they knew few other details about him. That he claimed to have grown up in the town and was proven during the trial to be a crack shot was the extent of the intelligence on him. While the police believed him to be responsible for at least a dozen highly placed assassinations, it was only with the investigation into the death of the property millionaire, Sir Anthony

Bidwell, at his home in Buckinghamshire, that they managed to assemble a case against him."

Pons then added, "I think you're in danger of underplaying your own role in the affair, Holmes." He turned to me, adding, "Our friend here was invited by Scotland Yard to attend the location of the crime, when all that they could determine was that Bidwell had been shot from a distance by a rifle of some kind. He had been seated at his dining table on the evening in question, and the killer had taken aim from somewhere within the grounds of the Bidwell estate. Holmes managed to work out the likely trajectory of the bullet, and discovered within the grounds where the marksman had taken aim. Footprints beneath one of the oak trees at the back of the house were later matched to the tread of some boots owned by Anstruther. It was suggested that the shooter had taken aim from a suitable height, and at a distance, which would enable him to operate without being seen. Furthermore, a single cigarette butt trampled into the mud nearby was found to contain the same unusual brand of Turkish tobacco favoured by the assassin."

Holmes smiled gently. "It required but a rudimentary understanding of ballistics. And as for the discarded cigarette, it was an uncharacteristic error of judgement on his part – a man who was customarily meticulous in his approach."

Bright sunlight had begun to stream into the room illuminating the thin wisps of cigarette smoke which now rose in layers above us. "What sentence did he receive?" I asked.

"It was recommended that he serve a minimum of twenty years, which appears to be all that he did endure, for his prison release occurred last October. Since that time, he has kept a very low profile. So this new information is extremely interesting."

"Why do you say *interesting*?"

"Well, it signals the need for me to be on my guard. After the trial, I received an unexpected visit from the man's sister, a Mrs. Emily Trenton. The lady had no regard for her brother, having learned of his despicable profession. The astute young woman said she felt compelled to share with me some gossip which had circulated within the family: Namely, that if Anstruther was ever released from prison, he would make it his mission to kill the private detective who had been instrumental in bringing about his downfall. So you see, Watson, I am, once again, something of a marked man."

If he had any concern about this, Holmes's countenance certainly displayed no sign of it. Pons asked what steps he would take in protecting himself. My friend responded in a familiar and confident tone, "I'll not sit back and wait for the man to act. I intend to take the fight to him."

"Good for you!" intoned Parker. "Can we assist?"

His response was an unexpected one. "On this occasion, I will decline your very kind offer of help. This may well be my last big investigation. If successful, I believe I will thereafter take retirement a little more seriously. With Watson at my side, we will put this small matter to rest. We have faced tougher challenges."

I felt a swell of pride and was touched by his words. Nothing in the world would have prevented me from standing squarely by his side, whatever the threats posed. Pons nodded and extended his hand towards Holmes. "Good luck. As ever, I have every faith in you. But should the need arise . . . ."

"Many thanks, both of you. I know that every moment is precious in a case of kidnapping, so I implore you to make haste. You have done me a great service in sharing this new information, so we too must act with some speed. Where are you heading now?"

"We have to revisit the boarding school in West Sussex where the abduction took place."

"Excellent! And with Watson as my most capable chauffeur, we will be heading to Chelsea!"

Half-an-hour later, Holmes and I were seated in the car. "Why Chelsea?" I asked.

"That is where Anstruther's sister lived at the time of his conviction. We will have to hope that she hasn't moved in the interim."

I chuckled. "You take me for a fool, Holmes! I saw you consult your *White's Directory* just before we left the cottage. You know perfectly well that she still resides there!"

"Of course. But it's nice to keep you on your toes!"

Our drive towards the capital was a pleasant one, along roads and country lanes which were relatively quiet for the time of year. Holmes chatted throughout the journey, and seemed excited about the prospect of heading back into the metropolis.

Mrs. Emily Trenton lived in a well-appointed four-storey house on Tite Street. Knocking on the door, we were greeted by an attractive young maid who took Holmes's calling card and scuttled off down the long hallway of the property. Returning some minutes later, she smiled and said that the lady of the house would be delighted to receive us.

Mrs. Trenton was a tall, elegant, woman in her early fifties, with a mass of curly blonde hair and the slenderest of figures. Her parlour testified to the Bohemian nature of her profession. She explained that she was a portrait painter who received commissions from many wealthy patrons. The walls of the room were adorned with paintings of all descriptions, and the general décor was bright and colourful, reflecting the lady's artistic flair.

When tea had been served, Holmes got down to business. "Mrs. Trenton, it is kind of you to make time for us, particularly when you are so busy with your artwork. We will endeavour to keep our visit short, so as not to inconvenience you."

The lady looked at him quizzically. "It's true that my work has been hectic of late, but how did you know that?"

"Your writing desk in the far corner tells me all that I need to know. The simple filing system you employ consists of just three trays. The one on the right is clearly for completed paintings, containing, as it does, a small pile of invoices and receipts for those works which have already been delivered to your patrons. The in-tray on the left appears to be full of more general correspondence, rough sketches, and calling cards, which hints at work which has yet to be formerly commissioned. But it is the sizeable stack of card folders in the middle tray which leads me to conclude that you aren't currently short of work. I would venture that there are at least a dozen such folders. That you were painting when we arrived is evident from the small splashes of oil paint on your nails. With all of that in mind, I would be loathe to take up too much of your time."

"Incredible!" replied the artist, "and all perfectly true. You have a rare gift, Mr. Holmes! Now, I am happy to make time to assist you in any way that I can. I'm guessing this has something to do with my recently released brother?"

"Indeed. You will remember that when you visited me in Baker Street all those years ago, you informed me that Carlton was likely to seek revenge if he was ever released from prison. I fear that he may now be intent on making good that promise, so I was hoping that you might be able to shed a little more light on his character – to enable me to be forearmed, as it were."

She smiled at the play on words, and her bright blue eyes lit up. "Yes, *forearmed*. How apt! I will tell you what I can, but I'm not sure how relevant it will be. I should add that I haven't seen or spoken to Carlton since his release."

"I would be grateful for anything you can share with us. Very little was disclosed at the trial."

She nodded. "That was because Carlton has, since childhood, been something of a loner. We lived with our father in a large, detached house in Maidstone. Mother died when I was six. Carlton was four at the time, and greatly affected by her passing. While I tried to be a caring older sister, he shunned any such attention. He retreated into his own space, an approach which he continued into adulthood. His relationship with our father didn't help."

Holmes was at once intrigued. "How so?"

"My father was a successful engineer and draughtsman, but an unrelenting bully. Having lost his wife, he too withdrew from the world, leaving the household servants to raise us as children. Whatever we said or did, it never seemed to be quite good enough for him. He was a stickler for detail, fastidious in dress, and brusque in his manner. But to my brother, he was also persistently cruel. Carlton would be beaten for any perceived misdemeanour, starved of food for days, and occasionally locked in a coal cellar. The servants were told to ignore his pitiful cries for help.

"On one occasion, my father took exception to his handwriting. Seeing the smudges of ink on one of his school books, he said it was because Carlton was lazy, awkward, and left-handed. From that point on, whenever we sat in the parlour completing our homework, father would insist on strapping Carlton's left arm behind his back, forcing him to write with his other hand. He also contacted the school, demanding that they follow a similar regime.

"Despite his treatment, my brother did well in education, and proved to be an excellent scholar. He excelled at mathematics and science, and had good practical skills, particularly in woodwork and metalwork. When he left school at sixteen, he took up an apprenticeship with our Uncle Gareth – a gunsmith in Maidstone – and promptly left home to live in a small flat above the shop. From that point on, he was estranged from my father, but he did let me visit him on two or three occasions, until we too drifted apart. Carlton refused to attend father's funeral when he passed. And when I married my late husband, Gabriel Trenton, he ignored the invitation to our wedding. Beyond that, I saw him on only a couple of occasions."

"So, a pretty tough, independent, and resourceful character?" I ventured.

"Yes. And a man lacking compassion. I'm not aware that he ever had any romantic inclinations, although I cannot be sure, for I know very little of his adult life prior to his incarceration. He certainly cultivated very few friendships as a child, beyond that of our cousin, John Pugh."

"Would that be the same cousin who was called to give evidence at the trial?" asked Holmes.

"Yes. Another solitary character. You may remember that the defence barrister described him as a diligent, hard-working, and trustworthy cousin who had grown up with Carlton, and had gone on to work with him. In calling him to the stand, I imagine they were keen for John to present my brother in something of a favourable light. Yet in focusing a little too much on Carlton's skills as a gunsmith, and his considerable abilities in stalking and shooting wild game, I believe his testimony may have had the opposite effect."

"Indeed," replied Holmes. "You mentioned that John Pugh was a similarly 'solitary character'. What do you mean by that?"

"Like Carlton, he could be incredibly insular. I had no rapport with him whatsoever. While I had a great deal of affection for Aunt Jenny, my father's sister, and my Uncle Gareth, I wasn't close to John. He would only speak when forced to, and would never look me in the eye. He and Carlton formed an unlikely bond, spending all their school holidays together building camps and hunting with catapults and airguns. Later, they worked together in the workshop of my uncle's business."

"I see. And how long did they work together?"

"Carlton's apprenticeship lasted for seven years – he left when he was twenty-three. As my uncle's son, John wasn't formally registered as an apprentice, but had from an early age been tutored in all aspects of gunsmithing. It was always understood that he would take over the business at some point, and he did the same year that Carlton left."

I raised an eyebrow. "Were the two events connected?"

She reflected on this, before responding. "I don't think so. I wasn't aware of any bad blood between the two. From the little I know, I believe that Carlton wanted to spread his wings and create his own business in London."

Holmes neatly anticipated the question I was about to ask. "And did he have any success in doing so? I cannot recollect any mention of a business during the trial."

"Smoke and mirrors, it would seem, Mr. Holmes. From the gossip which filtered back to us in Maidstone, it was said that Carlton had established a successful enterprise in Walthamstow. Certainly, on the rare occasions I saw him, he gave every impression that he was working hard and earning good money. I now realise that his not-inconsiderable income was being derived from more nefarious means."

Holmes nodded. "Yes. Carlton was taken under the wing of a man named Claude Dewalt, an aging East End gangster close to some of the most notorious contract killers. How their criminal relationship developed isn't clear, but certainly by the time of his twenty-fifth birthday, Carlton was known to be Dewalt's killer of choice. In fact, I have heard it said that it was the older man who first dubbed Carlton 'The Marksman of Maidstone'.

Mrs. Trenton grimaced at the reference. "A moniker which sickens me every time I hear it!"

Holmes clearly sensed that it was a good time to bring our visit to an end. "A final question for you, Mrs. Trenton: Is your uncle still alive and residing in Maidstone?"

"Oh, yes. He's on his own now, as my aunt died five years back. The man is in his late seventies, but remains as fit as a fiddle. It's just as well, for he still runs the business."

My colleague seemed a little surprised at this. "You will forgive me, but I thought you said earlier that his son, John, had taken over the venture in the year that Carlton left?"

"Yes, he did. I apologise, Mr. Holmes, for I think our conversation had moved on before I could clarify what happened. John took over the reigns of the business for six months, but while technically proficient in his trade, he clashed frequently with his father, who wanted things to be run as they always had. John had some colourful ideas for expanding the scope of their work into expensive precision pistols, but my uncle would hear none of it. In the end, John up and left, heading to London as my brother had done."

While we remained with Mrs. Trenton for a short while longer, it seemed that we had learned all that we might in our quest to understand more about the enigmatic Carlton Anstruther. Twenty minutes later, with the car parked safely, we sat enjoying a pint of ale in the taproom of The Cross Keys.

"Some valuable insights into the man, Watson! Certainly worth the time spent."

"Yes, Mrs. Trenton was most helpful. But I don't like the sound of Anstruther one bit. How do you propose to proceed?"

Holmes took a swig of his ale and paused to wipe the froth from his top lip. "Small steps, my friend. If you are game, I propose that we stop overnight at your house, and head towards Maidstone as soon as we have breakfasted. I'm keen to speak to Gareth Pugh, the gunsmith. As tomorrow is a Sunday, he is unlikely to be working, so it should be a good time to call. In the meantime, I have some telephone calls to make. Most importantly, I will ask our old friend, Charlie Wiggins, to keep an eye on Carlton Anstruther."

"Charlie Wiggins! Now, there's a name I haven't heard for some time! And he's still in the game?"

Holmes chortled. "I'm delighted to say that he is. From those early days as a ragamuffin irregular, Wiggins has built a very successful private enquiry agency from an office in Tooley Street. He now employs twenty staff, and always tries to call me at least once a month. A finer gentleman you could not hope to meet!

"His agents will have no trouble in locating Anstruther and trailing him for the next week or so. I need the confirmation that he has obtained the purloined pistols from his contact at the Dorchester. Then I'll be able to take more active steps in thwarting any attack he plans to make."

The next morning dawned bright and clear. My elderly housekeeper, Mrs. Halliday, had gone out of her way to make my friend's short stay a very pleasant one. The breakfast was a delight, with thickly cut bacon, sausages, fried eggs, mushrooms, and tomatoes. It was a rare treat – the sort of breakfast I regularly craved, but was reluctant to eat, given my expanding waistline.

We set off just after nine o'clock to travel the forty odd miles to Maidstone in Kent. Less than two hours later, we pulled up at Gareth Pugh's premises on Mill Street. The ageing gunmaker seemed a little bemused in receiving us, but was amiable enough when Holmes explained the nature of our call.

"Please, come in gentlemen. I have just made a pot of tea which should serve three." He viewed us over the top of his wire-framed glasses, which sat, somewhat incongruously, well south of the bridge of his nose. While he had clearly been a tall man in earlier years, the stoop which now afflicted him severely diminished his stature.

We entered through the main door of the shop, the interior of which proved to be smaller than I might have imagined. All the available wall space was taken up with weapons and the paraphernalia of hunting and shooting. A small counter at the back of the shop was the only other fitting in the room. We passed beyond this, through a narrow hallway, and into a more expansive workshop area full of benches, vices, lathes, and milling machines. Pugh beckoned for us to take a seat in one corner, which appeared to serve as a rest area, containing a small wooden coffee table and three low and extremely threadbare chairs. He headed off to the right into a small kitchen area. Presently, he returned with the aforementioned teapot and some ill-matched crockery.

"You will have to forgive the state of the place, Mr. Holmes. While I employ a maid to keep the shop and upstairs living quarters spick and span, her remit doesn't extend to the workshop. My young apprentice occasionally sweeps up, but for the most part, we are content to work around the untidiness!" His language and manner were curiously old-fashioned, putting me in mind of a character from a Dicken's novel.

With the tea poured, Holmes reiterated that we were keen to speak to him about his nephew. He asked, firstly, if the gunsmith had seen Anstruther since the man's release from prison. "No," came the reply. "I did visit him in prison in his first year. We had an awkward and unsatisfactory conversation, which consisted mainly of me telling him how his family were doing back home. Before I left, he told me never to visit again. I haven't set eyes on Carlton since."

"Were you surprised at his reaction?" I asked.

"Yes. I spent many happy hours guiding him as an apprentice, for he was a keen and talented young man. My wife and I treated him like a son, and we were pleased to have him live with us when his relationship with his father deteriorated. I had imagined that that might have counted for something, but it seems I was mistaken."

He seemed saddened at the disclosure and turned away from us momentarily. In doing so, he leaned backwards towards a bookcase positioned to his left. From this he retrieved a large photographic album from one of the shelves and placed it down on the table before us. "If you care to glance through some of those pictures, you'll see how joyful those times were."

Holmes and I leafed through the contents. The first full-page image showed two young boys, no more than ten years of age, in identical poses, clutching air rifles and displaying the bodies of the rabbits they had clearly shot with the weapons. Holmes pointed towards the lad on the left to indicate that it was Anstruther. Both boys were of comparable height and shared similar familial features: A long, gaunt face, dark hair, intense-looking eyes, and a high forehead.

A further photograph, which looked to have been taken a few years later, displayed a rather different image. The tall, muscular lads stood facing each other, four or five feet apart, with the same intense stares as before. Each had an outstretched arm in the foreground holding an ornate duelling pistol, the barrel of which was pointed at the head of the other. This time, Anstruther was on the right of the image.

Seeing our particular interest, the gunsmith sought to explain. "The pistols were the first weapons my son and Carlton completed on their own. Until then, they had always assisted me with the smithing. John took the lead in designing and crafting the first pistol, while Carlton worked under his supervision to replicate the second piece as part of his apprenticeship. Their work was exemplary. The pistols were constructed to replicate traditional flintlock weapons, but fire .22 calibre cartridges."

Holmes finished what remained of his tea and then asked, "What happened to the pistols?"

"They were purchased as a pair by Dr. Victor Gurney, one of my best customers at that time. He is long-since retired, but used to be the best family doctor in Maidstone."

"And he still resides in the town?"

371

"Yes, indeed, Mr. Holmes. I saw him only last week, outside his house on Lower Stone Street."

Holmes seemed content with this information and brought the conversation back to Anstruther. "I understand that Carlton completed his apprenticeship and then moved to London. Why was that?"

"It was straightforward enough. As a qualified gunsmith, Carlton could expect to see a ten-fold increase in his wages. I simply couldn't afford to pay him that amount, on top of what I was already paying myself and my son. Given the choice, I would have kept him on in preference to John, but had already promised my son that he would inherit the business."

I was a little surprised at the revelation. "Why do you say that, Mr. Pugh?"

"Oh, don't get me wrong. John was an expert craftsman, but had no head for figures. He also had something of a temper and would take to arguing with me in front of Carlton. His cousin shined in all aspects of the business, including the accounts and administrative work. He was always quiet and content to work with a large degree of autonomy – something I valued greatly."

"Yet, in the end, you saw both of them depart in the same year," observed Holmes. "Why did your son leave?"

"I'll be frank with you, for there seems little point in tiptoeing around the facts: I discovered that John was *cooking the books*, as it were. He was keeping company with some of the young roughs in the town and had taken to stealing to fund his excessive drinking and gambling habits. When Carlton left, I let John take over the running of the business, and from that moment on, he had his hand in the till. It didn't take me long to work out what he was doing, and when I confronted him, an argument ensued. That same night, he packed his bags and left for London."

"How is your relationship with him now?" I asked.

"Steady. He visits occasionally, although we usually have little to say to each other. He has a family of his own, and a successful business in London. In some respects, our falling out was the making of him. It made him stand on his own two feet."

"And what is it that John does?" I continued.

"He's still in the gun trade, and has premises in Turnmill Street near Farringdon Station. While he no longer does any smithing, he imports and sells hunting rifles and precision pistols."

Holmes returned to the question of Anstruther's departure. "Were you not tempted to invite Carlton back into the business following your son's departure?"

Pugh smiled and accepted one of the cigarettes which Holmes now offered him. "Of course, but having left Maidstone, my nephew had apparently secured a good position with a businessman in Walthamstow. A Mr. *Dewinter*, I think his name was."

"Could it have been *Dewalt*?

"Yes, that's the fellow. At my invitation, Carlton visited Maidstone and I offered him a salaried position. He was surprised to hear of John's departure, but said that his own prospects lay elsewhere. I saw little of him thereafter."

"Do you know if he and your son remained in contact?"

"Oh, yes. There was some business connection between them for six or seven years, but I believe it turned sour when Carlton refused to pay my son some money he was owed. There was considerable enmity between them."

Holmes was interested in this. "Did you know that your son was called as a character witness during Carlton's trial? It seems odd that the defence should call upon him, if what you say is true."

"I thought so myself when I read of the trial in the newspapers. But I think they were keen to find someone who had been close to Carlton, personally and professionally, in his earlier years. I couldn't attend, you see."

Holmes looked at him enquiringly. "No, I'm not sure I do see. Were you asked by the defence to attend court?"

"I was, but had been struck down with a debilitating bout of typhoid fever a week before the trial. It seems they approached John in my absence."

"Has your son ever talked about this?"

"Not really. He wouldn't be drawn on the matter, but did once say to me that Carlton got everything he deserved."

On this note, our conversation with Pugh came to a natural conclusion. We thanked the man for his time, and Holmes parted by asking the gunsmith to say nothing of our enquiries if he were to have any communications with either his son or the ex-convict. Pugh nodded reassuringly.

Back in the car, Holmes seemed pleased with all that he had discovered. "We have been pulling at a few loose threads, Watson, and it seems as if this whole criminal escapade is beginning to unravel!"

"Well, I'm glad to hear you say that, but I'm not so sure that we're any further forward in preventing Anstruther from exacting his revenge."

"Oh, we are. I'm beginning to understand exactly why the man is so embittered and the lengths to which he might go."

He refused to elaborate any further, but directed me instead to drive to Lower Stone Street. After stepping out of the car for a few seconds to ask a passing pedestrian for directions, I realised that our destination lay not five minutes away by foot. We left the car where it was, and a short while later found ourselves outside what had clearly once been a doctor's surgery – the brass plaque to the right of the door still displaying the name "*Dr. Victor Gurney*".

I had no idea why Holmes wished to talk to the aged surgeon, but knew from years of experience that he would have his reasons. It took some time for the man to answer the door, and when he did, it was clear that the doctor couldn't move at any great pace. He looked at us quizzically when the door was finally opened.

Holmes explained who we were and presented a calling card – an introduction which brought about an immediate change in the gentleman's demeanour. "A very warm welcome to you both! I have followed your exploits for many years, Mr. Holmes, as a result of Dr. Watson's marvellous narratives. Never did I imagine that you might call on me in person!"

Once seated within Dr. Gurney's spacious conservatory, Holmes contrived to explain the reason for our impromptu visit. "It may not surprise you to learn, Dr. Gurney, that I have always had a fascination with firearms, and maintain something of a collection myself – mainly shotguns and duelling pistols. I have in mind to commission dear Mr. Pugh on Mill Street to create for me two fine .22 calibre weapons which replicate the famous duelling pistols once used by the infamous highwayman, Dick Turpin. In talking to the gunsmith this morning, he mentioned that you have something of a prized collection yourself, including two finely crafted duelling pistols of that type which were made in his workshop. I know that I'm taking a very great liberty in turning up on your doorstep without invitation, but wondered if I might be permitted to view this most extraordinary pair of firearms?"

Gurney jumped up in a fashion which belied his serious lack of mobility and gestured towards a door on our right. "It would be my pleasure, sir! Please step this way!" He pulled a key from his waistcoat pocket and proceeded to unlock the sturdy oak-framed door which led us into a study housing over a dozen glass-fronted display cases. In total, there looked to be around forty firearms of all types, housed with the well-lit room. Gurney paused in front of a case standing at waist height and produced a second, much smaller, key from his pocket to enable the lid to be unlocked and lifted. Donning a pair of white surgical gloves which he pulled from his left trouser pocket, he retrieved one of the pistols from the case and placed it down gently upon the glass for our inspection.

Holmes scrutinised the pistol with some intensity before slipping on some white gloves of his own which he always carried within his jacket. Gurney nodded approvingly, and my friend then began to examine every detail of the decoration and workings of the firearm before announcing, with some enthusiasm, that it was one of the best pieces he had ever seen. "Exceptional quality, Dr. Gurney, simply exceptional!"

Gurney beamed with pride and stated that the second pistol was of a similar quality and identical to the first. Holmes corrected him without being impolite. "Yes, the workmanship is again first-rate, although they do differ in just one small respect."

Our host regarded him keenly. "Really? And how is that?"

Holmes turned his wrist and pointed towards some of the filigree decoration on the underneath of the barrel. "While the intricate scrollwork may look similar, you will note that hidden within this section are the tiny initials '*CA*', the maker's mark. I have no doubt that the same section on the other barrel will display the initials '*JP*'."

Gurney was at once fascinated. He reached in to retrieve the second pistol and turned it over in his hand. "Well, I never! In all the years that I have enjoyed firing and displaying these guns, I have never noticed that. Still, it doesn't diminish their appeal!"

"Indeed," replied Holmes. "Now, we will not impinge any further on your time, Doctor. You have been most helpful. I will leave you with my calling card. Should the need arise, I would be pleased to return the favour by assisting you with any troubles or conundrums you may face in the future."

With this curious conclusion, we headed off down Lower Stone Street to reach the car for our journey back to London. Holmes was tight-lipped about the whole episode, saying only that it had proved useful, and he had no doubt that Dr. Gurney would at some point take him up on his offer.

Holmes stayed at my home for a second night, and while I sat down at a little after seven o'clock that evening to eat one of Mrs. Halliday's excellent chicken roasts, Holmes made his apologies and said that he had a few matters to sort out while he was in town. In particular, he said he wanted to catch up with Wiggins and add another job to the irregular's task list – namely, to investigate the business affairs of John Pugh.

It wasn't until breakfast the following day that I was able to ask Holmes what progress had been made.

"All positive, my friend. Wiggins has three good men watching Anstruther's movements. They have learned that the former gunsmith has been accepted back into the criminal fraternity which used to be headed up by Claude Dewalt. While the latter died some years back, the gang is now being led by his son, Lennox.

"Anstruther is living in a dingy ground-floor apartment in Camden Town, owned by Dewalt. His new role is to source any firearms the gang require for their criminal activities. Stanley Westhall, whom we already know to be a concierge at the Dorchester Hotel, is likely to be just one of his many contacts.

"While trailing Anstruther, Wiggins's men have, on three occasions, followed him to Lincoln's Inn, close to the Royal Courts of Justice. Here he has spent time looking around the area and talking casually to some of the doormen who protect the entrances to the chambers and apartments of the complex."

"What do you think he's up to?" I asked. "Are these likely to be more associates with access to weapons?"

"I think not. I believe his objective is a little more direct. In short, he appears to be scouting out the whereabouts and working routines of a particular barrister – namely Arthur Quirrell."

"Of course! The defence barrister at his trial. You believe that Quirrell is also under threat?"

"Yes. Anstruther has had years to reflect on how poorly the man handled the defence. Whether it was professional negligence or something more sinister, Quirrell made the biggest mistake in calling John Pugh to the witness stand. Anstruther isn't the sort of man to let that go unpunished."

"True, but by the same reasoning, he might well blame Pugh himself for the debacle. We already know that there was some enmity between the cousins prior to the trial."

"You have hit the nail squarely on the head there, Watson! It's one of the reasons why Wiggins's men will need to shadow Pugh in the coming days. His life is most definitely threatened."

Later that day, I drove Holmes back to his farm and then set off to Brighton to meet my wife after her long weekend. It was agreed that Holmes would ring me if there were any major developments in the case.

On the Wednesday, there was such a development, but one which I hadn't anticipated. Holmes telephoned me at my surgery to say that he had received a frantic call from dear old Victor Gurney in Maidstone. A break-in had occurred at the doctor's house the previous evening. Entering the study through the French windows leading to the garden, the thief had apparently stolen just two items – the replica pistols which had been crafted years earlier by John Pugh and Carlton Anstruther. Gurney was desperate for Holmes to assist him in tracking down the whereabouts of the stolen pistols, something which the detective readily agreed to.

"That cannot be a coincidence!" I spluttered. "You knew all along that those pistols would be targeted. By the logic of this, the guns are likely to be the same pair that Anstruther is to collect from Stanley Westhall on Saturday night."

"Of course. For Anstruther, revenge is to be a ritualistic activity. What better than to use the very first firearm that he crafted himself as an apprentice? In visiting Gurney, I wanted to be sure that the guns hadn't already been taken. Having seen them, I was even more convinced that our man had arranged for them to be stolen to order. We will have our confirmation on Saturday night when Wiggins's men follow him to the hotel."

"What is the plan? Are you arranging to have him detained when he is in possession of the guns?"

"No, that wouldn't solve my problem. I want him to be detained for much more than the possession of a pair of stolen replica pistols. But in the eyes of the law, there is little to support my assertion that three lives are under threat. I need Anstruther to be caught in the act of attempting to murder someone."

I was troubled by the thought. "I understand that, but you cannot let Arthur Quirrell and John Pugh face such risks."

"I don't intend to. Arthur Quirrell has already been spoken to. He has travelled across to France in the company of one of Wiggins's men for a hastily arranged two-week summer holiday. As for Pugh, he will be warned as soon as we have confirmed that Anstruther has collected the weapons."

I wasn't sure why Pugh's safety should be treated any differently to that of Quirrell and voiced my concern. Holmes responded enigmatically, saying that there were "other forces at work here, which might jeopardise the entire plan." Beyond that, we would concede no more.

At my house, on the Sunday morning following this, I received a short telegram from Holmes, saying simply, "*Collection at hotel confirmed. The game is afoot.*" I felt a little uneasy at the news, hoping that Holmes had taken adequate precautions to protect himself.

At eleven o'clock on the Monday morning, the telephone in my surgery rang. Picking it up, I was surprised to hear Holmes in a state of some agitation. "Forgive me, Watson, but it is imperative that you drop whatever you are doing and meet me in Camden Town within the hour." I sprang into action, desperately hoping that my colleague was in no immediate danger. My old service revolver was already housed within an inside pocket of my jacket, which was hanging on the coat rail behind me.

After a couple of hasty calls to two of my patients, I was able to leave the surgery and hail a cab without delay. I joined Holmes some fifty minutes later at an agreed location in Albert Street. He had asked me to be discreet, so I requested that the taxi driver drop me off a short distance from where we were to meet.

377

I joined Holmes in a narrow alleyway opposite a large, run-down, detached house sitting between two larger industrial buildings. I was relieved to see that he looked to be unharmed.

He greeted me in a hushed tone and pointed quickly towards the house. "Anstruther's digs – the ground floor room on the right. There are four other rented rooms in the house, so the front door is kept unlocked during the day. The property can also be accessed from the rear. By eight-thirty this morning, only Anstruther was left in the house, the other tenants having left for work. Wiggins's men watched them depart. It was shortly after that when the shooting occurred."

"A shooting! Of whom?"

"Anstruther himself. The police believe he took his own life. A single bullet from a pistol, fired from below the chin. The officers are in there now and I have been invited to attend the scene. I wanted you to be with me, given your involvement to date."

I was flattered, but a little confused. "Wiggins's men were keeping watch when the suicide occurred?"

"Aaron Daly was watching from where we are standing now. Two of his colleagues were holed up in a property overlooking the back of the house. After hearing the single shot, Daly ran across the road and entered through the front of the house. He found the door to Anstruther's lodgings shut but unlocked. Armed with a pistol, he carefully opened the door and stepped into the room. There was no one else present, and Anstruther lay on his back in the manner I described, a pistol still in his hand."

"What did Daly do?"

"Having determined that the gunsmith was dead, he retreated from the premises, for fear that he might be implicated in the death. He made his way around to the back of the property and met with his two colleagues. They agreed to report back to Wiggins in Tooley Street. I was with their boss when they arrived back. We agreed a plan of action.

"An anonymous call was made to Scotland Yard, saying that a gunshot had been heard at the property in Albert Street. That was sufficient to prompt a visit by two detectives. They found the body and ascertained who the dead man was. One of the officers then left to find a police telephone to communicate the information back to an Inspector Laverne at Scotland Yard. Realising that the deceased was the recently released convict Carlton Anstruther, Laverne acted quickly. First, he asked his officers to protect the scene of the shooting until he could attend. He then called a number he had been given by the Chief Constable of the Criminal Investigation Department to speak to me, informing me of the shooting. That number belonged to Wiggins."

I was confused. "Why would the Chief Constable have Charlie Wiggins telephone number? And why would he use it to try to speak to you?"

"I have known Fred Wensley for many years. In the early part of his career, I helped him to solve several notable murders in Westminster. Since that time, he has been a useful contact, only too willing to assist me whenever I requested his help. You may remember that after our visit to Mrs. Trenton, I made some telephone calls. One was to Wensley, explaining that Anstruther might be out for revenge, and asking him to let me know of any reports he received about the shooter. Knowing that I might be hard to track down, I had given him Wiggins's number, explaining that he could be entrusted to forward any message on to me. It was fortuitous that when Laverne called, I was seated beside Wiggins.

"When I heard the news, I asked Laverne if it would be possible for me to visit the scene. He knew of my history with Anstruther and was only too willing to provide such an invitation."

"Then why all this cloak-and-dagger activity?" I asked, still bewildered as to what had happened. "Could you not have waited for me in the house?"

"No. I wanted the chance to explain to you all that had occurred. I'm doing my best to shield Wiggins and his men. I'm reluctant to reveal to Laverne that Anstruther's movements have been tracked for the past week. Their work has been invaluable. They have also discovered a lot more about John Pugh's activities at well. I'll share that with you a little later."

So saying, he set off across the street and knocked at the door of the detached house. A detective in plain clothes answered the door and ushered us in when a shout was received from Inspector Laverne. I let Holmes lead the way.

After some hasty introductions, Laverne spoke. "As you requested, Mr. Holmes, we haven't disturbed the body or the weapon, but I think you'll find it's an open-and-shut case of suicide. Single shot through the head from that rather antiquated pistol. Would have died instantly. He even left a suicide note to his sister on the desk in the corner."

Holmes received the note that was passed to him and scanned it quickly. "Most instructive," was all he had to say at that point. He began to circle, scrutinising everything around him in the sparsely decorated room before stooping to focus specifically on the body, magnifying glass in hand. Laverne and the other detective looked on.

"Yes, single shot beneath the chin. The .22 bullet exited the back of the head causing catastrophic, almost immediately fatal, damage."

"A .22, you say?" asked Laverne. "Isn't that a standard flintlock pistol?"

379

Holmes didn't look up but continued to focus on the body. "No, it's an adapted weapon, made to look like an old firearm. Anstruther himself made the gun over twenty years ago when he was still an apprentice gunsmith. I believe it had both sentimental and symbolic importance to him. He arranged for it to be stolen recently, alongside another pistol, from a collector in Maidstone. The .22 bullet is lodged in the wall just above the curtain pole over the front window."

Laverne walked over to the window and looked up. "Heaven's above! How did we miss that?!"

"The location of the bullet and the position of the body tells us that he was facing the door when the shot was fired," Holmes continued. "His body fell backwards, and yet the heavy pistol was still retained in his right hand. We might have expected the gun to be wrenched from his grip as he hit the floor, but it is positioned perfectly."

With that, the detective looked up at Laverne and asked if he might be permitted to remove the pistol from Anstruther's grasp.

"Certainly," came the reply. "I don't think there's much more to be learned from it, in any case."

"Without insulting you, Inspector, I'm afraid that you couldn't be more mistaken. I have gloves on and will be careful in retrieving the weapon and placing it in this bag, for it has both finger and thumb prints on it which will need to be examined. Those should confirm the identity of the shooter."

He walked over to the writing desk which sat just inside the door of the room to the left. Apart from a bed and a small wardrobe on the far wall, it was the only furniture in the room. Pulling open the single drawer beneath the desk, he revealed a second pistol, some metal working tools, a pen and ink, and a box of .22 ammunition. "Oh, Dr. Gurney will be pleased!" he said, lifting the pistol from the drawer.

Laverne looked incredulous as my colleague held the pistol upside down in his hand, paying particular attention to the scrollwork beneath the barrel. "As I thought, this pistol is etched with the initials '*CA*', showing that it was made by Anstruther himself. The companion piece which killed our man is etched with the initials of John Pugh."

With some dexterity, he gently broke the barrel of the pistol to reveal a round chamber which could be loaded with six .22 bullets. He chuckled to himself as he noted that it had been loaded with only three rounds. His laughter grew louder as he removed these one by one and examined the casing of each. "It seems I was correct in believing that Anstruther was out for revenge, gentlemen. With some of the tools in this desk, our gunsmith has etched tiny initials on each of these bullet cases. The first was intended for his ineffective defence barrister, Arthur Quirrell. The '*SH*' on the second shows that I was to be his second victim, while the initials '*JP*' tells us that he intended to kill his cousin, John Pugh, last. The biggest irony of course, is that Pugh got to him first, using the pistol which he made all those years ago."

I was quick to realise the significance of what he had just said. "Then this is no suicide. You're saying that Anstruther was murdered."

"Indeed. The suicide note is a fake, written by someone who is right-handed. It was written this morning using the pen and ink in the drawer. A natural left-hander like Anstruther would have dragged some of the ink across the page."

I raised something of a challenge. "But Holmes, while Anstruther's sister indicated that he had been left-handed, she did tell us that their father bullied him into using his right hand. And when we visited Gareth Pugh, and were shown photographs of the boys. I seem to recollect that in one of them the lads were in identical poses, holding air rifles in their right hands."

"They were, but in the second image we focused on, which was taken just after these replica flintlocks were made, Anstruther was captured on the right of the frame holding the gun in his left hand. It isn't uncommon for some left-handers to be ambidextrous and to play racket sports with their right arm, for example, while naturally preferring to write with their left hand. Similarly, Anstruther may have been conditioned to hold a rifle in his right arm because of the cruel treatment he received at the hands of his father. Either way, John Pugh managed to overlook such a detail. In trying to make the shooting look like a suicide, he inadvertently placed the weapon in Anstruther's right hand and then fabricated the note. The finger-marks on the gun will prove as much."

Laverne looked even more confused. "Anstruther was clearly obsessed with the idea of revenge and wanted to punish the three men who had contributed to his downfall. That I can see. But why would John Pugh, a respectable businessman, seek to kill his cousin?"

Holmes addressed the challenge directly. "Because, like me, he knew Anstruther's character and recognised that that man would literally be gunning for him. Some of my associates have been looking into Pugh's business affairs. He isn't the *respectable businessman* you have portrayed. For two decades, he has been running an import business supplying specialist weapons. Some of these have been falling into the hands of criminals in the metropolis, including some hired assassins. Through his friendship with Anstruther, Pugh began to sell guns to Claude Dewalt, the former East End gangster. But when Anstruther defaulted on a large payment owed to Pugh, the two parted company. Pugh set out to get even

381

with his cousin, but struggled because of the protection which Dewalt provided for the so-called 'Marksman of Maidstone'.

"In the years since Anstruther's trial, I have reflected on the flimsy, circumstantial, evidence presented against him. Those thoughts have often centred on the role played by John Pugh. It was his testimony that seemed to weigh heavily in the jury's mind. I believe it was he who used the murder of the property millionaire, Sir Anthony Bidwell, to finally get even. We will have to piece together a little more of the story to be certain, Inspector, but I would suggest that your next course of action is to arrest John Pugh."

With the arrest that followed, the final few outstanding details of the case were laid to rest. Holmes was obliged to tell Inspector Laverne about the work that Wiggins's men had done in pursing both Anstruther and Pugh. The latter had, in fact, been followed by another employee of the private enquiry agency on the day of the murder. He, like, Aaron Daly had seen the man enter the front door of the Albert Street property shortly before the fatal gunshot. Unlike Daly, he had decided not to linger around the property. The two other employees had seen Pugh leave the building by the back entrance and had noted the time. It was crucial evidence in the case against the Pugh.

The finger-marks discovered upon the pistol were found to match those of the firearms dealer. Presented with this information, and the knowledge that witnesses had seen him enter and leave the house, Pugh finally confessed to the murder. He also acknowledged that it was he, and not Anstruther, who had killed Sir Anthony Bidwell.

Holmes was allowed to sit in on the questioning. He heard how Pugh had learned of the planned assassination and had used it to implicate his cousin. On the night before the shooting was due to take place, Pugh carried out the killing himself. He knew that Anstruther was in Oxford, and had broken into the marksman's house in Walthamstow, stealing a precision rifle, a pair of boots, and a cheroot filled with Turkish tobacco. His rifle skills matched those of Anstruther, and, having carried out the job, he made sure that the police would see both the boot prints and the discarded cigarette in the mud around the tree. Later that night, he returned to Walthamstow to replace the boots and rifle before anonymously tipping off the police that Anstruther had carried out the killing.

As cousins, the two men were of a similar height and could have passed as brothers. Knowing this, Pugh took few precautions in travelling to and from Buckinghamshire. The witnesses who remembered seeing him travelling by train later testified that the man they had seen looked to be Carlton Anstruther.

With the opportunity to replace his father as a character witness at the trial, Pugh was able to completely undermine his cousin's defence, helping to send the man away for twenty years. He said that he felt no remorse and admitted that he visited Anstruther in prison a month after the trial, telling him what he had done. The convict had apparently responded surprisingly calmly, saying only that Pugh was "a dead man walking".

When Anstruther was released from prison, Pugh knew he had to act to protect himself. He found out where his cousin was living and, shortly before carrying out the murder, had received information that his former workmate had taken possession of two stolen pistols. * He acted without realising he was being followed by one of Wiggins's men.

Finding the front door to the house unlocked, he slipped quietly into the hallway carrying a small handgun. He listened for a short while at Anstruther's door before turning the handle and entering the room. He caught his cousin completely by surprise, his prey having no option but to back into the room as directed. It was then that Pugh saw the replica flintlock pistols on the desk. He laughed as he realised what they were. Keeping a careful watch on Anstruther, he took one of the pistols and loaded it with a single round from a box which was also sat the desk. He then placed the box and the second pistol in the drawer. Now brandishing both the handgun and the replica flintlock, he advanced towards Anstruther and placed the pistol up under his chin. He then fired off the single round, sending the man reeling backwards. Finally, he wrapped the dead man's fingers around the grip of the gun to make it look as if he had taken his own life. He left by the back door of the house, believing he hadn't been seen by anyone.

At his trial, Pugh was found guilty of the murders of both Carlton Anstruther and Sir Anthony Bidwell. He was sentenced to death, but two days before his planned execution, he was found dead in his cell, having hanged himself with two bedsheets.

I was with Holmes in the living room of his cottage when we learned of the death. Reading the news from a column in *The Times*, my colleague remained impassive. "I feel for the man's family, Watson, but the world is well rid of the likes of Pugh and Anstruther. I have to admit to the mistake of not realising that the evidence against Anstruther was fake, but I will not shed a tear for either man. After all, it could have been me looking down the barrel of that gun!"

I was not to be outdone. "Well, you know what they say, Holmes: 'The only bullets you have to worry about are those with your name on them!' In this case, you genuinely dodged that bullet!"

NOTE

*   Holmes admitted to me much later that it was he who had passed this information anonymously to Pugh.

About the Contributors

The following contributors appear in this volume:
The MX Book of New Sherlock Holmes Stories
Part XLVIII – Occupants of the Canonical Realm (1899-1924)

Dan Andriacco BSI, editor of *The Baker Street Journal*, is also a mystery writer. His long-running Sebastian McCabe – Jeff Cody series, starting with *No Police Like Holmes*, features a Sherlockian amateur sleuth and numerous Canonical references. He also wrote the Sherlock pastiche novels *House of the Doomed* and *The Sword of Death*. His scholarly articles have appeared in the *BSJ*, *The Sherlock Holmes Journal*, *Canadian Holmes*, *Sherlock Holmes Mystery Magazine*, and in numerous books. As leader of *The Tankerville Club of Cincinnati* scion society, he holds the title "Most Scandalous Member". He is also "Top Knot" of *His Last Bow*, a BSI scion for bow tie wearers.

Donald I. Baxter has practiced medicine for over forty years. He resides in Erie Pennsylvania with his wife and their dog. His family and his friends are for the most part lawyers who have given him the ability to make stuff up just as they do.

Brian Belanger, PSI, is a publisher, illustrator, graphic designer, editor, and author. In 2015, he co-founded Belanger Books publishing company along with his brother, author Derrick Belanger. His illustrations have appeared in *The Essential Sherlock Holmes* and *Sherlock Holmes: A Three-Pipe Christmas*, and in children's books such as *The MacDougall Twins with Sherlock Holmes* series, *Dragonella*, and *Scones and Bones on Baker Street*. Brian has published a number of Sherlock Holmes anthologies and novels through Belanger Books, as well as new editions of August Derleth's classic Solar Pons mysteries. Brian continues to design all of the covers for Belanger Books, and since 2016 he has designed the majority of book covers for MX Publishing. In 2019, Brian received his investiture in the PSI as "Sir Ronald Duveen." More recently, he illustrated a comic book featuring the band The Moonlight Initiative, created the logo for the Arthur Conan Doyle Society and designed *The Great Game of Sherlock Holmes* card game. Find him online at:
www.belangerbooks.com and
www.redbubble.com/people/zhahadun and
zhahadun.wixsite.com/221b

Gustavo Bondoni is a novelist and short story writer with over four-hundred stories published in fifteen countries, in seven languages. He has published six science fiction novels including one trilogy, four monster books, a dark military fantasy and a thriller. His short fiction is collected in *Pale Reflection* (2020), *Off the Beaten Path* (2019), *Tenth Orbit and Other Faraway Places* (2010) and *Virtuoso and Other Stories* (2011). In 2019, Gustavo was awarded second place in The Jim Baen Memorial Contest, and in 2018 he received a Judges Commendation (and second place) in The James White Award. He was also a 2019 finalist in the Writers of the Future Contest. His website is at *www.gustavobondoni.com*

Craig Stephen Copland confesses that he discovered Sherlock Holmes when, sometime in the muddled early 1960's, he pinched his older brother's copy of the immortal stories and was forever afterward thoroughly hooked. He is very grateful to his high school English teachers in Toronto who inculcated in him a love of literature and writing, and even inspired him to be an English major at the University of Toronto. There he was blessed to sit at the feet of both Northrup Frye and Marshall McLuhan, and other great literary professors, who led him to believe that he was called to be a high school English teacher. It was his good fortune to come to his pecuniary senses, abandon that goal, and pursue a varied professional career that took him to over one-hundred countries and endless adventures. He considers himself to have been and to continue to be one of the luckiest men on God's good earth. A few years back he took a step in the direction of Sherlockian studies and joined *The Sherlock Holmes Society of Canada* – also known as *The Toronto Bootmakers*. In May of 2014, this esteemed group of scholars announced a contest for the writing of a new Sherlock Holmes mystery. Although he had never tried his hand at fiction before, Craig entered and was pleasantly surprised to be selected as one of the winners. Having enjoyed the experience, he decided to write more of the same, and he has now written new Sherlock Holmes mysteries related to and inspired by each of the sixty stories in the original Canon, along with a number of others.

Martin Daley was born in Carlisle, Cumbria in 1964. His thirty-year writing career has seen over twenty books and numerous short stories published. Inevitably, Holmes and Watson remain his favourite literary characters, and they continue to inspire his own detective writing. In 2010, Martin created Inspector Cornelius Armstrong, who carries out his police work against the backdrop of Edwardian Carlisle. With the publication of the first *Inspector Armstrong Casebook* (published by MX Publishing), Martin became a member of the Crime Writers' Association. Most recently, he published *The Selected Cases of Sherlock Holmes*. He lives with his wife Wendy, in Kirkcudbrightshire, in Southwest.

Sir Arthur Conan Doyle (1859-1930) *Holmes Chronicler Emeritus*. If not for him, this anthology would not exist. Author, physician, patriot, sportsman, spiritualist, husband and father, and advocate for the oppressed. He is remembered and honored for the purposes of this collection by being the man who introduced Sherlock Holmes to the world. Through fifty-six Holmes short stories, four novels, and additional Apocryphal entries, Doyle revolutionized mystery stories and also greatly influenced and improved police forensic methods and techniques for the betterment of all. *Steel True Blade Straight.*

Steve Emecz's main field is technology, in which he has been working for about twenty-five years. Steve is a regular speaker at trade shows and his tech career has taken him to more than fifty countries – so he's no stranger to planes and airports. In 2008, MX published its first Sherlock Holmes book, and MX has gone on to become the largest specialist Holmes publisher in the world with over 500 books. MX is a social enterprise and supports three main causes. The first is Happy Life, a children's rescue project in Nairobi, Kenya, where he and his wife, Sharon, spend every Christmas at the rescue centre in Kasarani. They have written two editions of a short book about the project, *The Happy Life Story*. The second is Undershaw, Sir Arthur Conan Doyle's former home, which is a school for children with learning disabilities for which Steve is a patron. Steve has been a mentor for the World Food Programme for several years, and was part of the Nobel Peace Prize winning team in 2020.

Mark A. Gagen BSI is co-founder of Wessex Press, sponsor of the popular *From Gillette to Brett* conferences, and publisher of *The Sherlock Holmes Reference Library* and many other fine Sherlockian titles. A life-long Holmes enthusiast, he is a member of *The Baker Street Irregulars* and *The Illustrious Clients of Indianapolis*. A graphic artist by profession, his work is often seen on the covers of *The Baker Street Journal* and various BSI books.

John Atkinson Grimshaw (1836-1893) was born in Leeds, England. His amazing paintings, usually featuring twilight or night scenes illuminated by gas-lamps or moonlight, are easily recognizable, and are often used on the covers of books about The Great Detective to set the mood, as shadowy figures move in the distance through misty mysterious settings and over rain-slicked streets.

Arthur Hall was born in Aston, Birmingham, UK, in 1944. He discovered his interest in writing during his schooldays, along with a love of fictional adventure and suspense. His first novel, *Sole Contact*, was an espionage story about an ultra-secret government department known as "Sector Three", and was followed, to date, by three sequels. Other works include seven Sherlock Holmes novels, *The Demon of the Dusk, The One Hundred Percent Society, The Secret Assassin, The Phantom Killer, In Pursuit of the Dead, The Justice Master*, and *The Experience Club* as well as three collections of Holmes *Further Little-Known Cases of Sherlock* Holmes, *Tales from the Annals of Sherlock* Holmes, and *The Additional Investigations of Sherlock Holmes.* He has also written other short stories and a modern detective novel. He lives in the West Midlands, United Kingdom.

Paul Hiscock is an author of crime, fantasy, horror, and science fiction tales. His short stories have appeared in a variety of anthologies, and include a seventeenth-century whodunnit, a science fiction western, a clockpunk fairytale, and numerous Sherlock Holmes pastiches. He lives with his family in Kent (England) and spends his days taking care of his two children. You can find out more about Paul's writing at: *www.detectivesanddragons.uk.*

Jeremy Holstein has had a lifelong infatuation with Sherlock Holmes. He is the current Artistic Director for the Post-Meridian Radio Players theater company out of Cambridge, Mass., which has produced Sherlock Holmes dramas on stage every summer for the last decade, most of which Jeremy both wrote and directed. He lives near Boston with his wife and daughter, who both tolerate his obsession with The Great Detective.

Christopher James was born in 1975 in Paisley, Scotland. Educated at Newcastle and UEA, he was a winner of the UK's National Poetry Competition in 2008. He has written three full length Sherlock Holmes novels, *The Adventure of the Ruby Elephant, The Jeweller of Florence*, and *The Adventure of the Beer Barons*, all published by MX.

Roger Johnson, BSI, ASH, PSI, etc, is a member of more Holmesian societies than he can remember, thanks to his (so far) 16 years as editor of *The Sherlock Holmes Journal*, and thirty-two years as editor of *The District Messenger*, the newsletter of *The Sherlock Holmes Society of London*. He collaborated with his wife, Jean Upton, on the well-received book, *The Sherlock Holmes Miscellany*. Roger is resigned to the fact that he will never match the Duke of Holdernesse, whose name was followed by "*half the alphabet*".

David Marcum plays *The Game* with deadly seriousness. He first discovered Sherlock Holmes in 1975 at the age of ten, and since that time, he has collected, read, and chronologicized literally thousands of traditional Holmes pastiches in the form of novels, short stories, radio and television episodes, movies and scripts, comics, fan-fiction, and unpublished manuscripts. He is the author of over one-hundred-thirty Sherlockian pastiches, some published in anthologies and magazines such as *The Best Mystery Stories of the Year 2021* and *The Strand*, and others collected in his own books, *The Papers of Sherlock Holmes, Sherlock Holmes and A Quantity of Debt, Sherlock Holmes – Tangled Skeins, Sherlock Holmes and The Eye of Heka*, and *The Collected Papers of Sherlock*

389

Holmes – six volumes and more to come. He has won back-to-back first place fiction awards from *The Arthur Conan Doyle Society* (2023 and 2024) and the Nero Wolfe *Wolfe Pack*. He has edited over 1,100 Holmes adventures and ninety books, including dozens of traditional Sherlockian anthologies, such as the ongoing series *The MX Book of New Sherlock Holmes Stories*, which he created in 2015 to promote traditional Canonical Holmes. This collection is now at forty-eight volumes, with more in preparation. He was responsible for bringing back August Derleth's Solar Pons for a new generation with his collections of authorized Pons stories, *The Papers of Solar Pons* and *The Further Papers of Solar Pons*. Pons's return was further assisted by his editing of the reissued authorized versions of the original Pons books, and then several volumes of new Pons adventures. He has done the same for the adventures of Dr. Thorndyke, and has plans for similar projects in the future. He has contributed numerous essays to various publications, and is a member of a number of Sherlockian groups and Scions, as well as *The Mystery Writers of America*. His irregular Sherlockian blog, *A Seventeen Step Program*, addresses various topics related to his favorite book friends (as his son used to call them when he was small), and can be found at *http://17stepprogram.blogspot.com/* He is a licensed Civil Engineer, living in Tennessee with his wife and son. Since the age of nineteen, he has worn a deerstalker as his regular-and-only hat. In 2013, he and his deerstalker were finally able make his first trip-of-a-lifetime Holmes Pilgrimage to England, with return Pilgrimages in 2015, 2016, and 2024, where you may have spotted him. Another is planned in mid-2025. If you ever run into him and his deerstalker out and about, feel free to say hello!

Mark Mower is a long-standing member of the *Crime Writers' Association*, *The Sherlock Holmes Society of London*, and *The Solar Pons Society of London*. His pastiche collections include *Sherlock Holmes: The Baker Street Case-Files*, *Sherlock Holmes: The Baker Street Legacy*, *Sherlock Holmes: The Baker Street Epilogue*, and *Sherlock Holmes: The Baker Street Archive* (all with MX Publishing). His non-fiction works include the bestselling book *Zeppelin Over Suffolk: The Final Raid of the L48* (Pen & Sword Books). Alongside his writing, Mark maintains a sizeable collection of pastiches, and never tires of discovering new stories about Sherlock Holmes and Dr. Watson.

Sidney Paget (1860-1908), a few of whose illustrations are used within this anthology, was born in London, and like his two older brothers, became a famed illustrator and painter. He completed over three-hundred-and-fifty drawings for the Sherlock Holmes stories that were first published in *The Strand* magazine, defining Holmes's image forever after in the public mind.

Ember Pepper was born and raised in San Diego, CA. She has an M.F.A. degree in Creative Fiction Writing. She has been a fan of The Great Detective since she was a pre-teen and her greatest artistic enjoyment is challenging herself to write quality pastiches of Sherlock Holmes and his stalwart biographer and friend, John Watson.

Tracy J. Revels, BSI, a Sherlockian from the age of eleven, is a professor of history at Wofford College in Spartanburg, South Carolina. She is a member of *The Survivors of the Gloria Scott* and *The Studious Scarlets Society*, and is a past recipient of the Beacon Society Award. Almost every semester, she teaches a class that covers The Canon, either to college students or to senior citizens. She is also the author of three supernatural Sherlockian pastiches with MX (*Shadowfall*, *Shadowblood*, and *Shadowwraith*), and most recently, the three-volume pastiche set, *Tales of Light*, *Tales of Shadow*, and *Tales of Darkness*. She is a regular contributor to her scion's newsletter. She also has some notoriety as an author of very silly skits: For proof, see "The Adventure of the Adversarial Adventuress" and

"Occupy Baker Street" on YouTube. When not studying Sherlock, she can be found researching the history of her native state, and has written books on Florida in the Civil War and on the development of Florida's tourism industry.

Roger Riccard's family history has Scottish roots, which trace his lineage back to Highland Scotland. This ancestry encouraged his interest in the writings of Sir Arthur Conan Doyle. He has authored the novels, *Sherlock Holmes & The Case of the Poisoned Lilly*, and *Sherlock Holmes & The Case of the Twain Papers*, which was featured at the Museum of London Sherlock Holmes Exhibit in 2015. In addition, he has produced dozens of short stories, and has now joined the Sherlock Holmes 60+ Club, having exceeded Sir Arthur Conan Doyle's number of original Sherlock Holmes stories. All of his books have been published by Baker Street Studios and can be found at his website: *www.sherlockriccard.com* He credits his success to the encouragement of his wife/editor/inspiration and Sherlock Holmes fan, Rosilyn. She passed in 2021, and it is in her memory that he continues to contribute to the legacy of the *"man who never lived and will never die"*.

Dan Rowley practiced law for over forty years in private practice and with a large international corporation. He is retired and lives in Erie, Pennsylvania, with his wife Judy, who puts her artistic eye to his transcription of Watson's manuscripts. He inherited his writing ability and creativity from his children, Jim and Katy, and his love of mysteries from his parents, Jim and Ruth.

Shane Simmons is the author of the occult detective novels *necropolis* and *Epitaph*, and the crime collection *Raw and Other Stories.* An award-winning screenwriter and graphic novelist, his work has appeared in international film festivals, museums, and lectures about design and structure. He was born in Lachine, a suburb of Montreal best known for being massacred in 1689 and having a joke name. Visit Shane's homepage at *eyestrainproductions.com* for more information.

Emma West joined Undershaw in April 2021 as the Director of Education with a brief to ensure that qualifications formed the bedrock of our provision, whilst facilitating a positive balance between academia, pastoral care, and well-being. She quickly took on the role of Acting Headteacher from early summer 2021. Under her leadership, Undershaw has embraced its new name, new vision, and consequently we have seen an exponential increase in demand for places. There is a buzz in the air as we invite prospective students and families through the doors. Emma has overseen a strategic review, re-cemented relationships with Local Authorities, and positioned Undershaw at the helm of SEND education in Surrey and beyond. Undershaw has a wide appeal: Our students present to us with mild to moderate learning needs and therefore may have some very recent memories of poor experiences in their previous schools. Emma's background as a senior leader within the independent school sector has meant she is well-versed in brokering relationships between the key stakeholders, our many interdependences, local businesses, families, and staff, and all this while ensuring Undershaw remains relentlessly child-centric in its approach. Emma's energetic smile and boundless enthusiasm for Undershaw is inspiring.

I.A. Watson's first professional publishing credit was with a Sherlock Holmes story. The tale in this book will be his 50th (counting his novel *Holmes and Houdini*, and one or two short stories in publishers' queues). He is constantly surprised at how many ways there are to tell Sherlock Holmes adventures, which he holds to be a sign of Sir Arthur Conan Doyle's genius in developing so flexible and resilient a format for such a compelling cast

of characters. A full list of I.A. Watson's 100+ published works including twenty or so novels is available at:
http://www.chillwater.org.uk/writing/iawatsonhome.htm

Part XLVI– Occupants of the Canonical Realm (1861-1889)
Part XLVII – Occupants of the Canonical Realm (1890-1898)

Ian Ableson is an ecologist by training and a writer by choice. When not reading or writing, he can reliably be found scowling at a clipboard while ankle-deep in a marsh somewhere in Michigan. His love for the stories of Arthur Conan Doyle started when his grandfather gave him a copy of *The Original Illustrated Sherlock Holmes* when he was in high school, and he's proud to have been able to contribute to the continuation of the tales of Sherlock Holmes and Dr. Watson.

Mike Adamson holds a Doctoral degree from Flinders University of South Australia. After early aspirations in art and writing, Mike secured qualifications in both marine biology and archaeology. Mike has been a university educator since 2006, has worked in the replication of convincing ancient fossils, is a passionate photographer, master-level hobbyist, and journalist for international magazines. Short fiction sales include to *Metastellar*, *Strand Magazine*, *Little Blue Marble*, *Abyss*, and *Apex*, *Daily Science Fiction*, *Compelling Science Fiction*, and *Nature Futures*. Mike has placed some two-hundred stories to date, totaling over a million words. Mike has completed his first Sherlock Holmes novel with Belanger Books, and will be appearing in translation in European magazines. You can catch up with his journey at his blog "The View From the Keyboard"
http://mike-adamson.blogspot.com

Tim Newton Anderson is a former senior daily newspaper journalist and PR manager who has recently started writing fiction. In the past six months, he has placed fourteen stories in publications including *Parsec Magazine*, *Tales of the Shadowmen*, *SF Writers Guild*, *Zoetic Press*, *Dark Lane Books*, *Dark Horses Magazine*, *Emanations*, and *Planet Bizarro*.

"Anon." is a devoted Sherlockian and player of The Game.

Chris Chan is a writer, educator, and historian. He works as a researcher and "International Goodwill Ambassador" for Agatha Christie Ltd. His true crime articles, reviews, and short fiction have appeared (or will soon appear) in *The Strand*, *The Wisconsin Magazine of History*, *Mystery Weekly*, *Gilbert!*, *Nerd HQ*, Akashic Books' *Mondays are Murder* web series, *The Baker Street Journal*, *The MX Book of New Sherlock Holmes Stories*, *Masthead: The Best New England Crime Stories*, *Sherlock Holmes Mystery Magazine*, and multiple Belanger Books anthologies. He is the creator of the Funderburke mysteries, a series featuring a private investigator who works for a school and helps students during times of crisis. The Funderburke short story "The Six-Year-Old Serial Killer" was nominated for a Derringer Award. His books include *Sherlock & Irene: The Secret Truth Behind "A Scandal in Bohemia"*, *Murder Most Grotesque: The Comedic Crime Fiction of Joyce Porter*, *Sherlock's Secretary*, *Of Course He Pushed Him*, *Nessie's Nemesis*, *Ghosting My Friend*, She *Ruined Our Lives*, and *The Autistic Sleuth*.

Steven Connelly was born in Scotland, and lived for twenty years in London. When first visiting London, his first excited touristic trip was not Buckingham Palace or the Houses of Parliament, but Baker Street. This is his first Sherlock Pastiche but won't be the last.

Alan Dimes was born in Northwest London and graduated from Sussex University with a BA in English Literature. He has spent most of his working life teaching English. Living in the Czech Republic since 2003, he is now semi-retired and divides his time between Prague and his country cottage. He has also written some fifty stories of horror and fantasy and thirty stories about his husband-and-wife detectives, Peter and Deirdre Creighton, set in the 1930's.

Arthur Hall was born in Aston, Birmingham, UK, in 1944. He discovered his interest in writing during his schooldays, along with a love of fictional adventure and suspense. His first novel, *Sole Contact*, was an espionage story about an ultra-secret government department known as "Sector Three", and was followed, to date, by three sequels. Other works include seven Sherlock Holmes novels, *The Demon of the Dusk, The One Hundred Percent Society, The Secret Assassin, The Phantom Killer, In Pursuit of the Dead, The Justice Master,* and *The Experience Club* as well as three collections of Holmes *Further Little-Known Cases of Sherlock* Holmes, *Tales from the Annals of Sherlock* Holmes, and *The Additional Investigations of Sherlock Holmes.* He has also written other short stories and a modern detective novel. He lives in the West Midlands, United Kingdom.

Paula Hammond has written over sixty fiction and non-fiction books, as well as short stories, comics, poetry, and scripts for educational DVD's. When not glued to the keyboard, she can usually be found prowling round second-hand books shops or hunkered down in a hide, soaking up the joys of the natural world.

Stephen Herczeg is an IT Geek, writer, actor, and film-maker based in Canberra Australia. He has been writing for over twenty years and has completed a couple of dodgy novels, sixteen feature-length screenplays, and numerous short stories and scripts. Stephen was very successful in 2017's International Horror Hotel screenplay competition, with his scripts *TITAN* winning the Sci-Fi category and *Dark are the Woods* placing second in the horror category. His three-volume short story collection, *The Curious Cases of Sherlock Holmes*, will be published in 2021. His work has featured in *Sproutlings – A Compendium of Little Fictions* from Hunter Anthologies, the *Hells Bells* Christmas horror anthology published by the Australasian Horror Writers Association, and the *Below the Stairs, Trickster's Treats, Shades of Santa, Behind the Mask,* and *Beyond the Infinite* anthologies from *OzHorror.Com, The Body Horror Book, Anemone Enemy,* and *Petrified Punks* from Oscillate Wildly Press, and *Sherlock Holmes In the Realms of H.G. Wells* and *Sherlock Holmes: Adventures Beyond the Canon* from Belanger Books.

Naching T. Kassa is a wife, mother, and writer. She's created short stories, novellas, poems, and co-created three children. She resides in Eastern Washington State with her husband, Dan Kassa. Naching is a member of *The Horror Writers Association, Mystery Writers of America, The Sound of the Baskervilles, The ACD Society, The Crew of the Barque Lone Star,* and *The Sherlock Holmes Society of London.* She works in Talent Relations at Crystal Lake Publishing and was a recipient of the 2022 HWA Diversity Grant. You can find her work on Amazon.
https://www.amazon.com/Naching-T-Kassa/e/B005ZGHTI0

Susan Knight's newest novel, *Death in the Harem,* is forthcoming from MX publishing, is the latest in a series which began with her collection of stories, *Mrs. Hudson Investigates* (2019), and the novels *Mrs. Hudson goes to Ireland* (2020), *Mrs. Hudson Goes to Paris* (2022) and *Death in the Garden of England* (2023) She has contributed to many recent MX anthologies of new Sherlock Holmes short stories and enjoys writing as Dr. Watson as much as she does Mrs. Hudson. Nine of these stories comprised *The Strange Case of the Pale Boy and Other Mysteries* (2023). Susan is the author of two other non-Sherlockian story collections, as well as three novels, a book of non-fiction, and several plays, and has won several prizes for her writing. Susan lives in Dublin.

Gordon Linzner is founder and former editor of *Space and Time Magazine*, and author of four published novels and dozens of short stories in *F&SF*, *Twilight Zone*, *Sherlock Holmes Mystery Magazine*, and numerous other magazines and anthologies. He is a full member of the *Horror Writers Association* and a lifetime member of *Science Fiction and Fantasy Writers Association*.

David MacGregor is a playwright, screenwriter, novelist, and nonfiction writer. He is a resident artist at The Purple Rose Theatre in Michigan, where a number of his plays have been produced. His plays have been performed from New York to Tasmania, and his work has been published by Dramatic Publishing, Playscripts, Smith & Kraus, Applause, Heuer Publishing, and Theatrical Rights Worldwide (TRW). He adapted his dark comedy, *Vino Veritas*, for the silver screen, and it stars Carrie Preston (Emmy-winner for *The Good Wife*). Several of his short plays have also been adapted into films. He is the author of three Sherlock Holmes plays: *Sherlock Holmes and the Adventure of the Elusive Ear*, *Sherlock Holmes and the Adventure of the Fallen Soufflé*, and *Sherlock Holmes and the Adventure of the Ghost Machine*. He adapted all three plays into novels for Orange Pip Books, and also wrote the two-volume nonfiction *Sherlock Holmes: The Hero with a Thousand Faces* for MX Publishing. He teaches writing at Wayne State University in Detroit and is inordinately fond of cheese and terriers.

Michael Mallory is the author of the "Amelia Watson" and "Dave Beauchamp" mystery series, and the stand-alone novels *The Mural, Death Walks Skid Row*, and *The Ambulance*. His short stories – some 185 to date (including more than fifty in the Sherlockian realm) – have been published everywhere from *Alfred Hitchcock's Mystery Magazine* to *Fox Kids Magazine*. His story "What the Cat Dragged In," first published in *The Strand Magazine*, was selected for inclusion in *The Mysterious Bookshop Presents the Best Mystery Stories of 2023*. In the realm of nonfiction, Mike has authored eleven books on popular culture subjects, including the bestselling *Universal Studios Monsters: A Legacy of Horror*, and hundreds of articles for *Variety*, *The Los Angeles Times*, *Animation Magazine*, *Mystery Scene*, and scores of other publications. A former actor whose credits include the television shows *Mad Men*, *Vegas*, *Mob City*, and *Angie Tribeca*, Mike lives in the Greater Los Angeles area.

David Marcum *also has stories in Parts XLVI and XLVII*

Will Murray is the author of some 75 novels, including some 20 posthumous Doc Savage collaborations with Lester Dent, and 40 books in the long-running Destroyer series. Other Murray novels star the Executioner, Tarzan of the Apes, The Spider, Pat Savage and the Mars Attacks characters. His book, *Nick Fury, Agent of S.H.I.E.L.D.: Empyre* (2000) foreshadowed the 9/11 terrorist attacks. Murray has penned more than 45 Sherlock Holmes short stories. Twenty of Murray's Holmes short stories have been collected as *The Wild Adventures of Sherlock Holmes*, Vols 1 and 2. His novelette, "The Adventure of the Vengeful Viscount", in which Tarzan of the Apes, otherwise Lord Greystoke, hires Sherlock Holmes to solve a mystery, was approved by both the Estate of Sir Arthur Conan Doyle and Edgar Rice Burroughs, Inc. Murray is the author of the non-fiction book, *Master of Mystery: The Rise of The Shadow*, which is an exploration of the famous radio and magazine character, and a sequel, *Dark Avenger: The Strange Saga of The Shadow. The Wild Adventures of Cthulhu* Vols 1 & 2 collect Murray's Lovecraftan short stories. For Marvel Comics, Murray created the Unbeatable Squirrel Girl with legendary artist Steve Ditko. Website: *www.adventuresinbronze.com*

Tracy J. Revels *also contributed stories to Parts XLVI and XLVII*

Roger Riccard *also contributed to Parts XLVI and XLVII*

Jane Rubino is the author of *A Jersey Shore* mystery series, featuring a Jane Austen-loving amateur sleuth and a Sherlock Holmes-quoting detective, *Knight Errant, Lady Vernon and Her Daughter*, (a novel-length adaptation of Jane Austen's novella *Lady Susan*, co-authored with her daughter Caitlen Rubino-Bradway, *What Would Austen Do?*, also co-authored with her daughter, a short story in the anthology *Jane Austen Made Me Do It, The Rucastles' Pawn, The Copper Beeches from Violet Turner's POV*, and, of course, there's the Sherlockian novel *Hidden Fires.* Jane lives on a barrier island at the New Jersey shore.

Fifteen of **Brenda Seabrooke**'s Sherlock Holmes pastiches have been anthologized in MX Publishing and Belanger Books, six in *Best Crime Stories of New England*, one in *Destination: Mystery* and *Mystery Tribune*, and twelve in literary reviews such as *Yemassee, Confrontation*, and one in *Redbook*. Twenty-two of her books for young readers have been published at Penguin, Clarion, *etc.*, and won awards such as a Notable from the National Council of Social Studies, Junior Literary Guild, Hornbook Honor, an Edgar finalist, *etc.* She received a grant from the National Endowment for the Arts, and The Robie Macauley Award from Emerson College. In 2022, MX published her collection, *Sherlock Holmes: The Persian Slipper and Other Stories.*

Peter Shumway is a retired computer professional residing in Pennsylvania with his wife, Patty. They have been married forty-one years and have two daughters and four grandchildren. In the early 1970's, Peter performed magic with Bill Baker's World of Magic, John Bundy's Magic Concert, and traded secrets with David Copperfield when they were teenagers. Peter read the original Sherlock Holmes stories while in college in 1979, and has enjoyed rereading them many times since. He published his pastiche *Sherlock Holmes and The Kiss of Death* in 2005 and *Gullible's Journey* in 2023. When he was offered the opportunity to write a short story for the MX Series, he picked up his pen one more time.

Elbert Smith is a small-town writer, filmmaker, and illustrator, studying for his M.F.A. in screenwriting at The University Of Georgia. He has won multiple awards for his film *Murder in Black Satin*, and worked for Troma Entertainment as a video editor. When he is not writing or making movies, he can be found creating art for a Doctor Who magazine called *The Celestial Toyroom*. He has done illustration work for *Thunderbirds Are Go!* and *Space 1999* fiftieth anniversary sketch card lines. He also believes that Jeremy Brett is the ultimate Sherlock.

Robert V. Stapleton was born and brought up in Leeds, Yorkshire, England, and studied at Durham University. After working in various parts of the country as an Anglican parish priest, he is now retired and lives with his wife in North Yorkshire. As a member of his local writing group, he now has time to develop his other life as a writer of adventure stories. He has published a number of short stories, and he is hoping to have a couple of completed novels published at some time in the future.

Award winning poet and author **Joseph W. Svec III** enjoys writing, poetry, and stories, and creating new adventures for Holmes and Watson that take them into the worlds of famous literary authors and scientists. His *Missing Authors* trilogy introduced Holmes to Lewis Carroll, Jules Verne, H.G. Wells, and Alfred Lord Tennyson, as well as many of their characters. His transitional story *Sherlock Holmes and the Mystery of the First Unicorn* involved several historical figures, besides a Unicorn or two. He has also written the rhymed and metered Sherlock Holmes Christmas adventure, *The Night Before Christmas in 221b*, sure to be a delight for Sherlock Holmes enthusiasts of all ages. Joseph won the Amador Arts Council 2021 Original Poetry Contest, with his Rhymed and metered story poem, "The Homecoming". Joseph has presented a literary paper on Sherlock Holmes/Alice in Wonderland crossover literature to the Lewis Carroll Society of North America, as well as given several presentations to the Amador County Holmes Hounds, Sherlockian Society. He is currently working on his first book in the Missing Scientist Trilogy, *Sherlock Holmes and the Adventure of the Demonstrative Dinosaur*, in which Sherlock meets Professor George Edward Challenger. Joseph has Masters Degrees in Systems Engineering and Human Organization Management, and has written numerous technical papers on Aerospace Testing. In addition to writing, Joseph enjoys creating miniature dioramas based on music, literature, and history from many different eras. His dioramas have been featured in magazine articles and many different blogs, including the North American Jules Verne society newsletter. He currently has 57 dioramas set up in his display area, and has written a reference book on toy castles and knights from around the world. An avid tea enthusiast, his tea cabinet contains over 500 different varieties, and he delights in sharing afternoon tea with his childhood sweetheart and wonderful wife, who has inspired and coauthored several books with him.

A Sherlock Holmes fan since reading *The Hound of the Baskervilles* at about age twelve, **Tom Turley** has been writing pastiches since 2006. Most have appeared in previous volumes of *The MX Book of New Sherlock Holmes Stories*. All except the latest two have been collected in two books available from MX Publishing and Amazon. *Sherlock Holmes and the Crowned Heads of Europe* (2021) is a collection of four historical novellas that involve Holmes and Watson in the events leading up to World War I. The four stories are also available individually on Audible. As its title indicates, *Watson's Wives and Other Tales of Sherlock Holmes* (2023) focuses primarily on the Doctor's marriages. It likewise will soon be available on Audible. Currently, Tom is at work on a Sherlockian novel. A retired historian and archivist, he resides with his wife Paula in Montgomery, Alabama.

DJ Tyrer is the person behind Atlantean Publishing and has had fiction featuring Sherlock Holmes published in volumes from MX Publishing and Belanger Books, and an issue of *Awesome Tales*, and has a forthcoming story in *Sherlock Holmes Mystery Magazine*. DJ's non-Sherlockian mysteries can be found in anthologies such as *Mardi Gras Mysteries* (Mystery and Horror LLC) and *The Trench Coat Chronicles* (Celestial Echo Press), and on *Mystery Tribune*.
DJ Tyrer's website is at *https://djtyrer.blogspot.co.uk/*
DJ's Facebook page is at *https://www.facebook.com/DJTyrerwriter/*
The Atlantean Publishing website is at *https://atlanteanpublishing.wordpress.com/*

Margaret Walsh was born Auckland, New Zealand and now lives in Melbourne, Australia. She is the author of *Sherlock Holmes and the Molly-Boy Murders*, *Sherlock*

Holmes and the Case of the Perplexed Politician, *Sherlock Holmes and the Case of the London Dock Deaths*, *The Adventure of the Bloody Duck and Other Tales of Sherlock Holmes*, *Sherlock Holmes and the Curse of Neb-Heka-Ra*, and *Sherlock Holmes and the Hellfire Heirs*, all published by MX Publishing. She is currently working on her seventh book, *Sherlock Holmes and the Deathly Clairvoyant*. Margaret has been a devotee of Sherlock Holmes since childhood and has had several Holmesian related essays printed in anthologies, and is a member of the online society *Doyle's Rotary Coffin*, as well as being a member of *Sisters of Crime Australia*. She has an ongoing love affair with the city of London. When she's not working or planning trips to London. Margaret can be found frequenting the many and varied bookshops of Melbourne.

More than forty of **Vicki Weisfeld**'s short stories have appeared in leading mystery magazines and anthologies, most recently in the 2023 Bouchercon anthology (*Killin' Time in San Diego*), *Yellow Mama*, *Sherlock Holmes: A Year of Mystery 1884* and *1885*, and *Alfred Hitchcock Mystery Magazine*. They've won awards from the *Short Mystery Fiction Society* and *Public Safety Writers Association*. Her first mystery novel, *Architect of Courage*, was published June 2022 by Black Opal Books. She blogs regularly at *www.vweisfeld.com* and is a book reviewer for the UK website, *crimefictionlover.com*

Marcia Wilson is a freelance researcher and illustrator who likes to work in a style compatible for the color blind and visually impaired. She is Canon-centric, and her first MX offering, *You Buy Bones*, uses the point-of-view of Scotland Yard to show the unique talents of Dr. Watson. This continued with the publication of *Test of the Professionals: The Adventure of the Flying Blue Pidgeon* and *The Peaceful Night Poisonings*. She can be contacted at: *gravelgirty.deviantart.com*

The MX Book of New Sherlock Holmes Stories

Edited by David Marcum

(MX Publishing, 2015-   )

"This is the finest volume of Sherlockian fiction I have ever read, and I have read, literally, thousands." – Philip K. Jones

"Beyond Impressive . . . This is a splendid venture for a great cause!"
– Roger Johnson, Editor, *The Sherlock Holmes Journal*,
The Sherlock Holmes Society of London

Part I: 1881-1889; Part II: 1890-1895; Part III: 1896-1929

Part IV: 2016 Annual

Part V: Christmas Adventures

Part VI: 2017 Annual

Eliminate the Impossible
Part VII: (1880-1891); Part VIII: (1892-1905)

2018 Annual
Part IX: (1879-1895); Part X: (1896-1916)

Some Untold Cases
Part XI: (1880-1891); Part XII: (1894-1902)

2019 Annual
Part XIII: (1881-1890); Part XIV: (1891-1897); Part XV: (1898-1917)

Whatever Remains . . . Must be the Truth
Part XVI: (1881-1890); Part XVII: (1891-1898); Part XVIII: (1898-1925)

2020 Annual
Part XIX: (1882-1890); Part XX: (1891-1897); Part XXI: (1898-1923)·

Some More Untold Cases
Part XXII: (1877-1887); Part XXIII: (1888-1894); Part XXIV: (1895-1903)

2021 Annual
Part XXV: (1881-1888); Part XXVI: (1889-1897); Part XXVII: (1898-1928)

More Christmas Adventures
Part XXVIII: (1869-1888); Part XXIX: (1889-1896); Part XXX: (1897-1928)

2022 Annual
Part XXXI: (1875-1887); Part XXXII: (1888-1895); Part XXXIII: (1896-1919)

"However Improbable . . . ."
Part XXXIV: (1878-1888); Part XXXV: (1889-1896); Part XXXVI: (1897-1919)

2023 Annual
Parts XXXVII (1875-1889), XXXVIII (1889-1896), and XXXIX (1897-1923)

Further Untold Cases
Part XL: (1879-1886), Part XLI: (1887-1892) and Part XLII: (1894-1922)

2024 Annual
Parts XLIII (1874-1888), XLIV (1889-1897), and XLV (1898-1917)

Occupants of the Canonical Realm
Parts XLVI (1861-1889), XLVII (1890-1898), and XLVIII (1899-1924)

And in Preparation . . . The Final Volumes of
The MX Book of New Sherlock Holmes Stories: Parts XLIX and L

The MX Book of New Sherlock Holmes Stories
Edited by David Marcum
(MX Publishing, 2015-)

Publishers Weekly says:

Part VI: *The traditional pastiche is alive and well . . . .*

Part VII: *Sherlockians eager for faithful-to-the-canon plots and characters will be delighted.*

Part VIII: *The imagination of the contributors in coming up with variations on the volume's theme is matched by their ingenious resolutions.*

Part IX: *The 18 stories . . . will satisfy fans of Conan Doyle's originals. Sherlockians will rejoice that more volumes are on the way.*

Part X: *. . . new Sherlock Holmes adventures of consistently high quality.*

Part XI: *. . . an essential volume for Sherlock Holmes fans.*

Part XII: *. . . continues to amaze with the number of high-quality pastiches.*

Part XIII: *. . . Amazingly, Marcum has found 22 superb pastiches . . . his is more catnip for fans of stories faithful to Conan Doyle's original*

Part XIV: *. . . this standout anthology of 21 short stories written in the spirit of Conan Doyle's originals.*

Part XV: *Stories pitting Sherlock Holmes against seemingly supernatural phenomena highlight Marcum's 15th anthology of superior short pastiches.*

Part XVI: *Marcum has once again done fans of Conan Doyle's originals a service.*

Part XVII: *This is yet another impressive array of new but traditional Holmes stories.*

Part XVIII: *Sherlockians will again be grateful to Marcum and MX for high-quality new Holmes tales.*

Part XIX: *Inventive plots and intriguing explorations of aspects of Dr. Watson's life and beliefs lift the 24 pastiches in Marcum's impressive 19th Sherlock Holmes anthology*

Part XX: *Marcum's reserve of high-quality new Holmes exploits seems endless.*

Part XXI: *This is another must-have for Sherlockians.*

Part XXII: *Marcum's superlative 22nd Sherlock Holmes pastiche anthology features 21 short stories that successfully emulate the spirit of Conan Doyle's originals while expanding on the canon's tantalizing references to mysteries Dr. Watson never got around to chronicling.*

Part XXIII: *Marcum's well of talented authors able to mimic the feel of The Canon seems bottomless.*

Part XXIV: *Marcum's expertise at selecting high-quality pastiches remains impressive.*

Part XXVIII: *All entries adhere to the spirit, language, and characterizations of Conan Doyle's originals, evincing the deep pool of talent Marcum has access to. Against the odds, this series remains strong, hundreds of stories in.*

Part XXXI: *. . . yet another stellar anthology of 21 short pastiches that effectively mimic the originals . . . Marcum's diligent searches for high-quality stories has again paid off for Sherlockians.*

Part XXXIV: *Mind-bending puzzles are the highlight of Marcum's fully satisfying 34th anthology, which again demonstrates that multiple authors are capable of giving Sherlock Holmes and Watson innovative mysteries to tackle while staying in character. Marcum's inventory of canonical pastiches shows no signs of being exhausted any time soon.*

The MX Book of New Sherlock Holmes Stories
Edited by David Marcum
(MX Publishing, 2015-   )

402

An Investees' Anthology
Edited by David Marcum
(MX Publishing, 2022)

Selected Contributions to
The MX Book of New Sherlock Holmes Stories
by Members of
The Baker Street Irregulars

*All royalties from this collection are being donated
for the benefit of the preservation of Undershaw,
a school for special needs students located at
one of the former homes of Sir Arthur Conan Doyle*

Stories, Forewords, and Poems in this volume
have previously appeared in Parts I – XXXVI of
The MX Book of New Sherlock Holmes Stories

Featuring Contributions by:

Mark Alberstat, Marino C. Alvarez, Peter Calamai, Catherine Cooke, Carla Coupe, David Stuart Davies, John Farrell, Lyndsay Faye, Sonia Fetherston, Jayantika Ganguly, Jeffrey Hatcher, Roger Johnson, Leslie S. Klinger, Ann Margaret Lewis, Bonnie MacBird, Stephen Mason, Julie McKuras Nicholas Meyer, Jacquelynn Morris, Otto Penzler, Christopher Redmond, Tracy J. Revels, Steven Rothman, Nancy Holder, Mark Levy (and Arlene Mantin Levy), Nicholas Utechin, and Sean M. Wright (and DeForeest B. Wright, III)

MX Publishing

MX Publishing is the world's largest specialist Sherlock Holmes publisher, with over six-hundred titles and over two-hundred authors creating the latest in Sherlock Holmes fiction and non-fiction

The catalogue includes several award winning books, and over four-hundred-and-fifty have been converted into audio.

MX Publishing also has one of the largest communities of Holmes fans on Facebook, with regular contributions from dozens of authors.

www.mxpublishing.com

@mxpublishing on Facebook, Twitter, and Instagram

www.ingramcontent.com/pod-product-compliance
Lightning Source LLC
Chambersburg PA
CBHW020923020726
47495CB00002B/323